This book should be returned to any branch of the
Lancashire County Library on or before the date

Lancashire County Library
Bowran Street
Preston PR1 2UX

www.lancashire.gov.uk/libraries
Lancashire County Library

D0550078

Dear Readers:

Since the 1996 release of **HOME SWEET HOME** I've been bombarded with requests for Quintin Lord's youngest sister's story. My response was that I had to wait for Lydia to grow up and come into her own. It appears that not only has she grown up, but that she gets to realize all of her dreams in **ALL MY TOMORROWS**, with Kennedy Fletcher as an added bonus.

I hope you will enjoy Lydia, Kennedy, and the extended Camp Six Nations family while reuniting with the Lords—especially Quintin, Victoria, and their children.

There will be another reunion when a central character from **HAPPILY EVER AFTER** will solve a cold case, find love and discover passion in the Louisiana bayou. Look for journalist Gwendolyn Taylor and her sexy lawman Shiloh Harper, scheduled for a June 2006 release.

Here's hoping I will continue to bring you the characters and plots you've come to expect from me.

Peace,
Rochelle Alers

All My Tomorrows

Rochelle Alers

ARABESQUE

★BET
BOOKS

BET Publications, LLC
http://www.bet.com
http://www.arabesquebooks.com

ARABESQUE BOOKS are published by

BET Publications, LLC
c/o BET BOOKS
One BET Plaza
1900 W Place NE
Washington, DC 20018-1211

All Kensington Titles, Imprints, and Distributed Lines are available at special quantity discounts for bulk purchases for sales promotions, premiums, fund-raising, and educational or institutional use. Special book excerpts or customized printings can also be created to fit specific needs. For details, write or phone the office of the Kensington special sales manager: Kensington Publishing Corp., 850 Third Avenue, New York, NY 10022, attn: Special Sales Department, Phone: 1-800-221-2647.

ISBN: 1-58314-653-9

First Printing: August 2005
10 9 8 7 6 5 4 3 2

Printed in the United States of America

CONTENTS

ALL MY
TOMORROWS

Do not worry about anything, but in all your prayers ask God for what you need, always asking him with a thankful heart.

—Philippians 4:6

One

Lydia Lord touched a button on the dashboard of her late-model Nissan Pathfinder, turning off the air-conditioning. Reaching over, she pressed another button, then lowered the driver's-side window.

She'd left Baltimore's hot, hazy, humid weather behind miles ago. The cooler, pine-scented air, the steep incline of the winding road, and the massive pine and birch trees growing closely together as if forming a natural fortress against intruders were constant reminders that she was now in the Appalachian Mountain region.

She had signed on to cook for one hundred boys and girls and the counselors and staff of Camp Six Nations for the next eight weeks. The sleepaway camp, east of West Virginia and south of Pennsylvania, was a far cry from Kinkeads, the popular high-end restaurant in Washington, D.C. But on the other hand, Lydia looked forward to the experience with the same anticipation of a young child on Christmas morning.

Camp Six Nations was far away from D.C. and Justin Banks, and the next two months would provide enough time for her to adjust to life without him and her prestigious position at the restaurant, where she had been passed over not

once but twice for a promotion she believed she'd rightfully
deserved.

After discussing her first professional setback with her
sister-in-law, master chef Victoria Jones-Lord, Lydia sensed
ambition was getting the better of her and clouding her judgment. However, after the second time she knew it was a
game—one best played out in the nation's capital. She had
had enough of the "politricks." A month later she tendered
her resignation. The first morning she woke up realizing she
did not have a job to go to was the morning she decided it
was time she worked for herself.

She decelerated, maneuvering the SUV on the paved road
along a lake; painted wooden stakes bearing Native American
symbols and the number of miles to the campsite were positioned every quarter of a mile. Within minutes her drive ended
as she slowed and stopped at a clearing. Glancing at printed
directions taped to the dashboard, Lydia bore right, following the signs for STAFF HOUSING and CAMP PARKING.

She pulled into a space between a gleaming black Range
Rover and a minivan, parked, and cut off the engine. She had
less than an hour to settle into her cabin before meeting with
other staff members for an orientation session.

Alighting, she opened the hatch and grasped the handles
of a large duffel bag and hoisted the strap over her shoulder.
Her body sagged under the weight as she climbed a wooden
stairway to a clearing where a large two-story house sat on a
hill overlooking the lake. Two smaller cabins with screened-
in porches were erected nearby under a copse of towering
pine trees.

"Let me get that for you."

Lydia went completely still before a slight tremor swept
over her. She was as entranced by the velvety masculine
voice as she was from the intoxicating scent of an unfamiliar
men's cologne floating around her. Shifting slightly, she

stared at a pair of broad shoulders straining against the fabric of a navy blue cotton golf shirt. She knew the man was tall, very, very tall, because there weren't *that* many men she had to tilt her head and lean back to look up at. At five eight and a half she was taller than the average woman.

"Why, thank you," she said, smiling, letting the strap slide off her shoulder.

Her father had helped her load her SUV with enough clothes, books, and personal items for the summer. Moving back, she glimpsed the profile of the man assisting her. A baseball cap bearing the camp's name covered his head, a pair of sunglasses was perched on the bridge of his prominent nose, and faded jeans clung to his slim hips and long legs like a second skin.

There was something about his strong brown jaw that was vaguely familiar, and she knew if she saw all of his face she would then be able to recall where she'd seen him.

"My pleasure."

Where have I heard that voice before? she mused, staring at the flexing muscles in the man's upper arms as he deftly hoisted the bag as if it were a five-pound sack of potatoes. His voice was musical, melodious. The timbre reminded her of the low, soothing notes from a muted trombone.

Quickening her step, Lydia mounted the porch to the cabin she'd been assigned, opening the door. The man brushed past her as he walked into the cabin, leaving the subtle, sensual, masculine scent trailing behind him.

She had gone to a sleepaway camp during her preteen years, and although she'd learned to swim, exceled in arts and crafts, and gotten along well with her camp mates, what she remembered most were the smells: wet bathing suits, grass, mildewed clothes, and the occasional unwashed camper who refused to comply with the rule of a daily shower.

This time she would not have to share her living quarters or shower with eight or ten other girls. The responsibility of planning meals for one hundred campers, twenty counselors, and an administrative staff of twelve afforded her private housing.

She walked into a cabin that was no larger than her first studio apartment. A double bed in an alcove took up more than half the space. The floor plan in her orientation packet indicated a bathroom with a sink, a commode and shower, and a utility kitchen.

The man who had appointed himself her baggage handler turned and stared at her from behind his dark lenses after placing her luggage on the floor in front of a pair of sliding doors.

"How many more bags do you have?"

Lydia went completely still when she saw the hint of a smile curving the corners of his mouth upward. "Why would you think I have more bags?"

His smile curved into a full grin as he displayed a mouth filled with perfectly aligned large white teeth. Her stomach muscles contracted and her eyelids fluttered. There was something about the sexy smile that was so familiar she wanted to scream, *Who are you?*

"You're a woman and that bag certainly isn't heavy enough to hold all of the gadgets and doodads you'd need for eight weeks."

What was he talking about? The bag had to weigh at least twenty-five pounds, while the other one was even heavier. Resting her hands on slim hips, she tilted her chin.

"Do I detect a hint of sexism in that remark, Mr. . . ." Her words trailed off. She didn't even know his name.

He crossed his arms over his chest and rocked back on the heels of his hiking boots in what she could only interpret as a challenging gesture.

"Ken," he supplied.

Affecting a similar pose, Lydia stared up at him. "It's Mr. Ken?"

His smile faded. "No. It's Kennedy Fletcher, but most people call me Ken."

Realization rocked her. "Kennedy Fletcher," she whispered softly.

His striking good looks and magnificent body had most women gasping whenever his image appeared on the television screen. She had once openly referred to him as an African god. The remark elicited strange stares from her six brothers before they teased her mercilessly about turning into a groupie.

The man standing less than five feet away was the elusive former running back for the Baltimore Ravens. Known in the world of sports as the "Juggernaut," Kennedy Fletcher had retired from professional football at the height of his career. Sportscasters could not stop talking about the former rookie and defensive player of the year who had walked away from his career at a time when he'd become the highest-paid player in the game with endorsements that far exceeded his seven-figure salary. Rumors abounded about gambling losses, substance abuse, and an unsubstantiated paternity suit with a high-fashion model.

Her lush mouth softened as she offered him a smile. "Well, you *do* live and breathe."

Kennedy stared at the tall, slim figure in a pair of body-hugging jeans, a crisp white man-tailored shirt, and low-heeled black leather boots. Her flawless gold-brown complexion, shoulder-length hair pulled into a ponytail, and casual attire afforded her an overall look that was an alluring combination of exotic and classic.

Lowering his arms, he splayed his fingers on his waist, smiling. "And I hope to live and breathe for a long time, Miss . . ."

Lydia closed the distance between them, extending her right hand. "Lydia Lord, chef," she said.

Kennedy wanted to tell Lydia he knew who she was. He shook her hand, finding it cool and soft to the touch.

"My pleasure, Lydia. I'm the sports director."

Her expression stilled and grew serious. Maybe it was just a figure of speech, but it was the second time Kennedy said, "My pleasure." What she wanted to remind him of was that she was not at Camp Six Nations for his *pleasure*. There had been a time when she had been available for a man's pleasure. After she ended that relationship she'd promised herself it would never happen again—and it hadn't.

She eased her fingers from his firm grip. "It's nice meeting you."

Kennedy's penetrating gaze was fixed on Lydia's slender face. He wanted to remove his sunglasses to see the exact shade of her large eyes. As it was he had the advantage of staring openly at her.

"Do you have more stuff to bring in from your car?" There was a hint of laughter in his soothing voice.

Lydia raised her chin and flashed a facetious smile. "Yes. I do happen to have another bag."

Kennedy successfully bit back a grin, extending his hand. "Give me your key and I'll bring it in."

Reaching into the back pocket of her jeans, she dropped a key in his palm. "It's the silver Pathfinder."

She stared at his retreating back, then turned to survey what was to become her living quarters for the next two months. The cabin was half the size of her one-bedroom Silver Spring, Maryland condo, but it would do for the next eight weeks. In addition to the bed, there was a chest of drawers, a chair that matched one on the porch, and a small round table. The kitchen had a microwave, a two-burner stove, and a built-in cupboard. She counted the number of electrical outlets. There were four.

She hadn't planned to work the summer, but when her brother's best friend, Ethan Bennington, asked if she would supervise the kitchen staff at a sleepaway camp for economically disadvantaged boys and girls from the Baltimore/D.C. area, she hadn't hesitated.

She'd accepted the position, then decided to forgo a salary when told that it was the camp's inaugural season. Her decision to become a volunteer affected the fate of the last two wait-listed campers. Instead of spending their summer vacation playing on sidewalks or getting into trouble they would be given the opportunity to interact with other children in an environment that could possibly change their young lives forever.

Kennedy returned with a matching duffel bag slung over one shoulder and a small canvas case in his right hand to find Lydia sitting on a straight-back chair on the porch. He had removed his glasses and when his gaze met and fused with hers he felt as if a three-hundred-pound defensive linebacker had tackled him, knocking the air from his lungs.

Her eyes were beautiful. Framed by long, thick lashes, they were a peculiar shade of a burnished gold with dark brown centers that reminded him of shimmering liquid citrines. She rose to her feet and the soft fragrance of her perfume wafted into his nostrils.

He swallowed to relieve his constricted throat. "I'll take these inside for you."

Lydia nodded. "Thank you very much."

Kennedy gave her a sidelong glance as he walked into her cabin. He could've bitten off his tongue seconds after he'd uttered his sexist remark about her packing more than she would need for her stay. He did not want Lydia Lord to think of him as a misogynist.

During college and the years he'd played pro ball, he had always kept his private life very, very private, which had added to the mystique regarding his association with the opposite sex.

There were rumors as to his sexual preferences, but those remained unfounded rumors. He'd made it a practice to select women who were content to remain out of the spotlight, not flaunting their status as Ken Fletcher's girlfriend.

"Would you like a quick tour of the campgrounds before the staff gathers for orientation?" he asked, once he joined Lydia on the porch.

She glanced at her watch. It was now 1:20. Staff orientation had been set for 2:00. "Sure." Lydia knew she could not realistically unpack and put everything away in forty minutes.

Kennedy led her off the porch and across a grassy meadow. He pointed at the large two-story structure. "The camp directors, physician's assistant, and social workers will live in what is referred to as the main house. There are four larger cabins on the east side of the main house for the rest of the administrative staff."

"Where are you staying?"

"In the cabin next to yours."

Lydia stared straight ahead. "So, you're going to be my neighbor."

Kennedy chuckled softly. "No," he countered, "you're going to be *my* neighbor. After all, I moved in first."

Turning her head, she met his amused stare. "When did you move in?"

"Three days ago."

"Why so early?"

"Roger and Grace Evans decided it would be best that I inspect the play areas and sports equipment before the campers arrive."

Lydia nodded. She had met with the middle-aged couple for an interview; in a subsequent meeting a week later she signed papers authorizing a background investigation as mandated by the state's department of child protective services.

"Is that the alarm clock?" She pointed to a large bell perched atop a pole rising more than thirty feet in the air.

Kennedy chuckled again. "Yes."

"I'm willing to bet that someone will climb the pole and remove the clapper before the end of the season."

He stopped, reached out, and caught her forearm. "Do you realize how high that pole is?"

She nodded. "I'm still willing to bet that someone will climb it."

"What are you willing to bet?"

Vertical lines appeared between Lydia's eyes. "I only said *bet* as a figure of speech."

Kennedy dropped his hand, took a step, bringing them only inches apart, and within seconds Lydia felt light-headed. It was the first time in twenty-seven years that she found herself besieged by an overwhelming, tangible masculinity. She'd grown up with a lot of brothers—six, to be exact—and although they were the quintessential alpha males they always treated her as their equal.

She'd never been drawn to athletes, viewing them as pompous, arrogant, and manipulative. But she was aware that the Ravens had selected Kennedy in a first-round draft, offering the Olympic-gold-medal sprinter a contract that gave him instant multimillionaire status.

His penetrating eyes crinkled in a smile. "Are you *that* certain a camper will try to climb the pole and remove the clapper?"

"Very certain," Lydia countered. The two words were filled with a note of defiance, as well as a subtle challenge.

She *was* confident some camper would make the attempt, because it had happened every year she went to sleepaway camp. Once she'd turned thirteen she had been the one to shimmy up the pole and remove the clapper. She'd earned the distinction of being the only girl in camp history to successfully achieve the feat at that time.

"Okay," Kennedy drawled, his gaze lowering along with his mellifluous voice. "If no one removes the clapper before the end of the season, then you'll have to wine and dine me at a restaurant of my choice."

Lydia stared up at the man with the chiseled features and magnificent body. A slight frown marred her smooth forehead. "I don't date athletes."

He cocked his head at an angle. "Who said it would be a date? And, for your information," he added quickly, "I am not an athlete." He was a *former* athlete and now the owner of Camp Six Nations. But, on second thought, he wouldn't mind dating Lydia Lord, wondering how long it would take to make her see that there was no reason to take life so seriously.

Heat searing her face, Lydia prayed for the earth to open up and swallow her whole. Why, because he'd mentioned their dining together, did she liken it to a date?

"And if it is removed," she countered smoothly, "then I'll expect the same."

Kennedy nodded. He extended his hand. "You've got yourself a bet."

She placed her hand on his broad palm, his fingers closing over hers; but once she attempted to withdraw her fingers she found herself captive. Her eyes narrowed as she boldly met his gaze.

"Please let go of my hand, Kennedy."

He eased his grip, but instead of releasing her hand he tucked it into the bend of his elbow. "That building over there is the barn where everyone will gather for meetings," he continued smoothly.

Lydia knew she was no match for Kennedy's superior strength, so she relaxed her fingers. A sense of calm settled over her and she resisted an urge to lean against him.

She found herself swept up in the bucolic landscape as Kennedy identified the many buildings that made up Camp Six Nations: the playhouse, the arts and crafts hogan, the chapel, the infirmary, and the dining hall. Several buildings close to the lake were filled with life jackets, canoes, kayaks, and several motorboats that would be used for water skiing. A baseball diamond, basketball and tennis courts, and a soccer field were set up in an area three hundred feet from the camper cabins.

"Do you want to see inside the dining hall?"

Lydia glanced at her watch. It was now 1:50. "Do we have time?" She was fanatical about being punctual.

"Yes. The meeting is scheduled for two, but Roger is allowing extra time for latecomers. Even with printed directions this place is not that easy to find."

"It is out of the way," she concurred. If she had made a wrong turn, she would've wound up in Pennsylvania.

Kennedy affected a mysterious grin. "Don't you want to see your kitchen?"

Returning his sexy smile with one that silently shouted *blatant sensuality*, Lydia said, "Lead the way."

She followed Kennedy into a space filled with tables, benches, and cafeteria-style counters. Gleaming stainless steel waste receptacles were positioned in every corner. He flipped a switch and tracks of overhead lights flooded the building in brilliant illumination.

As Kennedy stared at her, Lydia made her way through a pair of swinging doors. She hadn't realized how fast her heart was beating until she felt the warmth of another body close to hers. The pristine state-of-the-art kitchen contained industrial ovens, grills, a walk-in refrigerator/freezer, a dishwasher, and gleaming pots, pans, and utensils.

"What do you think?"

She shivered as his moist breath feathered over her ear. He'd come up behind her without making a sound. "It's incredible."

And it was. The kitchen rivaled any in some of the world's finest hotels, restaurants, and culinary schools.

"You approve?"

Shifting, she smiled up at Kennedy and gloried briefly in the shared moment. "It's more than I expected."

Kennedy wanted to tell Lydia she was more than he had expected. Roger and Grace had shared her curriculum vitae with him. A single glance confirmed that Lydia Lord was overqualified. However, Grace alleviated his concern once she told him that Lydia's plans included setting up her own business and that she would volunteer her services to the camp as her way of giving back to the children in Baltimore and D.C. neighborhoods.

It had been nearly four years, but she was the first woman whom he thought enough of to want to know more about— much more than he had gleaned from her personnel file.

He stared at the wall clock at the far end of the kitchen. "I think we'd better start back."

Lydia knew Kennedy was right, and it was with great reluctance that she walked out of the building where she would have the final word on what would be prepared. Her imagination was operating at warp speed when she thought of the dishes she planned to offer.

TWO

Lydia and Kennedy walked through an expansive entry-way and into another room, encountering curious stares from a group of men and women sitting around a large round table.

Roger Evans stood up, adjusted a pair of round black wire-rimmed glasses on the bridge of his nose. "Now we can begin."

Lydia elbowed Kennedy in the ribs. "We are late," she hissed between her teeth.

Smiling, he cupped her elbow and led her to the last two remaining chairs. "Relax, darling, it's not as if they can start without us." His *da-ha-lin'* came in three syllables instead of two. Whenever he was completely relaxed, his speech pattern reverted to the slow deep-southern drawl he'd grown up with in his hometown of Smoky Junction, Alabama.

Lydia wanted to tell him she wasn't his *darling* and that she did not like being late. Forcing a smile and nodding at the others seated around the table, she let Kennedy seat her. She sucked in her breath as his shoulder brushed hers when he reached up and removed his baseball cap. Stubbles of dark hair dotted his well-shaped head. It was obvious he'd recently shaved his scalp.

A serving table against a wall groaned under enormous platters of sliced fresh fruit, vegetables, bread, condiments, chicken cutlets, thinly sliced roast beef, ham, turkey, bowls of potato, and macaroni and three-bean salads.

Roger, a bespectacled Jimi Hendrix look-alike, sat down and nodded to his wife. They were definitely throwbacks to the seventies. Grace exemplified the quintessential flower child with her waist-length straight salt-and-pepper hair, pale face, colorful beaded necklace, ankle-length skirt, and tie-dyed T-shirt.

Her laser-blue eyes crinkled in a friendly smile. "Because of the lateness of the hour I suggest we eat while discussing business."

Kennedy leaned closer to Lydia. "Will you forgive me if I fix you a plate?"

The intoxicatingly sensual fragrance of his body swept over her. Did he not know how potent he was? He should've been labeled X-rated, hazardous material, and highly contagious. She wasn't an ingénue when it came to the opposite sex, but there was something about the ex-ballplayer that disturbed her more than she wanted to be.

Lydia wasn't looking for someone to replace Justin. All she wanted to do was spend the summer testing the limits of her culinary creativity, and at the end of eight weeks she would know whether she would be ready to go into business for herself.

She wanted to open a restaurant on the lower level of an office building in downtown Baltimore not far from the Inner Harbor. After mulling over a name in her head for several weeks, she decided she would call it Lady Day in honor of Baltimore native Eleanora Fagan who later achieved fame as Billie Holiday.

Shifting on her chair, she met Kennedy's stare. His high cheekbones, chiseled jaw, and firm upper and lower lip were so undeniably masculine that she wanted to look away, but couldn't. There was a mysterious shimmer in his deep-set dark eyes that held her mesmerized. His likeness had appeared on the covers of *GQ*, *Sports Illustrated*, *Time*, and *Esquire*—all within a twelve-month period. Ken Fletcher had become the media's latest heartthrob and role model for America's youth.

He'd lent his face and body to designers in magazine layouts for Gianfranco Ferre, Façonnable, Dolce & Gabbanna, and Hilfiger. A televised interview with sportscaster Bob Costas revealed his refusal to endorse advertising for liquor, cigars, or cigarettes.

Whatever Kennedy Fletcher's reason was for hiding out at a campsite in the Appalachian Mountains was of no consequence to Lydia Charlene Lord.

Her eyes narrowed. "You may bring me a plate. But don't think I'm going to let you off the hook that easily. I don't like being late."

A slow, sexy smile flattened his upper lip against the ridge of his teeth. "I suppose I'll have to come up with something a bit more noble to receive complete absolution for what I believe is a mere transgression on my part."

Jaw dropping slightly, Lydia felt a wave of heat suffuse her face as Kennedy pushed back his chair and made his way to the buffet table. He had just reminded her that he was not a dim-witted jock.

Her gaze swept around the table as she waited to be served. Most of the administrative staff appeared to be in their thirties and forties. The camp director husband and wife team of Roger and Grace was the exception. The man on her left tapped her arm to get her attention.

"Hi. I'm Jeff Wiggins, drama and musical theater."

She flashed a friendly smile. Jeff looked like a West Coast surfer: rakishly long sun-streaked hair and eyebrows and a deeply tanned face. "Lydia Lord, chef."

Jeff cocked his head at an angle. "I detect a slight southern accent. Where are you from?"

"Maryland. And you?"

"Hawaii."

Her eyebrows lifted. "You came all the way from Hawaii to work here?"

Whatever Jeff was going to say was preempted by Kennedy's return. Balancing several dishes, he set two plates in front of Lydia. One was filled with melon wedges and sliced pineapple and the other with turkey, julienne carrots, and potato salad.

"I brought you two plates. Am I forgiven now?" he whispered close to her ear.

She rolled her eyes at him. "You wish."

Successfully masking a frown, Kennedy took his seat. Lydia Lord was a challenge—a beautiful, stubborn, intriguing challenge.

Lydia forced herself to concentrate on Roger Evans and not on the man sitting on her right. Although she had averted her gaze, she still remembered everything about Kennedy: the fabric of his shirt stretched over his chest and shoulders, his large, well-groomed hands, and his smell. The scent of his cologne wrapped itself around her like a sensual protective cloak. She found his presence disturbing and exciting.

Roger's evenly modulated voice broke into her thoughts. "Instead of Grace and me waxing eloquently about everyone's experience and credentials, I'd like each of you to introduce yourselves and give an overview of what you propose to offer the campers. Ken, we'll begin with you, then Lydia, Jeff, and so on."

Kennedy's features were composed as he stared at the people with whom he would spend the next two months. "I'm Ken Fletcher—" A spattering of applause interrupted his introduction. Lowering his chin, he stared at the crudités on his plate.

He had hoped that after four years since his retirement from pro football, he would be granted a modicum of anonymity, could become a private citizen, that he wouldn't be besieged by autograph seekers or photographers while working in a remote area of western Maryland.

His head came up. "I'm Kennedy Fletcher," he repeated, "sports director, *not ballplayer*." He stressed the last two words. "I've set up a program with a dual focus on individuality and teamwork. Each camper will be given the option of selecting another sport besides the required swimming and water safety. They will be taught the importance of competitiveness rather than aggression and violence. The result should build stronger minds and bodies."

Lydia took in the expressions of those sitting around the table. Kennedy had everyone's rapt attention, especially the women. Flushed cheeks, heaving bosoms, and longing stares said it all—they were enthralled with him. She did not know whether it was his superstar status, his looks, or his voice, but whatever it was she knew what they were experiencing because she felt it, too. However, she had a distinct advantage because she could feel his heat and also smell him. His cologne hinted of sandalwood, bergamot, and another unfamiliar scent that blended sensuously with his natural masculine aroma.

"The theme for the sports program will be "One Camp, One Family," Kennedy said, concluding his overview. Nodding, he turned to Lydia. "You're up next."

A smile softened her mouth as her gaze swept around the table. "I'm Lydia Lord, and I'm responsible for supervising the kitchen. What I plan to do is offer everyone a respite from the usual institutional cuisine. Because Camp Six Nations' mission is to celebrate diversity, I've established themed menus for each day of the week to expose our campers to different foods and cultures.

"Sunday dinners will be southern and the following days will include Italian, Mediterranean, Chinese, all-American, Caribbean, and Tex-Mex. I believe—"

Applause and whistles filled the room, stopping her delivery. Several exchanged high-five handshakes. She felt the rock-hard muscle in Kennedy's shoulder as he leaned into her.

"Hot *damn*, darling," he whispered, grinning. She wrinkled her nose at him. The expression may have been cute on another woman, but on Lydia it was downright sexy.

She held up a hand. "Because this is a camp catering to children I want to make certain they are offered meals that aren't loaded with calories, fat, additives, and preservatives. There will also be dishes set aside for those with dietary or religious restrictions.

"Breakfast selections will be whole-grain cereals, fresh fruit, yogurt, and baked goods. Lunch will include a salad bar and beverage choices. A midafternoon snack of cookies, homemade ice cream or gelato, and seasonal fruits will be available for the children, and smoothies, iced coffees, teas, lattes, and cappuccino for adults."

This announcement elicited another round of applause, and Lydia felt a warm glow flow through her. She'd worked diligently on her proposal, but she had not anticipated that it would be met with that much enthusiasm.

The uncertainty and self-doubt that had lingered after her resignation evaporated like a drop of water on a heated skillet. Even after Victoria insisted that she possessed the talent to rise quickly in the culinary world, the doubt had remained.

She felt elated by her new objectivity. "I'm certain that my staff and I will make the most of our training and experience to make Camp Six Nations' first season a memorable one. Thank you."

Jeff sat up straighter, clearing his throat. "Now, what can I say to top lattes?"

"You can't."

"Don't even bother."

"Forget about it."

Jeff appeared shocked by the comments coming from the people sitting around the table, but recovered quickly, saying, "You'll eat those words once you see my would-be thespians rocking the house."

He lowered his voice to a James Earl Jones timbre, smiling at everyone's reaction, and crooned about putting on a hip-hop version of *West Side Story.*

Artisans, an interdenominational minister, a team of social workers, medical personnel, and a recent culinary school graduate, who would become Lydia's assistant, spent the next two hours recounting their experience and how they would affect the lives of the campers.

A camp calendar, outlining camp regulations and daily activities, was distributed along with a schedule of personnel hours and their days off. Lydia's rotation was six days on, then two half days off. Her first days off would be a Friday and Saturday. A delivery of produce and meat was scheduled for the following morning. Sorting her papers, she rose to her feet. The man assigned to assist her headed her way.

Tall, lanky, with raven-black hair cut in a buzz style, he flashed a warm smile. "Neil Lane. I loved your presentation."

She took his hand, surprised when he brought it to his mouth, kissing her knuckles. She drew in a sharp breath. "Thank you, Neil."

Neil tightened his grip. "Can we go somewhere and talk?"

Her eyebrows lifted. "Now?"

He released her hand, seemingly embarrassed that he'd held it longer than was necessary. "It doesn't have to be right now."

"I still need to unpack and settle in. Why don't you come by my cabin in a couple of hours?"

Glancing at his watch, Neil said, "What if I come by around seven?"

Lydia nodded. "Seven is good."

He smiled. "Thanks."

"You're welcome. I'll see you at seven."

Turning to gather up the orientation material, Lydia met Kennedy's gaze over the ash-blond head of the physician's assistant, who clung to his arm as if he were a lifeline keeping her from drowning.

Lydia acknowledged his plea by lifting her eyebrows before turning and walking out of the main building. If Kennedy wanted her to rescue him from his admirer, then he was out of luck. Superstardom came with an astronomical sacrifice: anonymity.

Temporarily dismissing all thoughts of Kennedy Fletcher, Lydia made her way to her cabin. It was crucial that she unpack and make the small space feel like home. Her mother lectured her constantly about being too rigid, aggressive, and uncompromising, but what Etta Mae Lord did not understand was as the youngest in a family of nine children, Lydia had learned at an early age that if she wanted to be heard and acknowledged, then she had to assert herself.

Unlike most of her single girlfriends who trolled clubs for potential husbands and her past involvement with Justin notwithstanding, business success topped her wish list, not marriage.

Lydia lay down on one of the two cushioned recliners she always stored in the cargo area of her SUV. She had managed to unpack, add personal touches to the cabin, shower, and change into a pair of comfortable walking shorts and a tank top in record time. She'd thought about driving into town to find a grocery store to stock the small refrigerator with bottled water and yogurt, but decided against it because of her appointment with Neil.

Sighing audibly, she closed her eyes. The delicate wind chime hanging from the porch ceiling swayed and tinkled in the light breeze. She'd become captivated with wind chimes after seeing *Body Heat*, the film noir featuring Kathleen Turner in her screen debut.

The hauntingly beautiful sound of an acoustic piano accompanying Brenda Russell as she crooned "Piano in the Dark" came from the speakers of a portable stereo unit sitting on the floor. Lydia had ordered the complete Time-Life *Body and Soul* CD series more than a year ago, yet hadn't taken the cellophane wrapper off a single compact disc.

Now she would take the time to relax, listen to music, and catch up on her reading. She'd asked her attorney to keep her posted on the negotiations to rent space at a construction site that would contain several office buildings and an underground mall. The project was scheduled for completion in early spring next year.

She opened her eyes and sat up straighter when she registered a soft tapping sound. "Please come in and sit down."

Neil opened the porch door and lowered his lanky frame down to the other chair. His near-black gaze swept around the porch, cataloguing everything. The music, the delicate sounds from the wind chime, and the flickering votive candles in a three-tiered, brass candleholder added a delicate touch to the rustic structure.

He smiled. "You've settled in nicely."

Lydia nodded. "I'm trying to make it feel a little like home."

"Everyone is going into town in about half an hour to hang out and get better acquainted. I hope you'll join us."

She wanted to tell him that all she wanted to do was sit on the porch and listen to music and watch the sunset. However, she didn't want to appear antisocial.

"Of course." Leaning over, she turned off the CD player. "What is it you want to talk about?"

Neil sat forward, his hands clasped together. "I graduated from culinary school two months ago, and this will be my first job as a chef."

A flash of recognition crossed Lydia's face. She knew Neil was anxious over rumors he'd heard in culinary school about egotistical executive chefs, whose sole mission was to bully, terrorize, and intimidate their apprentices to tears. She hadn't been exempt, except that she refused to cry in front of the others.

"Relax, Neil." Her voice was soft, comforting. "I'm not going to scream or throw things. I know what that feels like, and I would never do it to someone else. You were hired to assist me, and that's what I need you to do."

Neil exhaled a sigh of relief and ran a hand over his cropped hair. "I've risked everything to follow my dream. I quit my job as a bean counter for the General Accounting Office the day after I had spent twenty years there. My wife moved out, took our daughters, and is now living with her mother because she believes I'm going through a midlife crisis. My father says 'a real man wouldn't be caught swishing around a kitchen.' "

"Do you really like cooking?" Lydia asked, deftly directing the conversation away from Neil's family. If they were going to work together she preferred not knowing about his private life.

His expression changed, becoming animated. "I don't know if I can explain it, but I feel . . ." His words trailed off.

"A rush," she supplied.

"Yes! That's it. A rush. A high. It's all the same emotion."

Lydia had experienced the same emotion. The few times she'd concocted a new dish that subsequently appeared on the restaurant's menu earning good reviews, she expected more than "nice work" from the executive chef.

Times had changed and so had she. The urge to please, while demonstrating that she was a talented chef, was no longer important. Cooking for the camp would prove one thing: either she would or wouldn't be able to supervise a kitchen.

She and Neil had something in common. He'd left a secure position as a government worker, while she had walked away from a prestigious position with one of D.C.'s most popular restaurants.

"Where are you working now?" he asked after a comfortable silence.

She stared at a bug crawling down the screen. "I'm not."

"What do you plan to do after the camp season is over?"

"I'm thinking about going into business for myself."

"Good for you," he said.

They talked about restaurants in the capital district, northern Virginia and eastern Maryland, until Neil stole a glance at his watch. "It's time we head out."

Lydia swung her legs over the side of the recliner. "Where are we going?"

"Ken said there's a place called the Roadhouse not too far from here. Dining and dress are casual."

She stood up, Neil following suit. "Give me a few minutes to change." Casual or not, she felt a skirt would be more appropriate than shorts.

"Do you mind going with him?"

Neil's question caught her off guard. "You want me to go with Kennedy?" He nodded. "Why?" If Kennedy wanted her to ride with him, then he should've asked her.

"I have a two-seater, and I promised Jill that she could ride with me."

She tried matching the name Jill with the face, but came up blank. It would take her several days before she would be able to identify everyone on sight.

"No, I don't mind." She did mind, but she wasn't going to let Neil know that. "I'll see you there."

"Good. I'll let him know you'll be going with him."

Her jaw dropped. "He doesn't know?"

"Not yet. I'll tell him on the way back to my cabin."

Mouth gaping, she stared at her assistant as he made his way off the porch. She didn't want Kennedy to think she *wanted* to ride with him. If she'd known where the restaurant was, she would drive herself.

However, there was something about the man living fifty feet away that made her uncomfortable, and the less contact she had with him the better. Turning, she walked into her cabin as a gentle breeze rustled the wind chime.

She unbuttoned the waistband on her shorts, stepped out of them, then reached into the closet for a slim black skirt. Slipping out of her clogs, she slid her bare feet into a pair of strappy sandals with a two-inch heel.

Reaching for a small leather purse, she took out a tube of gloss and drew the brush over her lips before smoothing back wisps of hair that had escaped the twist on the nape of her neck.

She headed for the door, closing it behind her. As she made her way off the porch she noticed Kennedy waiting for her, massive arms crossed over his chest. He'd changed out of his jeans and golf shirt.

Her breath caught in her throat as she surveyed his tall physique in a pair of black slacks and silk T-shirt. A pair of imported slip-ons had replaced his hiking boots.

Dropping his arms, he cleared his throat. "Neil said you needed a ride."

Lydia wanted to tell Kennedy that Neil had lied as she watched him staring at her. His gaze swept from her head to her feet in seconds. The uneasiness was back. Was her skirt too short, tight? Did her top reveal too much flesh? Were her nipples showing through the sheer fabric of her bra?

Girl, you'd better pull yourself together before you lose it, she chided. There was no way she wanted Kennedy Fletcher to think she was some bubble-headed groupie or video ho lusting after him.

"I can always follow you in my SUV."

"That's not necessary. I made reservations for eight o'clock, so we'd better head out before the locals take all the parking spaces."

"It's that popular?"

Kennedy extended his hand, and he wasn't disappointed when Lydia took it. "It's been called western Maryland's Studio 54."

Lydia smiled up at him. "No!"

He returned her smile. "Yes. Some of the sights you'll see will make you go 'humm-mmm.' "

"Give me a clue," she said, falling in step beside him.

"Beehive hairdos, platform shoes, bell-bottom pants, and an occasional Mohawk."

She laughed, the tinkling sound carrying in the quietness of the evening like her wind chime. "What aren't you telling me, Kennedy?"

"Most of the kids who work at the Roadhouse are drama students who live in the area for the summer. They double as wait staff and entertainers."

"It sounds like fun."

Kennedy gave her hand a gentle squeeze. "It is."

Those were the last two words they exchanged as he helped her into his SUV.

Three

Lydia stared out the passenger-side window of Kennedy's Range Rover, admiring the lush, verdant landscape flaunting its summer dress.

Jeff, who had flown in from Hawaii and did not have a vehicle for his use on the mainland, sat on the second row of seats. Leaning forward, he tapped her shoulder.

"Will you consider a special menu request?"

Shifting, she peered at him. "It depends on what you want."

"A luau."

Kennedy peered up in the rearview mirror. "I'm with you, Jeff. A luau would be perfect for the farewell celebration dinner." He returned his attention to the narrow, winding road.

Lydia's gaze shifted between the two men. "A luau means roast pig. Where am I going to cook a pig? I stand corrected—pigs."

The ovens weren't large enough to roast the half a dozen suckling pigs needed to feed a minimum of a hundred people. Her father always used an in-ground pit to roast a large pig for the Lord family's annual Memorial Day get-together.

Kennedy winked at her. "Why don't you run the idea past

Roger? It shouldn't be that difficult to have a pit constructed before the end of the summer."

"I'll do that," she said, quickly warming to the idea.

"We're here," he announced seconds before the Roadhouse came into view.

The Roadhouse was housed in a converted barn. Loud music floated from an open loft. Couples, spilling out of cars, pickups, and SUVs, gyrated to the upbeat tempo as they headed toward the entrance.

Kennedy pulled into one of the last remaining parking spaces and cut off the engine. He got out, came around, and opened the passenger-side door. Curving an arm around Lydia's waist, he scooped her off the seat, as if she were a small child, holding her aloft before lowering her slowly until her shoes touched the blacktop. If she registered his hesitation in releasing her, nothing in her expression indicated she had.

Since coming face-to-face with Lydia Lord, Kennedy felt as if he'd been ensnared in a web of curiosity. He wanted and needed to know what it was about the camp's chef that had him thinking about her when he did not want to. He knew it wasn't her looks, because he had dated women who made their living based solely on their faces and bodies. But there was something about Lydia that went beyond beauty. She seemed to possess a strength that in no way compromised her femininity.

What intrigued him most was that although she'd recognized his name she hadn't tried coming on to him like a lot of women had done during his football playing days, and now a few at the camp. A wry smile touched his mouth. Unlike a lot of his male friends, he never liked being chased, preferring instead to do the chasing.

Reaching for her hand, he squeezed her fingers. "Are you ready to go in?"

Tilting her chin, Lydia did what she wanted to do earlier

that day—she leaned into Kennedy's massive strength. "Yes."

They were still holding hands when a waiter dressed like a Shakespearean character directed them to a table where the camp staff had gathered. Kennedy seated Lydia on a long bench before rounding the table to sit opposite her. Their gazes met, fused, communicating an awareness of each other as if they were the only two people in the room. She offered him a shy smile, he acknowledged the gesture with a wink.

Her lids slipped down over her eyes, thick lashes sweeping the soft curve of high cheekbones. The demure expression, and the woman who made his senses spin out of control, enchanted Kennedy.

His eyes traced the planes of her face like a painter with a fine-tipped brush, moving slowly, feathering over the arch of her eyebrows, the bridge of her short nose, the hollow of delicate cheekbones, the lush, soft fullness of a petulant lower lip, and a minute dip in her delicate chin—the perfect spot on which to breathe a kiss.

"Captain Fletcher?" Kennedy shifted his gaze and attention from Lydia to a waitress dressed as a tavern-serving wench.

She smiled, displaying several blackened teeth. She leaned over, eliciting gasps from the men. The amount of flesh spilling from her revealing décolletage screamed *scanda-lous!*

"Do you still want the Monstrosity for your crew?" Her affected Cockney accent was flawless. He nodded mutely. "Grog, sir?" He nodded again, not realizing he'd been holding his breath until she sashayed over to the bar to put in their beverage order.

"Dam-yum," Jeff whispered under his breath at the same time he shook his head.

"I hear you, my man," Neil concurred.

Epithets of "tramp," "strumpet," and "harlot" were volleyed

about the table by the women, their reactions drawing hoots and high fives from the men. Lydia met Kennedy's amused gaze as she rolled her eyes at him.

"Are you sure this place isn't Hooters in disguise?" Jill, the very attractive ash-blond physician's assistant who had clung to Kennedy's arm as if she were an appendage, openly voiced her disapproval.

A social worker tapped Jill's arm, pointing at three men approaching the table clutching pitchers of beer, wine, and soft drinks. Bare-chested, they wore black skintight leggings, ballet-type slippers, and bow ties. The only competition for their toned pectorals and rock-hard abs were perfectly chiseled soap opera features.

Jill was practically salivating. "Who picked this place?"

Roger chuckled softly. "Ken."

"Nice choice," she crooned, giving him a thumbs-up sign.

Everyone at the table laughed. The tense moment behind them, mugs and glasses were filled and held aloft in a toast.

Roger adjusted his glasses. "Here's to good food, drink, and the best camp staff in the state."

"Hear, hear!" came a chorus of voices from those lining both sides of the long wooden table.

Hoisting his mug brimming over with frothy beer, Roger flashed a wide grin. "A special toast to Ken for offering to pick up tonight's tab."

"Hear, hear!" boomed the staff loud enough to be heard over the raucous sounds of music and conversations. The DJ had turned up the volume on Usher's "Yeah."

Jeff swallowed a mouthful of white wine. Snapping his fingers in time to the catchy tune, he reached for Lydia. "May I have this dance?"

Before she could accept or decline his invitation, he'd grabbed her hand. She was on her feet and following him to the platform stage set up as a dance floor. Two other couples from their group joined them.

Kennedy, refusing to dance, sat and watched Lydia's slender body swaying sensually as if seducing Jeff and every man whose gaze touched her. His lids lowered, he stared intently at her, hypnotized by the perfection of her long, shapely bare legs in high heel sandals with thin leather straps crisscrossing her narrow feet.

She raised her arms and clapped her hands, singing along with the lyrics, "make your booty go . . ."

As Usher's former blockbuster hit segued into OutKast's "The Way You Move," the wait staff and bartenders joined the customers on the dance floor. Everyone at the Roadhouse was up dancing, leaving Kennedy no excuse but to follow suit. He made his way over to Lydia. She smiled at him and he offered her his trademark matinee-idol smile.

At thirty-six, he wasn't too old to have been part of the MTV generation, but the most noticeable change was that he'd appreciably curtailed his social life. There had been a time when he'd been able to party as hard as he'd trained for a career as an athlete. However, it had only taken a single incident to change him, his career, his life, and his future.

The DJ was relentless, spinning another old hit from the *Bad Boy II* soundtrack, "Shake Your Tailfeather." As if on cue, the restaurant's personnel resumed their duties as the volume lowered.

"This is your DJ, Road Dawg, spinning the jams tonight." The sonorous voice floated from hidden speakers like watered silk. "We're going to take it down a notch, give you time to catch your breath, order a little sumptum, sumptum from the bar, or sample the house special of catfish fritters. Now, hold on to your favorite lady or gent and give a listen to an old Evanescence favorite, 'My Immortal.' "

"Please dance with me." Kennedy's arm curved around Lydia's waist, pulling her against his middle.

Closing her eyes, Lydia rested her head on Kennedy's chest, all of her senses on high alert. She listened to the strong, slow, steady beating of his heart over the hauntingly beautiful voice of Amy Lee, Evanescence's lead singer. Curving her arms under his massive shoulders, she breathed in the essence of the cologne that had become an aphrodisiac, and languished in the solidness of the body curving into hers. Her heels put the top of her head at his shoulder, making them a perfect fit.

Kennedy curbed an urge to tighten his hold on Lydia's slender body. If possible, he sought to absorb her into himself. He memorized everything about her: the silky feel of her skin, the floral scent clinging to her hair, clothes, and flesh, and the soft crush of her full breasts against his chest.

I want her!

The unspoken realization caught him off guard. He hadn't known Lydia Lord a day, yet he wanted her. And the wanting wasn't based solely on physical gratification—which he could get from any woman. Lydia posed a challenge, the perfect foil in a battle of the sexes.

"Were you serious about not dating athletes?" he whispered near her ear.

Lydia nodded. "Very serious."

"Why?"

Easing back slightly, she stared up at him staring down at her. "Once burned, twice shy."

He lifted a thick, black eyebrow. "So, you had a bad experience with a jock." The question was posed as a statement.

Her gaze did not waver. She wanted to tell Kennedy it was devastating. How could she disclose to a stranger that the man to whom she had offered her innocence had betrayed her? The deceit was compounded because he was sleeping with her best friend at the same time.

She saw the heartrending tenderness in his gaze. Her lids fluttered wildly as she struggled to maintain her composure. His query had opened the door she had closed years before, a door she did not want to open again.

"Yes," she whispered, the word pregnant with pain and resignation.

"Not all of them are SOBs."

She managed a wry smile. "I know. Just the one I knew."

Lowering his chin, Kennedy pressed a kiss on the top of

Lydia's head. "There comes a time when you have to put your past to rest, Lydia."

"I have," she mumbled against his shoulder. "I no longer date athletes."

Kennedy wanted to tell Lydia that he was no longer an athlete, and that he wanted to date her. Neither would have a great deal of free time because of their camp responsibilities, but he did want to take her to a movie, or on a leisurely drive in the country. He wanted to spend time with her in order to uncover why she, and not some other woman, pulled him back into a game where losing was not an option.

The song ended and he escorted Lydia back to the table. Kilt-clad waiters balancing trays with dishes piled high with crispy fried chicken, catfish fritters, Maryland crab cakes, chow-chow, steamed okra, corn on the cob, mixed greens, candied sweet potatoes, black-eyed peas, Creole vegetable gumbo, and barbecued short ribs set them on the table. Pitchers of iced tea and water were added to the other beverages.

Mugs overflowed with liquid refreshment and plates groaned under monstrous portions. Conversation was practically nonexistent as the camp's staff consumed copious amounts of food.

Lydia was impressed with the presentation and taste of what was commonly referred to as the Roadhouse "Monstrosity." Although she preferred oven-fried chicken to the deep-fry method, she approved of the taste.

Neil held up a chicken leg, garnering her attention. "Soybean veggie oil," he mouthed. Nodding, she confirmed his assessment. The soybeans added a sweet, flavorful essence.

Jill emptied her glass of red wine and extended it to Neil for a refill, her bare shoulder pressed intimately close to his. Lydia wondered if the chatty, flirtatious physician's assistant was aware of Neil's marital status. He'd admitted to being separated, not divorced.

Mind your business, Lydia Lord, the voice in her head chastised her. What Neil did with other women was not her concern. She knew spending eight weeks with the same people twenty-four-seven was temptation of the highest order.

"Have you decided on a dessert menu, Lydia?" Jeff asked, dabbing the corners of his mouth with a napkin.

Redheaded, green-eyed Megan Gallagher, a renowned potter, stared at Jeff in disbelief. "How can you talk about more food at a time like this?" she asked in a distinct Irish brogue. "Ye must have a belly like a bottomless pit."

A rush of blood darkened Jeff's face under his deep tan. "I happen to have a serious jones for desserts."

Megan looked perplexed. "Who is this Jones person?" A chorus of chuckles and sniggles followed her query.

"I could've said *feenin'*," Jeff teased, flashing a wide grin.

"Me sister is married to Liam Feeney," Megan announced proudly.

The staff laughed uncontrollably, fists pounding the table while others hiccupped, trying to hold their breath. Tears rolled down many of their cheeks.

Lydia, laughing as hard as the others, dabbed at her damp face with a napkin. Kennedy's motto of "One Camp, One Family" was evidenced by the camaraderie cementing the group who'd met for the first time only eight hours before.

"I'm with Jeff," Grace announced. "What are the desserts?"

All gazes were directed at Lydia, who had affected a mysterious smile. "You'll have to ask Neil about that."

Eyes wide, mouth gaping, Neil struggled to come to terms with what he'd just heard. It was apparent Lydia wanted him to be responsible for the dessert station. How, he mused, did she know his passion was to become a pastry chef?

Recovering quickly, he cleared his throat. "In keeping with Lydia's idea of themed menus, I plan for the desserts to be representative of each region. Tiramisu for Italy, flan for Latin America, baklava for the Mediterranean, and of course sweet potato and apple pie for the good old U. S. of A." Hard pressed not to smile, he stared at Lydia, who acknowledged her approval with a slight nod.

During their discussion of popular restaurants, Neil had

stressed which ones served the best desserts, which led Lydia to believe he would eventually become a patisserie.

"Speaking of dessert, would anyone like any?" Kennedy asked, reaching into the pocket of his slacks for a credit card. No one accepted the offer, and he signaled a waiter for the check. It had taken a little more than two hours for them to devour everything on the table.

As if on cue, everyone stood up, thanked Kennedy for dinner, and filed out of the Roadhouse several pounds heavier.

Lydia followed the others into the parking lot, breathing in the pungent odor of burning mesquite wood. She looked up at a star-filled sky with a near-full moon. The nighttime temperatures in this part of the state were at least ten degrees cooler than Baltimore, and the absence of the oppressive humidity was most noticeable.

Jeff headed toward her, Megan following. "Let Ken know that I'm going back with Megan. I told her I would give her a crash course in American slang."

She smiled. "A couple of months of BET and MTV music videos will give her all she needs to understand our vernacular."

As she watched the camp staff getting into trucks and cars, Lydia thought about the campers scheduled to arrive in another two days. Would some of them have trouble adjusting to living in the woods for two months? Would they bemoan the loss of their music videos and games that bombarded them constantly during their waking hours? How many, she wondered, would complete the eight-week season?

The last thought hadn't completed itself when she felt a presence behind her. How was Kennedy able to move so quietly for a man his size? She knew he weighed over two hundred pounds, and stood at least six four, maybe five.

"Do you need a ride, miss?" he whispered close to her ear.

Lydia shivered as much from the timbre of his voice as

from his moist breath sweeping over the side of her neck. Smiling, she said, "As a matter of fact I do."

"Where are you going, miss?"

"Camp Six Nations."

Kennedy moved closer, resisting the urge to touch Lydia. He wanted to touch her again, and not under the pretense of dancing with her. "I'm not familiar with the place," he teased softly.

Turning, Lydia tilted her chin and stared up at him. The lights ringing the parking lot cast shadows over the upper portion of his face. "I'll show you where it is." There was a hint of laughter in her voice.

A half smile parted his mouth. "I'll take you, but only if you allow me to take a slight detour."

"Where?" A slight frown appeared between her eyes.

"I need to stop at an all-night convenience store to pick up some bottled water."

"I need water, too," she said quickly.

Reaching for her elbow, Kennedy led Lydia to his Range Rover. He unlocked it with a remote device, then spanning her waist with both hands, lifted her effortlessly and set her down on the passenger-side seat.

Lydia secured her seat belt and adjusted the hem of her skirt. The skirt ended above her knees when standing, but rode up considerably once she sat.

Kennedy got in beside her, his warmth and smell nearly overwhelming her as she closed her eyes. His nearness elicited a slow warming heat that began in her face before moving down her body like a swath of slow-moving lava. How was she going to spend the summer with a man whose very presence sent her senses and now her hormones into overdrive?

Biting down hard on her lower lip, she prayed she wouldn't succumb to the sensual magnetism radiating from Kennedy Fletcher like radioactive waves.

At that moment it did not matter whether he had a wife

secreted away somewhere, or a girlfriend waiting for him to come back to her at the end of the summer. What did matter was that Lydia found herself mesmerized by a man she did not want to lust after.

Kennedy maneuvered into the parking lot of a convenience store several miles off the interstate. Neon lights from another establishment sharing the property flashed the outline of a woman's body crouched on her hands and knees. He left the engine running.

"Do you need anything else besides water?"

"Yogurt, but only if they carry it."

He unsnapped his seat belt. "What kind of yogurt?"

"I'll go in with you."

Kennedy reached over and covered her hand when she attempted to undo her belt. "No. I want you to stay here."

"Why should I?" She'd folded her hands on her hips.

"I don't want to expose you to *that*." He pointed to his right. A few men had stumbled out of the Doll House, one losing the contents of his stomach. Another unzipped his pants and urinated, while the third weaved and pointed at the ground.

Lydia averted her gaze. "I'll stay here."

Kennedy thought he was in for an argument once Lydia rested her hands on her hips and rolled her neck at him. She was safer inside the SUV than outside. It would take only a word or crude remark and he would revert to his football days, knocking down two-hundred-pound-plus men like matchsticks.

"What kind of yogurt?" he asked again.

"Fruit or plain. It doesn't matter."

"Don't run away," he said smoothly, with no expression on his face.

Lydia nodded. She certainly had no intention of leaving the Range Rover as more men staggered out of the club.

The Doll House was apparently a regular Friday night

hangout where the predominately male patrons tossed back a few drinks, downed several beers while they were entertained by naked women swinging around poles and executing full splits for their amusement.

A girl Lydia had gone to high school with had become an exotic dancer to earn extra money to supplement her child support payments. Lydia had asked Victoria to hire her as a waitress for her catered parties, but Belinda said she made more money stripping at a club in a seedy, crime-infested neighborhood where most law-abiding people refused to venture out after dark. Belinda swore she would quit as soon as she saved enough money to buy a house for her three children. The last time Lydia ran into her, Belinda was still dancing because some guy she'd dated had stolen her money.

All thoughts of Belinda vanished when Lydia spied Kennedy coming out of the store, balancing a plastic sack atop a case of water. As he came closer she realized he was carrying two cases of water. Most times she struggled with one, while he carried two with no visible struggle. He motioned for her to open the hatch, and she reached over and pressed a button on the vehicle's remote.

He placed his purchases in the cargo area and came around to sit beside her. "Is there any other place you'd like to go before I head back?"

Lydia glanced at the clock on the dashboard. It was close to eleven. She wanted to get into bed before midnight because she had to be up early for the food delivery.

She shook her head. "No." Shifting into gear, Kennedy backed out of the parking lot.

"How do you know this area so well?" Lydia asked ten minutes into the return trip. Kennedy had taken a different route back to the camp.

"I have a little place around here."

Sitting up straighter, she stared at his distinctive profile. "You live here?"

His eyes crinkled in a smile. "Not year-round."

"If you don't mind my asking, where *do* you live?"

He gave her a quick glance. "Friendship Heights."

Lydia's left eyebrow flickered. Kennedy lived in one of suburban Maryland's affluent communities. "Will your family spend the summer in Friendship Heights, or do they plan to join you here?"

"No," he said after a slight pause. "It's almost impossible to get my parents to leave Alabama. But, if you're alluding to a wife or girlfriend, then the answer is no. I have neither."

"Did I ask you if you were married or involved with a woman?"

Kennedy ignored her sharp tone. "No."

"Then, why did you tell me?"

"I'm hoping that by being honest and open with you you'll change your opinion of athletes."

"My opinion, or the fact that I won't date them?"

"Both."

"Does what I think of athletes mean that much to you?"

"Yes."

There came a deafening silence inside the vehicle as Lydia, stunned by his bluntness, struggled to compose her thoughts. She was aware of her personality, and stubbornness and being opinionated weren't her most admirable characteristics.

Perhaps she was being unfair to Kennedy. She'd tried and judged him without cause. She'd done to him what so many people did to others outside their racial, religious, and ethnic groups, basing their dislike and mistrust on stereotyping.

Kennedy slowed at an intersection, looking both ways before accelerating. He'd tried everything with Lydia except pleading with her. That he would never do because of his pride, a pride that was unyielding, a pride that had cost him the love of a woman, whom at one time he had loved more than himself.

"Okay, Kennedy."

His right foot hit the brake so quickly that the SUV nearly went into a spin. Shifting into park, he turned and stared at Lydia, complete surprise freezing his features.

"What?" The word exploded from his mouth.

Lydia closed her eyes as her heart pumped a runaway rhythm. Counting to three, she opened them. "I'm not saying I'll go out with you, but then I can't say I won't go out with you."

He leaned closer. "What are you saying, Lydia?"

"I'm saying I'll try and change my opinion of jocks—athletes."

Resting his right arm over the back of her seat, he smiled. "What about former jocks?"

"Those, too," she said softly, peering up at him through her lashes.

Removing his arm, Kennedy shifted into gear. "Good. At least we can start at one and move forward."

Sinking back into her seat, Lydia felt a new and unexpected warmth ripple through her. When she'd arrived at the camp earlier that afternoon she never would've imagined meeting the mysterious, reclusive Kennedy Fletcher.

Not only was he alive and well, he was more drop-dead gorgeous than before. He was also single and not in a committed relationship; the last thought made Lydia smile.

Perhaps she'd judged Mr. Fletcher prematurely. It was apparent he wanted to play, and play she would. She would see what he was offering, then decide whether it was worth accepting. Like the tourism slogan for Las Vegas: *what happens here, stays here.* The same could be said for Camp Six Nations.

Once they arrived at the camp, Lydia directed Kennedy to leave her water on the porch. "How much do I owe you?" she asked him.

"For what?"

"The water and the yogurt."

Kennedy shook his head. "Nothing."

They stood motionlessly, staring at each other for several seconds. She was the first to break the silence. "Good night, Kennedy. Thank you for dinner."

He angled his head, smiling. "It was my pleasure. Good night, Lydia."

She waited until he walked the short distance to his cabin before she turned and went inside. Her first day was nothing like she'd imagined it would be.

It was quite remarkable, and she knew Kennedy Fletcher had something to do with that.

Four

It was nature's alarm clock that woke Lydia before dawn, and not her travel clock or the camp bell. The chatter of birds nesting on several trees outside her cabin began calling to one another as soon as streaks of light pierced the night sky, heralding the beginning of a new day. She did not linger in bed.

Sunlight had filtered through the leaves by the time she'd made her bed, showered, and changed into a pair of sweatpants, an oversize T-shirt, and running shoes.

The delivery of meat and poultry was scheduled for seven, canned foods at nine, and produce at noon. Lydia was certain she and Neil would be able to organize the kitchen in time to prepare dinner for the staff and counselors.

The campers were expected on Sunday morning. She planned to have a snack available on arrival, followed by a southern-style Sunday dinner with all of the fixings.

She walked out of the cabin and off the porch. A cool breeze whispered over her face. The weather was ideal for an early morning walk. What she'd regretted most about selling her condo and moving back with her parents was not having access to a twenty-four-hour on-site health facility. She usually took advantage of the heated pool and treadmill.

Heading in the direction of the lake, Lydia realized she wasn't the only early riser. Wearing headsets, Jeff and Megan jogged leisurely across an open field. She reached the lake, but hadn't gone more than fifty feet when she saw Kennedy swimming toward the pier.

He hoisted himself out of the water and sat down, his feet dangling in the water. She was transfixed by the play of light over his naked upper body. He truly was an African god come to life. The droplets of water dotting his tanned brown shoulders shimmered like precious gems on dark brown velvet.

Lydia hadn't realized she'd been holding her breath until she felt a band constricting her chest. A wave of shame assailed her. What had she become? Watching Kennedy made her feel like a voyeur. Moving quickly, quietly, she walked back the way she'd come, away from Kennedy and away from temptation.

Perched on tall stools at a stainless steel counter, Lydia and Neil pored over pages of typed items. The pantry, refrigerator, and freezer were stocked with enough food and meat to last a week.

She gave her assistant a sidelong glance. "We need a computerized inventory. There's no way we're going to need this much food every week. We're not going to need a standing order for fifty pounds of onions."

Neil turned and met her gaze. A network of pale blue spidery veins around his penetrating dark eyes enhanced the paleness of his face.

"Who's going to do it?"

Lydia sighed softly. "I'll do it."

"When?"

"Before dinner."

"Where?"

"I'll buy a laptop."

"Why don't you use the one at the main house?" Neil asked.

"I could do that, but we're still going to need a terminal here."

Pressing the heels of his hands to his forehead, Neil grimaced. "I forgot about that."

Deep in thought, Lydia chewed her lower lip. "I remember seeing a Staples in a small shopping center not too far from here. Let's plan our dinner menu and then I'm going shopping for a computer. What do you suggest we prepare?" she asked, a mysterious smile crinkling her eyes.

Neil stared at Lydia, complete surprise on his face. "You want me to put together the menu?"

"Why not?"

His gaze narrowed. "Are you testing me?"

Lifting finely arched eyebrows, she stared at him, her expression deceptively neutral. "Now, why would I do that?"

He shrugged a shoulder. "I don't know."

"Are you going to show me what you've got, Mr. Neil?" She was going to offer Neil what had been withheld from her: an opportunity to showcase his talent and creativity.

"We're cooking for a little more than thirty, so I'd go with grilled London broil in a cilantro mint vinaigrette, grilled veggies, and a salad."

Lydia nodded. "What about those who don't eat beef?"

"Grilled chicken."

She nodded again. "What type of salad? Caesar? Waldorf?"

Excitement flushed Neil's normally pale face. "What about a mixed citrus with red onions and escarole?"

"Good choice," Lydia said, complimenting him. "I suggest two salads. The other can be apples or pears, walnuts, and blue cheese."

"I like your style, Lydia. You're definitely top-shelf."

"It's not so much what you prepare as it is working with what you have. We have bushels of seasonal fruit that should be eaten before it spoils. We can serve it for all three meals and snacks." Baskets of fresh raspberries, blackberries, blueberries, and strawberries were stored on shelves in the walk-in refrigerator.

"What about dessert, Lydia?"

Tilting her head at an angle, she smiled at him. "What about it, Neil?" she asked, answering his question with one of her own.

He flashed a warm, open smile . . . for the first time. "Trifle."

Reaching over, she squeezed his hand. "You just earned yourself a gold star."

Lydia sat down on the side of her bed, a towel wrapped around her damp body. Votive candles flickered, throwing low and short shadows over the walls. She ached, neck, back, and wrists, from spending hours hunched over the laptop entering every description and quantity of provisions in the kitchen after helping Neil prepare dinner. He had concocted a marinade with an Asian flavor that tantalized the palate. She was more than impressed by his trifle. Everything from the pound cake to the whipped cream and toasted almond garnish was made from scratch.

Neil's cooking ability was only surpassed by his speed. Lydia hoped his wife would realize that his passion was cooking and not sitting in a cubicle auditing government agencies.

Her own love affair with cooking began at age four. Etta Mae had sat her on a kitchen stool, hoping to keep her amused. Amusement became curiosity and finally an obsession. Cooking had become as vital to Lydia as breathing. And to succeed in her field had become an all-consuming drive that could only be assuaged by owning and operating her own restaurant.

She wanted to sit out on the porch and listen to music, but decided against it. In a few hours it would be Sunday. Removing the towel, she lay across the bed and within minutes fell asleep.

* * *

Kennedy stared through the screen, watching Lydia walk across the meadow. Although they were living close to each other he'd found it odd that he hadn't caught a glimpse of her since the night they'd gone to the Roadhouse.

A slow smile parted his lips as he slipped his hands into the pockets of his shorts. The memory of her soft body pressed intimately to his, the hauntingly sensual fragrance of her perfume, and her exquisite, fragile beauty had lingered. His smiled widened. She was dressed for work. Instead of jeans or a revealing slim skirt, the luscious curves of her body were concealed under a pair of loose-fitting black pin-striped pants and a white tunic; a black-and-white-patterned bandana covered her hair.

The vibrating motion of the cell phone clipped to his waistband broke into his musings. Peering at the display, he saw his mother's number. Vertical lines appeared between his eyes. Diane Fletcher-Anderson did not make it a practice to call him this early. He picked up the phone.

"Good morning, Mama." The slow Alabama drawl from his youth was back.

A soft laugh came through the earpiece. "Good morning, son."

"How are you feeling?"

"I'm mighty fine, Kennedy. It's your father who's not doing so good."

"What's wrong with Dad?"

There came a slight pause before Diane said, "It's not Philip."

If it wasn't his stepfather, Philip Anderson, then that meant it had to be Marvin Kennedy—the man who had fathered him, a man who had rejected him before his birth, a man whom he met for the first time a week after he'd inked a multi-million-dollar contract with a signing bonus to play for the NFL. Closing his eyes, Kennedy girded himself for bad news.

"What does he want?" A thread of hardness had crept into his voice.

There was another pause from Diane. "It's not what he wants, Kennedy, but what he needs."

He opened his eyes. "Okay, Mama, what does he *need*?" The last time Marvin contacted him it was because he needed money. He'd lost his job and the bank had threatened to foreclose on his house.

"A kidney."

"A what?"

"A kidney, son."

On shaking knees, Kennedy made his way over to a cushioned wicker love seat and sat down. He ran a free hand over his face. "He wants me to give him a kidney?"

"No. He only called to say that his doctor said he's going to need another kidney."

"How much time does he have?"

"Six to nine months. A year, if he's lucky."

Bitterness welled up in Kennedy's throat like bile, resentment smoldering with the weight of a soaked blanket. Why couldn't Marvin come to him? Why did he continue to go through Diane? Hadn't he hurt her enough over the years?

"Tell him to call me."

"You know he won't do that."

A muscle in Kennedy's lean jaw twitched as he clenched his teeth. "Either he calls me, or this topic is moot."

A soft sigh whispered through the earpiece. "I'll try to convince him to call you."

"You shouldn't have to convince him, Mama. Just tell him."

"You're both so much alike that it—"

"Makes you want to scream," Kennedy said, cutting off his mother and completing her statement. "I'm going to have to hang up because I need to go to work."

"How's the camp?"

Smiling for the first time since answering the call, he gave Diane an update. "The kids are coming in today."

"I think it's very noble of you to build a camp for less fortunate children, but I still would like to see you married with children of your own. I want a grandchild."

"Bye, Mama."

"Don't you dare hang up on me, Kennedy Marvin Fletcher," Diane warned.

"Love you a bunch." He pressed a button, ending the call.

Getting to his feet, Kennedy reattached the phone to his waistband. Diane Fletcher-Anderson's call disturbed him more than he wanted to admit. Just when he thought he'd straightened out his life it was about to be torn asunder with the news that his biological father needed a kidney.

Temporarily dismissing Marvin's medical condition, he pushed open the porch door, descended the steps, and headed for the kitchen. He needed a cup of coffee—black and very strong.

Lydia felt a presence and her head came up. Kennedy stood on the inside of the double doors. Her gaze moved leisurely from his stoic expression to his strong legs in a pair of khaki walking shorts.

She smiled. "Good morning."

"Good morning." His expression did not change. The smell of grilling bacon and brewing coffee filled the expansive kitchen. "Is the coffee ready?"

"Not yet. Which one do you want? Leaded or unleaded?"

A hint of a smile softened out the sharp angles in his face. "Leaded, please."

She took a quick glance at the urn. "Give it a few minutes."

Moving closer, Kennedy studied Lydia as she quickly, deftly chopped the ingredients for omelets. "Where's Neil?"

"I told him he could sleep in late this morning."

"He should be here working, not sleeping late."

Lydia's hands stilled. "I told you I gave him the morning off."

"You have no right—"

"I have every right, Kennedy," she said sharply, cutting him off. Turning, she stared at his thunderous expression, but refused to back down. The table of organization in the orientation packet indicated Kennedy shared equal administrative management status with Roger and Grace Evans.

"When I signed on I was told that I have absolute power to run the kitchen. And I interpreted that to mean on my terms, and that I set up my own schedule."

Kennedy was aware that Lydia had only accepted the position if she was given total control. She was talking about absolute power as if it were a divine right.

"Just make certain he doesn't slack off on you."

"I don't believe Neil Lane has a slack bone in his body. He proved that last night. He prepared everything."

Kennedy was momentarily speechless in his surprise. "He cooked last night?"

Crossing her arms under her breasts, Lydia nodded slowly. "*Everything*," she crooned, drawing out the word into four distinctive syllables.

"Damn! The dude is good."

"Neil is better than good. He's incredible." She went back to dicing red, green, and yellow bell peppers. "I decided we take turns cooking last night and this morning because we won't have a full camp until later on today."

"What's on tonight's menu?"

She gave him a sidelong glance. "You're as bad as Jeff. Do you think of anything else other than food?"

Kennedy's lids lowered and he gave her a direct stare. "Yes, I do."

"What?"

"You."

Lydia hesitated in dicing for a millisecond, her heart beating a double-time rhythm. Her eyebrows lifted. "You think about me?"

Crossing his arms over his chest, Kennedy propped a hip against a counter. "Yes."

"Why?"

"I'm curious."

Moving to the grill, she turned over strips of bacon. "What do you want to know about me?"

He shrugged a broad shoulder under his navy blue camp shirt. "Why are you working here when you could work at any three- or four-star restaurant?"

"That's a long story, Kennedy."

Smiling, he angled his head. "Will it take longer than eight weeks to tell?"

It was Lydia's turn to smile. Kennedy Fletcher was a study in contrasts—he was smooth, smooth as creamy peanut butter in his demeanor, but about as subtle as a sledgehammer in his pursuit of her.

"No," she said softly. Straightening, he moved closer—close enough for her to feel his breath feather over the top of her ear.

"How long, Lydia?"

It took all of her resolve not to lean into him as she'd done before, because there was something about the man standing a breath away that made her feel protected, safe. And all of her life men had protected her: her father and six brothers.

The only exception was Justin. She'd dated him because he was predictable and monogamous. The physical aspect of their relationship hadn't been extraordinary. Justin never complained, but on several occasions Lydia was left feeling unfulfilled, and whenever she broached the subject with him he blamed it on her hormones or libido. He mentioned her hormones once too often, and it was one of the deciding factors that led to her ending their relationship.

A mysterious smile curved the corners of her mouth upward. "Not long." He leaned even closer, his warmth and scent eliciting a shiver of longing. "Probably no longer than twenty minutes."

"You're right. That's not long. Where do you want to talk?"

Lydia's hands stilled; she stared at the kaleidoscope of

diced peppers on the cutting board. "You can either meet me on my porch, or we can go for a drive."

"What if we go for a walk?"

Her head came up slowly. "Walk where?"

"Around the lake."

She nodded. "Okay."

"I'll come for you around seven-thirty if that's not too early."

She gave him a long, penetrating look. "It's not too early." She'd scheduled Sunday dinner for three in the afternoon, which left her time to relax for the rest of the evening. "I want you to remember something, Kennedy."

He blinked once. "What's that?"

"It's not a date."

Kennedy successfully stopped the beginnings of what would've become a wide grin. "I'll try and remember that." He pointed at the urn of percolating coffee. "Is it ready yet?"

Lydia noticed that a button had changed from red to green. "Yes." Reaching for a mug stacked on a shelf under a counter, she filled it with coffee. "How would you like it?"

"Black, please."

She handed him the mug, their fingertips touching. Her body tingled from the contact. She watched him bring the steaming liquid to his mouth, watching its shape change as he took furtive sips. Waves of curiosity washed over her, and she wondered how she would react to the pressure of his mouth on hers. How would he taste? Would his kisses be gentle? Persuasive? Forceful?

For the second time in as many days she turned away from Kennedy, because she did not want him to see the lust radiating from her eyes. If there was something wrong with her hormones it was because they were at that moment raging out of control.

Kennedy savored the warmth spreading throughout his chest. He had avoided the coffee drinking habit because of its bitter aftertaste. But this cup claimed a rich fruity flavor.

"The coffee's good," he remarked, taking another deep swallow.

"Thank you."

Lydia did not want to concentrate on the man sharing her kitchen, so she busied herself placing sausage links on the grill, turning on the flame under a large pot of water for grits, and placing a pan of biscuits and a tin filled with batter for miniature cranberry and blueberry muffins into an oven.

She was certain Kennedy heard her sigh the moment two adolescent boys walked in. Roger had offered to give her two counselors-in-training on a rotating basis to put out serving trays, stack dishes in the industrial dishwasher, and clean up after every meal.

Kennedy set his mug on a counter. "Thanks for the coffee." Not waiting for Lydia's rejoinder, he nodded to the two boys and left the kitchen.

"What do you want me to do, Miss Lydia?"

She winced at the form of address, but the camp directors insisted every adult's name be preceded by Miss or Mr.

"You can begin putting out plates and utensils."

Forty minutes later the serving station was filled with trays of breakfast selections ranging from grits, scrambled eggs, bacon, and sausage to waffles, fruit toppings, and sliced melon and fruit.

By the time the first person walked in, Lydia stood behind a portable stove ready to take requests for omelets.

Neil arrived in time to man the omelet station, and Lydia returned to the kitchen to begin preparations for dinner.

Five

The buses carrying the campers arrived at eleven-thirty. Wide-eyed stares mirrored their apprehension about spending the next two months away from everything and everyone familiar to them in their young lives.

Kennedy stood with Roger and Grace, welcoming each camper with a smile and a handshake. He was fascinated by the reactions of the six-year-olds. They huddled together as if close contact with one another would protect them. All wore colored wristbands identifying them by name, age group, allergies, and an emergency telephone number.

His heart went out to a little girl with a profusion of curly braids crying that she missed her mother. She wouldn't move as the campers in her group made their way toward the dining hall where a snack awaited them. The impasse ended once her counselor picked her up and carried her. Exhausted from weeping, she laid her head on the counselor's shoulder, stuck her thumb in her mouth, and fell asleep.

Kennedy felt a strange numbing comfort despite the telephone call from his mother. Satisfaction shimmered in his eyes. He'd waited a long time for this day. The inspiration to set up a camp for under privileged children came during a fund-raiser in Baltimore. He'd remained behind after the gathering to sign autographs, and the complaint he heard from parents was that their children had no safe place to play during their summer vacation.

Kennedy had discussed the possibility of financing a community center with his investment banker, but it was his mother, Diane, who had suggested the sleepaway camp.

His agent had called the major networks, requesting time for a press conference, announcing Kennedy Fletcher's untimely retirement from the NFL. He left the game he loved, managed to avoid the media spotlight, and returned to college to earn a master's and put into motion his plan for the camp. His life was back on track because one of his dreams was now a reality.

If his focus on Camp Six Nations was unshakable he was not able to make the same claim when it came to Lydia Lord. He liked her because she was a challenge, more challenging than the only woman he had believed he loved enough to sacrifice everything for. But in the end the sacrifice was unwarranted. Nila had left him.

Lydia stood with the administrative staff as Roger explained the camp's mission to the children lining the many benches in the dining hall. She and Neil had prepared individual snack boxes filled with sliced fruit, cheese, juice, water, pudding, and stone-ground wheat crackers. Later that afternoon they would be served a traditional southern Sunday dinner with regional desserts.

"I'd like to welcome all of you to Camp Six Nations and what I know will become a wonderful summer experience. I don't want you to think of yourselves as a group of boys and girls ranging in age from six to twelve, but as one camp, one family. And before you leave here I want all of you to think of your fellow camper as a family member." Roger had adopted Kennedy's slogan as the camp's motto.

"You will be supervised by a staff whose sole mission is to help you become the best that you can be. All adults will be addressed as Mr. or Miss. Once you settle into your cabin your counselor will review the list of rules that were sent to you with your acceptance letter. I cannot stress enough that each infraction is followed by a consequence. Imagine the fun you'll have hanging out with me listening to music from way, way back in the day when everyone else is either at an overnight campout, watching a movie, or hanging out at the campfire jamboree."

"No!" shouted the chorus of campers as they shook their heads and slapped palms.

Roger threw back his head and laughed. "I thought not. You are encouraged to write letters to your families. Mailboxes are located around the camp and will be emptied twice a week. Mail will be distributed every Monday, Wednesday, and Friday. Your parents are aware they are not to send you food, so if they forget and send you snacks or candy it will be confiscated." Murmurs and grumbling followed this announcement.

"I'm going to introduce you to some people whose responsibility it is to make certain you enjoy your summer." Adjusting his glasses, Roger directed his attention to the table filled with camp staff.

"Miss Brianna is one of our social workers, who along with Mr. Lucas will be available if you're having a problem with anything or anyone." Brianna and Luke stood up and nodded. "Next is Mr. Jeff, who is our drama instructor. For those of who are interested in singing, dancing, or exploring your theatrical talents, please let your counselor know and he or she will sign you up." Jeff rose to his feet and gestured with a flourish, then bowed from the waist. His actions elicited laughs and a round of applause.

"Camp Six Nations is very fortunate to have the next great artist with us. Miss Megan has made a name for herself as a world-famous potter and glassmaker. None of you will want to leave here without making at least one item using Miss Megan's trademark technique.

"I suppose some of you have wondered why your camp is

called Six Nations. The answer will come from our interdenominational minister, Reverend Alfonso, who is also a Choctaw shaman or holy man.

"We have experienced medical personnel, whom I hope none of you will have to visit during your stay. But in case of a few scrapes and bruises Dr. Richard and Miss Jill will be available twenty-four-seven.

"Next up are two people we must always keep happy—the *cooks*!"

There came thunderous rounds of applause. "Please, please, please don't ever make Miss Lydia and Mr. Neil upset, because we don't want them to tell us that they forgot to turn off the oven and burned the food."

Lydia stared at Kennedy through her lashes, smiling when he winked at her.

"Last, but certainly not least," Roger continued, "is our sports director, Mr. Ken." He nodded to Kennedy. "I'd like for you to say a few words."

Kennedy swung his legs over the bench and stood up. Some of the children gasped, craning their necks to look up at him as he offered them his two-hundred-watt grin.

"I'd like to welcome everyone to Camp Six Nations. You are very special because this is our first season, which means you will be responsible for establishing a tradition for next year and all those to come.

"I've only set one goal, and that is that everyone will learn to swim before the end of the season. Swimming is mandatory, but you will have a choice of any other sport listed in your camp folder. All sports will focus on teamwork, sportsmanship, and respect. You are here because you are special. Don't ever forget that."

Kennedy, his gaze fixed on Lydia, sat down to a smattering of applause. Something intense flowed through him, and he wanted to tell Lydia she was special, special enough to make him forget his promise never to become involved with another woman.

* * *

Lydia stepped out onto the porch closing the front door; then she went completely still. Kennedy lay on her recliner, eyes closed, head cradled on folded arms, while the distinctive voice of Patti LaBelle singing "If Only You Knew" came through the stereo speakers. She was hard pressed not to smile. He'd made himself at home.

She moved closer and his eyes opened. He stared up at her as if she were a complete stranger. "Enjoying yourself?"

A mysterious smile softened his mouth. "You can't imagine how much," he said cryptically. Sitting up, he swung his legs over the recliner and stood up. "I like the wind chime and the candles. They add a very nice touch."

Kennedy liked the aesthetics *and* he liked Lydia Lord. He liked everything about her: face, body, voice, cooking ability. She claimed a refreshing femininity missing in many of the women he'd known, most of whom he'd discovered were either too vapid or too needy.

It wasn't vanity that made him cognizant of his ability to attract the opposite sex, but the numbers escalated once he'd become a ballplayer earning eight and sometimes nine figures from an NFL contract and product endorsements.

What had set him apart from many of the young instant millionaires and made him an anomaly in the sports world was that he wasn't a dumb jock blessed with only superior physical talent. He'd worked hard to dispel that myth, and now that Camp Six Nations was fully operational he'd become an entrepreneur.

Lydia flashed a dreamy smile. "They help me relax."

Lowering his chin, he angled his head. "Would you prefer we talk here?"

She shook her head. "No. I'm looking forward to walking." Sitting on her porch with Kennedy was far too tempting an offer.

His gaze moved slowly from Lydia's face to her feet in a pair of sandals before reversing itself. She'd brushed her hair off her face and secured it in a knot on the nape of her neck.

On another woman the style could be interpreted as matronly, but on her it was sleek, sophisticated. Her staid hairdo was incongruent to a magenta tank top and black slacks. An expanse of coffee-colored brown flesh was visible between the hem of her top and waistband of her hip-hugging pants.

"You look nice, Lydia."

The heat singeing Lydia's face swept downward like a sirocco and pooled between her thighs. It wasn't Kennedy's compliment that had aroused her, but the smoldering invitation in his gaze that seemly undressed her.

Why, she mused, did she feel like a girl on her first date? What was there about Kennedy Fletcher that melted her composure? His presence set her nerves on edge, heightened her sexual awareness of him, and stirred her libido.

She peered up at him through her lashes, unaware of the sensuality in the gesture. "Thank you."

The beginnings of a smile parted his lips. "You're welcome." Reaching for her hand, he gave her fingers a gentle squeeze. "Are you ready?"

"Yes."

She was ready for Kennedy and whatever they would offer each other over the summer, and more than ready for all of her tomorrows.

"Let me put out the candles first."

Kennedy released her hand, watching as Lydia used a snuffer to extinguish the flickering flames. Within seconds the objects on the porch were shadowed in the diffused light from a setting sun. Twilight had cloaked the camp with a diaphanous veil through which the subtle colors of red, orange, blue, and gray shimmered.

Completing the task, she returned to his side and took his hand. "I'm ready now."

Are you really ready, Lydia? he asked silently. Kennedy wanted to know if she was ready for the chase, his pursuit of her. They walked hand in hand across the meadow and down the path leading to the lake.

Camp Six Nations was settling down for the night. Lights

were going out in the cabins of the younger campers, while the older ones were filing out of the barn where they'd viewed *Lord of the Rings: Fellowship of the Ring*.

"When did you decide you wanted to become a chef?" Kennedy's sonorous voice broke the comfortable silence.

Lydia took a quick glance at his distinctive profile in the waning daylight. "I must have been four when I announced to my parents that I wanted to cook when I grew up."

Attractive lines fanned out around Kennedy's eyes. "You never changed your mind?"

"Nope. I grew up in the kitchen. I went from a high chair to a playpen and finally to a tall stool, watching my mother prepare three incredibly delicious meals a day for her husband and nine children."

Kennedy stopped suddenly and Lydia would've lost her balance if he hadn't caught her waist. "You're one of nine?"

She bit back a smile. His reaction was similar to most whenever she revealed the size of her family. "I'm the youngest."

"Are you the only girl?"

"No. I have six brothers and two sisters."

Pulling her closer, Kennedy shook his head. "What I would've given to have had a brother, a sister, or both."

Lydia, who knew nothing about the very private Kennedy Fletcher, said, "You're an only child." He nodded.

They continued along the path in silence as nightfall descended. A sprinkling of stars in the darkening sky was overshadowed by the brilliance of a near-full moon. Large round globes mounted on poles surrounding the lake were coming on in the encroaching darkness.

"How was it growing up with six older brothers?"

"It had its advantages."

"Did they scare away your potential suitors?"

Lydia wanted to tell Kennedy that she hadn't had many suitors. There was the college basketball player to whom she had given her love and innocence, and Justin Banks.

"By the time I began dating, most of my brothers were married with their own children. It was my father who'd earned a reputation as the intimidator. He scared away the paperboy who he thought was flirting with my sister Sharon."

"Where did you grow up?"

"We lived in a farmhouse about twenty miles outside of Baltimore. Our nearest neighbor raised milk cows. How about you, Kennedy? Where did you grow up?"

"Smoky Junction, Alabama."

Lydia's expression brightened. "I thought I detected a southern drawl."

"I worked very hard to get rid of my drawl."

"Why?"

"A television network had approached my publicist because they wanted a highly visible spokesperson for an anti-drug public service announcement. I went to the audition, but was rejected because it was hard to decipher some of what I was saying."

"How did you lose it?"

"I paid a speech coach to tutor me. Six months later I recorded the announcement."

"But isn't that a little like denying who you are?" she asked.

Kennedy shook his head. "Who I am has nothing to do with how I look or sound. I'm still a country boy from a mill town that's so small that if you go more than thirty miles an hour you'd see all of it in five minutes."

"How small is it?"

"The cotton mill employs almost all of the 958 folks who live there."

Lydia was mildly surprised by Kennedy's reference to his being a "country boy." Everything about him screamed *big-city elegance* and *sophistication*, and she wondered whether Kennedy's transformation was predicated on his publicist's desire to make his client a more marketable product.

"What are you going to do at the end of the summer, Lydia?"

"I don't know," she answered honestly. "I'm planning to open my own restaurant."

"When?"

"Hopefully next spring." She told him about the new construction site with the underground mall.

"Are you certain you'll be able to rent the space?"

"No. But, because I submitted an application as soon as the prospectus was announced, I believe I have a good chance of securing it."

Kennedy tightened his hold around Lydia's waist, bringing her closer. The soft curves of her body fit perfectly against his length. She stiffened slightly, then relaxed. He smiled.

"Running your own restaurant is an enormous responsibility."

She nodded. "I know, but I'm ready for it. I graduated from culinary school at twenty. I apprenticed in a hotel kitchen for a year, then spent the next two years in France, Italy, and Spain, learning how to cook their regional dishes.

"I came back to the States and went to work for a well-known D.C. restaurant that will remain nameless. I gave them four years. I was up for a promotion twice, and each time I was passed over. That's when I decided no more, not at twenty-seven."

"You quit?"

"You damn skippy I did. If I'm going to stand on my feet for hours over a hot stove, then it will be because I want to and not because someone else demands it."

Kennedy's mouth curved into an unconscious smile. There was just enough rebellion in Lydia to make her interesting. "I'm sorry you didn't get your promotion, but their loss is the camp's gain."

The campers had cheered and exchanged high fives once they realized they were going to be served a traditional Sunday dinner reflecting the American South: Cajun, Creole, soul, and just plain country dishes.

"I like cooking for children." Lydia gave Kennedy a sidelong glance. "Do you have any children?"

A low chuckle rumbled in his chest before he said, "No."

"Are you certain?"

Kennedy registered a quiver in Lydia's voice, knowing instinctively why she'd asked the question. He slowed his pace. "I'm not a monk, Lydia."

Her delicate jaw tightened. "How can you be sure you don't have a child somewhere that you don't know about?"

"I am sure, Lydia," he countered emphatically. "I've never slept with a woman without using protection. Now, why am I being interrogated?"

"I just don't want to contend with baby mama drama from an ex-chicken-head groupie or video ho if I decide to go out with you."

"I've never entertained groupies, hos, or chicken-heads." His voice was heavily sarcastic.

Lydia emitted an audible sigh over the incessant sounds of crickets and frogs mingling with other nocturnal wildlife serenading the countryside. She had agreed to go for a walk with Kennedy to talk about herself, but they'd compromised. He'd been forthcoming, answering her questions with a candor she had not expected. There was more she wanted to know about him, but that would come later.

"When do you want to go out?"

Stopping under the soft golden glow of a lamppost, Kennedy pulled her into the circle of his embrace. "Are you asking me out, Miss Lord?"

She gave him a saucy grin. "Yes, I am. We only have eight weeks, so I suggest we get this party started."

"Are you promising a party, Lydia?"

Her expression changed, sobering. "I never make promises, because I'm not certain I'll be able to keep them."

"Well, I do make promises," Kennedy said. His stare drilled into her, looking for a modicum of uneasiness in her gaze. But it was apparent Lydia Lord wasn't easily intimidated. "I promise to respect you." His voice lowered seductively. "And I promise to show you a good time."

Lydia found the man holding her to his heart vaguely disturbing as she tried separating Kennedy Fletcher, private citizen, from Ken Fletcher, celebrated running back. Tilting her chin, she studied his features one by one in the flattering light: a strong chin, the hollow beneath his cheekbones, and a full firm mouth that drew her gaze and lingered there.

"I like your promises."

"Good."

Lydia felt him coming closer although he hadn't moved. She knew Kennedy was going to kiss her, but there was nothing she could or would do to stop him. Her lids fluttered wildly, then closed as his mouth brushed hers tentatively before he staked his claim.

Kennedy forced himself to go slow. He dropped light kisses at the corners of Lydia's mouth as if it were a frothy confection to savor at a leisurely pace. Everything within him screamed for a release, but he managed to quell his desire for the woman in his arms. He'd promised her he would respect her—and he would. It would have to be her decision to take what they would share to another level. He deepened the kiss, his lips parting as he breathed in her moist breath and her scent.

Lydia curved her arms under Kennedy's shoulders, holding on to him as if she were a drowning swimmer. And she was swimming, feeling the power of the undertow from his slow, addictive kisses. She'd been kissed before, but not like this.

He held her as if she were a piece of fragile porcelain, his mouth brushing hers like the gossamer touch of a butterfly's wings. His nearness gave her comfort, the intoxicating smell of his cologne overwhelmed her, and for the first time in her life Lydia wanted to strip off her clothes and lie with a man she didn't know and damn the consequences.

Kennedy raised his head, but did not drop his gaze as a vaguely sensuous light passed between him and Lydia.

She rested her forehead against his shoulder. "You forgot one more promise."

His right hand moved up and down her spine in a soothing motion. "What's that?"

"Not to seduce me."

A deep rumbling laughter resounded in his chest. "That's one promise I can't make, Lydia."

He wouldn't promise, and Lydia did not want him to. As if on cue, they turned and retraced their steps. All of the lights in the camper cabins were out, while one light shone through the second-floor window at the main house. It was apparent everyone wanted to get enough sleep before the first full day of camp.

Lydia stopped in front of her cabin, easing her hand from Kennedy's firm grip. "Good night."

Kennedy nodded. "Good night, Lydia."

He stood motionless watching as Lydia climbed the steps, opened the door leading to the porch, then the inner door and closed it softly behind her.

Walking the short distance to his own cabin, Kennedy sank down on the love seat. A jumble of confused thoughts and emotions attacked him as he recalled kissing Lydia. The instant he tasted her mouth, he realized that was what he'd wanted to do when he saw her for the first time.

He'd promised her he would respect her and that they would have fun—lots of fun.

And they would—at least for the next eight weeks.

Six

Lydia had just completed the task of cutting up peaches and strawberries when a counselor with a little girl sporting a head filled with curly braids walked into the kitchen.

Keisha Middleton still had not adjusted to camp life. Kiki, as the children in her cabin called her, cried constantly, refused to eat, and would not participate in any of her scheduled activities.

The six-year-old was adorable, reminding Lydia of a doll that had become a favorite when she was a child: curly hair, flawless dark brown skin, large black eyes, and delicate features.

"Miss Lydia, Kiki hasn't eaten anything since yesterday afternoon," the counselor-in-training whispered.

Lydia washed her hands in a stainless steel sink, then dried them on the towel resting over her left shoulder. "Are you sure about that?"

"Yes. She didn't eat last night, and we tried coaxing her to eat something at breakfast."

"Leave her with me." Nodding, the counselor walked out.

Lydia knelt on one knee. "Come, doll baby." Keisha went into her embrace, chubby arms encircling her neck. Smiling, she asked, "Is there anything you want to eat, sweetheart?"

Tightening her hold on Lydia's neck, Keisha whispered close to her ear, "Ice cream."

Lydia's eyes widened. "Is that your favorite food?" The little girl nodded. "What flavor do you like?"

"Chocolate."

Lydia checked Keisha's wristband for food allergies. There weren't any. "I happen to have some chocolate ice cream." It wasn't the traditional ice cream Americans favored, but gelato. "I'll give you some, but first you must eat a little something." Resting her forehead against Keisha's, she winked at her. "I'm going to fix you a grilled cheese sandwich with sliced fruit and a glass of milk. Okay?" The child nodded again.

She placed Keisha on a stool as Etta Mae had done with her many years before. The child was enthralled as she watched the preparations for what would become her impromptu lunch. Half an hour later, Lydia and Keisha sat at a table in the dining hall, eating chocolate hazelnut gelato drizzled with a chocolate cream sauce.

Lydia reached over and dabbed Keisha's mouth with a paper napkin before she scrambled off the bench. "Wasn't that good?"

Keisha stood up, clapping her hands. "It was the best!"

Dropping a kiss on the fuzzy braids, Lydia smiled, saying, "I'm glad you liked it. Now I'm going to take you back to your cabin for rest hour."

Keisha frowned. "Do I have to go?"

"Yes, you have to."

"But I don't want to," she whined.

"You must play with your new friends, Kiki. Your mommy sent you to camp to have fun. Don't you want to learn how to swim and make a plate with your name on it?"

Keisha's brilliant black button eyes sparkled. "Can I make a plate for you, Miss Lydia?"

Smiling, Lydia hunkered down until her head was level with Keisha's. "I'd love for you to make a plate for me, Kiki. But I want you to start eating; otherwise you'll be too weak or sick to make anything for me. Okay?"

A slight frown dotted the space between Keisha's eyes as she appeared lost in thought. "Okay."

Negotiating with young children was something she had become accustomed to, because she'd become Aunt Liddie to nearly two dozen nieces and nephews.

Neil walked into the dining hall as Lydia and Keisha prepared to leave. Lydia nodded to him. "Please finish the gelato while I take Kiki back to her cabin."

He smiled, saluting. "No problem. I thought I'd tell you before you run into Ken. He's on the warpath."

Her eyebrows flickered. "Why?"

"Someone removed the bell's clapper. He told the counselors that he expects whoever took it to leave it in the barn. But if it's not returned before dinner, then they'll be remanded to their cabins after dinner for the next two weeks."

She winced. "Ouch." Extracurricular activities included playing video games, watching movies and television, and listening to music. "What happened to Roger's threat that they would have to listen to Jimi Hendrix, Janis Joplin, Bob Dylan, and the Doors?"

"Ken said that's hardly punishment, because the kids might actually enjoy Roger's music."

"I don't think the kids came to camp to be grounded."

"You're right about that."

A faint smile of satisfaction touched Lydia's lips as she curbed an urge to pump her fist in triumph. She'd won the bet.

"Thanks for the heads-up."

Kennedy waited for Lydia to sit on his love seat before settling down beside her. He had slipped a note under her door asking to see her before she retired for bed. Leisurely, he stretched out his long legs, crossing his feet at the ankles.

"It's all right if you gloat."

A flash of confusion crossed Lydia's face. "I don't know what you're talking about."

"You won the bet."

As she shifted and stared at Kennedy's grim expression, Lydia's grin was wide enough for him to see her molars. "I tried to tell you, Kennedy. Nobody wants to be startled from their sleep by a stupid clanging bell day after day."

Eyes narrowing and realization dawning, Kennedy peered closely at Lydia. "You knew it would happen because you'd gone to sleepaway camp," he said accusingly.

"Not only did I go, but one year I took the clapper," she admitted.

"You're kidding, aren't you?"

"Nope."

"I just can't imagine you shimmying up a pole."

"Why not?"

"Because you seem so prim and proper, Miss Lord."

"Prim and proper or female?"

Kennedy shook his head. "Don't go there, Lydia. Being female has nothing to do with being physically challenged."

She cupped a hand over an ear. "Do I hear another wager coming up?"

He gave Lydia a long, penetrating look. She was not only beautiful, but also competitive—a trait so apparent in his own personality, a trait he had learned to temper with age.

He crossed his arms over his chest. "Let me pay up on the first one before we bet again. Where do you want to eat?"

"You don't have to take me out."

"Why?"

"Because my favorite restaurant is nowhere near here."

"Where is it?"

"Forget it, Kennedy."

"Why?"

"Because we can't drive there."

"A name," he demanded softly.

"Alfonso's."

Kennedy leaned closer. "Where is Alfonso's, Lydia?" Her name came out like a caress.

"Mexico," she said after a noticeable pause.

He lifted an eyebrow. "Where in Mexico?"

"Cabo San Lucas."

Kennedy closed his eyes. She had selected a restaurant in a region of Baja California that had become a popular playground for those willing to pay any price for absolute privacy and anonymity.

He opened his eyes. "I'll make good on the wager."

Lydia shook her head. "No, Kennedy. I'm not going to hold you to the wager."

His expression stilled and grew serious. "You can't back out now."

"Kennedy, I—"

"I nothing," he interrupted quietly.

Lydia moved to stand up, but was thwarted when Kennedy's fingers snaked around her upper arm. She lost her balance, and with her breasts heaving she landed heavily on his lap.

"I don't want you to take me to Mexico."

"I promise not to seduce you," he said with a wide grin.

"Don't flatter yourself, Kennedy," she shot back.

"Then, that settles it. We'll decide on a date at the end of the summer."

A flicker of apprehension coursed through Lydia as she met Kennedy's unwavering stare. The man was actually serious. He hadn't known her a week, yet he wanted to take her out of the country.

"I'm not a gold digger, Kennedy, so please don't confuse me with your other women."

Kennedy recoiled as if Lydia had slapped him, as he attempted to control his temper. "What's with you and the innuendoes about my involvement with other women? There are *no* other women." His voice was cold, exacting.

She closed her eyes. "I don't want to . . ." Her words trailed off and were swallowed up by Kennedy as he moved his mouth over hers.

Lydia's heart lurched, her pulse pounded, the tingling in

the pit of her stomach tightened until she felt herself slipping away from reality.

"Stop wiggling, darling," Kennedy whispered against her parted lips.

Pushing against the wall of muscle, Lydia was unable to free herself. His heat eased into her thighs, her hips rocking back and forth of their own volition, setting a rhythm in a dance of desire screaming to be assuaged. The hardness pressing up against her buttocks made her aware of where she was and on whose lap she writhed.

Lydia did free herself from his marauding mouth, her breathing coming in long, deep gasps as if she'd run a grueling race. She closed her eyes and took pleasure in the strong pulsing between her legs.

"There's a flag on the field, Kennedy."

"For what?"

"Illegal holding."

Smiling, he buried his face along the column of Lydia's scented neck. "What's the penalty?"

Easing back, she gave him a steady, penetrating stare. "A loss of two yards—offense."

Circling her waist with both hands, Kennedy lifted her effortlessly off his lap and stood up. "That's not much of a penalty."

She gave him a slow, sexy smile. "That's because the referee is in a good mood tonight."

Kennedy's large hand took Lydia's face and held it gently. Lowering his head, he brushed her lips with his. "I hope I'm not penalized for attempting to influence the referee, but are you free next Sunday afternoon?"

Lydia felt an invisible magnetism pulling her to the man holding her to his heart, a pull she could not resist. She successfully masked the feelings surging through her with a deceptive calmness.

"What do you have in mind?"

"Do you like county fairs?"

Her large eyes crinkled in a smile. "Yes, I do."

"Will you come with me?"

Lydia stared at Kennedy staring back at her in silent expectation. She recognized vulnerability in the former superstar football player that hadn't been there in any of their prior encounters. It was not the first time she asked herself why had he left the NFL when he was at the top of his game. What secret was he hiding from the world? Who or what had affected his life so that he was forced to give up what he'd openly professed was an obsession?

Lydia knew the answers to her silent queries could only come from the person in question—Kennedy Fletcher. She was not only intrigued by him as an athlete, but enthralled with him as the camp's sports director.

Peering up at him through her lashes, she smiled and said softly, "Yes. I'd like very much to go with you."

Kennedy emitted a sigh of relief. Although Lydia had agreed to go out with him, he knew she hadn't completely let go of her distrust of athletes, and she still viewed him as a jock, although he'd left the game four years before.

Despite a few setbacks in his personal life he was where he wanted to be. He would celebrate his thirty-sixth birthday in three weeks and had accomplished much more than men twice his age. He'd amassed a fortune capitalizing on his face, body, and physical abilities. He'd invested well, well enough to live comfortably, given his current lifestyle, for the rest of his life.

He'd realized his dream of becoming a professional athlete, provided financial security for his parents, and established a sleepaway camp for children. There had been a time when he planned to marry and hopefully father children, but rejection and vindictiveness ended an impending engagement and his football career.

"Thank you, Lydia."

Lydia smiled when she registered the drawl Kennedy had sought to lose, the cadence leisurely, sensual, and hypnotic.

"Good night, Kennedy."

Shifting slightly, he stood behind her, lowered his head, and trailed his lips along the nape of her neck. "What are little girls made of? Sugar, spice, and everything nice."

". . . Snakes, snails, and puppy dog tails," she said, laughing softly and reciting the popular nursery rhyme along with Kennedy. Moving out of arm's reach, Lydia waved to him. "Good night."

Smiling, he returned her wave. "Good night."

Lydia descended the porch steps and headed for her cabin, feeling the heat of Kennedy's gaze on her retreating back. She curbed the urge to turn around to see whether he was watching her. It wasn't until she closed and locked the door behind that she was able to draw a normal breath.

Stripping off her clothes, she slipped under a sheet and lightweight blanket, her mind reliving her body's reaction to the intimacy of Kennedy's kiss; the harder she tried to ignore the truth, the more it persisted. She was attracted to Kennedy and her vow not to become involved with an athlete had been shattered completely.

Seven

The clapper was back several hours after it was removed allegedly by an eleven-year-old female camper. And to discourage a repeat of the incident, John Philip Souza military marches blared from speakers attached to poles around the camp alternating with the clanging of the insufferable bell.

Kennedy had established a routine of observing every counselor and staff member, monitoring their interaction with campers and supervision of their subordinates. In his role as sports director he was able to make the most of his degree in physical and recreational education.

Standing on the pier, he watched the fast-moving dark clouds in the distance. Meteorologists had predicted late afternoon thunderstorms for the region. A group of eight-year-old boys swam out to a marker before turning and swimming back to the bank. Three of the six wore life vests.

Of the one hundred boys and girls who'd been accepted for camp, more than half were unable to swim. Two weeks into the season the percentage of swimmers had increased appreciably.

Raising the whistle hanging from a chain around his neck to his mouth, Kennedy blew into it, the piercing sound stopping all movement in the water. He pointed to a counselor and made a cutting motion across his neck. Within seconds the campers were ordered out of the lake.

Reaching for a palm-size pager, he pressed a button. "Get everyone indoors."

"Take shelter! Take shelter! Everyone take shelter!" The command boomed from the public address system. Footsteps were muffled in the carpet of grass as all of Camp Six Nations sought shelter from the impending storm.

Kennedy checked the basketball and tennis courts, making certain no one had ignored the warning. A roll of thunder shook the earth, followed by a deafening crash of lightning as he sprinted toward the dining hall. The sky darkened. It looked like midnight instead of early afternoon. Everything was shrouded in an eerie gunmetal gray seconds before the heavens opened up. Rainwater pasted Kennedy's shirt to his upper body as he raced inside the nearest structure to escape the storm. Taking off his cap, he shook off the water.

The mood inside the dining hall was festive, a direct contrast to the dark, ominous weather outside. The brilliance of overhead track lighting, voices raised in song by Jeff Wiggins and his theatrical group, and Lydia and Neil serving steaming cups of beverages beckoned him closer.

Kennedy watched Lydia top off a mug with a froth of whipped cream. His gaze softening, he stared at the curling ends of a ponytail resting over one shoulder. She appeared slimmer, more delicate in the white T-shirt tucked into the drawstring waist of a pair of loose-fitting houndstooth-pattern pants. This was the first time he'd observed her in the dining hall without her tunic and bandana.

Neil whispered something close to her ear and she threw back her head and laughed, the sound drowned out by the campers singing a hip-hop version of "America," with a distinctive Spanish accent.

Seeing her laugh with such abandon as she threw her head back, arching her neck, sent a quiver of desire rushing through Kennedy. He'd kissed that neck, inhaled the intoxicating fragrance clinging to the velvety skin. His gaze moved lower. The outline of a pair of small breasts was ardently displayed against the cotton T-shirt.

What was there about Lydia that made her so damn sexy in a T-shirt and baggy pants? Her face was bare and her hairstyle was better suited for an adolescent, yet despite her youthful appearance there was something fervently womanly about her. At twenty-seven she was hardly a girl, yet a girl-like vulnerability surfaced at times.

Kennedy hadn't seen Lydia since the night he'd kissed her on his porch, not even when he took his meals in the dining hall. He'd hoped to find her on her porch at night, but each time he glanced over at her cabin he found it dark and the jalousie windows closed.

He crossed the room and came up behind her as she turned to fill a tall mug from a coffee urn. "Have you been avoiding me?"

Lydia froze. She hadn't heard Kennedy's approach. A slow smile parted her lips. How had she missed the scent of his cologne? "Don't flatter yourself, Kennedy." It was the same thing she'd said to him the night on his porch when he'd promised not to seduce her.

"Then, why is that we live fifty feet apart but don't run into each other?"

"I don't know. Maybe it's because I'm the one working."

Kennedy stared at her hair. The thick lustrous strands weren't black but a rich dark brown with reddish highlights. He wondered what her hair would look like spread out over his pillow. The instant the thought entered his head he knew he wanted to sleep with Lydia Lord. And he did not know how he knew, but he was certain they would be good to and for each other.

"Are you calling me a slacker?"

Lydia filled the mug, then turned and stared up at Kennedy, her breath catching in her chest. He looked different. His face was darker, leaner, his cheekbones more defined. Her gaze shifted to his head. His hair was growing out. The stubble now curled over his scalp.

"No," she said softly. "I wouldn't know if you were slacking or not, because I would've been too busy to notice."

Despite working well together, she and Neil still put in long hours. She planned menus days in advance and they prepared the next day's entrées the night before. She was up at dawn, and usually retired for bed sixteen hours later.

"Are we still on for Sunday?" he asked.

"Yes, unless you decide to cancel."

A slow smile parted his lips. "Never happen."

Her smile matched his. "Good."

His eyebrows shot up in surprise. "Good?"

Lydia nodded. "I'm really looking forward to going, because I can't remember the last time I've been to a fair."

She wanted to tell Kennedy that she was looking forward to going out with *him*, because he ignited a passion she did not know she had. With him she felt sexy—indisputably woman. She wanted to lose herself in his embrace, to wallow languidly under the onslaught of his kisses, and she wanted to experience why she'd been born female.

She'd come to Camp Six Nations to gain experience running her own kitchen. But if she were to become involved with Kennedy Fletcher, then that would be a bonus.

"Can I get you something, Ken?" Neil asked, wiping his hands on a towel.

"I'll take some gelato." The first time he'd eaten gelato he couldn't get enough of the custard-style Italian ice cream.

Neil turned to Lydia. "Do we have any more?"

"I know there's a pistachio, but I'm not certain about the mascarpone with toasted pine nuts or the chocolate hazelnut."

She always made extra hazelnut because it was Keisha's favorite. The dessert had also become a favorite with campers and counselors for their midafternoon snack, along with sliced fruit and whimsically shaped melon pieces.

"I'll take the pistachio with those delicious little wafers," Kennedy said.

Lydia folded her hands on her hips. "Would you like anything else, Mr. Fletcher?"

Leaning closer, Kennedy pressed his mouth to her ear. "Are you on the menu, Miss Lord?"

Her breath quickening and cheeks burning in embarrassment, Lydia glanced over at Neil, wondering whether he'd overheard Kennedy. Her fear was allayed because he was busy finishing off an iced latte, drizzling caramel over a fluff of freshly whipped cream.

Leaning against a counter she closed her eyes. Kennedy had just verbalized what she'd been feeling, what she'd felt when sitting on his lap. She opened her eyes, exhaling; she was back in control.

"Excuse me. I'll go get your gelato." Walking around him, she made her way toward the kitchen. From the very beginning, she'd known there was something special about Kennedy that had nothing to do with his celebrity status.

And the harder she tried to ignore the truth, the more it challenged her. She wanted Kennedy Fletcher—in *and* out of bed!

Lydia returned to the dining hall, placing a bowl on the table in front of Kennedy along with a small plate of paper-thin wafers filled with almond paste.

He stared up at her. "Aren't you going to join me?"

She shook her head. "I can't. I'm serving." Lydia knew as soon as the rain stopped the dining hall would be filled with campers looking for their afternoon snack.

Rising to his feet, Kennedy motioned for Neil. "I want you to serve while I talk to your boss, and please bring her whatever she wants to eat or drink."

Neil inclined his head to Lydia. "What do you want?"

She forced a smile she didn't quite feel, because she did not want to make a scene. Kennedy's arrival had disrupted her normal routine.

"Nothing, thank you."

"Are you sure?" Neil asked.

"Very sure."

Kennedy cupped her elbow. "Please sit down."

She sat, folding her hands together on the table. "What do you want?"

Kennedy scooped up a spoonful of gelato, extending it to Lydia. "Have a taste."

"No, thank you."

Rising, he rounded the table and sat beside her. "You can use a few extra pounds."

Lydia's delicate jaw dropped, giving Kennedy the advantage he sought, as he eased the spoon into her mouth. He stared at her as she swallowed the gelato. A satisfied smile crinkled the lines fanning out around his large eyes. Slowly, deliberately, and calculatingly he put the spoon to his mouth and licked it, his gaze meeting and fusing with her shocked one.

Lowering his gaze and his voice, he drawled, "*You* taste wonderful."

Lydia was grateful she was sitting because she didn't think her shaking knees would've supported her quaking body if she'd been standing. The intent in Kennedy's erotic gesture was not only blatant but also palpable. When she'd asked him what he wanted, he'd been forthcoming when he said he wanted her. He wanted her and she wanted him, and she knew it was only a matter of time before their dilemma would be resolved.

The corners of her mouth inched with a knowing smile. "There is a flag on the field, Mr. Fletcher."

"What's the call this time, Ms. Referee?"

Her smile widened. "Flagrant foul."

Kennedy rolled his eyes. "And your penalty?"

"A four-day suspension."

Kennedy stared at Lydia's profile, a lethal calmness in his eyes. "That's excessive."

"I don't want the others spreading gossip about the chef and the sports director not being able to keep their affair under wraps."

"I didn't know we were having an affair," he teased.

"We're not," she protested softly.

Kennedy took in her solemn expression. "Not—yet," he said in a quiet tone.

"Can we talk about something else?" There was a pulse beat of silence before she said, "I'm a little uncomfortable with public displays of affection."

He nodded, recalling her protests about going out with athletes. Had she been involved with one who had publicly humiliated her? "I promised that I wouldn't disrespect you. I've kissed you twice, and the only time I've ever touched you is when we danced at the Roadhouse. If you didn't want me to kiss or touch you, then you should've said something at that time."

"It's not that I don't like kissing you," she said in a hushed tone, "it's just that I don't want everyone to know that we're . . ." Her words trailed off.

"We're not doing anything, Lydia, at least not what *I'd* like to do with you. But if you want us to act like strangers when we're around the others, then so be it."

Lydia knew Kennedy was annoyed, but at that point she didn't care. They were over twenty-one, consenting adults, but she'd learned a hard lesson: do not flaunt your liaisons.

The sound of childish voices filled the dining hall. The rain had stopped and the campers had come for their afternoon snack. Lydia, ignoring Kennedy's order that Neil serve the campers, excused herself and went to help her assistant.

Kennedy ate the gelato, wondering how Lydia could run hot and cold so quickly. When hot she made him burn and ache for her, but once cold her tongue lashed out, cutting like the bite of a whip. Whether hot or cold he still hadn't uncovered why he wanted her.

Lydia felt what it meant to be bone tired. She'd been on her feet for more than twelve hours preparing trays of food for the next two days. In less than an hour it would be

Sunday, her day off—a day she looked forward to spending with Kennedy, and the first time she looked forward to spending time away from the camp.

Just putting one foot in front of the other seemed like a chore as she made her way up the porch and walked into her cabin. She stripped off her clothes, leaving them in the laundry bag in a corner of the bathroom. The counselors-in-training were responsible for doing the campers' laundry, but the staff had the option of using the machine at the main house. Lydia decided to drop hers off at a service in town, because she had no intention of spending her days off doing laundry.

Like an automaton, she brushed her teeth, showered, slipped into a nightgown, and crawled into bed. As she reached over to turn out the bedside lamp she checked her cell phone. The symbol for a voice mail message appeared on the display.

Pressing a button, she listened to the message. "Hi, kid." She smiled. Only her brother Quintin called her that. "Vicky and I are going to pick up Tamara next week. We're getting together at Mama's over the July Fourth weekend to officially welcome her into the family. Call me back and let us know whether you'll be able to join us."

Lydia pressed the End button and made a mental note to return her brother's call. Seven-year-old Tamara would become Quintin and Victoria's first daughter and third adopted child in their eight-year marriage; Lydia would be Aunt Liddie to yet another niece.

Smiling, she turned off the lamp. She'd just closed her eyes when a rustling noise jolted her into awareness. Blinking in the darkness, she listened intently. There was more rustling, followed by squeaking.

Lydia sprang from the bed, racing to the door. She flung it open, straight-armed the screen door with such force that it vibrated against the frame. There was no way she was going to share her cabin with an animal—one she couldn't see, one that could possibly be rabid. Heart beating uncontrollably, unmindful of her bare feet or state of undress, she pounded on Kennedy's door.

"Kennedy! Open the door! Plee-eeze!"

Without warning the door opened and she lost her balance, pitching forward. A wall of solidness and the firm grip on her shoulders halted her fall. She barely had time to catch her breath when she was scooped up in Kennedy's arms.

"There's something in my cabin," she gasped, trying to slow down her runaway pulse.

Kennedy shifted her slight weight. He'd thought he'd been dreaming, but once he opened his eyes he realized the person calling him was Lydia.

A fist of fear squeezed his heart. She was shaking uncontrollably. Pressing his mouth to her mussed hair, he breathed a kiss on her scalp. "What's in your cabin, baby?"

Lydia buried her face against Kennedy's bare chest. "An animal," she whispered hoarsely.

"Are you certain? Did you see it?"

She shook her head. "No. But I heard it."

Turning on his heels, he carried Lydia to his bed, lowering her to the mattress. "Stay here while I look for your *animal*."

Lydia could not see Kennedy's face, but she hadn't missed his facetious tone. "You think I'm hallucinating, don't you?"

"No," he said as he turned on a lamp, flooding the room with soft, warm light. "Something could've gotten into your place."

It was the second time in so many minutes that Lydia's heart pounded in her chest as she stared at Kennedy's beautifully proportioned nude body awash in ribbons of gold.

He bent over to pick up the jeans he'd tossed on an armchair. Her mouth went completely dry when she saw the ripple of muscles flexing sensuously under his skin.

A swath of heat swept over her, and she could not stop the

soft moan escaping her parted lips. A ball of fire settled between her thighs, roaring out of control.

Reason fled, insanity taking its place. She wanted Kennedy Fletcher to take her, make love to her, and erase the memory of every man she'd ever known in and out of bed.

"Kennedy."

He halted in zipping his jeans, turned, and stared at Lydia reclining on his bed. A knowing smile softened his mouth. His fantasy of having her in his bed and her hair spread out over his pillow had manifested itself. He lifted a questioning eyebrow.

"Yes, Lydia?"

Rising on an elbow, she reached out for him. "Don't leave me."

Kennedy went completely still, unable to believe what he was hearing. Lydia had come to him, trembling, her heart racing because she believed some form of wildlife had gotten into her cabin. He'd offered to go and look for it, but now she wanted him to stay. And if he stayed it would mean one thing.

Staring at her under lowered lids, he inhaled deeply. "Do you know what this means, darling?"

She nodded.

"If we make love to each other, then things cannot remain the same between us."

She nodded again.

Slowly, deliberately he pushed his jeans down his hips, stepping out of them, his gaze never leaving her face. Her eyelids fluttered when he stood before her naked, aroused. He was ready for Lydia, had been ready from the first time he saw her. Was she ready for him? he mused.

Uneasiness swooped at Lydia's innards, but this time it wasn't from fright but from the realization of what she had just initiated. She did not have time to analyze her actions as

Kennedy moved closer. She didn't know whether she was trying to prove that there was nothing wrong with her libido, that she and Justin were only compatible out of bed.

Everything about the man looming over her was large, massive, and she forced her gaze not to stray to the engorged flesh pulsing between muscled thighs.

"Turn off the light. Please," she added as he joined her on the bed.

Kennedy shook his head slowly. "No, Lydia. Not the first time. I want you to see how much pleasure you're going to bring me."

Her hand went to his chest, slender fingers splaying over his heart. "How can you be so certain that I will be able to satisfy you?"

A mysterious smile parted his full, firm lips as Kennedy, supporting his weight on his elbows, leaned closer. "Oh, you will, baby, because I'm not going to stop until I satisfy you."

"I need you to do something for me."

Dipping his head, he nuzzled her neck. "What?"

The pulse in her throat fluttered under the onslaught of his mouth, and she found it difficult to speak. "Protect me."

Kennedy froze. He'd told Lydia he'd never slept with a woman without using a condom. Why hadn't she believed him? "Don't worry. I'll take care of everything." He successfully tempered the edge that had crept into his voice.

He reached into the nightstand drawer and grasped a condom. His gaze fusing with Lydia's, he opened the packet and slipped the latex sheath over his arousal. She nodded, and they shared a smile.

Lydia sat up, curved her arms around Kennedy's neck, and pulled his head down as she opened her mouth to his. With their breaths mingling, she tasted his essence. The kiss deepened along with their breathing.

Kennedy forced himself to go slow as he caught the hem of Lydia's nightgown and eased it up over her head. He wanted her so badly that he feared spilling his passions before he could penetrate her. And his feelings for her ran too deep to take her quickly like a rutting bull in heat.

Sitting back on his heels, he surveyed her graceful, willowy body. Small, firm breasts were perched above a narrow rib cage that flowed into slender but rounded hips. Her skin was flawless, its smoothness and color calling to mind whipped chocolate mousse.

Cradling her face in his hands, he leaned closer, his tongue tracing the outline of her mouth. "You've been very stingy with your samples, Miss Lord. Right now I'm starving, which means I want everything on the menu. Are you ready to dine with me?"

Lydia's cheeks warmed. She stared up at Kennedy through her lashes. A quiver of wanting surged through her veins, heating her body and her blood. Pressing her forehead to his solid shoulder, she trailed kisses over his collarbone to the base of his throat.

She laughed softly. "Do we begin with an appetizer or go directly to dessert?"

"Appetizer," Kennedy said as he eased her down to the mattress. Anchoring his hands on Lydia's thighs, he spread them apart as he slid down the length of the bed. Smiling up at her perplexed expression, he crooned softly, "Aren't you going to tell me bon appetit, madam chef?"

The laughter bubbling up from the back of Lydia's throat halted, choked off by the loud gasp of shock mingling with a rush of pleasure that paralyzed her mind and body.

She'd had two lovers and neither had put his face between her legs. His tongue throbbed a passionate message that left her writhing and gasping for escape. She bit her lip to stifle the outcry of pleasure as waves of ecstasy rolled over her with the power of the moon's pull on the tide.

Lydia gasped, then sobbed for release as the sweetest bliss she had ever known swept her up in a tidal wave, refusing to let her go. She soared higher and higher until mindless desire hurtled her faster and faster to a sphere of no return.

Throwing back her head, she screamed, her body shaking and shuddering from the explosive spasms of a long-denied orgasm. The second followed, overlapping a third as her breath came in long, surrendering moans.

Her attempt to press her knees together was thwarted once Kennedy moved up and slowly eased his tumescence into her newly awakened flesh inch by inch until he was fully sheathed.

Burying his face between Lydia's neck and shoulder, he groaned in erotic torture. She was so tight he feared moving, but his desire for Lydia overrode everything else in his life at that moment.

He did move, establishing a rhythm that became a raw act of possession. As he roused her passion again, his own grew stronger until he lost himself in the scented arms of a woman who unknowingly made him forsake his vow never to open his heart again to offer more than his passion.

He quickened his motions, but when he felt the familiar tightening indicating he was going to spill his passion, he slowed because he wasn't ready to experience the exciting free fall that accompanied sexual gratification.

Not yet, and not when he hadn't had his fill. He had come to the banquet table a man who'd been long denied food and drink. He hadn't known he'd been waiting for someone like Lydia until the moment he saw her struggling under the weight of her luggage.

It had been her looks, then her sassiness that drew him to her. But once he tasted her mouth he was like an addict—hooked on a drug from which there was no escape or cure.

Lifting her legs, he wound them around his waist, allowing for deeper penetration. Kennedy raised his head, meeting her gaze, his near-black eyes widening as the pulse in her throat fluttered wildly. She closed her eyes against the carnality altering his features, and surrendered to a feeling of weightlessness, the tears pricking the backs of her eyelids and overflowing shamelessly down her cheeks.

When Kennedy felt Lydia's pulsing flesh squeezing his,

he knew he couldn't prolong his own gratification any longer or his heart would explode. He grasped the hair spread out on his pillow and bellowed as passion hot and unrestrained erupted like molten lava.

He lay motionless, helpless as a newborn, waiting for his heart to resume its normal rate before he reversed their positions. His hand grazed her spine as Lydia snuggled for a more comfortable position.

He kissed her moist forehead. "Did I hurt you?"

"No," she whispered. Her voice was low, sultry.

"Then why the tears, baby?" He'd tried to be gentle with her. When Lydia didn't answer, Kennedy eased back and stared at her. His mouth curved into an unconscious smile. She had fallen asleep.

He covered their damp bodies with a sheet before he reached over and turned off the lamp. He lay reveling in the aftermath of the exquisite pleasure he'd found in Lydia's scented embrace. Her smell, her passion, and the ecstasy she wrung from him were stamped on his skin, branded into his brain like a signature. He closed his eyes and sleep came stealing on whispered feet to offer him an infinite peace.

Eight

Lydia woke up startled. The side of the mattress had dipped and a solid object over her waist wouldn't permit her movement.

"Stop wiggling, darling."

The familiar soothing voice sent a shiver up her spine. A secret smile parted her lips when she recalled what she'd shared with Kennedy. He had proven one thing: there was nothing wrong with her libido. He had taken her to heights of passion she could not have imagined.

"What time is it?" Her voice was slightly hoarse. No light shone through the partially opened blinds.

Kennedy pulled her closer until her buttocks were pressed intimately to his groin. "It's too early to get up."

She lay in the darkness savoring his warmth and strength, remembering how she had come to be in Kennedy's bed. "There's an animal in my cabin, Kennedy."

"There *was* an animal. I got up a little while ago and checked. Your wild animal was a little bird that probably got in when you held the door open. I checked all of the windows and found the screens intact."

"Did you get him out?"

"It was too happy to fly the coop."

"Thank you, Kennedy."

He kissed the nape of her neck. "I want to thank you, too."

"For what?"

"The banquet feast."

"What?"

"You."

A wave of heat suffused her face, her cheeks burning in remembrance. "Oh, that."

Tightening his hold on her waist, Kennedy flipped her with a minimum of effort. She lay across his chest, her legs sandwiched between his. "Oh, that?" he repeated. "You didn't like it?"

Resting her head on his shoulder, Lydia traced the contours of his pectorals with her forefinger. Although he no longer played pro ball, Kennedy's body was in peak condition. It was obvious he worked out regularly.

"I loved it," she admitted. "I thought there was something wrong with me because I never really had an orgasm."

He went completely still. "You're kidding."

Lydia shook her head. "No, I'm not. I'd come close, but it was never like what I had with you. I thought maybe there was something wrong with me."

Kennedy kissed her hair. "There's nothing wrong with you. Whoever the clown was you were sleeping with was probably only concerned about himself."

"I know that now." She swallowed to relieve the dryness in her throat. "I hope I'm not getting sick."

"Why?"

"Because my throat is a little sore."

Kennedy laughed, the sound floating up from his chest until it was full-hearted. "You're not getting sick. Your throat hurts because you were screaming. I never pictured you for a screamer."

She slapped his chest with an open hand. "I never should've told you about my not having an orgasm."

Kennedy's fingers snaked around her wrist to keep her

from hitting him again. "What do you think I'm going to do with that information? Tell the world? What happens between us stays between us, Lydia. I've never been one to kiss and tell."

"There has been talk about you and other women."

"What kind of talk?"

Lydia paused, not wanting to sound accusatory. "That you weren't really into women, that you left football because some woman threatened you with a paternity suit."

Smiling, Kennedy closed his eyes. "Don't tell me you believe everything you read in the tabloids?"

"No, Kennedy. But you have to know that you were front-page news for months after you announced your retirement."

"Do you want to know why I retired?"

"You don't have to tell me if you don't want to."

"Do you want to know?" he asked again.

"Yes."

Lydia decided to be truthful. When all the network and sports channels carried the news that Kennedy Fletcher opted not to sign another contract with the Ravens, she'd taken a sudden interest in football. She'd never been an avid fan of the game, but was drawn into it whenever her father and brothers gathered in front of the television to debate plays and calls as if they were coaches and referees.

Kennedy was going to disclose something only his agent, his publicist, his parents, and three others knew. He felt he owed it to her not only because they were sleeping together, but also because his feelings for her had changed dramatically.

He opened his eyes. "I left the game for personal reasons," he said in a low, composed tone. "Lumel McClain and I were drafted the same year, and we hooked up as roomies whenever we were on the road. During the off-season I hung out at his house and vice versa. We met this girl at a club in Dallas after a game with the Cowboys, and to say she was aggressive is an understatement. Mac liked women a little wild, so I told him to go for it.

"A year later they were married and I stood in as his best man. Mac had his ups and downs with Cassandra because if he gave her a three-carat diamond ring she complained that it was too small. She kept upping the stakes until he couldn't keep his mind on the game.

"Meanwhile I met a woman who taught social studies at a Baltimore middle school where I'd been invited to speak to a group of young boys about career choices. I asked her out and we dated off and on for over a year. Off-season Nila and I hung out at either Mac's or my place. The four of us became inseparable."

"What happened, Kennedy?" Lydia asked after a pregnant pause.

"What's the phrase, 'familiarity breeds contempt'? Well, it came knocking with a vengeance. Mac came to me for money because a loan shark had put out a hit on him."

"How much did he need?"

"Three hundred."

"Three hundred dollars?"

"No, Lydia. Three hundred thousand."

"You're kidding."

"I wish I was."

"Did you give it to him?"

Kennedy nodded. "I had to. Mac had become the brother I never had, and there wasn't anything I wouldn't do for him. I told him he had to stop giving Cassandra everything she asked for. But the woman had his nose so wide open you could drive a freight train through it. He must have told her what I said, because she turned on me.

"All hell broke loose when she told Nila that I was sleeping with her and the baby she carried wasn't Mac's but mine. She told Nila this lie days before I'd planned to propose marriage."

"Did she know you planned to marry Nila?"

"Yes. I'd shown her and Mac the ring. Nila called me and

cursed me up the front and down the back. Once I got her to calm down she told me what Cassandra said about her carrying my baby. I swore I'd never touched Mac's wife, but it was too late. She said she never wanted to see me again, that she couldn't afford to ruin her reputation getting caught up in locker room BS."

Lydia felt tension tightening Kennedy's body. "There's more, isn't there?" she asked quietly.

"Yes." The single word was like an echo in an empty tomb. "I went to Mac's to confront Cassandra, but he met me at the door with a loaded shotgun. He ordered me off his property and said if I ever came near his wife again he'd kill me.

"Our last two games were home games, which meant I didn't have to room with Mac. As we were emptying our lockers he came at me. He got off a few good licks before I ducked and he smashed his fist against the locker. He broke five bones in his hand. The team fined him and the league sanctioned him for the first three games of the upcoming season. I was in negotiations for a new contract, so I decided to quit. I knew Mac and I could never play on the same team again, because one of us would've wound up a murderer."

"What happened with Cassandra?"

Kennedy smiled. "She gave birth to a son who looked exactly like his father. Mac called me, leaving a message on my answering machine that Cassandra admitted lying about having an affair and that he wanted us to meet to reconcile our differences."

"Did you?"

"No, I never called him back. I closed up my house in Friendship Heights and relocated to Alabama to escape the media. I stayed long enough to get a master's in physical education; then I came back to Maryland and bought a house not too far from here. I plan to spend my summers working at the camp, and next year I'll coach football at a New Carrollton high school."

Lydia closed her eyes and listened to the beating of

Kennedy's heart under her cheek. He'd trusted her enough to tell her what few knew about the very private ex–football player. Her heart turned over in pity. He'd lost a woman he'd loved enough to share his life with because of distrust, had become a sacrificial lamb, giving up his career for a friend— a friend so undeserving of his loyalty.

She pressed a kiss to his warm throat. "As a child I attended Sunday school, and we were required to memorize a verse of scripture a month. The one I always remembered is: *Do not worry about anything, but in all your prayers ask God for what you need, always asking him with a thankful heart.* It appears as if you've gotten what you need, Kennedy."

He chuckled softly. "You're right, Lydia. I do have what I need." He had what he needed, but didn't have all that he wanted. Reversing their positions, he brushed his mouth over hers. "I didn't tell you my sordid tale to make me look like the hero and Mac the villain. There were times when Cassandra came on to me and I was flattered by the attention because she was an incredibly beautiful woman. Before I got involved with Nila I only dated models. What I should've done was sit Cassandra down and tell her that there could never be anything between us."

Lydia could make out some of Kennedy's face from the rays of the rising sun filtering through the windows. She traced the curving shape of his eyebrows with her forefinger.

"If you'd been direct with her you probably would be playing ball today."

He smiled. "Maybe yes, maybe no. But if I was, then I probably never would've met you."

"Would that have been a bad thing?"

"Oh, hell yeah. A very bad thing." He pressed his middle against her, permitting her to feel his rising ardor. "Would you mind giving me seconds this morning?"

Raising her arms, Lydia clasped them tightly around his strong neck. "No. I don't mind," she whispered against his mouth.

They made love again, and this coming together was different as they took their time learning each other's body. Kennedy's large hands sculpted every curve of Lydia's body, she rising off the mattress when he suckled one breast before giving the other equal attention.

Pausing to protect her from an unplanned pregnancy, he entered her so slowly she pleaded with him to end her erotic torture. Her sobs became hiccupping sighs before he finally released her from an ecstasy that held her poised on a precipice where she prayed to fall, but couldn't. When she did fall he was there to catch her, both drowning in a flood tide of pleasure that was pure and explosive.

Lydia lay in her lover's protective embrace, peace and contentment flowing through her. Skin to skin, heart to heart, they'd become one. She sighed and snuggled closer to the man she not only wanted, but also needed.

She knew there was something special about him from the very beginning, and the harder she tried to ignore the truth, the more it nagged at her: she was falling hard for Kennedy Fletcher.

Lydia hadn't lingered in Kennedy's bed Sunday morning after their leisurely session of lovemaking. She went back to her cabin, completed her morning toilette, including washing her hair before blowing and curling the ends with a large-barrel curling iron. She returned her brother's call, confirming her attendance at his daughter's party. She planned to drive to Baltimore Friday night, stay over Saturday, and return the following morning for the camp's Family Reunion on Sunday.

Sunday activities were unstructured. Brunch was served between the hours of eight and eleven, and the campers were free to remain in their cabins or hang out in the barn playing board and video games. Many used the time to write letters, listen to their CD players, shoot hoops, or jump double Dutch before coming together for dinner. Sunday night movies at the playhouse had become a favorite pastime. The campers each selected a title from a listing and deposited their ballots into a box. A minor uprising ensued after the same film won for two consecutive weeks. The dilemma was remedied once the runner-up was shown.

Lydia stood in the middle of the living room at Kennedy's vacation hideaway, awed by the cathedral ceiling, the Palladian windows and skylights bringing the rugged mountain landscape indoors, and the eclectic furnishings. The four-bedroom structure overlooked a lake in a gated subdivision less than ten miles from the campsite. Each structure was set an acre apart, ensuring total privacy from its nearest neighbor.

Crossing the terra-cotta floor, she stopped in front of a massive stone fireplace spanning more than half of a fieldstone wall and peered at the photographs lining the mantel. There was one of a youthful Kennedy with a man and woman whom she assumed were his parents, several of him posing with a U.S. Olympic-gold-medal-winning relay team, and another with his high school football team. Missing were those depicting him as a Baltimore Raven. She felt Kennedy's warmth as he came behind her, wrapped an arm around her waist, pulling her against his chest.

She pointed to the photograph of him with his parents. "How old were you in this picture?"

"Twelve."

"Were you spoiled rotten?"

He chucked softly. "No. My mother did not believe in spare the rod and spoil the child."

"How about your dad?"

"He's a pussycat."

Lydia smiled at him over her shoulder. "He sounds like my father." Kennedy tunneled a hand through her hair, his fingers massaging her scalp. She shivered noticeably. "What are you doing, Kennedy?"

He nuzzled the side her neck. "Nothing," he whispered.

The arm around her waist inched up and Lydia closed her eyes, swallowing an erotic moan. "Don't. Please."

His hand closed over a breast. "Don't what, darling?"

"We can't," she gasped through parted lips. The area between her thighs thrummed an erotic rhythm that made her go pliant against Kennedy's body.

"Yes, we can, baby."

Lydia wanted him, needed him so badly that she clamped her jaw tightly to keep from blurting out her consent. They'd made love twice in less than twenty-four hours, and whenever she moved, there were muscles that reminded her of the unaccustomed activity.

"I can't now. You're going to have to give me a few more days to recuperate."

Kennedy's hands stilled. "I asked you if I'd hurt you and you said no."

Shifting in his loose embrace, Lydia saw his agonized expression. "You didn't hurt me. It's just that there are a few muscles that were put through a rigorous workout that hadn't been tested before."

Cradling her face in his hands, Kennedy lowered his head, his lips brushing against hers. "I won't touch you again until you're feeling better." He kissed her again. "Are you ready to leave?"

Nodding, she laid her head on his shoulder, her arms circling his trim waist. "I can see why you live here. It's so quiet, peaceful."

Kennedy pressed a kiss on her scalp. "I love it here and . . ." He stopped short of admitting that he loved her. There was nothing about Lydia he did not love: her femininity, passion, beauty, intelligence, talent, and selflessness. She worked long hours and had voluntarily forgone a salary in order to give two less fortunate children an extraordinary summer experience.

"I think we'd better get going before we have to wait in long lines to get on some of the rides," he continued smoothly.

Tilting her chin, Lydia smiled at him staring down at her. "You go for the rides?"

He returned her smile. "Of course. Don't you?"

"Of course not. I love sampling the jellies, jams, and pies."

Winking at her, he crooned, "Spoken like a true food connoisseur." He kissed her hair again, inhaling the lingering scent of a floral shampoo. "I like seeing your hair loose." His voice had dropped an octave to a seductive whisper.

Lydia wound a bouncy curl around her finger. "I wear it up so much that I'm considering cutting it in a very short style."

"Please don't cut it."

"Why not?"

"I love seeing your hair spread out over the pillow whenever I make love to you."

She closed her eyes to shut out his erotic stare. "You find that a turn-on?"

"No," Kennedy replied quietly. "I find *you* a turn-on. Everything about you turns me on. Sleeping with you has turned me into a sex machine."

"You'd better slow down, old man, or you'll find yourself popping Viagra or Levitra before you're forty."

"I doubt that. I'm hornier now than I was at sixteen."

Lydia opened her eyes and kissed his clean-shaven cheek. "How old are you?"

"I'll turn thirty-six next month."

"On what day?" she asked.

He flashed a slow, sensual smile, running a finger down the length of her nose. "No prying, sweetheart."

"Why is it a secret?"

"It's not a secret. But if you're predicting my well is going to dry up before I'm forty, then I'd better get busy now trying to produce a few little Fletchers."

Lydia rolled her eyes while sucking her teeth. "You don't even know if you can father a child."

He regarded her intently. "You're right. But you can help me find out whether I can or can't."

Lydia, caught off guard by the passion in his voice, said, "You must be crazy, Kennedy Fletcher. "I don't want a child. Not when I'm planning to start my own business."

"So, you'd rather sacrifice marriage and motherhood for a career?"

"Wouldn't you, Kennedy?" she countered. "Would you have given up football if your wife asked you to?"

"I don't know. I suppose I would've had to consider the circumstances."

Lydia glared at him. "You quit the game because of a friend, yet it would depend on the circumstances if your wife had asked."

His expression became a mask of stone. "I quit because I didn't want to spend the rest of my life in a six-by-eight prison cell. I let Mac hit me because I knew what he was going through with Cassandra. But I wasn't about to take another ass-whipping from him on or off the gridiron."

Lydia felt herself retreating from Kennedy. There was a primal look in his eyes that communicated he could be quite dangerous when crossed, and no doubt a formidable enemy. The comfortable camaraderie between them disappeared, replaced by tension and uneasiness.

Nine

Lydia burrowed against Kennedy's chest, her hair whipping around her face, as the roller coaster careened like a runaway freight train.

"This is not a kiddie ride," she shouted, to be heard over the grinding and clacking of the gears propelling the cars up, down, and around the winding track.

"Come on, Lydia, don't be such a baby."

Raising her head, she glared at him. "But you call me baby."

"When?" The word was snatched from his lips as the car lurched sideways around a sharp turn.

"When we were in bed together. You said, 'Yeah, baby. Give it to me good, baby. Oh, oh, yes, baby girl.' "

Chuckling, Kennedy pulled Lydia closer. "That's different. And I totally disavow anything said in the throes of passion."

"It's too late to offer a disclaimer, Love Daddy," she teased. Lydia was able to relax as the roller coaster slowed before coming to a complete stop. "No more rides, Kennedy."

He hopped nimbly out of the car, then reached for Lydia, setting her on her feet. "Just one more. Please," he added when she closed her eyes and turned away from him. "You said you wanted to ride before you ate anything."

Lydia had declared an unspoken truce with Kennedy. Their earlier confrontation behind them, she decided she was going to enjoy herself. She affected a pout. "Which one?"

The fair advertised as the largest in western Maryland was spread out over ten acres. The area set aside for parking was nearly filled to capacity. Vendors had set up booths, offering everything from clothes, household appliances, and pottery to electronic equipment.

A sea of tents, housing everything from farm animals raised by young children under the auspices of the 4-H Club to contests for chili and barbecue cook-offs and pie-eating contests. The tent featuring bingo overflowed with senior citizens who complained vehemently that the caller was too fast and they couldn't distinguish his B from G.

Kennedy curved an arm around Lydia's waist. "The Ferris wheel, baby." He'd crooned his plea.

"Don't even go there," she chided, rolling her eyes at him.

"I don't want you to think you're only my baby when we're making love."

Lydia shook her head. "What am I going to do with you?"

Kennedy looked at her and the message she read in his eyes was obvious. She tried ignoring the tingling in the pit of her stomach.

Without warning his expression changed until she did not recognize him as the sensual, easygoing man who with a single glance made her crave him.

"I don't know, Lydia. That's something you're going to have to figure out for yourself."

A jumble of confusing thoughts and emotions assailed her as she tried analyzing his cryptic statement. A cautious voice whispered to her to let the subject drop. Two weeks ago she would've goaded Kennedy into saying exactly what was on his mind, but she'd changed, matured. If she wanted to succeed in business, then she had to learn to play the game of give and take. This was one time when she would concede.

"Let's go before the line for the Ferris wheel gets too long."

Kennedy had expected Lydia to challenge him because he'd recognized a particular look in her eyes that always preceded her lashing him with the whip she called a tongue. He didn't know what had brought on the change, but he preferred her soft and purring instead of spitting and snarling.

Reaching for her hand, he led her in the direction of the towering wheel ablaze with colorful flashing lights against the darkening sky.

The noise level escalated with the approach of nightfall. Adolescents and young adults looking for a good time replaced older couples and mothers with young children. A uniformed officer stationed at the beer tent checked the IDs of everyone, regardless of their age. Lydia and Kennedy strolled arm in arm, sipping the ice-cold brew from plastic cups to counter the lingering taste of a chili-rubbed barbecued brisket.

A woman of indeterminate age waved to them, the many colorful bracelets lining her arms jangling musically. Her swarthy complexion, long black hair, and colorful blouse and skirt blatantly screamed *Gypsy*. Lydia had encountered many of them during her stay in Europe.

"Come, children. Let Mariska tell you your future." Her large black eyes surveyed them in one sweeping glance. "You pay for one and I will give you two fortunes."

Kennedy looked at Lydia. "Do you want to know your future?"

She moved closer to him. "How do you know she isn't a fake?"

"The only way you're going to know is to go into the tent with her."

Lydia had never had her palm or tarot cards read. "I'll go in, but only if you'll do it, too."

Kennedy smiled at Mariska. "Can we do it together?"

"No! Mariska will read the lady, then you." She held out a hand. Her curved fingernails looked like bird talons. "Pay first."

Kennedy shook his head. "I'll pay when you finish with both of us."

Mariska shot him a baleful look, then motioned for Lydia to come into the tent. She pointed to a chair pushed under a card table covered with a garish cloth in shocking colors of red and pink.

"Sit down and give me your hand."

Lydia obeyed. Mariska made clucking sounds with her tongue as she stared at Lydia's palm. "You have a nice hand." Her fingernail traced the line closest to her thumb. "You will live to be a very old lady." She pointed to another line. "You work very hard. Why do you work so hard when you will always have money?"

Lydia lifted her eyebrows, but did not interrupt as the fortune-teller shook her head from side to side. "I see two men in your life—one who will come to love you very much and one who will pretend to love you." She paused, squinting. "I see children. Two. Maybe three. Do not move!" she snapped when Lydia attempted to extract her hand.

"I see confusion, lots of confusion, and some disappointment. You will cry. You will smile." She released her hand. "Now, you can ask Mariska one question."

Lydia clasped her hands together, mentally replaying the fortune-teller's predictions. There weren't two men in her life. Her sleeping with Kennedy did not qualify as someone who was in her life. Justin Banks was now a nonentity, which meant the men had to be in her future. Mariska's reference to hard work meant that she would eventually run her own restaurant—one that would prove profitable. She also saw children in her future. Whose children would she bear?

Whom would she marry? Could she successfully balance motherhood and her career?

Deep in thought, she chewed her lower lip. Exhaling, she focused her gaze on the woman opposite her. "The two men in my life—how will I know which one to choose?"

Mariska gave her a narrow look. "They will tell you that they love you, but you must look behind the eyes to see the truth."

Lydia sat up straighter. "How do I look behind someone's eyes?"

"That is two questions. I am finished with you. Send in your friend."

She stared at the woman in shock. She'd been summarily dismissed. Rising, Lydia pushed back her chair and walked out of the tent. "You're next," she said to Kennedy, who stood at a nearby booth tossing a basketball into a net affixed to a board.

Kennedy tossed the last ball into the net. Leaning over, he kissed Lydia's cheek. "Pick out whatever you want." Plush toys, large and small, were suspended from hooks around the small booth. He winked at her. "Don't run away," he teased as he turned to walk into the tent.

Kennedy sat down opposite Mariska, a slight smile curving his mouth. He didn't need a fortune-teller to tell him what lay in his future.

"Your hand," Mariska demanded. Kennedy extended his hand. She held it, staring intently, before her head came up slowly. "You have money and health, but no love in your life." Her gaze returned to his upturned palm. "You take women because you do not want to be alone. I see an older man crying for you." She let go of his hand. "Ask Mariska one question."

Kennedy knew who the older man was: his father. His NFL contract had made him wealthy, and shrewd investments had more than doubled his net worth.

He had slept with women to pass the time, to provide temporary companionship. But that was his past. Now that he'd met and slept with Lydia he wanted her to be the last woman in his life.

"There is a woman now," he began slowly, "and I need to know if we will have a future together."

Mariska smiled. "Your feelings for this woman are different from the others. You can have her, but it will not be easy. You must be willing to fight for her."

Kennedy leaned forward. "Fight how?"

"No more questions." The hand with the clawlike fingers grazed his T-shirt. "Pay me."

Shifting and reaching into the pocket of his jeans, Kennedy withdrew a fifty-dollar bill and placed it in Mariska's hand. "Thank you." As he pushed back his chair, her fingers curled around his wrist.

"You will get her if you do not let anything or anyone stop you."

Kennedy gave her a long, penetrating stare before shaking off her grip. "Nothing can stop me." Standing, he walked out.

Smiling, Mariska pushed the bill into a deep pocket of her long skirt. The handsome young man had paid full price despite her offering him two for the price of one.

"Young fools," she whispered angrily. "So young and so blind to the truth."

Kennedy couldn't help smiling when he spied Lydia holding a small white teddy bear with its arms extended over its head. The bear was clad in a black-and-white-striped shirt with a white cap. She'd chosen a football referee.

"And the extra point is good," she drawled with a wide grin. "He's so cute."

Curving an arm around Lydia's waist, he pulled her to his side, smiling. "He's not as cute as you."

She wrinkled her nose at him. "That's because you're biased."

Kennedy nodded, his smile in place. "Hell yeah."

He led her down a path lined on both sides with booths filled with stuffed animals as prizes for games of chance that usually did not favor the player.

"How did you like Madame Mariska?" he asked Lydia.

"She was okay."

"Just okay?"

"Yes."

Lydia did not want to talk about the fortune-teller's prediction. She knew without a doubt that Kennedy wasn't one of the two so-called two men in her life. Even before Mariska's prediction, she had asked herself whether she wanted Kennedy Fletcher to become the last man in her life, or was he just passing through? Would their affair become just that—an affair? Or would it end like thousands of others—a summer romance?

The doubts tumbled over themselves in her head. Despite her protests to the contrary, did she really want to marry? Was she willing to sacrifice bearing children to further her career? Could she successfully manage both—motherhood and a restaurant?

The questions bombarded her until she wanted to scream at the top of her lungs to the two men in her future, *Who are you? Please reveal yourselves.*

A crowd surrounding a large DUNK THE CLOWN sign pulled Lydia from her reverie. A man dressed as a clown sat on a perch leering and gesturing to those staring at him to try and hit a bell with a hardball for a dollar a throw.

"Who's next?" a barker chanted over and over. "Mr. Giggles has been sitting in his chair for the past two hours, and right about now he needs a bath. All it takes is a dollar. Just one dollar to sink the clown and you'll have the pick of any prize on the shelf."

Lydia handed Kennedy her bear. "Please give the man a dollar."

He stared, complete surprise on his face. "There's no

way you're going to hit that bell from here." The bell was at least twenty feet from a white spray-painted line on the grass.

"Give me the dollar, or I'll ask another man for it," she said between her teeth. At his urging, she'd left her purse back at his house.

Cursing softly under his breath, Kennedy reached into his jeans, pulled out a dollar, and handed it to the barker. He, along with all of the others, held his breath, watching Lydia as she stepped behind the white line and took aim at the bell above Mr. Giggles's head.

She cradled the ball to her chest before going into a windup. Seconds later the missile whizzed by, hitting its target dead center. A loud roar ripped through the air as the clown went down into the shallow pool. The toes of his large yellow shoes wiggled like fishes out of water.

"She did it, Daddy!" screamed a little girl as she jumped up and down.

Lydia flashed a triumphant grin, while pumping her fists above her head. She turned to the child. "Which prize do you want?"

Large blue eyes regarded her. "I want the dolly with the red dress."

"Give the child her doll," Lydia ordered the barker.

The barker took the doll off the shelf as a soaked Mr. Giggles climbed back onto his chair to wait to be dunked again.

Lydia walked over to Kennedy with an exaggerated swagger. "Thought I couldn't do it, didn't ya!"

There was no expression on his face. "Where did you learn to throw like that?"

Looping her arm through his, she tilted her chin. "Whenever my family gets together for our annual Memorial Day reunion we always have a baseball competition with the girls against the guys. I'm always the pitcher for the Lord ladies. This year I pitched my first no-hitter. If I'd known my male relatives were going to spend the rest of the weekend pouting I would've deliberately given up one hit."

Dipping his head, Kennedy brushed his mouth over hers. "That's for giving that little girl your prize for dunking Mr. Giggles."

"One thing I don't need is another doll or stuffed animal to add the ones I've packed away in a steamer trunk."

"Are you going to pack away your referee bear?"

She shook her head. "No. I'll leave him out as a reminder of my summer at Camp Six Nations."

Kennedy angled his head. "You cook, throw a wicked curve ball, and climb poles. What else are you hiding from me?"

Shrugging her shoulders under the crisp fabric of a man-tailored white shirt, she said, "Nothing."

"Do you swim?" She nodded. "Canoe?" She nodded again. "Sing?"

"Oh no. When musical genes were being handed out I missed that boat."

"Speaking of music. The band over there sounds pretty good."

Listening intently, she recognized the piece they were playing, bobbing her head in time to the upbeat tune. "Let's see if we can't get closer."

They approached an area where a local band entertained a modest crowd with a repertoire of pop, country, and R&B favorites. Several couples had formed lines for the electric slide. Kennedy and Lydia were swept along with the others as they dipped, turned, and snapped their fingers. The lead singer segued into the updated cha-cha slide, and many dropped out, leaving those familiar with the steps to follow the calls.

Clutching her bear tightly, Lydia surrendered to the rollicking tempo. She'd danced more since coming to Camp Six Nations than she had in years, relying on her younger nieces and nephews who kept her up to date with the latest dance moves.

She shot a sidelong glance at Kennedy, who appeared to be caught up in his musical flight of fancy. For a man who exceeded six feet and two hundred pounds, he was as graceful as a professional dancer.

The band slowed the tempo, singing the past hit of The Dixie Chicks' reprise of Fleetwood Mac's "Landslide." Lydia peered up at Kennedy as he mouthed the words to Kenny Chesney's "Superstar." He waved his hand in the air and sang, "My Town," Montgomery Gentry's former number-one blockbuster hit.

Lydia fell in step with Kennedy as they made their way to the parking area. "How do you know those songs?"

He gave her hand a gentle squeeze. "I told you I'm a country boy. Every once in a while I mix my BET with CMT."

"Country and hip-hop?"

"Don't knock it until you try it, darling." His inflection was unadulterated Deep South.

Using the key chain remote, Kennedy unlocked the doors and helped Lydia into the Range Rover before placing her bear in the cargo area with a stack of handmade quilts and a case of homemade preserves and jellies. He rounded the vehicle and sat down behind the wheel, starting the engine with a flick of his wrist.

He waited in a long line of traffic before he was able to maneuver out of the parking lot and onto a local road. Then there was only the slip-slapping sound of the tires on the roadway.

I see an older man crying for you.

It's your father who's not doing so good.

His mother's words overlapped Mariska's. It had been two weeks since Diane's call and during that time Marvin Kennedy had not contacted him. The prognosis that he would not survive another year unless he underwent a second kidney transplant nagged at Kennedy.

He did not know whether he would be a compatible match, but the percentages were more than likely good because he was Marvin's only child. Glancing at his watch, he noted the time. It was ten o'clock in Smoky Junction.

He stared out the windshield, a look of determination on his face. He knew Marvin wouldn't call him, so it would be up to him to make the first overture.

Ten

Kennedy stood in front of a wall of glass overlooking the patio, a cordless phone pressed to his ear, listening for a break in the connection. Apprehension and frustration dogged him.

He was apprehensive because he feared losing a woman he had fallen in love with, a woman with whom he wanted to share his life and his future.

And his frustration stemmed from a man with whom he shared a bloodline, a man staring death in the face in less than a year if he did not get a much-needed kidney transplant.

Lydia fell asleep before they arrived home. She hadn't stirred even when he'd carried her into the house, undressed her, and put her into bed. He'd stood there, watching her sleep, while the image of her thick dark hair flowing in graceful curves over her shoulders, generously parted lips, and delicately carved facial features that made her appear feminine and fragile was imprinted on his brain.

At first he'd thought her pull was merely physical, but after spending the day with her, Kennedy knew it went beyond anything they'd shared in bed.

As the phone on the other end rang, his thoughts shifted

back to his father. He did not love Marvin, nor did he hate him, because he regarded him as a stranger.

"Hello," came a familiar voice through the earpiece.

His stepfather had answered the phone.

"Hi, Dad. How's it going?"

"Everything's good. If you're calling to talk to Diane, then you're going to have to call her tomorrow. She's out bowling with her girlfriends."

Kennedy smiled. He was glad his mother was out enjoying herself instead of moping around the house worrying about Marvin. "I just called to say hello," he half lied. He wanted Diane to give him Marvin's number.

He lingered on the phone. He and Philip talked about baseball standings and the older man's golf handicap, and Kennedy brought Philip up to date on the activities at Camp Six Nations. He hung up after a promise from Philip to let Diane know he'd called.

He replaced the telephone in its cradle and made his way toward the staircase leading to the master bedroom and Lydia.

"Where the hell have you been?"

The rosy feeling of love and loving faded with the acerbic question. Lydia glanced over her shoulder, not certain to whom Neil had spoken.

Realizing they were the only ones in the kitchen, she folded her hands on her hips as an expression of disbelief froze her features. "Say *what*?" The *what* exploded from her mouth like a torpedo.

The flush suffusing Neil's face receded, returning to its normal pallor with Lydia's defensive stance. He lowered his head and stared at the toe of his shoes. "I'm sorry I came at you like that," he apologized.

"Why?" she snapped, still smarting from his unorthodox greeting.

His head came up. "You haven't heard?"

"Heard what, Neil?"

"Last night's dinner was a complete disaster. Well, not all of it."

Two deep lines of worry appeared between Lydia's eyes. "What are you talking about? We prepared everything in advance. All you had to do was put the trays in the oven."

Neil's gaze darted nervously back and forth as he focused on a pot hanging from an overhead rack. "Something went wrong."

Lydia shook her head slowly. "Don't tell me you burned the food."

Running a hand over his spiked hair, the assistant chef bit down on his lower lip, nodding. "The chicken, ham, macaroni and cheese, and corn bread were unsalvageable."

Now Lydia knew why instructors and executive chefs threw tantrums whenever a chef overcooked a dish. Undercooked was salvageable, burnt wasn't.

And at that moment she wanted to scream, curse, and throw something. If Neil had worked for her she knew she would've fired him on the spot. She'd stood on her feet for eight hours without taking a break to prepare Sunday dinner, and it probably took less than an hour to ruin it.

She lowered her hands. "Didn't you check the thermostat?"

"I thought I had."

"You can't think, Neil," Lydia admonished tersely. "You have to know."

"I can't even think straight right now. I'd called my wife and asked her to bring the kids to camp for Family Reunion Sunday. She said no, because bringing the children would mean seeing me. And she doesn't want to see me again until we meet either in her lawyer's office or in divorce court." His eyes blazed with sudden anger. "She has no right to keep my children from me."

Lydia chewed the inside of her lower lip. She did not want

to become a participant in Neil's marital dilemma, nor did she want to work with someone who was currently an emotional basket case. She needed dependability and stability.

"What do you want to do, Neil?"

A muscle quivered at his jaw. "What do you mean?"

"You can leave and handle your business, or you can stay here and do the job you were hired to do. You're a very talented and competent chef, which means I shouldn't have to supervise you twenty-four-seven. I understand you have personal problems, we all do, but I'm not going to turn into Dr. Phil and hold your hand whenever you have an emotional meltdown.

"I've accepted the responsibility of running this kitchen, and that is something I will do either with you or by myself. Let me know what you intend to do before I close down the kitchen tonight."

Not waiting for a comeback from Neil, Lydia turned on her heel, walked out of the kitchen and dining hall, and into the blinding sunlight. She didn't see the tall figure in front of her as she collided against an immovable object.

A pair of strong hands caught her upper arms, steadying her. "Careful, darling."

"I'm sorry, Kennedy. I didn't see you with the sun in my eyes."

He dropped his hands, smiling. "That's all right. I was just coming to see you."

"I suppose it's about Neil and last night's dinner."

Kennedy's smile faded as he stared at Lydia's scowling expression. "He told you?"

"Yes, he did." She threw up both hands. "I don't understand what went wrong. I'd prepared everything in advance, which meant all he had to do was heat the food. There is nothing complicated about turning on an oven, checking the temperature, putting trays on a rack, and closing the door. I'm a chef, Kennedy, not a babysitter."

Kennedy heard the frustration and pain in her voice. He

and Lydia had returned to the camp before dawn and retreated to their respective cabins. He'd gotten a call from Roger at six-thirty, asking to see him.

Easygoing, laid-back Roger Evans strung together four-letter words Kennedy hadn't thought possible when he related Sunday afternoon's dining catastrophe. After Neil announced he'd burned the food, the campers' silence was eerily frightening. One child began crying that he was hungry, then the others joined in chanting, "We want food." Roger and Grace remedied the impending insurrection once they called a local restaurant to order enough pizzas and other side dishes to feed 125 people.

"It's all right, Lydia." Kennedy's voice was soft, comforting.

"It's not all right," she shot back. "What's going to happen Saturday?"

"What about Saturday?"

"I have to go home."

"Is everything all right?"

She nodded and offered a smile she did not feel at that moment. "Yes. My brother just adopted a young girl, and everyone's getting together to welcome her into the family."

Kennedy experienced a rush of envy. While Lydia had her brothers, sisters, nieces, and nephews—a large extended family that gathered for holidays and special occasions—he only had his mother and stepfather. There was no sister, brother, grandparents, aunts, or uncles. He did claim a few cousins on Marvin's side of the family, but he'd never met them.

"Will you be back in time for Family Reunion Sunday?"

"I'm coming back late Saturday night. Right now I don't trust Neil to handle the kitchen with guests coming." She'd changed her original plan to return early Sunday morning.

"Why not?"

Lydia paused, choosing her words carefully. She was Neil's direct supervisor, not Kennedy. "He's got a few things on his mind he needs to straighten out."

Kennedy lifted a questioning eyebrow. "And if he doesn't?"

"Then I'll handle it."

"How, Lydia?"

"In my time, and in my own way, Kennedy," she added defiantly.

Their gazes met, fused, a tension vibrating between them like static electricity. The seconds ticked off. "Just make certain you do. Everyone is allowed only one fumble in *my* game," Kennedy warned in a dangerously soft tone. A lethal calmness filled his eyes before his lids came down.

Lydia blinked once, then stared at Kennedy's broad shoulders as he turned and walked away. She was in the same position even after he'd disappeared over a rise.

Why did he seek to undermine her authority with Neil? Did he not believe she could successfully supervise her assistant? Were his doubts based on her age? Gender? And what did he mean about his game? He'd talked as if he were lord and master of Camp Six Nations. Wasn't he, she thought, a summer employee like herself—or was he something more than he represented? The camp season was nearing its halfway mark, which meant she had a little more than four weeks to uncover who the real Kennedy Fletcher was.

The instant she turned to go back to the dining hall, she vacillated. She really did not want to know Kennedy that well, because once the camp season ended she wanted no shadows across her heart. The fortune-teller had predicted she would have two men in her life vying for her love, and one thing she knew was that the camp's sports director would not be one of them.

It was Monday; the food theme was Mediterranean. Lydia had excluded Italy because she devoted one night entirely to Italian cuisine. This Monday her entrées included Moroccan couscous with lamb and seven vegetables; rice pilaf; assorted lamb kebabs with marinades from Greece, Turkey, and Tunisia; beef and okra stew from Egypt; Greek-style roast chicken with oregano and lemon; and another chicken entrée from Lebanon, roast chicken with rice stuffing. Soup selections included lentil, lamb, and bean and meatball, which were the perfect complement for Neil's sesame bread rings.

Closing her menu book, she glanced over at Neil, who was engrossed in preparing the dough mixture for the bread rings. "How do you feel about me making *sanbusak* to go along with the spinach pie for appetizers?"

Neil shut off the industrial mixer. "Please translate." He'd found himself asking her to translate the names of the foreign dishes quite a few times since becoming Lydia's assistant.

Lydia, deciding not to dwell on Neil's shortcomings, smiled at him. Although she'd never burned a dish, she had made enough mistakes as a student and an apprentice to elicit the wrath of her instructors and bosses.

"Little pastries filled with cheese or meat."

Neil's interest was piqued once he heard "pastries." "What kind of cheese and meat?"

"Feta and minced lamb. The feta is blended with eggs, fresh or chopped mint, and white pepper. The meat is mixed with olive oil, finely chopped onions, cinnamon, allspice, toasted pine nuts, and freshly ground salt and pepper."

"Baked or fried?"

"The cheese is usually baked and sprinkled with sesame seeds, and the meat-filled pastries are deep-fried."

Neil, always open to trying a new dish, nodded. "Let's do it."

"You're going to have to mix another batch of dough without the yeast."

Closing the distance between them, Neil extended his little finger. "Wanna bet the kids call the *sanbusaks* beef patties?"

Lydia shook her head. "No, because I *know* they are." She and Neil had made miniature Jamaican beef patties for

Caribbean night and they disappeared so quickly she thought everyone had inhaled them.

Lydia had taken a huge risk presenting the camp with her regional dishes, aware that most people usually ate what was most familiar to them. However, her proposal was successful because the campers always came to the dining room ravenous. And because presentation was a key component in cooking, she made certain all of the dishes were appealing.

She'd learned to gauge how much of each entrée and side dish was needed to feed one hundred children and twenty-five adults, and most nights there were little or no leftovers. Glancing at the clock on the far wall, she noted the time. It was time to put the meats in the oven. She loaded the chickens on several spits, leaving them for Neil to secure on the rotisserie.

Lydia turned her attention to a large uncovered bowl. Tabouli, a Mediterranean salad made with bulghur, tomatoes, fresh herbs, and lemon juice, had become an instant favorite. Several times a week she'd found a note taped to the kitchen door: *Miss Lydia, please make the salad with the little bumps.* They weren't familiar with bulghur.

She'd honored their requests and planned to make tabouli, gelato, melon and fresh fruit cut into funny shapes, low-fat ice-cream sandwiches, sodas, sundaes, and parfaits until the camp season ended.

The door leading into the kitchen opened slightly and a kitchen assistant leaned in. "Miss Lydia, you're wanted in the dining room."

Lydia smothered a sigh. She wanted to finish the task of cutting up the meats and vegetables for the following night's Chinese theme.

"Who wants me?"

"Mr. Roger."

"Tell him I'll be right out."

Moving over to the stainless steel sink, she rinsed her hands, dried them on the towel slung over her shoulder, and walked out of the kitchen to find everyone standing. Within seconds they launched into Mase's 2004 comeback rendition of "Welcome Back."

Lydia covered her face with her apron and laughed until tears rolled down her face. She was still laughing when Roger came over and patted her on the back.

He signaled for silence, and the assembly sat down. Although his mouth was smiling, his deep-set eyes were serious. "I don't know what the kids did to Mr. Neil to make him angry yesterday, but I've had a long talk with them and whatever it is they've all promised not to do it again." He gave Lydia a sly wink. "I know I speak for everyone when I say we much prefer your pizza to what we were forced to eat yesterday."

"It was mad nasty!" yelled a girl sitting in the back.

"Word," a boy confirmed at a nearby table.

Lydia had to admire Roger's attempt to publicly vindicate Neil. Her gaze swept over the sea of young faces staring at her. Just for an instant she met Kennedy's gaze and averted hers.

"Mr. Neil and I are very sorry about yesterday, and we hope it will not happen again. It's not easy cooking for so many people day after day. We work very hard to prepare different dishes because when you grow up and travel to other countries that don't have fast food restaurants on every corner, you'll be able to order and eat dishes that you've become familiar with.

"Next Sunday is the first of our two Family Reunion Sundays, and Mr. Neil and I have planned a very special dinner for your family members." She flashed a demure smile. "Before I go back to the kitchen, I'd like to thank you for your song."

Her gaze strayed back to Kennedy. He nodded and smiled

his approval. She acknowledged him with a perceptible nod before she retraced her steps.

Kennedy speared a forkful of Greek salad. Roger had informed him that he'd met with the campers earlier that morning to smooth over their ruffled feelings about their aborted southern-style Sunday dinner. Not wishing to openly blame Neil, and as a certified social worker, Roger spoke to them about compassion and forgiveness. The campers listened intently, then drew their own conclusions: the dinner was ruined because Miss Lydia hadn't been there to cook it.

Chewing thoughtfully on a kalamata olive, Kennedy had to agree with the campers. If Lydia had been there they would've eaten their favorite dishes instead of tasteless pizza with cardboardlike crusts.

But the fact remained she wasn't at the camp because she was with him. Spending time away from the camp with her was something he wanted to experience again. He wanted to take her to his lake house, and for a few precious hours pretend they were a couple.

Not waiting for dessert, he picked his tray off the table, emptied it, and walked out of the dining hall. The sun had dropped lower in the sky, taking with it the heat of the day.

Thrusting his hands into the pockets of his walking shorts, Kennedy made his way toward the lake.

Eleven

"I'm going to miss you, darling."

Lydia pressed her forehead to Kennedy's shoulder. "Don't be so dramatic. I'm only going to be away for a day."

Resting his chin on the top of her head, he buried his face in her fragrant hair. "Why don't you wait and leave in the morning? It's much safer than driving across the state at night."

Easing back in his embrace, Lydia stared up at the man whom she had come to love despite her resolve not to become involved with him. "I have to leave tonight." Her hairstylist sister-in-law, Gloria, had promised to keep her salon open in order to touch up Lydia's much-needed chemically relaxed hair.

Kennedy felt as if he was losing Lydia. This had begun the night they returned to the camp from his lakefront property. She'd informed him she was experiencing PMS and preferred sleeping alone during that time of the month. He'd wanted to tell her that they could share a bed without making love, but something in her tone silenced him. What he'd shared with her up to that point in their relationship was too new to override her protest.

As soon as he'd conceded to Lydia's request that they

sleep apart because she was menstruating he realized he'd become his stepfather. Although he and Philip Anderson were not related by blood, their personalities were quite similar. Philip always gave in to Diane, even when he knew she was wrong. His adage was: *she'll find out in her own good time that I'm right.* And whenever he proved his wife wrong he never said, *I told you so.*

What if he and Lydia were married, would she deign to move out of their bedroom once a month because she had her period?

Hell no! His inner voice was talking to him again after a four-year absence. The last time he'd wrestled with his conscience was when he'd been faced with the life-altering decision to leave the NFL.

"I'll call you when I get there," she promised, rising on tiptoe to kiss him.

"You have my cell phone number?"

"Yes," she whispered against his parted lips. "I've memorized it."

Tightening his hold on her body, Kennedy pressed her against the door to her SUV and drank from her mouth like a man dying of thirst. "I'm going to miss you."

Lydia closed her eyes against his intense stare. "Me too."

She opened her mouth to his probing tongue moving in and out in a rhythm that sent her pulse racing and her senses spinning out of control, and she knew if she hadn't been on her menses she would've begged Kennedy to take her back to his cabin and his bed.

Somehow she found the strength to pull out of his embrace and tear her mouth from the onslaught of his. "I have to go."

Nodding, Kennedy opened the driver's-side door, waiting until she was seated before he closed the door with a solid slam. Leaning into the window, he smiled. "Be safe, darling."

Lydia returned his smile with her own sensual one. "I will," she promised as she pushed a button, raising the window.

Kennedy gestured with his thumb and little finger against his ear. "Don't forget to call me."

Staring at him through the glass, she nodded, saying, "I will, baby."

He stepped away from her vehicle and she backed out of the space. Her hand tightening on the gearshift, she shifted and drove slowly away from Camp Six Nations and Kennedy Fletcher.

Moments before turning on to the road that ran around the lake, she glanced up in the rearview mirror to find him standing motionless, as she'd left him. Hot tears pricked her lids, but she blinked them back. She couldn't cry and drive at the same time.

Was this how it was going to be come summer's end? Would she feel as if she was leaving a small part of herself once she returned to Baltimore? Could she leave Kennedy without letting him know what was in her heart?

She switched on the radio, surfing stations until she found one featuring country music. A smile softened her expression when she heard "Sweet Home Alabama." The song reminded her of her sweet Alabama lover.

Kennedy Fletcher, the country boy as he referred to himself, who made her crumble like a flaky biscuit dipped in a bowl of warm molasses whenever he whispered her name in the throes of passion.

Mr. Ken, as the campers referred to him, who presented the perfect role model for young boys and girls who sought success with nothing more than focus, dedication, and hard work.

Darling, as she had begun to think of him, who displayed infinite patience whenever her temper flared without warning.

And last, but certainly not least—lover—a patient, passionate, drop-dead gorgeous, and sinfully sexy man who made her sing in bed although she couldn't carry a tune.

She stayed on the county road until she saw the sign for I-70. Barring delays on the interstate, she could expect to reach Baltimore in an hour.

As she neared Baltimore's city limits she'd listened to songs by Keith Urban, Kenny Chesney, Rascal Flatts, LeAnn Rimes, Tim McGraw, and Alan Jackson. There was no doubt Kennedy's country boy influence was rubbing off on her.

Lydia maneuvered into a parking space in front of her sister-in-law's upscale full-service salon in a strip mall. Reaching into her purse, she took out her cell phone and punched in Kennedy's programmed number.

"You made it."

She smiled. "What happened to hello?"

"Hey, baby," he crooned like the late Barry White.

Lydia, laughing softly, countered with an Eartha Kitt purr into the tiny mouthpiece. "I arrived safe and sound." Staring out the windshield, she saw Gloria peering through the vertical blinds. "I've got to go, Kennedy. I'll see you tomorrow night."

"I'll be waiting for you."

She nodded although he couldn't see her. "Good night, Kennedy."

"Good night, Lydia."

Ending the call, she got out of the Pathfinder and walked to the door of Le Chic Tresses, ringing the bell. Fingertips parted the drawn vertical blinds covering the door, and seconds later the door opened.

Gloria Lord, sporting a head filled with graying twists, smiled at her. "Girl, get yourself on up in here." Glo, as everyone called her, pulled Lydia to her ample bosom. "You know I only stay open this late on a Friday night for family."

Lydia kissed Gloria's cheek. "Thank goodness I'm family." Easing back, she parted her hair with her fingertips. "Take a look at the new growth."

Gloria wrinkled her short nose. "That's nothing. You should see some of my clients when they come in asking to pay touch-up prices when they need their whole head relaxed." She angled her head and stared at her husband's youngest sister. "Are you losing weight?"

Shaking her head, Lydia placed her handbag on a chair. "I don't think so."

Gloria rested her hands on wide hips that had carried four of Dwayne Lord's babies. "I don't understand you and Victoria."

"What don't you understand?"

"Why is it the two of you cook for a living, yet don't gain any weight? Look at me. I suck air and still can't lose a pound."

Lydia gave Gloria a sidelong glance as she sat down in a chair facing a wall of mirrors. Everyone teased her mercilessly about trying every diet on the market but refusing to give up eating dessert. "The fact that neither Vicky nor I have carried a baby may have something to do with it."

"Your mama had nine babies and she's still not overweight," Gloria complained. She picked up a cape, shook it out, and draped it over Lydia's shoulders.

"That's because Mama doesn't eat dessert."

"What you trying to say, Liddie Lord?"

Lydia met the stylist's glare in the reflection of the mirror. "Give up the red velvet and pound cakes. Step away from the coconut custard pie. Try a vegetable or fruit smoothie, Gloria. They're nutritional, energy-boosting, and many are low in calories. I blend them for the overweight kids at camp."

"Have they lost weight?"

"Most of them have lost an average of two pounds a week." The medical staff charted the campers' height and weight weekly.

Gloria's round, dark eyes in an equally round, dark face narrowed. "Can you give me some of the recipes? You know I'm willing to try anything."

Lydia smiled. "Of course."

Picking up a comb, Glo parted Lydia's hair into sections. "How's camp?"

"It's quite interesting."

Two hours later, Lydia unlocked the door to the large white farmhouse with the wraparound porch where she'd grown up with her sisters and brothers. An overhead fixture in the entryway provided enough light for her to navigate the staircase to her second-floor bedroom. She passed her parents' bedroom. No light shone from under the closed door. Even after more than fifty years of marriage, Charles and Etta Mae Lord were still passionately in love with each other.

She walked into the bedroom she'd once shared with her sister Sharon and stripped off her clothes. Covering her hair with a large plastic bonnet, she made her way to the bathroom. Gloria had relaxed her hair, shortened it by two inches, set it on large rollers, then wrapped and pinned it in a doobie hairstyle after she'd sat under a dryer.

She had less than twenty-four hours to reconnect with her family, and she intended to make the most of it. Spending the day away from the camp and Kennedy would give her the space she needed to be objective about her relationship with him.

She had to keep telling herself that what she had with Kennedy was temporary; it was only a summer fling.

Lydia was up at dawn, showered, dressed, and preparing breakfast, when her mother walked into the kitchen. Etta Mae's smile faded, her mouth turning downward in a frown as she stared at her daughter's body in a pair of black stretch capri pants and a matching tank top.

"You're bad for your business."

Turning on her heel, Lydia smiled at her mother. "Good morning, Mama." Seventy-year-old Etta Mae Lord was tall and large-boned without an ounce of excess fat. Her silver hair was stylishly cut to fit her evenly balanced features.

Etta moved closer. "Don't good morning me, Lydia Charlene Lord."

An expression of confusion settled into Lydia's features. Whenever her mother called any of her children by their full names it meant trouble—for them.

"What's up, Mama?"

"Certainly not your weight."

First Gloria, and now her mother, had remarked about her weight. Was she that thin? And hadn't Kennedy mentioned she could use a few more pounds?

"Are you eating, Lydia?"

"Of course I am," she snapped.

"Don't take that tone with me, young lady."

"What's going on here?" asked a deep male voice.

Lydia wiped her hands on a terry cloth towel. She crossed the kitchen and kissed her father. "Hi, Daddy."

Charles wrapped an arm around his youngest child's waist, pulling her close. "Hi, baby girl." His gaze shifted to his wife. "What's all the commotion about so early in the morning?"

Etta Mae pointed to Lydia. "Look at *your baby*, Charles."

Charles Lord stared at his daughter's upturned face as her coiffed hair rippled over the nape of her neck. "She looks beautiful." He winked at her. "I like your hair. Glo really out-did herself this time."

"I'm not talking about her hair, Charles. Look at her body. She's nothing but skin and bones."

"Who's skin and bones?" asked another familiar male voice.

Lydia pulled away from her father and turned around. Her brother Quintin stood under the arched entrance leading into the large kitchen, cradling a large plastic crate to his chest. He put it down and extended his arms. Except for a few strands of gray at the temples he hadn't changed at all. At his age of forty-seven, the years had been very kind to Quintin Lord. Tall, slender, and classically handsome, he'd become a much sought after photographer, who had married a woman who'd at one time been his neighbor, and who was now the father of two sons and a daughter.

He wasn't disappointed when Lydia rushed into his embrace. "Welcome home, kid."

Lydia brushed a kiss over his smooth jaw. "Thanks. What are you doing here so early? Where's the rest of your family?"

Smiling, Quintin displayed a mouth full of straight white teeth under a neatly barbered mustache. The brilliance of his smile matched the diamond studs in his pierced lobes.

"Mama decided we should gather early because you're not going to be here all day, and Vicky should be here momentarily. You know how hard it is to coax Chaz out of bed when he doesn't have to go to school."

Quintin and Victoria had adopted their middle child as an infant, deciding to name him Charles in honor of his maternal grandfather. Their older son had celebrated his fourth birthday when he'd officially become Micah William Lord. Victoria had given him her father's middle name.

Victoria, who hadn't been able to bear children, openly admitted she always wanted three children. Now with ten-year-old Micah, Chaz, five, and eight-year-old Tamara she felt her family was complete.

"Does Tamara know about the party?"

Quintin shook his head as he bent down to pick up the crate. "No. She believes it's going to be a pre–Fourth of July cookout."

The young girl had languished in foster homes because no one wanted to adopt an older child. But once Victoria decided she wanted a daughter, Tamara had become her first and only choice.

Lydia found her latest niece quiet and reflective when she wasn't playing with her brothers or younger cousins. There were times when Lydia found her own family overwhelming, and she could surely understand a newcomer's reaction to the large boisterous clan whenever they got together as a family unit.

Quintin set the crate on a tall stool at a cooking island as Sharon waddled in holding a hand under her very pregnant belly. A tiny black schnauzer puppy darted around her feet.

Etta Mae pointed at her daughter. "You know the rules, Sharon Ida Lord-Gibson. No animals in my kitchen!"

Lydia caught Quintin's gaze, nodding. She walked over to Etta Mae and kissed her cheek. "Go sit out on the porch while I start breakfast." She shot her father a knowing look. "You too, Daddy."

Charles caught her meaning immediately, hoping to diffuse a confrontation between his dog breeder daughter Sharon and Etta Mae, who liked animals but not in her kitchen.

"Come, dear," Charles said in a soft tone, cupping his wife's elbow, "Let's sit outside while Lydia starts breakfast."

"Please let me help her," Etta argued softly.

Charles pressed a kiss to her forehead. "Etta Mae. Lydia doesn't need your help. She's used to cooking for a lot of people."

Etta Mae smiled at her husband with whom she had fallen in love at a high school dance. Charles had given her her first kiss and made her his wife, and in turn she'd given him nine children. She was mother to nine, grandmother to twenty-two, and great-grandmother of five.

Lydia stared at Sharon. "Why did you bring that puppy in here?"

Sharon eased her bulk down to a chair. "I couldn't leave Fitzhugh in the car."

"You should've left Fitzhugh home," Quintin countered.

Sharon's sherry-colored eyes narrowed as she glared at Quintin. "I can't leave my baby by himself."

"Fitzhugh is a dog, not a baby, Sharon. What you have kicking in your belly is a baby," Lydia said pointedly.

Sharon's eyes welled up. "You're just picking on me because I'm fat and you're skinny."

Lydia and Quintin groaned in unison. Everyone walked on eggshells around Sharon because of her erratic mood swings.

Orlando Gibson strolled into the kitchen, encountering his wife's tears. He went to her side, gathering her off the chair. "What's the matter, honey?"

Sharon buried her face against her husband's chest. "I'm fat," she sobbed dramatically.

"You're not fat, sweetheart. You're pregnant, and pregnant women always put on weight."

Orlando had given the NBA fifteen years of his life as a point guard, then retired after marrying Sharon. He'd set up a public relations agency with another former basketball player.

Quintin raised a thumb, gesturing for Orlando to take Sharon out of the kitchen. The ex-ballplayer complied; Fitzhugh followed.

Lydia leaned against a countertop. "What's up with the family, Quintin?"

Crossing his arms over his chest, he assumed a similar pose. "There are so many changes going on that everyone's a little on edge. Sharon is anxious about having her first child, now that Dad's retired he's always under Mama's feet, and everyone is still upset because you left the restaurant when you were about to make it big."

Lydia stared at Quintin, complete surprise on her face. "Make it big? Did everyone forget that I was passed over twice for a promotion?"

"You're young, Lydia. Do you actually think an experienced executive chef is going to allow a twenty-seven-year-old neophyte to show him up? No," Quintin added, answering his own question.

"Vicky says you're very good, much better than she'll ever hope to be. And we both know my wife is no slouch in the kitchen. You need to slow down and stop working so hard, or you won't last long enough to enjoy it."

You work very hard. Why do you work so hard when you

will always have money? Mariska's words echoed in Lydia's mind as if the woman were there with her.

"And I'm afraid I have to agree with Mama about your weight," Quintin continued, frowning. "Are you feeling all right?"

"I'm fine, big brother. Now, please get out of the kitchen so I can start breakfast."

"Would you like some help, Madame Chef?" Victoria Lord said as she walked into the kitchen, followed by her three children.

Lydia closed the distance between her and her petite sister-in-law. Bending slightly, she kissed her cheek. "I'd love it." She smiled at her nephews. "You guys owe me a kiss." Micah and Chaz shook their heads as they backed away. At ten and five respectively, both thought kissing girls was horrifying.

Tall, willowy Tamara stepped forward. Her resemblance to her adoptive mother was startling, especially their eyes. They were large, dark, and mysterious. They even shared the same chestnut-brown coloring.

"I'll kiss you, Aunt Liddie."

Gathering Tamara in an embrace, Lydia kissed her neatly braided hair. "Thank you, beautiful. I love your hair," she whispered softly.

"Thanks. Aunt Glo did it yesterday."

"She did a wonderful job."

Quintin rested his hands on his sons' shoulders. "Let's go and unload your mama's van."

Chaz stared up at his father. "Do I have to, Dad?"

"No, you don't," Quintin answered, deadpan, "that is, if you don't want to eat."

Chaz tugged Micah's hand. "Help me bring in the food."

Victoria offered her husband a grateful smile. "What's for breakfast, Lydia?"

Opening the doors to a side-by-side refrigerator/freezer, Lydia peered at the foodstuff crowding the shelves. "It looks as if we can have French toast, eggs Benedict, waffles, pancakes, home fries, ham, bacon, sausage, and eggs cooked to order."

Making her way to the half bath to wash her hands, Victoria smiled over her shoulder. "That sounds good to me."

Twelve

Lydia raised her arm, peered at the watch strapped to her wrist, then closed her eyes. She planned to leave in half an hour.

After she'd heard, "Are you on a diet?" "Are you losing weight?" "Do you plan to audition for America's Next Top Model? once too often, she'd overindulged.

She and Victoria had assumed the responsibility for preparing breakfast, while the other women took care of the dishes for the afternoon cookout. The male family members were assigned to erect the tent, man the grills, replenish beverages, and the post-celebratory cleanup detail.

Tamara was shocked once she was informed that the family gathering was to celebrate her legally becoming a Lord. Lydia had given her niece one of the handmade quilts she'd purchased at the fair and a check earmarked for clothes for the upcoming school year. She'd purchased three quilts: one for Tamara's new canopy bed, a sunny yellow and mint-green crib-size quilt for Sharon's unborn child, and another for herself.

Lydia met with her oldest sister, Andrea, who brought her up-to-date on the plans for Sharon's surprise baby shower. She had also reconnected with Ethan Bennington, the executive director of the community center who had recruited her as Camp Six Nations' chef.

Ethan, Quintin's best friend, had married Victoria's best friend and business partner, Joanna. Ethan and Joanna also had three children. Ryan, their eldest son, had completed his first year at Morehouse as an economics major, while the histrionics exhibited by their active red-haired six-year-old twin girls foretold a future in the theater.

"Wake up, Lydia. You have company."

"Who is it, Glo?" she asked, not opening her eyes.

"Why don't you open your eyes and find out?" drawled a familiar masculine voice.

Lydia opened her eyes. Justin Banks stood over her, grinning. Sitting up, she swung her legs over the side of the recliner. "What are you doing here?" Her voice was void of emotion.

Justin leaned down, cupped her elbow, pulling her gently to her feet. "I ran into Lucien the other day and he told me you'd be here this weekend."

The two men leased office space in the same high-rise office building in downtown Baltimore. Until now, never had she wanted to wring her brother's neck for telling her business. However, she couldn't blame Lucien, not when she hadn't told her family that she and Justin were no longer a couple.

"I'm leaving now."

Justin moved closer. "Please hear me out, Lydia."

Lydia stared up at the tall, slender man whose cold urbane manner concealed an extraordinary intelligence. Justin and three other computer geeks had changed the face of gaming entertainment, blending music videos with video games. The result was mesmerizing and innovative.

"Wait for me near the garage. I want to tell my parents I'm leaving."

She found her mother and father relaxing on the porch in

matching chaises. She kissed her mother, then her father. "I'll be back in four weeks."

Retracing her steps, Lydia spied Justin leaning against his car's trunk. Everything about him screamed *elegance* and *sophistication*. And in spite of his business success, Justin had not curried favor with his upper-middle-class family after dropping out of medical school during his third year. His fixation with computer games had become an all-consuming passion.

She affected a polite smile that did not reach her eyes. "What do you want to talk about?"

Justin's expression darkened with an unreadable emotion. Even though Lydia looked the same he knew she was not the same woman with whom he'd fallen in love, seeing a hardness that had not been apparent before their break-up.

"Us."

Lydia blinked once. "There is no *us*, Justin."

"Because that's the way you wanted it."

Struggling to contain her temper, she counted slowly to three. "I'm not going to stand here and get into the blame game with you."

There was something in Lydia's gaze and tone that told Justin to reconsider his approach with her. She was the only woman with whom he'd been involved that he hadn't been able to intimidate, and he knew that was the reason why he'd been drawn to her. All of the other women in his past were either subservient or too willing not to do or say anything that would displease him.

He schooled his expression to conceal the rage roiling inside him like slow-moving lava. "I'm sorry, Lydia, but I didn't come here to fight with you."

"Why did you come?" Her voice was layered with neutral tones.

"To apologize, and to tell you that I love you."

Justin bit down on his lower lip to keep from grinning from ear to ear as her eyes widened and her jaw dropped. He knew he'd never mentioned the L word once during their two-year relationship. He did love her, her femininity, beauty, intelligence, and ambition—an all-consuming ambition that surpassed his.

She'd complained about their sexual incompatibility, wanting more when he was unable to offer her more. He knew he was unlike most men in their early thirties because he viewed sexual intercourse as a conduit not for gratification but procreation.

Lydia stared at Justin, tongue-tied. Her gaze moved slowly from his precise close-cropped hair, delicate features in a tanned narrow tawny-brown face, to his favored Ralph Lauren–tailored attire.

Although she wasn't superstitious and had never had a clairvoyant before Mariska read her palm, she couldn't shake the woman's prediction: *I see two men in your life— one who will come to love you very much and one who will pretend to love you.*

Which one was Justin? Was he sincere or a fraud?

She blinked once. "Why now?" she asked, recovering her voice. "We dated for more than two years, and now you tell me that you love me."

"I've always loved you, Lydia."

Shaking her head, she closed her eyes for several seconds. "It's not going to work, Justin."

He moved closer and took her hands. "Why? Because you say it won't?"

Lydia met his direct stare. "I've changed."

"Are you saying you don't have feelings for me?"

"No, I'm not."

Tightening his grip on her fingers, he leaned closer and kissed her cheek. He'd negotiated enough deals to know when to retreat. "Let's talk about this at another time. Better yet, I'll write you." He angled his head, smiling. "Campers shouldn't be the only folks to get mail."

She nodded. "Okay." Justin did not want to talk about their relationship and she didn't either.

Justin brushed his mouth over hers. There was just the slightest pressure before he pulled away. "Be safe, darling."

A wave of apprehension swept through Lydia, gnawing away at her confidence. Justin had repeated the same words Kennedy had said before she left the camp.

"I have to go." Pulling her hands from his loose grip, she walked over to her SUV, got in, and drove away without a backward glance.

What had she gotten herself into? A man whom she'd relegated to her past had openly confessed to loving her, while another whom she loved awaited her return.

She wanted to weep, as a fist of fear and disappointment squeezed her heart. If the fortune-teller's prediction boded the truth, then was she destined to spend the rest of her life with Justin—a man who failed to ignite the grand passion she'd experienced with Kennedy?

Lydia left the parking area and walked to her cabin. The smell of burning wood lingered in the air from the Saturday night campfire. A large oil drum was filled with kindling, set afire to the delight of the campers who roasted marshmallows while listening intently to Reverend Alfonso retell Native American folktales passed down through countless generations.

She chanced a glance at Kennedy's cabin. No light shone from the windows. Either he was at the campfire or he'd gone to bed.

She opened the screen door, and closed it quickly. After the bird had taken up residence in her cabin, she made certain not to leave the door ajar. If the creature had been a raccoon or a bat she would've relinquished her private lodgings without a second thought.

* * *

A feeling of weighted fatigue settled over Lydia as she lay on the recliner. She'd showered, brushed her teeth, slipped on a nightgown, but instead of crawling into bed she'd decided to take in the solitude of the warm summer night.

The cooling breeze rustling the trees and wind chime provided the natural accompaniment to the soft strains of a contemporary jazz number coming from the stereo's speakers. It had been a while since she enjoyed sitting out on her porch. Most nights she'd been too exhausted to do anything more than shower and fall, facedown, into bed. She must have fallen asleep, because the chiming of her cell phone jolted her into wakefulness. Patting the cushion, she located it and flipped the top.

"Hello."

"Are you back?"

Her pulse quickened. "Yes, Kennedy, I'm back."

"Good."

Sitting up, she peered over her shoulder. His cabin was still dark. "Where are you?"

A deep sensual chuckle came through the earpiece. "I'm home."

"Home, where?"

"Next door."

A teasing smile softened her mouth. "What are you wearing, handsome?" She'd affected the sultry timbre of a 1-900-4A GOOD-TIME telephone operator.

Kennedy gasped audibly. "What did you say?"

"You heard me, tiger. What's the matter? No woman has ever asked you that?"

"No!"

"Did I shock you?"

"A little. But I like it."

Lydia giggled, the sound as soft and tinkling as her wind chime. "Good. That's what I like—a secure man."

There came a pointed pause before Kennedy spoke again. "Do you really like me, Lydia?"

It was her turn to pause. "Of course I like you. Why else would I sleep with you?"

"I don't know. Perhaps you were curious?"

A slight frown marred her smooth forehead. She didn't like the direction the conversation was taking. "I've never been that curious, Kennedy. Not even the first time."

"Do you have anything planned for tomorrow night?" Kennedy asked, smoothly changing the topic.

"Why?"

"Because I'd like you to go out with me."

Lydia heard the change in his voice. It was soft, coaxing. "Where?"

"To a jazz club."

Her eyes crinkled as she smiled. "Don't tell me you're deserting your country music?"

"Never, darling." Lydia told him about the radio station she'd listened to during her drive. "You'd better be careful, sugah, or you're going to become a real country girl."

"Who's to say I'm not a country girl now? After all, I did grow up twenty miles outside Baltimore."

"That's a suburb, not the country."

Lydia laughed softly. "This place is in the country."

"Not," Kennedy drawled. "It's more like the wilderness."

"Is the jazz club in the wilderness?"

"Not quite."

"What's the occasion?"

Kennedy chuckled. "Does it have to be a special occasion for you to go out with me?"

"No."

"Good. Now, to answer your question as to what I'm wearing. Why don't you come over and find out?"

A wave of heat suffused her face in embarrassment. Lydia didn't know what had elicited her bold behavior. "I hadn't planned on a sleepover tonight."

She did not want to sleep with Kennedy, because she needed to be alone to sort out her feelings for him, had to ascertain whether what she felt for him was based on sex, or if it went beyond whatever they shared in bed.

"When do you want to have another sleepover?" Kennedy asked.

Her mouth softened in a smile. "Tomorrow night."

"Pack light," he said after a pregnant pause.

She nodded although he couldn't see her. There was no doubt they would spend Sunday night at his lakeside home. "Good night, Kennedy."

"Good night, sweetheart."

Pressing a button, Lydia ended the call and closed her eyes. Inhaling, she held her breath, then let it out slowly, repeating the action as her chest rose and fell in an even rhythm. She lay on the recliner, momentarily lost in her own reveries. She thought about the space she'd hoped to lease in the underground mall, about Justin's declaration of love, and she mentally relived the passion she'd discovered in Kennedy's embrace.

Thirteen

Kennedy felt the undercurrent of excitement sweeping over Camp Six Nations as staff, campers, and their family members filed into the eight-sided barn.

The campers' growth and development had exceeded the goals set for each age group. Roger Evans had provided direct oversight for the first session, but Kennedy would closely monitor the next four weeks.

The next four weeks were certain to become the most decisive. He would provide hands-on supervision of the campers and he knew he had to resolve his relationship with Lydia before driving down to Alabama to undergo tests to determine whether he was a compatible match to donate a kidney to Marvin.

Seconds after he'd ended his call to Lydia the night before, his cell phone rang. It had taken Marvin Kennedy three weeks to return his call. He spoke to his biological father as if he were a polite stranger, then told Marvin he would come to Alabama to confer with the older man's renal specialist about his medical condition.

The call, which hadn't lasted more than two minutes, left Kennedy restless, experiencing emotions he did not want to acknowledge—pity and compassion for a man so undeserving of the sentiment.

He checked his watch as the last of the counselors escorted their charges into the barn with a thirty-foot vaulted ceiling and capacity for three hundred. Everyone, except the chefs, wore a navy blue T-shirt with Camp Six Nations imprinted in white across the chest. Roger entered the barn, closed the door, sat down on a folding chair, and nodded.

Kennedy's gaze swept over the assembly as he raised the handheld microphone, then affected the smile that had been captured on countless occasions by sports photographers after a Ravens victory.

"I'm Ken Fletcher, the camp's sports director." A smattering of applause from adults followed his introduction. "I'd like to welcome all family members to Camp Six Nations' first Family Reunion Sunday," he continued smoothly as if there had been no interruption, his mellifluous voice carrying easily in the enormous space.

"I know many of you are surprised to see the changes in your children in just four short weeks. Some have grown several inches, gained weight, lost weight, and I'm proud to say that every camper has passed the water safety course and is now a certified swimmer." All of the campers stood up, applauding loudly.

Waiting until everyone quieted and retook their seats, he continued, "The goal of Camp Six Nations is to foster excellence, fairness, cooperation, responsibility, compassion, and citizenship. What good is a strong body without a strong mind? We've spent the past four weeks fostering teamwork, and the next four will be competition.

"Your sons and daughters have learned to respect and support others in their cabin, while relating to them as members of their camp family. Midweek the senior and junior boys will take part in a modified three-night survival training exercise based on the official U.S. Army Survival Manual. The following week it will be the senior and junior girls.

"I'm going to turn the mike over to our direct care staff, who will give you a brief overview of their day-to-day interactions with your children." His gaze swept over the five people sitting behind him on the stage. "Reverend Alfonso."

Reverend Al, as the kids called him, took the microphone from Kennedy. The shaman, a tall, spare man in his mid-fifties, wore his salt-and-pepper hair in a single braid. A necklace made of colorful beads and matching earrings in his pierced lobes enhanced his distinctive Native American features.

"Welcome to Camp Six Nations. I will make this quick, because there is a lot to see and do this afternoon. Our camp is called Six Nations in honor of those who inhabited this land centuries before the Europeans settled here. The name Iroquois, meaning 'real adders,' is of Algonquian origin. The Iroquois, who refer to themselves as 'we who are of the extended lodge,' are not a tribal group, but an alliance of tribes that dominated the vast area stretching from the Atlantic Coast to Lake Erie, and from Ontario down into North Carolina.

"The original Five Nations Confederacy was made up of the Mohawk, Oneida, Onondaga, Cayuga, and Seneca tribes. In 1715 the Tuscarora joined the league, and from that time, the Iroquois have been known as the Six Nations. Each cabin represents a tribe—male and female, an alliance of children from many tribes who have come together as one. Thus, our motto: One Camp, One Family.

"Before we begin our day, everyone gathers in the chapel for morning meditation, or they use the time to pray in their own way. For those who choose not to pray or reflect, they are exempt." He smiled and a network of lines fanned out around his dark eyes. "I'm happy to say no one has asked to be excused. I'll let your children tell you about our Saturday night campfire gatherings. Thank you very much for your attention."

The adults murmured their approval as Alfonso handed the microphone to Lydia.

The campers stood up, stomping and shouting, "Eat! Eat! Eat!" The entire barn was filled with laughter, and before Lydia composed herself enough to speak, tears had filled her eyes and rolled down her cheeks. She removed the white kerchief from around her neck and dabbed her face.

Her shoulders still shaking from laughing, she smiled, saying, "It's redundant to say I'm a chef. My partner and I have taken our campers on a culinary journey to countries as far away as Morocco and Greece. They may shock you when they ask to go to a restaurant serving couscous, pasticcio, pasta *fagioli*, or *arroz con carne de cerdo* rather than McDonald's or the local pizza parlor."

Her amused gaze moved slowly over the faces of the campers in hues ranging from creamy white to a deep rich sable brown. "I'm most proud of our campers because of the ease with which they've embraced diversity not only among themselves, but also with the international cuisine my partner and I have offered." Turning slightly, she glanced over her shoulder at Neil. "None of this would've been possible without Neil Lane."

Neil stood up and was rewarded with whistles and shouts from everyone in the barn. A wave of bright color moved from his neck to his face. The beginnings of a smile faded, then widened as the barn door opened and a petite woman with stylishly cut ash-blond hair walked in with two preteen girls whose inky black hair was a startling contrast to hers. She'd come. His estranged wife had brought his daughters to Family Reunion Sunday!

Lydia saw the direction of Neil's raven gaze and handed him the microphone. "It's all yours," she whispered softly.

Neil, who hadn't been scheduled to speak, cleared his throat. "I'm certain I speak for everyone when I say that we're blessed to have Lydia supervising the kitchen." Pausing, he gave his supervisor a forlorn look. "Please don't forget me when you open your restaurant." Grinning broadly, he handed off the microphone to Jeff Wiggins.

Kennedy stared at Lydia as she and Neil left to see to the

food that would be served following a tour of the camp by the visiting parents. He redirected his attention to Jeff as the drama instructor energized everyone when he talked about the theatrical numbers his drama students were rehearsing. Megan Gallagher followed Jeff, enchanting the crowd with her lilting Irish brogue. She invited everyone to come to the arts and crafts hogan to view the pieces of pottery she had put on display for viewing. After completing her brief presentation, she returned the microphone to Kennedy.

Rising he moved behind the lectern, replacing the microphone on its stand. "I'd like to thank everyone for their attention, and if you would be so kind as to follow the counselors wearing the red wristbands they will give you a tour of our campgrounds. Then, I'd like everyone to gather in the dining hall for Sunday dinner. This is just a reminder for those who came up on the bus, the driver would like to start loading at six-thirty. He will pull out at exactly seven o'clock and not one minute later."

Kennedy turned off the mike and followed the others out of the barn. He also planned to leave the camp at seven with Lydia. It had been a long time since he'd looked forward to going out with a woman who did not bore him to tears.

Nila hadn't been as superficially beautiful as the models he'd dated, but it was her intelligence and gentleness that had drawn him to her. He was playing pro ball, involved in product endorsements, traveling from city to city for away games, and he hadn't wanted any encumbrances in his life at that time.

Whenever he returned to Baltimore he called Nila, and she was always available. Even if she'd had a prior engagement, she canceled it to be with him. She was predictable, accommodating, and faithful—all the hallmarks for a woman who was certain to be a good wife. That was then, and this was now. He was older, wiser, and what he did not want in a woman was predictability.

Smiling, Kennedy put on his sunglasses. Lydia Lord was

anything but predictable. He'd found her incredibly sexy, despite her claim that he was the first man who'd brought her to complete sexual fulfillment. She'd become the first and only woman that made him want to lie with her without the benefit of contraception. He wanted Lydia as his wife and the mother of his children.

Neil pulled his daughters close to his side. "Lydia, I'd like you to meet my wife, Rachel, and our daughters Stacy and Jennifer. Girls, Rachel, my supervisor and mentor, Miss Lydia Lord."

Lydia removed her latex gloves, tucking them under her apron ties, and extended her right hand. "It's nice meeting you." Rachel Lane's fingers were cool and smooth as they touched hers.

Rachel's dark blue eyes studied the face of the tall, slender woman whose youthful appearance belied her culinary experience. "It's nice meeting you, too, Lydia."

"Is this where you work, Daddy?" asked the younger girl.

Nodding and smiling at his nine-year-old daughter, Neil said, "Yes, baby girl."

"It's nice, Daddy."

He ruffled her inky black hair. "I think it's nice, too."

Jennifer Lane had inherited her father's hair and eyes and her mother's petite frame. She smiled up at Neil. "I love this camp."

Stacy tugged on Neil's arm. "Can me and Jenny come here next summer, Daddy?"

Lydia's and Neil's gazes met and fused. Next summer was a long way off, and neither knew what direction their lives would take by that time.

"We'll see," he said noncommittally.

"I think I want to become a cook like Daddy," Jennifer announced, shocking both her parents.

Lydia slipped on her latex gloves. She wanted to finish up

with the watermelon boat salad. "Neil, why don't you give your family a tour of the kitchen while I take care of the fruit salad?"

She was anxious to leave the dining hall and prepare for her evening with Kennedy, and she also wanted to give Neil time to reconnect with his family.

Twenty minutes later, two halves of a large watermelon, cut lengthwise with a serrated border, were filled with balls of cantaloupe, honeydew, watermelon, blueberries, strawberries, kiwi, and white grapes.

Picking up one half, she pushed open the swinging door with her shoulder and walked into the dining hall. The noise level was deafening. She motioned to a kitchen assistant. "Please bring out the other half."

Pleasant and always cooperative, the teenager took the watermelon from Lydia, placing it on the refrigerated portion of the serving counter. "What else do you need for me to bring out?"

"That's it," she replied, smiling. She glanced down when she felt someone tugging on her apron. It was her favorite camper, Keisha Middleton. "Hi, Kiki."

Keisha touched her hair. "My mommy braided my hair."

Hunkering down to the child's height, Lydia ran a finger over her silken cheek. "You look beautiful, doll baby."

Clapping a hand over her mouth, Keisha giggled through her fingers. "I told my mommy you call me doll baby and she laughed. Do you want to meet my mommy, Miss Lydia?"

She smiled. "Of course I do, Kiki."

She had met many of the parents during their tour of the dining hall. All of them thanked her for weaning their children off greasy, fat-filled foods. Taking the child's hand, Lydia followed her across the dining hall, nodding and smiling at the many campers she'd come to recognize on sight.

Kennedy sat at a table with three senior Mohawks and six Senecas. The young boys, ranging in age from nine to twelve, were the first group to participate in the survival training exercise. The sight of Lydia and Keisha Middleton had captured his attention. He stared, unblinking, as Lydia touched the little girl's face. In that instant the pull of fatherhood nearly swallowed him whole.

He went completely still, unable to pull his gaze away when he saw them walk hand in hand to the table where Keisha's mother and older brothers and sister sat. He was still staring as Lydia sat next to Mrs. Middleton.

His penetrating gaze lingered on the omnipresent bandana covering her hair, the dewy sheen on her bare face, the enchanting tilt of her sherry-gold eyes whenever she smiled, and the lush lower lip he yearned to lick, kiss, and suckle.

"You didn't answer my question, Mr. K."

The camper calling his name pulled him from his reverie. He blinked once and turned back to the others at the table. "I'm sorry, Mustafa, I wasn't listening."

"I . . . we want to know if we're going to have to catch and cook our own food."

Kennedy affected a mysterious smile. "What do you think? After all, it will be a survival training expedition."

"Will we have to sleep out on the ground?" asked Angelo Quinn, who'd earned the distinction of being the first camper to pass the rigorous requirements for being a lifeguard.

"You will see in a couple of days." They were scheduled to hike a mile to a lodge and spend two nights learning how to survive in the wilderness, before returning to camp by canoe. "The only hint I'm going to give you is that you're going to have to rely on one another for everything."

"Come on, Mr. K.," one of the younger Senecas drawled. "You have to tell us more than that."

"No, I don't," countered Kennedy, unsuccessfully suppressing his amusement. "The survival exercise will come in handy once we have game week."

"Yo, Mr. K, you comin' wit' us?" asked Mustafa.

"Yo, Mustafa, yeah." The boys dissolving into a paroxysm of hysterics pounded the table and exchanged high fives. Kennedy was still smiling when he rose and walked out of the dining hall.

Lydia walked into the kitchen, slowing her pace when she saw Neil sitting on a stool at a counter flipping pages in a notebook. "I thought you'd be out of here."

His head came up. "I was just going over some recipes."

Moving closer, she sat down on a stool next to Neil and stared at his distinctive profile. His finely boned features made him appear fragile. But his looks were totally incongruent with his temperament, which was stubborn, determined. He possessed a willingness to sacrifice his job and family to pursue his passion.

"Which ones are you looking at?"

Neil met Lydia's steady gaze. He liked and respected her professionally. And as promised, she hadn't screamed or thrown objects. "I was thinking about our all-American menu."

Reaching up, Neil removed the black skullcap covering his spiky hair. "I'd like to make some suggestions."

Bracing an elbow on the countertop, Lydia rested her chin on a fist. "Talk to me, Neil."

"I'd like for us to amend the all-American by offering an entrée and desserts from several regional menus on a daily basis. One night we can offer a New England clambake with various chowders. I'm certain the kids will love Philadelphia cheese steak sandwiches, Buffalo wings, and on rainy days, Manhattan clam chowder for lunch. Pennsylvania pot roast can be a dinner entrée that can round out the Middle Atlantic states."

Arching her eyebrow, Lydia asked, "What about the rest of the country?"

Neil felt a jolt of excitement. So far his boss hadn't shot down his proposal. "The South will include Maryland crab cakes, gumbo, jambalaya, hoppin' John, and fried green tomatoes. The Midwest will feature Swedish meatballs, Kansas City barbecued ribs, sausage and kraut, and Chicago-style deep-dish spinach pizza. The Southwest menu can be vegetable-topped cheese quesadillas, green chili cheese spread, a taco salad, and Navajo fry bread.

"Chicken potpie, *kolaches*, sourdough bread, chicken with black bean sauce, and marinated grilled lamb can be featured from the West, and pumpkin soup, pineapple salsa, cream cheese and macadamia pie, and ginger-orange shrimp stir-fry for the Pacific Northwest, Alaska, and Hawaii."

"Are you suggesting we scrap our all-American theme in favor of daily regional dishes?"

"Oh no," he said quickly. "I just thought we'd add a few more choices to the daily theme."

"A theme means having a distinctive quality or characteristic. I believe we'll confuse everyone if we offer a Chicago-style deep-dish pizza when the menu reads Chinese." Neil glanced away rather than let Lydia see his disappointment. "But I do have a suggestion where we can use your idea," she said in a soft tone.

Excitement fired his raven gaze, his mood suddenly buoyant. "Talk to me, boss."

A flash of humor crossed Lydia's face. "We can modify our lunch schedule to include some of your choices. Keep in mind that our breakfast and lunch dishes require the least amount of preparation."

"I know," Neil concurred.

Lydia gave him a long, penetrating look. She did not want Neil to go through what she'd experienced with her last employer—an outright rejection of her proposals. But she also didn't want to spend more time in the kitchen than necessary. As it was, she spent an average of twelve hours a day at the dining hall.

"What if we compromise?"

"How?" he asked smoothly, with no expression on his face.

"You will become totally responsible for breakfast and lunch. Beginning tomorrow morning, you will supervise the kitchen for the next two weeks."

He stared at his supervisor, complete surprise on his face. "You . . . you want me to supervise *you*?"

A smug smile tugged at the corners of her mouth. "Me and the help. How else are you going to gain supervisory experience?"

Neil hesitated, measuring Lydia's expression for a hint of guile. "You're joking, aren't you?"

There was a moment of silence before she said softly, "No, I'm not, Neil. I never joke about anything that has to do with my job. You've risked everything you've worked for, and that includes your family, to follow your dream. I'm offering you what I wanted from the first day I walked into the lecture hall at the Culinary Institute of America, and you sit here asking me if I'm joking.

"You're a talented chef, Neil, and if I had a restaurant I'd hire you. I'm giving you the opportunity to supervise the kitchen because we won't be at full capacity for the next two weeks. The ten- to twelve-year-old boys will be away for three days, and the girls the following week. What's it going to be?" she challenged as hardness crept into her voice.

His forehead creased in consternation, Neil contemplated Lydia's proposition. He wanted to cook, not supervise. In more than twenty years with the General Accounting Office he passed on every supervisory position because he'd always felt uncomfortable monitoring others.

"I need your decision now, Neil."

The soft feminine voice broke into his musings as a smile found its way through an expression of uncertainty. "Okay."

A secret smile softened her mouth and lit up her liquid gold eyes. Kennedy had slipped a note under her door earlier that morning to let her know he would pick her up at seven. He'd added a postscript: *if possible—please have Neil cover breakfast.* The first time she'd stayed over at his house he'd complained about getting out of bed "at the crack of dawn" to return to camp. But when she reminded him that he usually got up early to swim in the lake he countered by saying it was either the cold lake water or a cold shower. His gaze had burned her face, and there was no mistaking his double meaning.

"If it's all right with you, *boss*, I'd like to start a little later tomorrow."

Neil threw back his head, laughter floating up from his throat. Becoming temporary executive chef for two weeks and reuniting with his family had changed his life in less than twenty-four hours.

"Yes, Lydia. Take the time, and don't forget to relax."

Slipping off the stool, Lydia wiggled her fingers. "I will."

Lydia wrapped narrow silk ribbons around her ankles, tying them neatly in a bow. The three-inch silk-covered sandals were the perfect complement to the halter-style black dress. A knock on the door shattered the silence, and she glanced at her travel clock on the bedside table. It was 6:50.

Rising to her feet, she made her way to the door, while removing the oversize pins from her wrapped hairdo. Peeking through the slats of the jalousie window, she spied Kennedy. She opened the door several inches and went completely still.

The fragrance of his cologne, the velvety smoothness of his clean-shaven jaw, the exquisite cut of a midnight-blue tailored suit caressing the lines of his powerful body made the muscles in her stomach contract.

There was an expression in his dark eyes that pulled her into a force field, holding her captive. He was making love to her without touching. Heat swept up her face, bringing with it a light sheen of moisture. Her breasts grew heavy, the nipples swelling against the fabric of her dress.

"As soon as I comb my hair I'll be ready." Lydia did not

recognize her own voice. It floated around her like a disembodied specter.

Bracing a hand on the door frame, Kennedy pushed it open, walked into the cabin, closed it, then reached for Lydia. Slowly, methodically he removed the last two pins and her hair fell over her forehead and down around the nape of her neck.

"You've cut your hair," he whispered against her ear.

"A little." Moving behind her, he tunneled a hand through the mussed strands, massaging her scalp. "You're too close, Kennedy," Lydia said, gasping, while attempting to slow down her runaway pulse.

His free arm circled her waist, bringing her hips to his groin. His hand went from her head to a breast. "We're not close enough, sweetheart."

Breathing through parted lips, she closed her eyes, going pliant in his embrace. Kennedy's hardness throbbing against her buttocks electrified her. She managed to swallow the first moan, but the second one slipped out of its own accord. A rush of moisture, which left her legs trembling so much she doubted whether she would've been able to stand if Kennedy hadn't held on to her, followed the flutters that began between her thighs. Her moans became a strangled gasp as she succumbed to the liquid fire bathing the soft core of her body.

Her breasts rising and falling heavily as if in the aftermath of passion would not permit her to move or speak. Lydia closed her eyes and rested her head on her lover's shoulder.

Kennedy felt the runaway beating of Lydia's heart under his splayed fingers. Burying his face in her hair, he breathed a kiss on the sweet-smelling strands. He loved her. He loved her so much that he feared blurting out what lay in his heart.

Lydia opened her eyes, smiling. "Please let me go. I need to get ready." She didn't have time to take another shower, but knew she had to wash away the evidence of the erotic pleasure Kennedy had roused in her.

Lowering his head, Kennedy brushed his mouth over the nape of her neck. "I'll wait on the porch."

Once he released her, she walked over to the chest of drawers, selected a pair of panties, and retreated to the bathroom.

Fourteen

Lydia stepped out onto the porch, unable to meet Kennedy's gaze. He knew she had no control over her traitorous body, knew that all he had to do was touch her and she'd melt like a pat of butter on a heated surface.

She, Lydia Charlene Lord, who'd prided herself on being in total control at all times, had surrendered the will of her flesh to a man whom she had fallen for and did not want to love.

She had accepted the position as chef for Camp Six Nations to test her culinary creativity, to prepare nutritious meals for what she considered the world's toughest critics: children.

She'd planned to spend eight weeks in western Maryland's unspoiled wilderness perfecting her craft, not preparing to spend the night with a man who made her forget her vow never to become involved with an athlete, or in Kennedy's case a former athlete.

They were four weeks into the camp season with another four before it ended, and Lydia told herself over and over that she could engage in a summer romance and then walk away with her emotions intact. That she would enjoy whatever she and Kennedy shared, then relegate it to her past, because her sole focus was setting up her restaurant.

Smiling, she pointed to the bag decorated in a needle-point design resting near the recliner. "Light enough?" She'd packed underwear, a nightgown, T-shirt, shorts, a pair of sandals, and her grooming products.

Bending down, Kennedy picked up the bag, testing its weight. It was very light. Straightening up, he turned and stared at Lydia, his eyes making love to her face. Her hair, parted off-center, framed her face—a face that bore the slightest trace of makeup that subtly enhanced her natural feminine beauty. She'd tilted her chin slightly, staring up at him through a fringe of long, full black lashes that framed her incredible sherry-colored eyes.

His eyes moved lower, caressing the graceful column of her bared neck, the soft swell of breasts rising and falling above the décolletage of her form-fitting dress that outlined every line of her slender, curvy body. He stared at her long bare legs in the heels that put her over the six-foot mark.

"You look incredible, darling." His voice was low, reverent, and blatantly seductive.

Lydia stared at the strong brown throat above the starched collar of a white shirt. "So do you." Taking a step closer, she took a deep breath and whispered, "What are you wearing?"

Kennedy lifted his eyebrows. "You want to know who designed my suit?"

She shook her head. "Not your clothes, Kennedy. What fragrance are you wearing? You always smell so delicious."

"Is that what you'd asked me last night?"

"No. Last night I wanted to know literally what you were wearing."

"I'm wearing Burberry Brit, and when I called last night I was in my birthday suit."

Curving her arms around his neck, she brushed her mouth over his. "Happy birthday."

Kennedy did not move, not even his eyes. "Who told you today's my birthday?"

"You just did."

His free arm curved around her waist. "I did not."

"The night at the fair you told me that you were going to be thirty-six next month. This is next month. And the fact that you asked me to go out with you on a Sunday night tells me that today is special," she said with an attractive pout. "Now, tell me I'm wrong."

Tightening his hold on her body, Kennedy lowered his head and pressed a kiss along the column of her neck. "You're not wrong, baby."

"You should've come clean with me, Kennedy. I could've gotten you something special for your born-day."

"I have all that I need. I have you."

Lydia sobered quickly. "You'll only have me for the next four weeks. I wanted to give you a small gift to remind you of our summer together."

"Do you really want to give me a little something?"

"Yes."

"When I take you to Cabo San Lucas I want to make it an extended stay."

A wave of momentary panic swept through Lydia, gnawing away at her confidence. She knew Kennedy could feel the runaway beating of her heart against his chest. What exactly did he want? Did he want to continue their liaison beyond the camp season?

"Extend it how?"

"A week or two."

Pulling out of his embrace, Lydia stared at Kennedy as if she'd never seen him before. "I can't," she said, shaking her head.

"Why not, Lydia? It's not as if you have to get up in the morning to go to work."

Her quick temper flared. "The last time I checked I was certain I didn't have someone hovering over me monitoring my daily comings and goings."

Kennedy knew he had made a grievous faux pas. Lydia had changed before his eyes like a reptile shedding its skin, and he wanted to shake her until she was too breathless to lash him with the whip she called a tongue. There was a time and place to argue, and he knew this time wasn't one of those times.

Fixing her with a lethal stare, he said, "I'm sorry, Lydia, if you misconstrued my meaning, but I would never attempt to monitor anyone's life, and certainly not yours." His tone was neutral, conciliatory. "*You* told me that you don't expect to open your restaurant until next spring. I interpreted that to mean you would have *some* free time before the end of *this* year."

Lydia stared at a spot over Kennedy's shoulder. Shame quickened her breath, singed her face, and she was angry for being embarrassed because never had she been chastised so eloquently.

Pulling back her shoulders, she tilted her chin in a defiant gesture and affected a half smile as Kennedy stared at her under hooded lids.

"I'm sorry I snapped at you. Will you forgive me . . . darling?"

Offering her a smile that sent her pulses racing, Kennedy cupped her elbow and led her off the porch. "I'll think about it . . . baby."

"I thought by now you would've cut me some slack."

Shifting her gaze from the side window, Lydia stared at Kennedy as he navigated a narrow road bordered on both sides with towering pine trees. She'd been content to watch the passing landscape while listening to the seductive voice of Will Downing coming through the SUV's speakers.

Kennedy had removed his suit jacket and laid it over the rear seats. The haunting scent of his cologne, the crisp fabric of the custom-made shirt with monogrammed French cuffs, and the heat from his body had become a sensual feast that ensnared her in a gluttonous web from which there was no escape.

"What are you talking about?"

"Do you still lump me in the same category as your ex?"

Kennedy took his gaze off the road for a second. Lydia's expression mirrored his confusion. "There are times when I must edit everything before I say it whenever I'm with you," he explained softly, as he concentrated on the winding stretch of asphalt. "Maybe I'm wrong, but I feel as if I'm being punished for the indiscretions perpetrated by the men in your past."

It was the second time in as many minutes that Kennedy had chastised her. Was he right? Was she punishing him for one man's infidelity and another's insensitivity?

Tears welled in her eyes, but did not fall. A tumble of confused thoughts and feelings weighed her down. Biting down on her lower lip, she tried to bring her fragile emotions under control. Against her will, she had fallen in love with Kennedy Fletcher. He was everything she had sought in a man, yet he had become the receptacle for her frustration and disappointments.

"I'm sorry, Kennedy. It is not my intention to lash out at you."

He lifted an eyebrow. "Apology accepted." He drove another quarter of a mile, made a sharp left, and continued along a one-lane road until he saw a sign indicating the number of miles to Pennsylvania.

"Do you want to tell me about him?" he asked softly.

"Who?"

"The jock that hurt you."

Lydia wanted to openly deny she was still carrying the pain of Vincent's deception, but did not want to lie to Kennedy or to herself.

She knew she had to stop punishing Kennedy because of her inability to move forward emotionally.

She stared out the windshield and exhaled. "I won't tell you his name, because he's still playing pro ball."

"Which league?"

"NBA. I met John Doe in high school. He was a year ahead of me. He was a point guard and captain of the basketball team and I was captain of the girls' softball team. To say he was popular is an understatement. He had looks, talent, and brains enough to get into Georgetown on a full scholarship.

"He never seemed that interested in me until he came back to speak at our annual sports award dinner. After I was selected best all-around female athlete he approached me and asked if I had a date for the senior prom. Up until that time, none of the boys had asked me because most of them believed the rumors that had been circulating for years about my brothers threatening guys with bodily harm if they even looked sideways at their sisters."

"Did you go to the prom with him?"

Lydia nodded as a sad smile softened her features. "Yes. We saw a lot of each that summer. I'd applied to a D.C. culinary school, so that fall John and I continued to see each other.

"I talked my folks into letting me share an apartment in D.C. with my best girlfriend who had enrolled at Howard. She had her boyfriend and I had John. When we weren't studying or when John wasn't playing ball, we'd all take turns getting together at our respective apartments. I always wound up with the cooking duties."

"How long did you date John?"

"Almost three years. I saw him for a year before going to bed with him. Meanwhile I'd bragged to my roommate that he was the greatest because he hadn't pressured me into sleeping with him. She always told me that I was the luckiest girl in the world.

"However, my luck ran out. The NBA came knocking at John's door, and he had to decide whether to finish college or turn pro. He opted to drop out. The lure of a multimillion-dollar contract with several product endorsements was too tempting to pass up.

"The day he turned pro, his agent held a press conference announcing John was planning to marry at the end of the month. My telephone never stopped ringing with everyone congratulating me on my upcoming nuptials. At first, I was pissed at John for using the media to propose when he hadn't given me a clue that he wanted to marry before he graduated from college. He called me and said he needed to talk. The fact that he said he needed and not wanted to talk should've put me on notice. Well, shame on me for assuming the woman he wanted to marry was me." Lydia closed her eyes, unable to continue.

"Who was she?" Kennedy asked after a prolonged silence.

"Who do you think?" she said, recovering her voice.

"Your roommate."

A wry smile twisted her mouth. "Give that man a cigar," she said cynically.

"What was his excuse for choosing your roommate over you?"

"Georgetown was one of the final four teams during March Madness, and I'd come down with the flu, so I couldn't make it to an off-campus party. My roommate went in my place. John claimed he and my roommate had a little too much to drink and wound up in bed together. He tried to absolve himself when he said it was only the first time they'd slept together."

Kennedy's right hand covered the gearshift in a deathlike grip. "I thought you told me she had a boyfriend."

"She did when we moved in together. After a while she began complaining about him because he would never have the earning potential John would. Poor Curtis finally had enough of her bitchin' and moanin' and moved on."

"Which opened the door for her to go after your man."

Lydia nodded, sighing audibly. "I suppose he wasn't my man if I was also sharing him with another woman—or maybe even other women. My roommate never came back to the apartment to pick up her things. I eventually packed everything and shipped it to her parents. I kept the apartment while I completed the internship; then I gave it up just before I went to Europe. My brother Quintin accused me of running away, and in a way I suppose I was. Living abroad forced me to grow up faster than I would have in the States. The other plus is that I'm fluent in three other languages."

"Whatever happened to your John and Jane Doe?"

"They were married, and she had a son, then a daughter a year later. Her fairy-tale marriage fell apart when her philandering husband was hit with a paternity suit not from one, but two women within the span of three months. He admitted to sleeping with both of them, so aside from baby mama drama he lost most of his endorsements, because he'd tarnished his role model image."

Kennedy winced. Whenever celebrities lent their name to a product, it always came with a caveat—behave! That was the reason he hadn't had a knock-down, drag-out brawl with Lumel McClain. Although he'd opted out of his football career, he had subsequently amassed a small fortune from endorsements and investments.

"Are they still together?"

Lydia smiled. "Oh yeah. I doubt if Jane would ever leave him, because it would mean not living as grand as she is now. They now have four children, and someone told me there's another one on the way. Seven children before you celebrate your thirtieth birthday must make John feel like quite the man. And I'm willing to bet he'll have a few more baby mamas before he finds himself broke. All of his children need a full-time father, not someone who'll drop by a couple of times during the year to play Santa when the mood hits him."

A pregnant silence filled the vehicle. The compact disc had finished, and there was only the slip-slap sound of the tires on the roadway.

"I'd like to ask you something, Lydia."

She glanced at Kennedy, wondering why his voice sounded so ominous. "What is it?"

"Do you still love him?"

Lydia was as startled by the question as she was with Kennedy's impassioned query. "No," she said softly. "I don't love him."

There was another moment of silence before he said, "Good."

A plethora of sounds and delicious smells greeted Lydia as she and Kennedy wound their way through a maze of small round tables in the dining establishment in rural southwestern Pennsylvania. The Music Shack catered to every musical genre from classical to zydeco, seven nights a week. Sunday nights featured classic and modern jazz.

A sax player went down on his knees amid rousing applause, holding a high-pitched note for more than two minutes as a chanteuse crooned a Dakota Stanton ballad.

"How did you find this place?" Lydia asked Kennedy once they were seated. The table was perfect. It was close enough to the stage and far enough away from the other diners to ensure a modicum of privacy.

The glow from a small votive on the table was flattering to his features. Lydia found herself transfixed by the hollows in his lean face, by his strong chin and penetrating large dark eyes.

"I found it by accident. Once I moved here I used to take day trips to check out the area. The night I found this place they were playing Delta blues and serving catfish fritters, fried okra, and hush puppies. It was enough to make me forget that I was in Pennsylvania and not Mississippi."

"Are you saying that the menu coincides with the music?"

Kennedy nodded. "Yes, ma'am. Zydeco night is Cajun and country is Texas-style ribs and fried chicken."

"What other types of music do they offer?"

"Pop, R-and-B, and Latin."

"They bring in a different band each night?"

Kennedy reached out and held her hand. "No, sweetheart. The same band plays every night."

"They're that versatile?"

"Not as versatile and talented as you."

Amusement flickered in the eyes that met Lydia's. "You

keep talking like that and I'm going to wind up with a swelled head."

He tightened his hold on her slender fingers. "You are incredible, Lydia." *In and out of bed*, he mused, holding her gaze. A momentary look of discomfort crossed her face before it faded behind a beguiling smile.

"Chef Lord thanks you."

Kennedy sobered quickly. "I'm not talking about your cooking, Lydia. I was referring to you."

She attempted to extract her hand, but the fingers clasping hers tightened like manacles. "Don't, Kennedy."

"Don't what?"

"Don't make it harder on me to leave you at the end of the summer."

"You, Lydia? Is this all about you? What about me? What about *us*?"

"I didn't know there was an us," she countered.

His eyes widened. "The night you came to my cabin and slept in my bed we became us."

"You know why I came to you that night."

"Yes, I know. But the moment you asked me not to leave you, the moment you opened your legs for me, it was no longer you and I, but us."

Lydia gave Kennedy a long, penetrating look. "What are you saying? What do you want?"

"We're a couple, Lydia. And to answer your second question—I want you."

"How?" she whispered, although there was no one close enough to overhear their conversation.

"That will have to be your decision."

"What if all I want is the summer? That at the end of the camp season I leave whatever we've shared together here?"

Shrugging a broad shoulder under his jacket, Kennedy lowered his gaze and his voice. "If that's your decision, then I have no other choice but to respect it."

Lydia felt a rush of dread. "Why are you making me out to be the villain, while you become the martyr?"

"Do you feel like a villain?"

Kennedy had eased his hold on her hand, making it easy for her to withdraw it from his warm, protective grasp. "Right now I don't know what I'm feeling," she admitted honestly. What she did not want to feel was like a lovesick groupie. When she least expected it, doubts assailed her that if Kennedy hadn't slept with her, he probably would've sought out another female staff member.

"I like you, Kennedy," she said in a soft, quiet voice, "in spite of my vow that I would never let myself get involved with another athlete. In your case, ex-athlete," she added quickly, correcting herself.

"That's my past and your John Doe is your past. What do you say we bury our pasts—right now, tonight?"

Lydia studied him thoughtfully for a moment. She had buried her past when Vincent Haddon walked out of her apartment after he'd informed her that another woman was carrying his child. A satisfied light came into her eyes. "Okay, Kennedy."

"What do you say we celebrate with a bottle of champagne?"

Her smile was dazzling. "I say yes, but only if you'll permit me to pay."

Kennedy shook his head. "The next time, darling."

"Ken . . . ne . . . dy." His name came out in three syllables. "Lighten up. It's your birthday."

"I'll still pay for it."

She stared at him, and something in his gaze indicated he would not relent. "Will you let me treat you the next time we go out?"

"No."

"No?"

Bracing an elbow on the table, he rested his chin on a fist. "Which letter don't you understand? The N or the O?"

"What can I give you for your birthday?"

"I told you, I want you."

Resting her chin on her hand, Lydia ran her tongue over

her lower lip, bringing Kennedy's gaze to linger there. "Then you will have me."

Kennedy felt his flesh between his legs stir with the erotic invitation. It had been more than a week since Lydia had shared his bed, and he wasn't certain how much longer he could see her and not touch, kiss, or make love to her before he went stark raving mad.

Everything about Lydia had crept under the barrier Kennedy had set up to avoid becoming involved with a woman. He'd loved and trusted Nila. However, she hadn't loved him enough to believe he could be faithful to her.

He hadn't lied to Lydia when he told her that he hadn't lived a monastic lifestyle. But when he shared a woman's bed it was only for physical gratification, not a declaration or promise of love.

A waiter came over and placed two menus on the table. "Ma'am, sir. I'm Billy and I'll be your server tonight. Can I start you off with a cocktail?"

Kennedy, staring directly at Lydia, said, "We'll have a bottle of champagne."

"Any particular brand, sir?"

"Do you have a preference?" Kennedy asked Lydia.

She smiled at the young server who sported multiple piercings in his left ear. "Do you have Bollinger or Tattinger?"

Billy nodded and smiled. "I know we carry Bollinger."

"Then, we'll take a bottle."

"Yes, ma'am. I'll be right back with your wine."

Lydia critically surveyed the restaurant as Kennedy perused the menu. The sextet who had taken a short break returned to the stage.

The singer, a pale woman with platinum blond hair styled in a becoming chignon, appeared to have been poured into her black-sequined gown.

She removed the microphone from its stand. "Good evening, ladies and gentlemen. My name is Verona and these guys behind me are some of the most talented musicians in the world." She waved her hand and each musician rose slightly to acknowledge the applause. "Tonight we're celebrating the great ladies of jazz: Ella Fitzgerald, Peggy Lee, Rosemary Clooney, Etta James, Julie London, and Billie Holiday. The next song I'd like to sing for you is one of the twentieth century's best-loved songs, and I'm certain many of you will agree with me.

"However, I'm going to need your help with this one. I'd like for husbands, wives, boyfriends and girlfriends, and those who are visiting the Music Shack for the first time to get up and dance to Etta's 'At Last.' "

Lydia was rooted to her chair as Kennedy pushed back his and rounded the table. He extended his hand. "Come, darling. Dance with me." She placed her hand in his, and he pulled her gently to her feet.

He led her to the area set aside for the dance floor and swung her into his embrace, her arms circling his neck. Everything—the minute particles, fragments, or molecules that had come together to make Kennedy Fletcher the being that he'd become—seeped into her, making them one. Closing her eyes, Lydia pressed her mouth to his throat.

I love this man!

And she did love him despite her vow not to become involved. She had known of the strong passion within her, but it had taken the man holding her close to his heart to ignite it. She had convinced herself that what she shared with Kennedy was nothing more than a summer fling, that she could walk away from him without a backward glance, back to a life and those who were safe and familiar.

Molded chest to thighs, she followed Kennedy as he eased her away from the other couples crowding the dance floor until they were in a corner not far from their table. They kept perfect rhythm—heartbeats, a dip, sway.

Without warning Lydia heard the fortune-teller's voice: *I see two men in your life—one who will come to love you very much and one who will pretend to love you.* She went completely still and would've fallen if Kennedy hadn't been holding her.

Kennedy tightened his hold on Lydia's waist. "What's the matter?" he whispered close to her ear.

Lydia forced herself to relax. "Nothing." She hadn't lied, but then she hadn't told him the truth either. She was faced with a dilemma—one she had to resolve on her own.

Tilting her chin, she smiled up at him. "Everything is good."

He returned her smile, executing a step and spinning her around as Verona crooned the ballad with all of the passion that made the song a trademark of the singer who had come to be known as Peaches.

Kennedy pulled Lydia closer. "It's more than good. It's perfect."

His life was perfect because he'd found a woman whose passion, dedication to children, and ambition were similar to his. Lydia was ardently feminine, confident, strong-willed, determined, and while her cool exterior was a foil for a quick temper that made her unpredictable, he knew instinctively she would never bore him.

Burying his face in her hair, he closed his eyes, losing himself in the moment and the woman he'd claimed as his own.

The song ended. Lydia applauded, while Kennedy's whistle joined those of the other men, who alternated whistling with hooting. The piercing sounds vibrated her eardrum. She gave him an incredulous stare and he flashed a Cheshire cat grin.

Curving an arm around her waist, Kennedy directed her toward their table. "Verona has an incredible voice. You have to hear her do Aretha and Gladys Knight."

"When is R-and-B night?"

"Thursday. We won't be able to come this week because I'm going on survival maneuvers with the older boys."

Lydia had overheard the older campers talking about the three-day expedition, but she hadn't expected Kennedy to join them. They were scheduled to leave Wednesday afternoon and return to camp Saturday morning.

He seated her, lingering over her head for several seconds. "Are you going to miss me?"

Glancing over her shoulder, she wrinkled her nose. "Now who has the swelled head?"

His hand circled her neck. "Are you going to miss me, baby?" he repeated.

There was a pregnant silence; then Lydia whispered softly, "Yes, Kennedy. I know I'll miss you." Lowering his head, Kennedy pressed his mouth to the nape of her neck, eliciting a noticeable shudder from her.

Billy approached the table and set down a large glass bowl filled with ice and a bottle of champagne. Within seconds the sensual spell between Kennedy and Lydia vanished like a puff of smoke on a frigid winter day.

Fifteen

Lydia floated in a state of absolute relaxation after her second glass of champagne. Her dining partner, the live music, and the casual, intimate ambience of the Music Shack had enveloped her in an aura of tranquility she hadn't thought possible.

She forgot that she'd walked away from a position most aspiring chefs would've sold their souls to obtain. She forgot Justin's shocking declaration of love and she temporarily forgot about the space where she'd hoped to establish Lady Day.

Leaning back in his chair, Kennedy watched Lydia as she catalogued the goings-on in the restaurant. "Do you have a floor plan for your restaurant?"

Smiling and nodding, she met his knowing gaze. "Yes."

He took a sip from his flute. He had barely touched the platter of appetizers, preferring instead to drink the excellent vintage and watch Lydia.

"How about the décor?"

"Contemporary and Asian."

"Nice combination. Do you have a name?"

"Lady Day."

Attractive lines fanned out around his eyes when he smiled.

"Aha! Quite fitting for Baltimore native Billie Holiday. What will be your seating capacity?"

"No more than sixty. The total capacity cannot exceed eighty-five. I'm projecting fifteen at the bar, and another ten in the waiting area. I've been on pins and needles ever since my attorney filed the application with the planning board. The last time I spoke to him he said we should expect to get the approval in a couple of weeks."

Kennedy was suddenly alert. He'd thought Lydia had inked the deal. "You still don't have the city's approval?"

"No."

"What if you don't get it?"

Her delicate jaw tightened. "I refuse to think of them declining my proposal."

"But what if you don't, Lydia? You must have a backup plan."

"The alternative is that I go back to work and look for another space."

"Do you have the required financing?"

Lydia angled her head and smiled at Kennedy. "Why? Are you thinking of investing in my dream?"

"If you need a partner, then let me know," he said noncommittally.

"Hands-on or behind the scenes?"

"A silent partner, of course."

Lydia's large expressive eyes widened perceptively. "Thank you, but no, thanks, Kennedy."

He leaned forward, took her hand, his thumb caressing the velvety skin on her knuckles. "I want you to promise me that you'll contact me if you find yourself short on funds."

She would not need Kennedy's money, because she'd been preapproved for a business loan to cover construction costs. The proceeds from the sale of her condo would cover furnishings and equipment.

Doubting whether she would see Kennedy beyond the summer, she smiled and said, "I promise." She placed her napkin on the table. "I'm sorry to be a party pooper, but if I don't get up I'm going to spend the night in this chair." Drinking champagne always made her sleepy.

Kennedy glanced at his watch. They'd been at the restaurant for more than two hours. He signaled their waiter for the check, settled the bill, and left Billy a generous tip.

Rounding the table, he pulled back Lydia's chair, wound an arm around her waist, and led her out of the restaurant to the parking lot. She gasped, but did not protest when he swung her up in his arms and carried her to where he'd parked his Range Rover.

He unlocked the doors with the remote control key chain, opened the passenger-side door, and placed Lydia on the seat with a minimum of motion or effort. Reaching for the seat belt, he secured it over her chest; the back of his hand brushed against her breasts. Both recoiled from the brief contact, their startled gazes meeting and fusing.

"Sorry."

"It's all right."

Kennedy and Lydia had spoken in unison. Even though Kennedy wanted to make love to Lydia, he did not want her to see him as a predator—someone who went after her for her body. If and when they came together for a sexual encounter he wanted it to be with mutual consent.

He closed the door, rounded the vehicle, and sat behind the wheel. Starting up the engine, he maneuvered out of the lot, heading south and estimating he would arrive home before midnight.

Lydia dozed off and on during the drive, coming awake when all movement stopped. Sitting up straighter, she stared through the windshield. Kennedy had parked his vehicle in a bay in the three-car garage. The other time he had left it in the driveway.

"Don't move," he cautioned in a soft voice. "I'll come

around and get you." Kennedy reached for Lydia's overnight bag, then scooped her off the leather seat.

"I can walk, Kennedy." Her protest sounded weak even to her ears.

He kissed her forehead. "You can walk once I get you inside."

Lydia curled her arms around Kennedy's neck and rested her head on his shoulder. He carried her with the same ease with which she picked up her toddler nieces and nephews.

Kennedy stopped at a door with a keypad. "Punch in these numbers, then the star key." He told her the four numbers that would deactivate the lock and turn on the lights on the first floor.

The door opened automatically, and he mounted the four steps that brought them into a mudroom off the kitchen. Once Kennedy stepped into the expansive gourmet kitchen, he set Lydia on her feet.

She turned and stared up at him with a strange expression on her face, and he wondered if she'd changed her mind about spending the night with him.

"What time do you want me to wake you up in the morning?"

A mysterious smile replaced her expression of indecision. "We don't have to get up that early. Neil is going to cover breakfast and lunch."

Buoyed by the news that they could linger in bed beyond sunrise, Kennedy reached for Lydia and swung her around and around until she pleaded with him to stop. He did stop, and she clung to him until the room stopped spinning.

When she had deactivated the security system it also turned on a stereo system with hidden speakers positioned throughout the house. The distinctive bass of Soul II Soul's "Back to Life" filled the space.

Grabbing Kennedy's left hand, Lydia said, "I love this song. Please dance with me."

He swayed from side to side, watching Lydia's slender

body moving sensuously to the upbeat song with a distinctive driving bass beat. Everything about her teased and seduced as she closed the distance between them.

Her hands went to his lapels, pushing the jacket off his shoulders. Kennedy froze, holding his breath, stunned as she removed his tie, gold-monogrammed cuff links, and watch, placing them on a countertop. His breath caught in his chest when she unbuttoned his shirt and relieved him of it, as the shirt joined his jacket and tie on the floor tiles. He was forced to exhale when he felt the pressure on his chest. He gasped sharply seconds later once the buckle of his belt hit the floor.

Kennedy couldn't believe it. The minx was stripping him in the middle of the kitchen without missing a beat. He could not remember when she relieved him of his shoes, socks, trousers, and boxers. What he did remember was a jolt of desire so strong that he groaned aloud.

Lydia placed her hands on Kennedy's smooth muscled chest and forced him back until a wall stopped his retreat. Seeing him naked and unable to conceal his arousal brought forth a throbbing between her thighs.

Her gaze moved slowly from his taut expression and lower. His clenched fists, half-closed eyes, labored breathing, and the swollen flesh jutting between tight, muscled thighs elicited a boldness that was as foreign as the act she contemplated initiating.

Resting her hands on his shoulders, Lydia molded her breasts to his chest. "I'm going to offer you a very special birthday present. Would you like it now?" she asked, her tongue flicking outward and tracing the outline of his mouth.

Unable to speak, Kennedy nodded like a bobble-head doll. He didn't know what it was that Lydia proposed doing to him, but he was helpless to resist her. He feared moving because he did not want to spill his passion on the kitchen tile, but in her hot, fragrant body.

Smiling, Lydia pressed a kiss over his left eyelid. "H," she whispered in a voice so sultry that Kennedy shivered. "A," she continued, kissing his right eyelid. P was the bridge of his nose, a second P his mouth, and his throat claimed the Y.

"B - I - R - T - H." These letters began with a series of light kisses starting at his breastbone and ending inches above his belly button. Grasping his hips, Lydia slid down his body. She went to her knees. "D," she crooned, flicking her tongue into the indentation of his belly button.

"A." This letter elicited a painful groan from Kennedy that erupted from the back of his throat.

Lydia buried her nose in the inverted triangle of hair cradling his blood-engorged flesh, and breathed her hot breath inches from his maleness.

She prayed she would be able to follow through with her plan to offer up herself to Kennedy as a special gift for his thirty-sixth birthday. One hand on his flat belly and the other cradling his inner thigh, she whispered, "Y."

Throwing back his head, Kennedy bellowed as if he'd been impaled with a spike as Lydia took him into her hot, wet mouth. Every nerve in his body short-circuited, every muscle quivered. He writhed and jerked as if he'd been hit with bolts of electricity.

Please don't let me lose it. The litany played over and over in his head as her mouth closed around his rigid flesh and created a rushing, turbulent rapture that weakened his knees.

In.

Out.

Deeper.

Up.

Down.

Around. Around again and again, then up and down his straining shaft.

Her magical tongue, her selflessness, her pure sensuousness hurtled Kennedy beyond himself where he'd become a voyeur in a private coupling he never wanted to end. But sanity surfaced and he knew if he did not stop her, it would be over much too quickly.

"No!" A swath of heat settling in his groin spread, threatening total incineration. "Stop, baby. Please."

Lydia heard Kennedy's fervent plea, making her aware of the power she yielded over him. She would stop, but not yet. She wanted him numb and mindless with an ecstasy he'd never experienced with any other woman. In a moment of selfishness, she wanted to imprint herself on his body and memory for all time.

Kennedy tunneled his fingers through Lydia's hair. Holding her head in a firm grip, he sank down to the floor, forcing her to release him.

"No," she moaned in protest.

Pressing her back to the floor, he held her captive as his mouth swooped down on hers with the ferocity of a hawk tearing into its prey. He devoured her mouth, his hands searching for the opening to her dress. He found it under her left arm.

"I want you," he chanted. "I want you so much."

Unaware she was writhing on the floor beneath her naked lover, Lydia pulled his head to her breasts. She was on fire! She wanted him so badly she bit down hard on her lower lip to keep from shaming herself, to keep from begging him to take her.

"Ah-h!" The gasp escaped her parted lips when Kennedy's hand moved up between her thighs and under the triangle of silk to find her wet and pulsing. "Love me," she pleaded in a hoarse whisper.

His eyes, glittering wildly, were fixed on the swell of breasts rising and falling above the revealing décolletage. "We can't, Lydia. Not here."

"Why?" Her voice was low, breathless.

"I don't want to get you pregnant." She'd asked him to protect her from unwanted pregnancy, and he would. Lydia's wide-eyed stare reminded him of a deer paralyzed by the brilliance of a car's headlights. "Do you want a baby?" he asked, thinking perhaps she'd changed her mind.

Lydia's breath seemed to have stopped in her throat, making speech difficult. The possibility of having Kennedy's child was not an option. Not at this time in her life, and not when she didn't know whether he loved her as much as she loved him.

Her eyelids fluttered. "No."

Successfully masking his disappointment, he swung Lydia up in his arms, stood up, walked out of the kitchen, and headed for the curving staircase leading to the second story.

Shifting her slight weight, he mounted the stairs and made his way along the catwalk and into his bedroom. There was enough light from a half-moon coming in through the clerestory windows and skylights to make out the large bed.

Kennedy placed Lydia on the bed and sat down beside her. He undid the silk ties around her ankles, slipped off her shoes, and dropped them on the carpet. Reaching into the drawer of the bedside table, he removed a condom and rolled the latex sheath down the length of his hardened flesh.

He moved over Lydia's prone body, cradling her face between his palms, kissing her mouth, the column of her neck, then lower to the base of her throat. He returned to her mouth, his tongue meeting hers in a slow, sensual dance of desire. Her taste, her smell, the silkiness of her skin held him captive, and he wanted to spend hours in her scented embrace and a lifetime in her bed.

Reaching down, Kennedy caught the hem of her dress and eased it up and over her head. Sitting back on his heels, he watched the play of silvered moonlight on her bare breasts, her flat belly, and the womanly flare of hips. He took his time taking off her black bikini panties, leaving her ardently naked for his admiring gaze.

His hand, inching upward, stopped and covered her mound. Her expression was one of bliss as he pressed the pad of his thumb against the swollen nub, massaging it gently. He achieved the reaction he sought as she rose several inches off the mattress.

Supporting his weight on one elbow, he parted her knees with his and pushed slowly into her tight body. Her erotic moan echoed his as he once again lost himself in the erotic torture clouding his brain.

Lydia's body vibrating liquid fire, she succumbed to the dizzying passion wrought by the hardness sliding in and out of her body in a powerful thrusting that stole the oxygen from her laboring lungs.

Kennedy Fletcher was a thief. He'd stolen her heart and imprisoned her body in a maelstrom of desire only he could assuage.

Kennedy felt the familiar sensation at the base of his spine and quickly reversed their position in order to delay the ecstasy struggling for escape.

Lydia liked being on top, setting a rhythm that quickened, slowed, and quickened again, until she felt his hardness touch her womb. She screamed once, then again and again before collapsing on his chest and melting over his thighs.

Kennedy licked Lydia's neck and throat, his teeth biting gently into the tender flesh as he yielded to an awesome ecstasy that stopped his heart for several seconds.

Lydia buried her face between her lover's neck and shoulder, breathing a kiss on his moist skin. "Happy birthday, darling."

Cupping Lydia's hips in his hands, he massaged the soft skin on her buttocks. "If I live to be a hundred I'll never forget this day."

Snuggling closer, Lydia closed her eyes. "And I don't want you to."

Kennedy waited until Lydia was asleep before he gently eased her off his body. She moaned but did not wake up. Pulling a sheet up over their moist bodies, he wrapped an arm around her waist and pressed his groin to her hips. He had never expected the wantonness lurking beneath the surface of the cool exterior of the woman with whom he had fallen in love, the woman he wanted to marry, the woman whom he wanted to bear his children.

Closing his eyes, he joined her in a sated sleep reserved for lovers.

Sixteen

Lydia, who awoke before Kennedy, lay motionless as she studied his face in the weak light coming in through the clerestory windows. The shades covering the skylights were drawn, and it was apparent he had gotten up during the night and closed them.

He lay on his side, one muscular arm thrown over her hip. Her gaze shifted upward to his head. The stubble covering his scalp when she first came to the camp had grown out enough for Kennedy to have needed to visit a barber to give him a clean haircut. The color on his upper body was a shade lighter than his face. Peering closer, she saw a spray of freckles across the bridge of his nose. She found it odd that she'd never noticed them before.

As she studied his features she found it odd that he did not resemble either the man or the woman in any of his family photographs on the mantel of the living room fireplace. Had he been adopted like her brother Quintin's children? He did admit to being an only child.

Lydia stretched out her leg, hoping to ease the pressure of Kennedy's arm on her hip, and when she looked up she found him watching her.

"Good morning, lover."

He smiled, and tiny lines fanned out around his large dark eyes. He wrapped his arms around her midriff, bringing her closer to him as they rolled over and over on the king-size bed, stopping near the edge of the mattress.

Burying his face in her hair, he nuzzled her neck. "Good morning, beautiful."

She giggled like a little girl. "How does it feel to be four years closer to middle age?"

Kenneth cupped her sex, eliciting a shriek from her. "You've got jokes?"

Closing her eyes and shaking her head, Lydia gasped. "No-ooo!"

Instead of releasing her, Kennedy eased a finger inside her. "Apologize, baby."

Instinctively, her body pushed against his hand. "No," she whispered, a dreamy expression softening her features. Aroused, desire clouding her brain, Lydia couldn't disguise her body's reaction as heat rippled under her skin.

As Kennedy stirred Lydia's passion, his own surfaced. Leaning over, he reached for a condom. Using his teeth, he tore open the packet. He withdrew from Lydia long enough to protect her, and when he joined their bodies he knew this coming together was more than sexual desire.

It was love.

Lydia moved around the gourmet kitchen with the familiarity of someone who'd spent hours there. What had surprised her when she opened the side-by-side refrigerator-freezer was that it was well stocked with what she needed to prepare an unconventional breakfast.

After their early morning lovemaking, she and Kennedy shared a bath in an oversized tub with pulsing jets, splashing each other like children. The contest ended in a draw when her hair hung limply around her face in wilted strands. She'd offered to cook breakfast, leaving Kennedy to clean up the bathroom and change the bed.

Kennedy walked into the kitchen with one hand behind his back. He stopped short, staring at Lydia as she stood at the cooking island. It was an image he wanted to relive every day for the rest of his life. He wanted to tell her what was in his heart, but decided to wait—wait until he had gained her complete trust. She looked more like a high school student, with her bare feet, oversized T-shirt, and baggy shorts, than a chef. He closed the distance between them, lowered his head, and kissed the side of her neck.

Lydia smiled up at Kennedy over her shoulder. "Where have you been?"

He rested his hands on her shoulders. "Don't tell me you're going to be one of those nagging wives?"

"No," she said quickly, "because I'm not going to become some man's wife for a long, long time." She turned to face him. Moisture dotted his forehead, while his T-shirt was pasted to his chest. Her eyes drank in the sensuality of his magnificent physique.

"What were you doing?"

"Working out."

"Where?"

"There's a sports club with an indoor track on the property."

"I miss jogging." Lydia told him about the sports club in the complex where she'd owned a condominium.

"The next time you come, you can work out with me."

Lydia met his steady gaze. "There's not going to be enough time for you to take me to the Music Shack, or come back here to work out. I don't have a lot of time off, and we only have another four weeks before camp ends."

Kennedy moved closer. "But does it have to end?"

Her eyebrows lifted. "Camp?"

He shook his head. "No, Lydia. Us. Does it really have to end in four weeks?"

Lydia's face clouded with uneasiness. Kennedy had just asked a question she couldn't answer. "I don't know. Why don't we talk about this later?"

"Later?"

Resting a hand on the middle of his chest, she felt the steady pumping of his heart under her palm. "Before the end of camp."

He nodded his approval and placed a bouquet of sweet pea on the countertop. "These should liven up the table."

Lydia's gold-flecked eyes brightened with pleasure. "They're beautiful. Where did you get them?"

"In the field behind the fence the developer put up to keep deer and other wildlife from wandering onto the property. A month after I moved in I got up one morning and found a doe on the patio. I tried chasing her off, and it walked about a hundred feet before collapsing. I called animal control, and by the time they arrived a small crowd had gathered. It became something of a spectacle because the doe had gone into labor."

"What happened to her?"

"A vet came and assisted birthing two fawns. The authorities transported the entire family back to the forest, and within a month the fence was up." Kennedy placed his hand on Lydia's shoulder, the gesture blatantly possessive. "What's for breakfast?"

"Eggs Benedict."

"Hot damn! Why don't you make them at camp?"

"Because I'd never make partially cooked eggs for children. I could always make them safer by heating them to a temperature of one forty for three and a half minutes, but the consistency is not quite the same as poached."

He dropped a kiss on her shoulder. "I'm going up to shower; then I'll be back to help you."

Standing on tiptoe, she touched her lips to his. "Okay."

Lydia walked into the dining hall kitchen, her step jaunty. She was blissfully happy. The time she'd spent with Kennedy made her feel like a fairy-tale princess.

* * *

"What are you smiling about?" Neil's voice broke into her musings.

"I just remembered something."

Eyes sparkling like onyx and crossing his arms over his chest, Neil regarded her intently. "It must be something very good."

She sobered. "Why would you say that?"

Pointing to his throat, the assistant chef winked at her. "You're wearing it."

Putting a hand over her throat, Lydia made her way over to a mirror. A tiny bruise was visible where Kennedy had bitten her. She dropped her hand. "Please let me use your kerchief."

"No way."

"Come on, Neil. I don't have time to go back to my cabin and get one."

"I can hear the kids now. Miss Lydia has a hickey."

She took several steps in his direction as he backed away from her. "Give it to me," she hissed between her teeth. "That is a direct order." Lydia reached for him, but he ducked, wrapping an arm around her waist and lifting her off her feet.

"Lydia has a hickey," he crooned in singsong fashion, tickling her in the ribs.

Giggling uncontrollably, she swatted at him. "Stop, Neil! Please."

"What the hell is going on in here?"

Lydia froze and Neil set her on her feet. They turned slowly and saw Kennedy glaring at them, his dark face set in a vicious frown.

"We were just fooling around," Neil said.

Kennedy's frown deepened. "Fool around on your own time, Lane."

A shiver of annoyance snaked its way up Lydia's spine. He had no right to reprimand a member of her staff. Eyes narrowing, she rested her hands on her hips. "Look here, Kennedy—"

"Look nothing, Lydia," he countered angrily. "I left the list of foodstuffs for the three-day outing with your *assistant* last week. I told Mr. Lane I needed a breakdown on the number of meals, including restricted diets, by noon today. It is now two-thirty."

Neil flushed a deep crimson. "I have it."

Lydia watched, seething, speechless, as Kennedy held out his hand and waited for Neil to give him the information he'd requested. This was a Kennedy she didn't know, someone who'd become a stranger to her. Even when Neil had warned, "Ken is on the warpath," following the missing bell clapper, she hadn't witnessed his temper firsthand.

Neil, glaring at Kennedy, slapped an envelope on his outstretched palm. A tense moment ensued when the two men regarded each other with hostile stares. Neil, the first one to end the stalemate, turned on his heel and disappeared into the walk-in freezer.

The sound of the door closing behind Neil pulled Lydia from her stupor and she rounded on Kennedy. "You have some nerve coming in here—"

"Nerve?" he retorted, interrupting her. "The next time Lane decides to feel you up, have him do it where no one can walk in on you."

Shock rendered Lydia motionless and speechless as she watched Kennedy turn to leave. She was too stunned by his accusation to scream or cry. They'd parted less than half an hour ago with smiles and caresses that promised a repeat of what they'd shared earlier.

Her love for him was so overwhelming that she had had to bite down on her lower lip to keep from blurting out how much she loved him. Tears pricked the back of her eyelids, and one found its way down her cheek. She swatted at it with her fingertips.

How could she have fallen in love with a man whose generosity and passion were limitless? A man who had taken her to heights of ecstasy she hadn't known existed. A man who made her forget her vow, a man who'd slipped under the wall she'd erected, refusing to consider marriage and motherhood before she set up her restaurant, and a man who believed she'd deceived him because he saw her in the arms of another.

There was nothing going on between her and Neil except trust—something obviously missing in her fragile relationship with Kennedy.

Trust had sustained her parents' marriage for more than fifty years, had kept her brothers and sisters and their spouses in healthy relationships, and trust was what she sought from a man more than passion or a declaration of love.

Annoyance replaced her shock. She'd come to Camp Six Nations to gain experience supervising a kitchen, yet she'd allowed herself to be distracted by romantic notions.

A sense of strength came to Lydia. She had only four weeks in which to fulfill her obligation as camp chef. Then she would close this chapter of her life on Camp Six Nations and Kennedy Fletcher, never reopening the book again to relive that experience.

Reaching for an apron, she slipped it over her tunic and secured the ties around her waist. She'd washed her hands in one of four stainless steel sinks when Neil exited the freezer carrying a crate filled with vegetables and herbs for the night's Chinese theme. His face had regained its normal pallor.

"I'm sorry about that," she apologized softly.

Neil waved a hand. "I should be the one doing the apologizing. I shouldn't have touched you."

Lydia dried her hands on a towel before placing it over her left shoulder. "We were just playing around."

"I know that and you know that," he argued softly. "But think of how it must have looked to Ken. I'm willing to suspect that if it had been anyone else, the camp grapevine would be buzzing that I'm hitting on my boss."

"As long we both know that's not true, then I'm not even going to think about it."

"I don't want Ken chewing you out because of something I've done."

She gave him a steady look. "If I don't chew you out, then he has no right to do it either."

Neil began emptying the crate. Chinese white, flowering, and celery cabbage, mustard greens, sugar peas, and bean sprouts filled the preparation table that was expressly for vegetables.

"That's where you're wrong, Lydia."

"Why would you say that?"

Reaching for a cleaver from an overhead hook, Lydia picked up a head of celery cabbage. Using a rocking motion, she sliced it into thin strips for stir-frying.

Neil gave her an incredulous look. "I can't believe you're sleeping with the man and he hasn't told you that he owns this place."

The cleaver fell to the butcher block with a dull thud. It took all of her self-control not to let Neil see her hands shaking. "What! And who told you I was sleeping with Kennedy?"

Taking several steps closer, narrowing the distance between them, Neil placed his hands on her shoulders. "Me and my big mouth."

"You better tell me . . ." Her words trailed off. What could she do to Neil if he decided not to tell her?

"Come, sit down, Lydia." Neil led her to a pair of stools where they usually sat to discuss menus and recipes.

And like a lamb being led to the slaughter, she followed him. Not only were her hands shaking, but also her heart. It fluttered in her chest like a leaf in a storm.

I've been sleeping with my boss. The realization twisted her gut. It was compounded because now others were privy to their affair.

Neil ran his hand over his head, removing his skullcap. "I never should've said anything."

Lydia stared him down. "But you did. Please talk to me, Neil."

"Jill told me she overheard a conversation between Roger and Ken in which Roger told Ken that the final decision rested with him because he owned Camp Six Nations."

Now it all made sense to Lydia why Kennedy's name shared the same position as Roger's and Grace's on the table of organization. Why he'd picked up the tab for dinner at the Roadhouse. He must have given himself a gold star for getting her into his bed so easily.

"Who told you I was sleeping with him?"

Neil shook his head. "No one in particular. It came down to coincidence. You and Ken were always away at the same time, and I've seen the way he looks at you, Lydia, and you at him. The love is there—big time. I only walked away because I didn't want to say something that would ruin what you have going with him."

Lydia placed her hand over Neil's. "There's nothing to ruin. Kennedy and I are friends."

"Sure, boss," he drawled, his voice heavy with sarcasm.

She still hadn't confirmed or denied to Neil that she was sleeping with Kennedy, and wouldn't.

"Remember, you're the boss for the next two weeks." She'd deftly changed the subject. "If it's all right with you, I'll handle dinner."

Neil smiled. "I'll take you up on your offer after I cut up the vegetables." He removed the handkerchief from his neck, looped it around Lydia's, tying it neatly over the love bite. "That should silence the wagging tongues."

Seeing the amusement in Neil's eyes, she laughed. "Thanks, partner."

He winked at her. "Don't mention it, partner."

They slipped off the stools and began preparations for dinner.

The notion that he'd become like a few of the men with whom he'd played football who took special glee in causing serious injuries to players from opposing teams frightened Kennedy. Their mantra was: if you can't take the pain, then get the hell out of the game.

He had played the game of love for the second time in his life, and this time it was he who'd inflicted pain. The look on Lydia's face when he'd accused her of carrying on with Neil Lane was one he would never forget or want to witness again.

Clenching his teeth tight enough to make his jaw ache, he ran a hand over his face. *Maybe I'm not cut out for this love thing*, he mused. First Nila and now Lydia.

You take women because you do not want to be alone. The words from the fortune-teller stabbed at his conscience. Was she telling him that he was doomed to repeat Marvin Kennedy's mistakes? His biological father had spent his life loving and leaving a trail of women so numerous he was unable to recall their names or faces. Marvin, who was content not to marry or father children because he didn't want to feel "trapped," made two grievous mistakes—he fell in love with Diane Fletcher and got her pregnant. And despite pressure from his and her family to marry Diane, he deserted her and enlisted in the army, becoming a lifer.

Lowering his hand and letting out his breath in an audible sigh, Kennedy walked up the stairs leading into the main house. He looked enough like Marvin to have been his clone, but that's where the resemblance ended. He had no intention of spending the rest of his life sleeping with nameless, faceless women to assuage his sexual frustration.

As he opened the screen door and stepped into the spacious entryway he swore a solemn vow: Lydia Lord would become the last woman in his life.

Seventeen

Kennedy retook the chair he'd vacated when he went to the dining hall to retrieve the information he needed from Neil. His gaze swept around the table, lingering on those taking part in the three-day survival-training mission.

"People, let's finish this up." His sonorous voice, filled with an authoritative edge, brought the conversations floating around the table to an abrupt halt.

Forcing a smile he didn't feel at that moment, he read from the report that Neil had put together for him: "We will transport the following food items to the fortress tomorrow morning: powdered milk, eggs, dehydrated potatoes, canned beans, fruit, meatless chili, sardines, and hash. We'll also take vegetable oil, cornmeal, ten five-gallon bottles of water, bottled reconstituted lemon juice, and baking soda."

"What about meat?" asked the head counselor for the Mohawks.

Kennedy gave him a level stare. "What about it, Kareem?"

"It sounds as if we're going to have to be vegetarians for a couple of days."

"The first thing this expedition will teach you is how to overcome your desire for comfort. It is about learning to survive, not filling up on steak and fries. What we are going to do is a modified version originally commissioned by the Department of the Army to train its special forces in all-climate, all-terrain survival tactics.

"My personal belief is that this type of training should be mandatory for campers, hikers, pilots, and others whose vocation or avocation requires familiarity with the out-of-doors. Most times, if someone is stranded, they won't have one-tenth of what we're taking. I hope this answers your question, Kareem."

Kareem nodded. "It does."

"Speaking of comfort," Kennedy continued, "I'd like to inform everyone that we will not have to sleep outdoors on the ground." A series of high-five handshakes followed this disclosure. "But before you congratulate yourselves, hear me out. The place we've named the Fortress will have a wood-burning stove and indoor plumbing with *cold* running water."

The head counselor for the Seneca boys raised his hand. "I don't think the boys will complain too much, but the girls are going to freak if they have to shower in cold water."

"You *ain't* lying," Roger agreed, laughing with the others.

Kennedy lifted his eyebrows. "Now you guys are thinking like men."

"That's because we are men," Kareem said proudly.

"Didn't you hear me say wood-burning stove?"

Realization dawning, the men nodded. "Anyone want to place a wager that they'll heat the water?" Roger asked, smiling.

"No!" came a chorus of deep voices from around the table.

Kennedy laced his fingers together on the table. "The food, canoes, life jackets, first-aid equipment, and medical personnel will go up in the truck Tuesday morning. Remember, counselors, that there are no beds or bunks, which means you'll have to use sleeping bags. Please check all backpacks to make certain your campers pack enough clothes to sustain them for at least five days. And I don't have to tell you to confiscate all Walkmen and CD players. Each of you will be given a cellular phone programmed with numbers to the camp and state police in case of an extreme emergency."

James Bennett, the Seneca counselor, raised his hand again. "Are you going with the truck or hiking up with us?"

Rising to his feet and pushing back his chair, Kennedy clasped his hands together, flexing his massive biceps. "What do you think, Jimmy?"

James held up a hand in supplication. "Oh–kay," he drawled.

Laughing easily for the first time since witnessing Neil and Lydia together, Kennedy exhaled a normal breath. He had to laugh or joke; otherwise he would return to the dining hall and snap Neil Lane's neck as easily as he would a pencil.

"We're done here, folks. Thank you."

Everyone filed out of the meeting room except Roger. Bracing his hands on the back of a chair, he smiled at Kennedy. "It sounds as if you guys are going to have fun roughing it."

Nodding, Kennedy returned his smile. "Why don't you come along with us?"

"I'd consider it if I didn't have to hike up there."

"You can always go up with the truck."

"I don't think so. There's no way I'm going to have the campers think of me as a candy-ass."

Folding his arms over his chest, Kennedy studied the slender, bookish-looking social worker. "But you are a candy-ass, Roger." He held up a hand when Roger opened his mouth to refute his assessment of him. "You were the one who always bowed out whenever we chose sides for a football game."

Roger tapped his forehead. "That's because I'm smart enough not to have you guys open my noggin like a melon, especially you. There was no way I was going to let you tackle me."

"You still haven't learned the game. I played offense, not defense."

"Whatever," Roger drawled. Like quicksilver, he sobered. "I don't think I've ever asked you this, but do you miss the fame?"

"Don't you mean the game?"

"No. I meant the *fame*."

A hint of a smile softened Kennedy's strong mouth. "Now, if you'd asked me if I miss the game I'd say yes. Ah, the fame," he said, shaking his head. "I'm ambivalent about that. I liked what it brought me—money, enough money to fulfill most of what is on my wish list. But then, the flip side was that I had to give up any semblance of a normal life. Most times I felt as if I existed in a fishbowl with everybody watching and waiting for me to mess up. There was one sportswriter who couldn't find any dirt on me, so he decided to fabricate a story about me and an underage girl in a Kansas City restaurant bathroom. The story was killed because someone at his paper called me before it was printed. That was the ugly side of fame."

Roger stared at the ex-ballplayer whom he regarded as family. They didn't share the same bloodline, yet had become cousins once his uncle Philip married Diane Fletcher.

Kennedy had approached him asking his help in establishing a sleepaway camp for underserved inner-city children three years before. His cousin's enthusiasm was contagious, and before he knew it Roger had agreed to head the planning committee.

Kennedy showed him another side of his personality once he revealed to a landowner the reason he wanted to purchase eight hundred acres of a twelve-hundred-acre plot. Kennedy, aware that the man wouldn't be able to sell the remaining four hundred acres, offered to buy the entire plot for half the asking price. The elderly man, grateful to unload the property, agreed.

The Camp Six Nations campsite encompassed less than sixty acres, and a developer who wanted to buy a portion of the land to build houses for a retirement community had approached Kennedy with an offer that would become a financial boon.

Roger removed his glasses, pinching the bridge of his nose with his thumb and forefinger. He knew Kennedy wanted to provide financial stability for his parents, and he'd done that. He owned an elegant home in Friendship Heights and a vacation retreat twenty minutes from the campsite. He hadn't squandered his money supporting an entourage of hangers-on and gold-digging women, or on ostentatious jewelry and cars. He'd become an anomaly among the young athletes who had become instant millionaires with a scrawl of their signature.

Reporters and photographers loved him. He was always approachable and accommodating, but in the end they vilified him once he left the game without an explanation.

"How many more items are left on your wish list?"

Kennedy's expression did not reveal what he was feeling at that moment. "A few." And one of the few had a name: Lydia Lord.

"Does she have a name?" Roger asked, reading his mind.

"She does."

Squinting at a speck of lint on his glasses, Roger rubbed the lens over the front of his shirt. "Do you care to share it with me?"

"I can't."

"You can't or you won't?"

"Both."

"Why not, Ken?"

"Because I'm not certain it's going to work out."

Replacing his glasses, Roger gave him an incredulous look. "You're kidding, aren't you?"

"No, I'm not kidding," he snapped angrily.

"Yo, cuz, don't jump down my throat. I'm not your enemy."

"You're right. I'm sorry, cuz. I'm going to hang out at my place tonight. I'll see you in the morning."

"You've been hanging out there a lot, Ken."

"Yeah, I know. I go there when I need to think."

"It doesn't pay to think too much."

"Save the social work spiel for your clients, Roger."

"You could use a few sessions on my couch. I won't charge you."

"If you think I'm going to spill my guts to you, then you're crazier than I am."

Roger's eyebrows shot up. "Are you crazy?"

"Of course," Kennedy said glibly. "Falling in love is a bitch!"

He walked out of the meeting room, leaving Roger staring at his back. Kennedy knew Roger wasn't his enemy. He was family, a friend, and business partner. But on the other hand, jealousy and frustration had become his closest friends, living with him day in and day out.

Why, he mused as he made his way to the parking area, whenever his life spun out of control, was a woman at the center of the morass? It had begun with Cassandra lying to her husband that she'd had an affair with him, Nila's rejection because she said she couldn't trust him, and now Lydia. Had he just used up his last strike?

He got into his SUV, started it up, and drove away from the campsite without a backward glance. He needed to put some distance between him and Lydia so that he could think objectively.

Lydia sat in the middle of her bed, Justin's unopened letter on her lap. She hadn't seen Kennedy in days, and knew she would not see him again until Saturday.

When she'd returned to her cabin Monday night, his was dark. No light shone through the windows Tuesday night. Wednesday dawned with nervous excitement floating throughout the camp. Twenty-six campers, head counselors, counselors-in-training, and several staff members were hiking to a remote campsite in the Appalachians for a three-day survival training mission. The campers who didn't take part in this year's expedition expressed their impatience with not being old enough to go along.

I miss him. I love him, the voice of truth whispered to her, and Lydia choked back the tears blurring her vision. Just when she'd let go of the pain and bitterness making it impossible to open her heart to love freely, the door had been slammed shut with Kennedy's unfounded accusation that she was involved with Neil. Could he believe that she was sleeping with him and her assistant? Had he dealt with so many fickle, promiscuous women that he'd lumped her into the same category?

She closed her eyes and let the tears flow. She cried until she was spent, then slipped off the bed and went into the bathroom to wash her face. Instead of returning to the bed, she picked up Justin's letter and went out to the porch. There was still enough daylight to read the typed words:

Dearest Lydia,

I hadn't realized how much I'd missed you until I saw you Saturday. I know we've had our differences in the past, but I'd like to offer an olive branch.

I know you think I've not been supportive of you in your quest to go into business for yourself, but nothing could be further from the truth. I understand more than you'll ever know, because of my own pursuit, not only to achieve business success, but to prove to my family that I can make it on my own, that I don't have to become a clone of my father, grandfather, and great-grandfather. How many more Dr. Bankses are needed to deify the Banks name in the annals of medical history?

Lydia smiled. "How right you are," she said, answering Justin's query. Her eyes scanned the rest of the page before continuing.

I know I haven't been very demonstrative when it comes to showing my love for you. The fact remains that I do love you—very, very much. And although we haven't slept together in nearly a year, I want so much to believe that what we share goes beyond our platonic relationship. I'm totally committed to you—in every way. Remember I'll always be here if you need me.

Write back soon.

Love, Justin.

P.S. HURRY HOME!

Hurry home? What on earth did Justin mean? When she'd lived in Silver Spring it was either *her place*, or *his place* in north Baltimore, and never home.

Justin's letter disturbed her because it was filled with innuendoes. It was the second time he'd confessed to loving her. Justin loved her and she didn't love him—at least not the way she loved Kennedy. And she loved Kennedy when he hadn't told her that he loved her. What a lopsided love triangle if ever there was one.

Leaving Justin's letter on the recliner, Lydia went into the cabin. As soon as she stepped into the one-room structure she felt as if the walls were closing in on her. Why did the space now appear so claustrophobic?

Removing her cell phone from its charger, she picked up a lightweight blanket and returned to the porch. Sinking down to the recliner, she punched in a programmed number. Her call was answered after the second ring.

"Hello."

Lydia smiled. "Hi, Victoria."

"Lydia, I . . ."

Whatever her sister-in-law was going to say dissolved in a spasm of giggles.

"No-o-o-o, Quintin. Don't. Please don't."

"I told you not to answer the phone. Hang it up, darling, and let me . . ."

Lydia ended the call, heat stealing into her face. It was apparent her telephone call had interrupted Quintin and Victoria's lovemaking.

The phone rang, startling her. Peering at the display, she recognized the number and answered the call. "Victoria?"

"I'm sorry about that, Lydia. Did you want to talk to your brother?"

"No. I wanted to talk to you. But I can call back another time."

"Talk now. Quintin's gone."

"Are you sure?"

"What do you want to talk about?"

She'd called Victoria because she found her easier to talk to than her own sisters. Her sister-in-law was more objective and less judgmental than Sharon or Andrea.

"I need your advice."

"What about?"

A flicker of apprehension flickered through Lydia as she composed her thoughts. "I met someone . . . I've met a man." There. She said it.

Victoria's soft laughter came through the tiny earpiece. "Are you saying you went to camp and got bit by the love bug?"

Wrinkling her nose, Lydia could not stop the grin spreading across her face. "Big time."

"Good for you. Who is he?"

Her grin vanished as quickly as it had appeared. "I can't tell you. Not yet." Lydia was forthcoming when she told Victoria about her dates with Kennedy, his promise to take her to Cabo San Lucas, his offer to invest in her restaurant, the fortune-teller's prediction, and Justin's declaration of love.

"Has your mystery man told you that he loves you?"

"No."

"Have you let him know how you feel?"

"No."

"When are you going to tell him?"

"I'm not. He thinks I'm carrying on with my assistant."

"He thinks?" Victoria asked.

"He saw us together—"

"Doing *what*, Lydia?" Victoria interrupted.

"Wrestling."

"What were you thinking about? How do you think you'd have reacted if you saw him with his hands roaming over another woman's body?"

Lydia reined in her temper. Victoria had chastised her as if she were an errant child. "I get the picture." She wasn't certain how she would've reacted if she'd witnessed Kennedy with another woman.

"What are you going to do with Justin?"

"Nothing has changed between me and Justin."

"You're going to continue to see him although you're in love with another man?"

"I broke up with Justin before moving back home."

"Why?"

"He refused to support me when I told him I was going into business for myself."

"Lydia, you don't need his support or his approval. Has he ever asked for yours?"

"No."

"I rest my case."

Lydia smiled in spite of the disquiet that would not permit her the ease she sought and needed. "Thanks, Victoria, for listening to me bitch and moan."

"You're not bitchin' and moanin.' You are in love. And love makes all of us a little crazy at times. I fell in love with your brother, yet I wasn't able to commit because I knew I'd never be able to give him a child. Once I told him of my infertility he said he wanted me for myself, not for the children I couldn't give him. If your mystery man is willing to support your business venture and take you away, then I'd say he more than likes you."

A demure smile lit up Lydia's eyes. "I suppose you're right."

"I know I'm right. Now, are you going to go to your man and explain about you and your assistant?"

Her smile vanished. "Of course not. There's nothing to explain."

"Agh! You stubborn Lords and your insufferably stiff-necked pride."

"Sticks and stones may break my bones, but names will never harm me."

Victoria laughed. "I think you need some adult company right about now."

"You're right about that. Thanks for listening."

"Not a problem. Call whenever you need to talk."

"I will. Good night."

"Good night, Lydia."

Lydia ended the call, leaving the cell phone on the recliner. Rising to her feet, she walked off the porch toward the flickering flames from the oil drum. The campfire storytelling had begun. She found most of the younger campers sitting together on the carpet of grass listening to Reverend Al as he read *Fiddlefingers* to his enraptured charges.

She sat down and within minutes the spooky tale of Captain Brassbuttons and his colorful crew of ghost pirates mesmerized her, too.

Eighteen

Eight campers gathered around Kennedy as he knelt on the ground angling a convex lens to catch the sun's rays on a pile of kindling.

"You must hold the lens so that the sun's rays stay directed over the same spot until the tinder begins to smolder," he instructed.

"It's smoking, Mr. Ken!"

Kennedy nodded. The kindling had begun to smolder. "Blow it gently, Tarik."

Kneeling down, Tarik blew on the kindling until a flame appeared. A loud cheer went up from the other seven. "We won!" they crowed in triumph, pumping their fists in the air.

Kennedy placed several branches on the kindling, waiting until they caught fire. Coming to his feet, he smiled and touched fists with the campers who'd lined up to congratulate their team leader.

The campers, divided into three teams, were adjusting to roughing it in the woods. The Fortress, built in the 1920s, was used as a hunting lodge. The family of the original owner, who'd made his wealth in West Virginia coal mining, abandoned the property because recurrent strikes by the miners bankrupted the company. The furnishings were stolen, and anything saleable removed, leaving only the shell.

Kennedy purchased the property for a fraction of the back taxes, refurbished it, and made certain it did not lose its rustic charm. There was no modern heating system or any beds because he wanted to discourage squatters from taking up residence when camp wasn't in session.

The day of their arrival was spent sweeping, dusting, and chopping and gathering wood for the massive stove in the middle of the great room and the fireplaces in each of the other rooms. Aching backs and arms and blistered hands from the unaccustomed heavy labor were all but forgotten once everyone bedded down in spaces warmed and illuminated by the fire in the stone fireplaces. One or two commented about the eerie sounds coming from outside the lodge. The distinctive hoot of owls and the howling of coyotes sent all of them burrowing deeper into their sleeping bags.

Kennedy pointed to two brothers. "Juan and Manuel, go take the fish out of the water. Gregory, are you finished cleaning the leaves?"

Gregory popped up like a jack-in-the box. "Yes, sir, Mr. Ken," he said, uncovering a square of a canvas lined with large fanlike leaves that would be used to cook the fish they'd caught earlier that morning.

Kennedy beckoned another boy closer. "I want you to put more sunblock on your face and arms." The boy's face was almost as red as his flaming orange-red hair.

Kennedy's chest filled with pride. The boys had come together as a team, working and supporting each other in every assigned task. He only had to demonstrate something once and they understood what he wanted from them.

They'd learned to fashion spearheads from small stones they'd sharpened by rubbing them against rough-surfaced rocks. The pointed stones were lashed to the tips of sturdy branches with vines or strips of fabric. They'd sat patiently in canoes until spying a fish, then struck with precise accuracy over and over. They'd attached their catch to a line fashioned by tying shoelaces together.

Reaching into the pocket of his shorts, Kennedy removed a multipurpose knife. "Now we'll clean our lunch."

"No fair, Mr. K," Mustafa wailed, pointing to the knife. "You said we had to make our tools."

Kennedy stared at the boy. "Either I use this knife or you won't eat until you make your own knife. What's it going to be?"

"Yo, Mustafa, shut up!" shouted a fellow camper.

Kennedy shot the camper a warning stare. "Watch your language."

"Sorry," he said, apologizing.

The group sat on the ground, watching Kennedy as he removed the heads, then split and gutted ten largemouth bass. "We'll bury the heads and entrails for scavengers."

The fish seasoned with herbs from the camp's kitchen were wrapped in leaves and cooked over the open fire. Mouthwatering smells filled the air as everyone enjoyed a midday meal of broiled fish and a salad of fresh-picked dandelion leaves, wild onions, and blackberries with a tart lemon dressing.

Propping his back against the trunk of a massive tree, Kennedy kept watch while everyone settled down before heading back to the Fortress. It would be the last night they'd sleep in the mountain retreat.

He'd been so involved with the campers that he hadn't had time to think about Lydia—at least not until he retired for bed. As he lay in his sleeping bag, everything about her came rushing back as if she were lying beside him.

Even with his eyes closed he still could see the delicate bones in her face, the temptingly curved mouth he wanted to kiss over and over, the length of her lashes that concealed her large gold-brown eyes; still could sense her smell, a sweet haunting fragrance that had become a hypnotic aphrodisiac. He forced himself not to think of her body for fear his own would betray him. The first night he'd lain awake for hours waiting for his flesh to return to a flaccid state.

The expression on her face when she realized he'd seen her and Neil together was one he would carry to his grave. It was an expression of openness, innocence, a plea for understanding, while he'd been too incensed to register it at the time. It said she had done nothing wrong.

His life had come full circle.

Four years ago Nila had walked out on him because she believed he had been involved with another woman.

And now he had walked away from Lydia because he believed she was involved with another man.

When had he become so self-absorbed, believing it had to be either his way or no way?

Did he still believe the hype that had been so pervasive during his football career? That he could have any- and everything he wanted because he was Kennedy Fletcher? Had the feeling of entitlement persisted although he was no longer a sports icon? Had he sought to hold on to Lydia beyond the summer when he'd offered to invest in her business venture?

The questions bombarded him relentlessly, and he knew he had to resolve his dilemma before he returned to the campsite. Lydia wanted to wait until just before the end of the camp season to talk about their relationship. There were three weeks left, and as far as Kennedy was concerned, it was close enough to the end to where their relationship had to be resolved one way or the other.

Lydia stared at the blinking cursor on the laptop screen, calm and resolute in her intent. A call from her attorney the night before delivered bad news. The building's owner had rejected her proposal. Now she would have to begin the process all over again. She sulked for an hour before deciding it was time to move forward. And moving forward meant reconciling with her past.

Justin Banks was her past. He'd written her twice, the second letter more passionate and intense than the first.

Her fingers poised on the keyboard, she composed her thoughts, before she typed:

Justin,

I received both your letters. Thank you for taking time from your busy schedule to write.

I'm flattered by your declaration of love and marriage proposal; however, I'm unable to reciprocate in kind. I'd be a liar if I said I don't have feelings for you. I like and respect you and will always value our friendship. But that is all we have: friendship.

I would've preferred telling you this in person because I don't want to appear cowardly. I've always been direct with you, sometimes much too direct, but I implore you to move on, Justin. I have.

This is not about us.

It is about me, me finding my center, me coming to grips about what I want for my future and myself. I'm unable to accomplish this as long as I'm involved with you on any level.

I humbly ask you to respect my wishes.

I remain,
Lydia.

She read the message once, twice, then hit the Send button before she could change her mind. She hadn't wanted to tell Justin to move on, yet she'd never been able to deal with innuendoes with him. Once Justin received her e-mail she knew he would cease being one of the two men in her life.

Logging off, she put away the laptop at the same time a loud roar came from the direction of the dining hall. It was obvious Kennedy, the Mohawk and Seneca boys, and their counselors had returned.

Neil walked through the swinging doors, smiling. "They're back."

She nodded, returning his smile. "I can hear them."

"They look like lean, mean fighting machines."

"Three days without snacks will do that."

Neil washed his hands in a sink with an antibacterial soap, his sharp midnight gaze fixed on Lydia as she lined a large pan with pieces of marinated chicken for the next day's dinner.

"I just spoke to Kennedy," he said without preamble.

Lydia's hands did not falter as she continued filling the baking pan. "What about?" Her voice was calm and neutral as if they were discussing the weather.

"About us."

She froze, then turned slowly to meet Neil's direct stare. "What about us, Neil?"

"I told Kennedy there was nothing going on between us. I also told him that I'm attempting to reconcile with my wife, and I'd never do anything to jeopardize that."

Pulses racing, Lydia tried to control her fragile emotions as a dizzying mixture of hope and fear held her captive. "What did he say?"

"He said, 'thank you.' "

"That's all he said?"

"Do you want me to go back and ask him to elaborate further?"

"No," she said quickly. "Please don't."

She would wait, wait for Kennedy to come to her.

Kennedy stood on the top step, staring through the screen at Lydia as she slept on the recliner. She hadn't lit the votives or turned on the stereo, leaving the porch in silence and in the shadows.

He felt like a voyeur watching her sleep, but he needed to drink his fill before making his presence known. Opening the screen door, he stepped up onto the porch, holding the door until it closed with a soft click. The sound was enough to alert Lydia that she was not alone. Why hadn't he noticed she was a light sleeper?

Lydia sat up. She stared wordlessly at Kennedy, her heart pounding a runaway rhythm that left her light-headed. Neil was right. He was leaner, the angles in his face more pronounced.

"Hello." Her husky greeting shattered the suffocating silence.

Kennedy inclined his head. "Good evening, Lydia."

She gestured to the matching recliner. "Would you like to sit down?"

"Thank you."

We've become polite strangers. The realization rocked him as he lowered his tall frame down to the recliner. He had no one to blame but himself for the abrupt shift in their relationship.

Lydia pressed her head to the cushioned back and schooled her features not to reveal her inner turmoil. She wanted to crawl onto his lap, curve her arms around his strong neck, while inhaling his potent masculine scent. She wanted Kennedy, but needed him more.

"How was roughing it in the mountains?" She had to say something, anything to break the silence.

"It was good. The boys really enjoyed it."

"Will the girls go through the same training?"

A slight smile parted Kennedy's lips. "Yes. I don't want to be accused of gender bias." There was enough light to make out Lydia's face in the shadowed twilight that draped the landscape in a blue-gray veil. "I've come to apologize for the comments I made about you and Neil."

To her surprise, Lydia felt no joy or victory from his admission of guilt. It was her turn to incline her head. "I accept your apology."

Kennedy stared at her long bare legs under a pair of cutoffs. "I'd like to talk about us."

"Talk, Kennedy," she urged softly.

Giving her a long, penetrating stare, he said, "I love you."

An audible gasp slipped past her lips. Wide-eyed, she stared at Kennedy. He loved her, and she loved him.

I see two men in your life—one who will come to love you very much and one who will pretend to love you. I see confusion, lots of confusion, and some disappointment. You will cry. You will smile.

Why was it she could remember Mariska's prediction verbatim when she sometimes struggled to remember the ingredients that made up her favorite dish?

Was Kennedy the man who would pretend to love her? Had he admitted loving her because he didn't want her to stop sleeping with him?

A tense silence enveloped the porch as Lydia wrestled with her conscience as to whether she would be able to reveal to Kennedy what was in her heart, yet something cautioned her not to speak.

Kennedy knew he'd shocked Lydia with his unexpected declaration of love, but he would've thought she would say something. Anything. A rejection was preferable to complete silence.

Pushing off the recliner, he stood up. "Good night."

Lydia did not move when she heard the soft click of the door closing behind Kennedy, sitting in the same position and recalling the events in her life as if viewing frames of film.

Night covered Camp Six Nations like a quiet, warm blanket, and she took comfort in its darkness. It hid her fears, insecurities, and false bravado. As the youngest of nine it had always been, "look at me," "listen to me," "why can't I go with you?" or "I'm not too young." She had been so pampered, protected, and overindulged that at thirteen she'd seriously considered running away to seek her fortune. The only time she felt completely secure was in the kitchen. She was in control whether whisking, sautéing, frying, baking, broiling, or braising.

It took over an hour of self-reflection for her to equate loving a man with the loss of her independence and identity, because she had never been able to give herself completely to any man—any except Kennedy. She knew it was the reason she'd never experienced sexual fulfillment with the men in her past. She'd been the one to hold back for fear of losing a part of herself.

The harder she tried to ignore the truth, the more it nagged at her: she loved Kennedy Fletcher enough to spend the rest of her life with him. He had come to her baring his soul and she'd sat mute, unable to form a response.

She'd taken the coward's way out and e-mailed a rejection to Justin, but she didn't intend to be a coward twice in one day. Swinging her legs over the side of the recliner, she stood up and pushed open the screen door with a force that left it banging against the frame.

Lydia hadn't taken more than twenty steps when a tall form loomed over her. "Where are you going?"

Tilting her chin, she stared boldly up at Kennedy. She could tell he'd showered, because the smell of soap lingered on his body. "I was coming to see you."

"Why?"

"I have to tell you something."

"Make it quick, because I'm going for a walk."

She swallowed to relieve her suddenly dry throat. "I love you, Kennedy Fletcher."

And as casually as she would tell someone the time of day, she turned and made her way back to her cabin. Her retreat was thwarted by the firm grip on her upper arm.

Kennedy spun her around, pulling her up close to his chest. "Don't play games with me—"

"I'm not playing a game," she said, cutting him off. "I love you even when I don't want to love you."

His hands moved up and cradled her face as gently as one would delicate crystal. "Why don't you want to love me, baby?"

Tears flooded her eyes with the endearment. "Because I don't want to lose my independence."

The pads of Kennedy's thumbs moved over her cheeks in

an attempt to wipe away her tears. "Is that really what you believe?" She nodded. Lowering his head, he kissed her parted lips. "Wrong, sweetheart. I fell in love with you because of your beauty, passion, talent, and independence. I have no use for a needy, insecure woman who'll bore the hell out of me because she feels I'm not giving her enough attention."

"I used to be like that," Lydia admitted softly, smiling through her tears. "Once my brothers were old enough to drive and date, I used to throw tantrums because I was no longer the center of their universe. But once my body began maturing, everything changed. They, along with my father, scared away every boy who had enough nerve to glance my way. That's why I was so inexperienced with Vince . . ." She'd caught herself just in time.

"Vincent Haddon."

Her jaw dropped. "You knew who I was referring to?"

"Yes. The only thing I'll say about him is that he's a very talented jackass. Now, back to your brothers. Are any of them my height or weight?"

She shook her head. "No. How tall are you?"

"I'm six five and weigh 224."

Lydia shook her head again. "Dwayne has gained at least fifteen pounds, but I still don't think he weighs as much as you do. Why did you ask about my brothers?"

"I like to know what to expect before I meet them."

"Are you talking about mixing it up with my brothers?"

Kennedy angled his head. "Won't be none, if they don't start none."

She pulled out of his loose embrace. "Oh no, Kennedy. I'll not have you brawling with my brothers."

He lifted an eyebrow. "There won't be any need for a brawl as long as they're not penalized for interference." Reaching for Lydia again, Kennedy pulled her to his chest. "All I want to do is rush for one more touchdown with you as the extra point."

"What are you talking about?"

Kennedy knew what he was about to say would change him, Lydia, them—forever. "Will you marry me, Lydia Lord?"

Her eyes filled again. "I came here to cook, not pick up a husband." Brushing his lips over hers, Kennedy tenderly kissed the corners of her mouth. "That's an illegal play," she gasped as he nibbled her lower lip.

"There's no flag on the field," he countered, breathing heavily.

Lydia giggled, her arms tightening around his neck. "And there won't be."

Bending at the knees, Kennedy swept her up into his arms, carrying her back to her cabin. He sat on the recliner, bringing her down to straddle his lap. "I'm still waiting for an answer."

Smiling, Lydia rested her forehead against his. "I thought I said yes."

"No, you didn't."

"Yes, I did," she argued softly.

Cupping her hips, he pulled her closer. "Say it, baby."

Lydia moved her hips in a rocking motion, eliciting the reaction she sought as Kennedy groaned as if in pain.

"I said yes, yes, yes, *yes*!"

Kennedy buried his face in her hair, breathing a kiss on her scalp. If possible, he would marry Lydia the next day, but knew he couldn't. It would be another three weeks before camp ended, and he had to go to Alabama to see if he was a donor match for Marvin.

"Thank you, thank you, thank you, thank you," he whispered over and over. Once his heart resumed its normal rate, he said, "I'd like to marry you before the end of the year."

Pulling back, Lydia tried making out his expression in the darkness. "Why the rush?"

"If I'm not giving you enough time, then we'll hire a wedding planner to put everything together."

"I don't need a wedding planner, Kennedy. I just thought you'd want a longer engagement."

"Four and a half months is long enough." He winked at her. "If I give you too much time you'll bolt. Something tells me you might be a flight risk."

She slapped playfully at his shoulder. "No, I'm not. Once I commit to something I go all the way."

"I don't ever want you to believe that I'm not totally committed to you," he said in a tone filled with raw emotion. The love he felt for the woman on his lap radiated from his adoring gaze. "What's your ring size?"

"Five. Look, Kennedy, I—"

He stopped her protest with an explosive kiss that left both of them breathing heavily. "Whenever you say, 'look, Kennedy,' I know I'm in for a tongue-lashing, so I suggest you think before you speak, because once we're married you'll find yourself on your back so often that you'll forget how to walk upright."

She placed one hand over his mouth and the other over his groin, squeezing gently. "You can't threaten the referee, darling. Do you know why?" Unable to speak, he shook his head. "Because the penalty will be the happy birthday song." Eyes widening, Kennedy bolted off the recliner, bringing her up with him.

When Lydia had taken him into her mouth she had stripped him bare, leaving him vulnerable as a newborn and malleable as soft clay. Each time he lay in her scented embrace he surrendered all he had, all he was to her.

"I don't want to make love to you again until we're married," he whispered close to her ear.

Her face clouded with uneasiness. "Why not?"

"I want you for *you*." He placed a hand over her heart. "I want what comes from here to be the most important thing in our marriage, not what is between your legs. Remember, you're my fiancée, not my groupie."

"What would I have to do to be a groupie?"

"Hang around stadium exits after the games, in hotel lobbies, and of course at the bars and clubs where the players usually get together. Most of the women are looking for husbands, a few want babies just to say they're someone's baby mama, while others sleep with the players just because they can. Now, do you think you can wait?"

Her smile was dazzling. "I waited for you, didn't I?"

He chuckled, the sound coming from his chest. "Yes, you did." Like quicksilver, Kennedy sobered. "It may be a while before I will be able to meet your family. I have to go to Alabama, and I'm not certain how long I'll be there."

Vertical lines appeared between Lydia's eyes. "Are you all right?"

"I'm fine." He was in the best condition that he'd been in for years. The exception was his first year in college when he'd trained for the Olympics, qualifying for the two- and four-hundred-meter runs and the four-hundred-meter relay. He won the bronze medal in the two-hundred-meter and the gold in the relay.

Reaching up, she trailed her fingertips over the stubble on his jaw. "You're not hiding anything from me, are you?"

"Don't tell me you're going to be one of those nagging wives?" As soon as the question left his lips, he realized it was the same thing he'd asked Lydia the morning she'd prepared breakfast at his house. Her comeback had been that she wasn't going to become some man's wife for a long, long time. However, within the span of a week she'd changed her mind.

Flashing a sensual pout, she crooned, "Now, you know you wouldn't love me any other way."

"You're right about that. Come, let's get you into bed. I don't want you to have bags under those golden eyes because I've kept you from your beauty sleep."

She put her fingers to her lips before pressing them to his. "The proposal for my Lady Day was rejected."

Kennedy gave her a level stare. "Don't worry about it, baby. We'll talk about it later." He kissed her tenderly. "Good night."

"Good night."

Kennedy stood on Lydia's porch, waiting for her to turn

off the light. Then he returned to his own cabin, this time to sleep. When he'd decided to go for a walk he never knew it would result in a marriage proposal.

Lydia had asked him if he was all right. He was better than all right. His life was as close to perfect as it could get.

Nineteen

It took Lydia more than twenty-four hours to accept that she would change her marital status before the end of the year.

She told Kennedy that she wouldn't tell her family of their engagement until he concluded his business in Alabama. What she didn't want was a repeat of the humiliation she'd endured after Vincent's publicized engagement.

Her whole being seemed to be filled with waiting—waiting for the end of the camp season, waiting for approval of her restaurant proposal, waiting for the day when Kennedy would meet the Lords, and waiting for the moment when she would exchange vows and become Lydia Lord-Fletcher.

She sensed a change in Kennedy, too. He appeared calmer, less reflective. His interaction with the campers became almost paternal. Many of the boys who had little or no contact with their fathers came to him with their doubts and fears instead of seeking out the on-site social workers. Kennedy asked one of the social workers to talk to nine-year-old Seneca Mustafa Johnson after the boy refused to get out of bed one morning because he didn't want to return to his group home.

Mustafa wasn't the only camper who had begun acting

out. Many of the others also feared leaving their summer home and new friends in less than three weeks.

Lydia sat on a stool in the kitchen in a corner where she'd set up her makeshift office, checking her meat inventory on the laptop. She'd decided to hold the second Family Reunion Sunday outdoors, taking advantage of the warmer weather.

The work on the massive barbecue pit completed, its chimney rising ten feet, it stood ready for the half dozen suckling pigs she'd ordered for the farewell dinner.

She checked off her meat selections, then went online to send it electronically, noting she had mail. She clicked on the icon. Justin had answered her e-mail.

Lydia,

It was cowardly to e-mail me when a telephone call would've been more socially correct. And I'm certain your mother brought you up better than that. Speaking of mothers—when I told my mother that I'd asked you to marry me she appeared quite pleased with my choice. She feels because you come from a good family that she would be proud to have you as her daughter-in-law, but since your last e-mail her impression of you has changed drastically. I don't need you to tell me to move on. I have.

Justin.

"Well, thank you very much, Mr. Banks," she said to the computer monitor.

"Who are you thanking?" Neil said, leaning over her shoulder.

"No peeking," she chided, deleting the message.

Neil straightened. "Do you want coffee?"

Lydia gave him a skeptical look. "You're making coffee this morning?" Neil had never brewed coffee.

"Sure. Why not?"

"I don't know. This is the first time you've volunteered to do it."

Reaching for his skullcap, he covered his head. "There's a first time for everything."

"Speaking of first time, I'm going to use the outdoor barbecue for tonight's dinner and tomorrow's family reunion gathering."

Neil gave her a bright smile. "Good move. Will the kids eat out tonight, too?"

"Yes. We'll set up some of the tables and benches for those who prefer eating outdoors. It's time we go into wind-down mode."

"What do you want for tonight?"

Lydia met Neil's gaze, holding it. "Let's go with a tailgate party theme. Burgers, franks, giant heroes, wraps, stuffed pitas, and salads."

Neil nodded. "I'll take care of today, and you can start on tomorrow's menu."

She saluted him. "Aye-aye, boss."

He blushed to the roots of his coal-black hair. "Don't go there, Lydia."

"Why not? You're a good supervisor, Neil."

"I don't want to supervise anyone. I just want to cook."

"Would you work for me?"

"In a heartbeat," he said quickly.

Moving off the stool, Lydia rested her hip against a serving table. "I'm planning to open a downtown restaurant next spring. I'd like you to come work with me."

Neil smiled. "Let me know when, and I'll be there with my toque in one hand and a whisk in the other."

Her smile matched his. "Thanks, partner."

Winking, Neil said, "No, thank *you*, partner."

Kennedy, the counselors, the female campers, and the support staff who had spent three days at the Fortress returned to Camp Six Nations late Saturday afternoon exhausted, but elated because of the expedition's success. The girls had learned to erect a swamp bed to counter sleeping on the wet ground.

Their spirits were revived after they sat on the grass rather than at the tables, eating, talking, and singing along with the upbeat music coming from overhead speakers.

Mustafa trailed behind Kennedy like a lost puppy, talking nonstop. He hadn't seen Mr. K for three days, and he wanted to tell him all that had happened at camp during his absence.

Kennedy placed a hand on Mustafa's head. "Excuse me for a few minutes, buddy. I have to talk to Miss Lydia."

"I'll go with you, Mr. K."

"No, you can't."

"Why? You don't want me to hear you talk to her?"

Kennedy turned his head to keep Mustafa from seeing his wide grin. "Miss Lydia and I have to talk about grown-folk things. Now I want you to go finish eating."

"Okay, Mr. K. I'll see you later."

"Later, Mustafa."

Walking toward Lydia, Kennedy thought about Mustafa. The child lost his mother after she died from injuries in a hit-and-run accident the year he turned six, and because there was no father listed on his birth certificate he became a ward of the state when no relatives came forth to claim the boy.

There were thousands of Mustafas, children in the foster care system falling between the cracks, who if given the right opportunity would flourish and become the brightest and best of their generation.

Picking up a plate, he stared at Lydia's back as she flipped burgers on the grill. Today she wore a toque instead of her usual bandana.

"I'd like a burger, please."

Turning slowly, Lydia smiled at her fiancé. Her smile faded quickly when she took in his appearance. He hadn't shaved. He sported a short beard. His face was leaner and much darker from all of his outdoor activity. She peered around him.

"Where's your buddy?"

"Who?"

"Mustafa."

Leaning closer, Kennedy whispered, "I told him that I had to talk to you."

"The kid is going to lose it when all of this ends."

Kennedy's brow furrowed. "I know. The social workers are going to have their work cut out for them helping the kids adjust to separating from their counselors and friends."

"I'm not talking about the other kids, Kennedy. I'm talking about Mustafa. The other children are going *home*. He's going back to a group home."

"I know that."

"I just want you to be aware of what's going to happen once he has to separate from you. You've coddled and protected him all summer. He sees you as a surrogate father."

"He doesn't have a father."

Lydia kept her features deceptively composed. "That's something you can't forget."

Kennedy frowned. "What are you implying, Lydia?"

She turned back to the grill, checking several burgers for doneness. Facing him again, she met his angry stare. "Don't mess with the kid's head. If you're going to play daddy, then go all the way with it. If not, then pull back *now*."

His frown vanished, wiped away by an expression of astonishment. "Are you saying you're willing to . . ." His words trailed off as he pointed to Lydia, to himself, and then signaled with his thumb over to where Mustafa sat with the other boys in his cabin.

Lydia nodded, saying brightly, "How would you like it, Mr. Ken?" Several counselors had gathered at the grill.

Kennedy's gaze moved with an agonizing slowness over her face, lingering briefly over her mouth before it eased lower to the pristine white tunic and apron and down to her black pin-striped pants and leather clogs.

"Medium-well."

She held his gaze. "Would you like anything else from the grill?"

"What do you have?"

"Hot dogs, kielbasa, and butterflied lamb."

"Give me one of each."

Lydia deftly caught the grilled meats between a pair of tongs, placing them on Kennedy's plate. "Hungry, Mr. Ken?"

Forcing back a smile, he winked at her. "Starved."

"Good. Then you should try the side dishes." She dismissed him without another glance, smiling at a counselor. "What can I get for you, Robin?"

Lydia sat on the edge of the pier next to Kennedy, her bare feet dangling in the water. The sun had begun to set and the sky was the same color as the bloodred oranges she used for her orange gelato.

Kennedy pulled his knees to his chest, clasped his arms around his legs, and stared at the small houses across the lake. Three sun-browned, towheaded children ran and jumped into the lake, frolicking like baby seals. "I bet they learned to swim before they could walk."

Lydia felt something brush her toes. She pulled her feet out of the cool water, leaned back on her hands, and stared at the young swimmers. "You're probably right. None of them are wearing life jackets."

An overhead screeching sound drowned out the children's laughter, and Lydia and Kennedy glanced up to find a circling red-tailed hawk.

"He's probably looking for his dinner," she said softly.

Straightening his legs and lying on his back, Kennedy stared up at the emerging constellations in the summer sky. "Speaking of dinner. Everyone liked eating outdoors."

Lydia glanced at Kennedy. He was so still he could've been a statue. "I wanted to make certain the grill was working before we have our family reunion gathering tomorrow."

"Two more Sundays, then it's over." There was a wistful quality in his voice.

"It's been good, Kennedy."

"Yes, it has."

"Did you know it would be this successful?"

Kennedy pondered her question. "Why would you ask me that?" He'd answered her question with one of his own.

She shifted her hips and faced him. "What made you come up with the idea to set up a camp?"

He sat up without using his arms to propel him forward. "Who told you? When did you find out?"

"Someone told someone else that they overhead Roger mention that you owned the camp. I found out the day after your birthday. Why didn't you tell me?"

His eyes burned her face with their intensity. "Would you have slept with me if you'd known?"

She shook her head. "No. I would never sleep with my boss."

A knowing smile softened the sharp angles in his bearded face. "That's why I didn't tell you," he drawled, returning to his reclining position.

Lydia rolled her eyes at him. "So, you knew all about me even before I got here. Whose idea was it to put me in the cabin next to yours?"

"Roger's. I may have financed the camp, but Roger and Grace run it. I didn't know you'd come on as a volunteer until Roger called and told me that he'd accepted the last two wait-listed campers. I'll admit that I was very curious about the woman who would work a twelve-hour day for no pay."

Lydia moved close enough to feel Kennedy's body heat seeping into hers. "I sold my condo and moved back home, so financially I'm not doing too badly. I was going to use the proceeds of the sale to furnish the restaurant if it had been approved."

"Put your money in tax-free municipal bonds for our children's college fund."

She went completely still. "What!"

"I'll finance the construction of your restaurant."

Lydia sprang off the pier as if a wire had jerked her up. "I can't take your money."

Closing his eyes, Kennedy rested his head on folded arms. "Why can't a husband underwrite the expenses for his wife's business venture?"

"Because it's my business venture, Kennedy."

His jaw tightened. "It's not your money or my money, your business venture or my business venture, your children or my children. It's ours, Lydia."

"I told you I wasn't a gold digger," she mumbled under her breath.

He opened his eyes, glaring at her. "If you keep running off at the mouth, then I'll have my attorney draw up a prenuptial agreement. If we split up, then you can walk away with whatever you brought to the marriage, and I'll take the rest."

Eyes narrowing, she thrust her face close to his. "I believe in death, not divorce."

Reaching for her hand, Kennedy held it firmly, as laughter rumbled in his broad chest. "I take that to mean that we'll be together for the rest of our lives."

"Yes, it does."

He tightened his grip on her fingers. "I want you to look for property where you'd like to build your Lady Day. Check with the zoning boards to make certain they'll approve your parking accommodations, ingress, and egress."

"You're really into real estate, aren't you?"

"I picked up what I know from my dad. He's an underwriter, but he has a nose like a hound dog when it comes to real estate. When I got my signing bonus his advice was not to squander it on cars, jewelry, or women, but invest in property."

"It sounds as if you've been a good son."

"Not as good as I've been obedient. Speaking of children. What was that comment about me and Mustafa?"

"Do you want him, Kennedy?"

Kennedy repeated Lydia's query to himself, his heart pounding against his ribs like the rumble of a runaway freight train. She had read his mind. There was something about Mustafa that pulled at his heart the way no other child he'd ever met had done. During his pro ball days, he'd visited schools, hospitals, and community centers to distribute toys, sign autographs, or present a check during a photo-op, meeting thousands of boys and girls who looked up to him as if he were an immortal being with superhuman powers. Not one of them, not even those with terminal illnesses, had touched him like Mustafa Johnson.

Holding his breath until he felt his lungs laboring, Kennedy let it out slowly "Yes, darling. I want him."

Lydia knew the state would have to conduct an exhaustive search to ascertain whether Mustafa had any surviving relatives who could possibly want to adopt him.

She rested her head on Kennedy's shoulder. "Then you should have him. I know someone who can help you with the legal paperwork. Her name is Caroline Bennington. She's the sister of a family friend who handled all of my brother's adoptions. Once she wades through all of the bureaucratic red tape, we might be able to finalize everything before the end of next year. Meanwhile, you can always petition social services to become a foster father."

Kennedy was so overwhelmed with emotion that he couldn't move, speak, or swallow. He'd fallen in love with an enigma, a woman who would continue to challenge, shock, and amaze him.

Two weeks into the camp season he had known he had to rescue Mustafa from the foster care system. He was prepared to become a single father, but having Lydia in their lives completed the family unit.

"Are you certain you want to start out with a ready-made family?" he asked, recovering his voice.

Lydia nodded. "It's no longer an oddity for couples to

marry and become a blended family. I'll never be able to take the place of Mustafa's mother, but you can be the father he's never had."

"I've seen you with Keisha, darling. I know you're going to be a wonderful mother."

"I hope so. I've had enough practice babysitting my nieces and nephews."

"How long do you want to wait before we make Mustafa an older brother?"

A secret smile stole its way over Lydia's face. "Not too long."

Rising slightly, Kennedy peered down at her, the tenderness in his expression making her heart turn over in love. "You want to start right away?"

Her eyelids fluttered. "Why not? If I'm going to build or renovate a place for Lady Day, then I project that should take at least a year. Which means you'd better be a straight shooter, darling, or we're going to have to wait until after we open the restaurant. If I have a baby before our grand opening, then I'll only serve dinner Tuesday through Sunday and add brunch on the weekends."

Kennedy stood up, offered his hand, and pulled her to her feet. "That sounds perfect. Speaking of babies, would you like a demonstration to see how straight I can shoot?"

Closing her eyes, Lydia shook her head. "No, Kennedy. There's no way I'm going to become your baby mama before we're married." She opened her eyes. "Besides, you said we wouldn't sleep together until we're married."

"I've changed my mind."

"No!"

"Please, baby."

Folding her hands on her hips, she rolled her eyes at him. "Look at you. Mr. Fine-ass, Superstar Juggernaut begging a woman for her *stuff*!"

The last word was barely out of her mouth when Lydia found herself lifted off her feet, the darkening sky spinning overhead. She managed one shriek, before falling into the lake with Kennedy.

"You didn't!" she screamed once she recovered her breath.

Kennedy, treading water, began swimming toward the opposite bank, Lydia in hot pursuit. They splashed each other until tiring, then floated back toward the pier.

Kennedy pulled himself up before reaching down to pull Lydia up. The white T-shirt she usually wore under her tunic was pasted to her upper body. His eyes widened when he saw the distinct outline of a pair of dark nipples showing ardently through the fabric of her bra and shirt.

He removed his camp shirt and pulled it over her head. "You were showing too much of your . . . stuff."

She wrinkled her nose at him. "Hanging out with you is dangerous."

He flashed a wide grin. "There may be some truth in that statement, but you have to admit, being dangerous is a lot of fun."

Picking up her sandals, she leaned against Kennedy and slipped them on. "Good night, darling."

He stood on the pier, bare-chested, watching her walk. "Good night, Lydia."

After she'd disappeared from his line of vision, he sat down again. In less than a year he would become a husband, and a year later possibly a father.

He exhaled a long sigh of contentment. He would complete every entry on his wish list before turning forty.

Twenty

An underlying excitement reached a fever pitch even before the buses arrived for the final Family Reunion Sunday. Lydia and Neil were up before dawn. Working silently side by side, the chefs marinated, basted, and baked chicken tenders, egg rolls, mozzarella sticks, mini–chicken cordon blue, and cheese poppers.

The eclectic menu featured finger foods: oven- and deep-fried chicken, Buffalo wings, sliced smoked salmon, succulent roasted chicken, spare ribs, tiny triangular finger sandwiches, and a platter of imported and domestic cheeses.

Neil had offered to man the carving table, slicing leg of lamb, turkey, and rib roast. He had outdone himself, baking pans of fluffy Parker House rolls and biscuits and a variety of fruit pies.

Lydia checked off the trays on a printed list—a rice medley, roasted potatoes and vegetables, stuffed cabbage, sausage and peppers, and baked ziti—as they were transported from the kitchen to an area where the counselors had erected a large tent to shield everyone from the brilliant summer sun.

* * *

Kennedy walked into the kitchen and found Lydia sitting on a stool, eyes closed, the back of her head pressed against a wall. Lines of worry furrowed his forehead.

He touched her arm and she opened her eyes. "Are you all right?"

She flashed a tired smile, her gaze caressing his face. He'd shaved off the short beard. "I'm trying to catch a few winks."

Wrapping his arms around her shoulders, he pulled her head to his chest. "What time did you get up this morning?"

"Four."

It was almost one, which meant she had been on her feet for nine hours. "Come, Lydia. I'm taking you back to your cabin."

Pushing against his chest, she pulled away from him. "For what?"

Kennedy glared at her. "So you can catch a few winks in bed instead of on a stool."

"I'm not going to bed in the middle of the day."

An expression of determination tightened his jaw. "Either you go back to your cabin under your own steam, or everyone will see Mr. Ken carry Miss Lydia under his arm like a football. It's your choice."

"You're delusional," she drawled, rolling her eyes at him. "You can't carry me like a—"

Kennedy never gave her the chance to say "football," when he gathered her off the stool with one arm and held her effortlessly against his side. "I said you had a choice, darling."

She pounded his back. "Let me go."

"Are you going to your cabin?"

She knew she was no match for his superior strength. "Yes," she said between clenched teeth. "This is what I meant about losing my independence," she whispered under her breath.

Kennedy set her on her feet. "I'll walk you," he said firmly. Untying her apron, Lydia placed it on the stool she'd just vacated. "Bully," she snorted under her breath, pushing past him and walking toward the double doors.

"Keep walking, Lydia," he drawled as he stared at her ramrod-straight back.

She made her way out of the dining hall and into the blazing sunlight. The smells wafting from the serving tables tantalized her olfactory senses, making her mouth water. A crowd had lined up, waiting to be served, while those who had plates filled with food sat on benches under the tent, or on the grass, eating and drinking.

Stopping, Lydia turned and faced Kennedy. "I'm going to my cabin, but can you bring me a plate?"

He gave her an incredulous look. "You haven't eaten?"

She shook her head. "I never eat when I'm cooking."

"You don't even sample?"

"Never."

"Damn it, Lydia! No wonder you're so tired and can't keep your eyes open. You're hungry!"

Lydia glared at Kennedy. "Just bring the food."

Turning, she headed for her cabin as he made his way over to the serving area.

Lydia didn't know when Kennedy walked into her cabin with a napkin-covered plate; she was totally unaware that he'd lain beside her for three-quarters of an hour, listening to her breathing as she slept.

She slept through the afternoon, into the night, not waking until streaks of light pierced the cover of darkness the following day. Her nap had become sixteen hours of deep, dreamless, uninterrupted sleep.

Lydia realized she was undergoing her own separation anxiety the closer it came to the end of Camp Six Nations' inaugural summer. Many of the campers had begun acting out, and the social workers went into crisis mode as they attempted to ease the transition as the campers prepared to go home, some to less than stable environments.

Megan Gallagher had erected an exhibit with pieces of pottery and painted clay masks festooned with ribbons and feathers reminiscent of those Lydia had seen in Venice during Carnival. Keisha had given her a plate decorated with her name and image in slip trailing—a liquid medium for drawing on ceramic ware. Keisha had signed her name with the date on the reverse side.

The survival training had honed the skills of the older boys and girls once they engaged in canoe and swimming competitions. They played a sophisticated version of a scavenger hunt with items hidden throughout the campground. The team who came up with the most was declared the winner.

Twelve hours before buses were scheduled to transport the campers back to Baltimore and Washington, D.C., everyone gathered in the playhouse for an awards ceremony followed by a theatrical program under the auspices of Jeff Wiggins. The day would conclude with a luau.

Lydia sat in the rear, staring at the man to whom she'd pledged her future as he took a position behind the podium. If he'd changed in eight weeks, so had she. He'd kept his promise not to make love to her, but that did not stop him from coming to her cabin after the camp settled down for the night to climb into bed with her.

These were the times when they talked—about everything. Kennedy shocked her once he disclosed the extent of his wealth. He'd admitted to receiving a signing bonus, but hadn't told her of other incentives, which included a percentage of ticket sales. Spectators came to the stadium to see him run. Not only was he fast, but unbelievably strong, strong enough to shake off any player's attempt to dislodge the ball or take him off his feet. She'd told him how she wanted to decorate Lady Day and the signature dishes she believed would become an instant favorite with diners.

Bringing her attention back to the present, she watched Grace pin a blue ribbon inscribed with *One Camp, One*

Family, on each camper's T-shirt as they all filed into the playhouse. Grace completed the task, then nodded to Kennedy.

Picking up the handheld microphone, he tapped it lightly. "Welcome to what will become our last night at Camp Six Nations. When you board the buses tomorrow that will take you back to your homes, I want you to remember that it will not be good-bye, but later. Next year we're going to do it all over again—bigger and better." The campers cheered wildly.

"I want the counselors to come up here and give out the awards to their campers, and before we close this afternoon's program, Mr. Jeff and his aspiring actors and actresses will entertain us with their extraordinary theatrical talent."

The counselor for the six-year-old girls and boys took the podium, giving awards to every camper: best swimmer, most improved swimmer, most congenial, best sense of humor, best dressed, and all-around camper. Every camper in every group was a winner.

Two of the older campers, one male and one female, stepped onto the stage. Evangeline smiled at her counter-part. "Antonio and I represent all of the campers, and we've come up with our own awards. Of course there was a lot of dialogue, a little arguing, and the slightest bit of coercion, but in the end we were all in agreement.

"The first award is the hot dog, and it goes to Mr. Neil, for grilling the best dogs on the planet." Neil pumped his fist and went up to pick up a ceramic frank in a bun.

Antonio took the microphone. "The next award goes to Miss Jill, who had not only an inexhaustible supply of ban-dages, but ones with the animated characters." He held up a ceramic bandage, eliciting guffaws from everyone. Chatty, flirty Jill wiped away tears as she got up to retrieve her award.

Evangeline and Antonio alternated, distributing awards to all of the counselors and staff members. Roger and Grace were each given a plate inscribed with *We're cool, do not disturb*.

Smiling, Antonio crooned into the microphone, "Will Mr.

Ken please take the stage?" All of the kids cheered as Kennedy returned to the stage.

"This award is the only one we all agreed on. Thanks to you, this city boy can swim, canoe, kayak, and build a fire without matches. You've taught us not only how to survive in the woods, but to depend on one another for the survival of the entire camp." Reaching into a large canvas bag, he withdrew a large platter inscribed with all the names of all of the campers. "We call this the Father Award, because each of us would be proud to have you as our dad twenty-four-seven." He and Kennedy exchanged handshakes and a hug.

Kennedy held the beautifully decorated platter above his head, his gaze fixed on Mustafa before it shifted to Lydia. He knew he was expected to say something, but the words lodged in his throat would not come out. Nodding his thanks, he walked off and retook his seat.

Antonio handed the microphone to Evangeline. "We have one more award. This one goes to Miss Lydia." Everyone shifted in their seats and stared at her seated in the back of the room. "Miss Lydia, will you please come up?"

She stood up and made her way to the front of the expansive building with near-perfect acoustics. All eyes were on her.

Antonio reached into the bag and took out another platter, this one with the names of the campers inscribed around a crest bearing a toque flanked with a knife and fork.

"This is the Mama Award, because all of us wish our mamas could cook like you," Evangeline continued. "I thought I'd never be able to go a week without my Big Mac and fries, but you showed me not only did I not have to eat them, but eating healthy is also delicious. Thank you, Miss Lydia, and we all hope you'll come back next summer." The campers rose as one, cheering and applauding.

Lydia took her platter, holding it above her head as if she'd won a sports trophy. Evangeline positioned the microphone near her mouth. "I'd like to thank everyone for this award. I will treasure it forever. I usually don't make promises, because I'm not certain whether I'll be able to keep them. But I promise this—I'll be back," she said in her best Arnold Schwarzenegger imitation.

Clapping and whistles accompanied her retreat to the rear of the playhouse. She and Neil had sat in the back because once the final production number began they would leave to start serving the dishes they'd prepared for the luau. Jeff, wearing his mask with the twin faces of comedy and tragedy, walked up onstage and slipped behind the curtain.

Megan dissolved into a fit of giggles after she'd opened the *Handbook of American Slang, Including Rap and Hip-Hop* the campers had compiled and printed, using a desktop publishing program.

The counselors, counselors-in-training, and administrative staff, impressed with the creativity coming from their charges, were effusive with their affection and praise. Within the span of eight weeks it had truly become one camp, one family.

The lights dimmed, the curtain opened, and Jeff stood onstage, sans mask, in front of a set decoration depicting the skyline of a large cosmopolitan city. An overhead spotlight shimmered on his pale light hair with flecks of diamond dust.

"I'd like to welcome everyone to Camp Six Nations' rendition of a *A Modern Walk Along Broadway.* Our camp's theater group will sing and perform a medley of songs from classic musicals, but with a modern spin. We'll begin with Leonard Bernstein and Stephen Sondheim's *West Side Story,* and move through the decades to Andrew Lloyd Weber musical masterpieces and conclude with Elton John's *Aida.*"

Prerecorded music filled the space as a boy and girl took the stage, holding hands and staring into each other's eyes as they sang an upbeat version of "Tonight," then segued into "Somewhere," scatting with an ease that would've made Ella Fitzgerald and Al Jarreau take notice. Break-dancers showing off the latest hip-hop steps accompanied selections from *The Wiz*. The production ended with the theme from *Fame,* and Lydia found herself on her feet, singing and dancing along with everyone.

The curtain came down and went up again to thunderous applause as the cast took their bows. It was during the third curtain call that Lydia and Neil slipped out.

"Hey, Mama," he teased Lydia, winking at her.

She wrinkled her nose at him. "Don't hate, Neil. You know the Mama Award beats the hot dog."

He looked serious, giving her a sidelong glance. "Do you think they've forgiven me for ruining their Sunday dinner?"

"I'm willing to bet they can't even remember it, especially now since they like eating outdoors so much."

"Are you really coming back next summer?"

Lydia was momentarily taken off guard by Neil's query. "I plan to. Why?"

"What about your restaurant?"

She told him her proposal had been rejected, but not about Kennedy's suggestion that she build her own eating establishment. "I'll probably either work part-time or help out my sister-in-law with her catering business. I can't commit to working full-time until I figure out what the future holds for me."

"You better call me when you open your place."

She touched his shoulder. "You'll be the first one I'll call."

The levity continued with R&B and hip-hop blaring from the speakers as everyone, sporting colorful plastic leis, lined up to sample the cuisine of the fiftieth state. The suckling pigs, roasted to perfection and displayed without their heads, had become the main attraction. Skewered ginger-orange shrimp ran a close second to the pigs' crispy skin and sweet, tender meat. Jeff had sampled and given his approval for the pineapple salsa, banana-macadamia nut bread, baked custard with a coffee sauce, and frosty Hawaiian nog made with buttermilk, crushed pineapples, sugar, and vanilla.

The smell of food lingered in the air hours later as the sun sank lower behind the trees, and still the campers lingered on the grass. Some of the younger ones played a vigorous game of tag, while others sat around in groups talking quietly with one another.

Lydia and Neil returned to the kitchen where they began the task of filling small plastic shopping bags with fruit, granola bars, juice boxes, and trail mix for the campers who were scheduled to board the buses at eight o'clock the following morning.

She and Neil had inventoried the kitchen and had packed up all of the leftover foodstuffs, which were to be transported in a refrigerated truck to a soup kitchen in West Virginia.

Sitting on stools, they looked at each other. "Well," Lydia said softly, "this is it, partner."

Neil nodded. "It's been good. Damn good, partner." He ran his hand over his hair. "Rachel said she's willing to try and make a go of our marriage, but on one condition."

The heavy lashes that shadowed Lydia's eyes flew up. Rachel and her daughters hadn't come to last week's family reunion. "What's that?"

"I do all of the cooking."

"Of course you said yes." She was barely able to keep the laughter from her voice.

"Oh, hell yeah. When she said that, I thought of the worst-case scenario like going to the mall with her. Every time I've gone to the mall with Rachel I've ended up with a headache. The woman has to visit every shoe store in the whole frigging place, and that also includes the department stores."

"She sounds like someone I can hang out with. I love shoes." She lifted a clog-shod foot. "These excluded." Glancing at the clock on the wall, Lydia noted the time. It was almost midnight, and she had to finish packing.

"I'm going to turn in. I don't want my coach to turn into a pumpkin if I'm not home before the clock strikes twelve." She slipped off the stool, smiling at Neil as he followed suit.

He extended his arms, and he wasn't disappointed when she went into his embrace. "Good luck with everything."

Tilting her chin, Lydia nodded. "You too." She pressed a light kiss to his cheek, pulled back, and walked out of the kitchen for the last time.

Twenty-one

Kennedy sat on a large boulder with Mustafa, his left hand resting on the boy's shoulder. "Your counselor said you wanted to see me."

Mustafa nodded, his gaze fixed on the ground, fighting back tears. "I'm going to miss you, Mr. K."

"You think I'm not going to miss you, too?" Mustafa's head came up. Kennedy smiled at the boy who remarkably looked like him when he was his age.

"You are?"

"Of course, Mustafa. You're going back to Baltimore tomorrow morning, and I'll be leaving for Alabama on Tuesday. I don't know how long I'm going to be there, but the minute I come back I'm coming to see you."

"Really?"

Kennedy nodded. "Really. I'm going to talk to the social worker at your home to see if we can spend some time together."

"At your house?"

"Yes. At my house."

"It must be a big house, because you're big."

Kennedy chuckled, shaking his head. "Yes, it is." He wanted to tell Mustafa a six-thousand-square-foot house was much too large for one person. "Whenever you sleep over you'll have your room."

"I haven't had my own room in a long time. When did you say you were coming back?"

"I don't know."

He couldn't tell Mustafa that he'd planned to adopt him, because if it never materialized, then he would be devastated. "I want you to promise me something."

Large, dark, trusting eyes stared up at him. "What?"

"I want you to be a good boy. No fighting, talking back, and most importantly, you have got to do well in school."

His jaw set in a stubborn line, Mustafa said, "I promise."

Resisting the urge to hug and kiss the child, Kennedy patted his shoulder. "Good. Now go inside and get ready for tomorrow."

"Can I write you, Mr. K?"

"Write the letters, but don't mail them. I want you to give them to me when I come for you."

Mustafa's solemn expression brightened. "Later, Mr. K." He raised his hand, and wasn't disappointed when Kennedy gave him a high-five handshake.

"Later, Mustafa."

Kennedy sat on the boulder long after the screen door slammed behind the boy. He was frightened—no, scared out of his wits! The fact that he contemplated adopting a child frightened him more than marriage. He loved Lydia, loved her enough to sacrifice everything he had for her, but he didn't love Mustafa—at least not yet.

He finally left the boulder and made his way across the open meadow to his cabin. He passed the cabin and walked another fifty feet to the neighboring one. As he opened the door to the porch he went completely still. The wind chime, votive candles, and porch furniture were missing.

He knocked on the cabin door, then tried the knob. It turned easily. A slight smile curved the corners of his mouth. Lydia had left the door unlocked. Light from the bathroom provided enough illumination for him to see the bags on the floor near the door.

Kennedy crossed the room and stood next to the bed. Lydia lay on her back, staring up at him. With the flick of her wrist, she swept back the sheet.

"Get in."

The husky command galvanized him into action. He held her gaze as he stripped off his clothes, slipped into the bed beside her, and cradled her spoon-fashion. Lydia reached up and turned off the lamp, plunging the space into darkness.

Pressing his mouth to the nape of her neck, Kennedy whispered, "I'll call you every night."

She laughed softly. "That won't be necessary. Call me on Sundays after nine and talk dirty to me."

It was Kennedy's turn to laugh. "I can't talk dirty to you on the Sabbath."

"Every day is the Sabbath, darling."

"You're right about that. I had a talk with Mustafa tonight."

"Did you tell him that you wanted to adopt him?"

"No. I don't want to get his hopes up when there is a possibility that it may not happen."

"The only thing that will stop it is if a distant relative contests it."

Kennedy let out an audible sigh. "This may sound awful, but I pray there are no relatives."

Closing her eyes, Lydia said, "Me too."

They lay together in the darkness, feeding on each other for emotional strength. Kennedy had told Lydia he had to go to Alabama to take care of some business. She'd waited for him to tell her the nature of his business, but when he wasn't forthcoming, she decided not to pry. Once they married, she prayed, there would no secrets between them.

Wrapped in her fiancé's arms and in a cocoon of love, she fell into a dreamless slumber.

When she awoke hours later, the space beside her was

empty and the bags she'd left near the door were gone. The keys to her SUV rested on the pillow that bore the imprint of Kennedy's head.

A knowing smile softened her mouth. The first time she came face-to-face with Kennedy Fletcher he'd offered to carry her bags. This time he hadn't asked. He just did it.

Kennedy climbed the steps to the wraparound porch, leaned over, and kissed his mother's cheek. He lowered his tall frame down to the glider beside Diane Anderson and stretched out his legs.

Her questioning gaze met his seconds before she pressed her lips together until they narrowed into a hard, tight line. "You're going to do it."

Kennedy nodded. "Yes."

Tears welled in Diane's eyes, and she turned her head so Kennedy couldn't see them. "When?" she asked, once her troubled spirits quieted.

"Two weeks."

This disclosure stunned Diane. She stared at her son's strained profile. "Why the delay?"

"Marvin's come down with a cold."

Pushing off the glider, Diane walked several feet and leaned a shoulder against a massive column supporting the porch. "I know I sound like a selfish old woman, but I don't want you to go through with it."

Kennedy went completely still, shock and surprise rendering him temporarily mute and motionless. He stared at his mother's petite figure, unable to believe what he'd just heard.

"You're not old, Mama."

Diane turned and glared at her son, unable to hide the pain and anguish in her tear-filled eyes. Her curly hair, cut to frame her tiny, smooth oval face that was the color of golden oak, and her large hazel eyes, full lush mouth, and slim figure belied her age. She could easily have passed for thirty-six, not fifty-six. There were a few occasions when people thought she was Kennedy's sister, and not his mother.

"I'm old enough to stop living in a world of fantasy, to know what I always wanted I will never have. And I'm much too old to continue to love a man whom I know is so undeserving of the most precious gift in the world." Her hands fisted. "It's taken me almost forty years to come to my senses to see Marvin Kennedy for what he is: a self-centered, manipulative bastard who doesn't care who he uses as long as he gets his way. What pains me is that I'm no different than he is."

Kennedy shot to his feet. "Yes, you are."

Tilting her head, Diane looked up at him towering above her. "No, I'm not." Her voice was soft, but held a thread of hardness. "I fell in love with your father—"

"He's not my father," Kennedy said angrily, cutting her off.

She nodded. "I fell in love with Marvin the year I turned sixteen, fantasizing that we would marry and live happily ever after. It didn't matter that every girl in Smoky Junction felt the same way. I threw myself at him, but he was kind enough to tell me to look him up once I turned eighteen. He didn't want to be charged with statutory rape."

"Why are you telling me this?"

"Because I want you to know who the man is whose life you're going to save. I called you to tell you about Marvin's condition because he'd asked me to. I could never deny him anything—and that included giving him myself when I didn't want to."

Wide-eyed, Kennedy stared at his mother. "You slept with him after you'd married Philip?"

A slight smile crinkled her luminous eyes. "No, son. I've never been an unfaithful wife."

"Then what do you mean about giving him yourself?"

Diane ignored Kennedy's sharp tone. "Whenever he

called me for something I either listened to him or helped him out. He said I was the only one he could count on or trust. I knew he was using me, but I didn't care.

"I didn't love Philip when I first married him, but grew to love him because I was afraid to be alone and I needed a father for my young son. Philip gave me everything I needed for emotional and financial stability, knowing I would never give him his own child." She saw Kennedy's eyes widen with this disclosure. "A year after I had you I slept with Marvin and got pregnant again. I knew something was wrong from the beginning, but ignored the cramping and spotting. I was about three months when I began hemorrhaging. I woke up in a hospital bed knowing instinctively that I would never have another child. In order to save my life, the doctors removed my uterus."

A muscle flicked in Kennedy's lean jaw. "Why are you telling me this?"

"It's about letting go, son. Before you told me that you planned to marry and adopt a child I prayed that you would be a donor match, but now . . ." Her words trailed off.

"Why have you changed your mind?"

She unclenched a fist and placed her cool palm against Kennedy's cheek. "You've given him enough. You've given all of us more than enough. It's time you secure your own happiness."

Kennedy covered the small hand with his much larger one. "Everything I've given has been given to me—material things. I'd always thought it absurd that I'd be paid millions for running down a field with a football under my arm, while teachers and cops have to picket and demonstrate for a lousy three-percent-a-year raise." He remembered his mother walking the picket line in the rain when she and the other teachers at her school had worked two years without a new contract.

"Yes, Mama, I've given away a lot of money because I felt if I couldn't be happy, at least I could make someone else happy."

"Are you happy now?"

His expression softened. "Delirious." Pulling Diane's hand from his face, he pressed a kiss to her fingers.

Her eyes filled again. "I don't want anything to happen to you."

"What's going to happen to me?"

"There is always a lot at risk whenever someone undergoes major surgery."

"I faced risk every time I suited up and took the field. One hit, one wrong fall, and within seconds I could've either lost my life or been crippled for life."

"But you got out before that happened," Diane argued softly.

"You know why I got out, Mama, and it had nothing to do with the risks of the game. After I give Marvin what he needs, then we're even. He gave me life, and now I'm returning the favor. He's never going to contact you again."

Diane shook her head and closed her eyes. "You know that's never going to happen."

Kennedy's expression hardened, becoming a mask of stone. "It has."

"What did you do, Kennedy?" The look in his eyes frightened Diane.

"Don't worry about what I did. Just know that he'll never call you again. The disrespect he's shown you, *my* father, and your marriage ended today." Wrapping his arms around her waist, he kissed her forehead. "Why don't you go inside and change into something pretty? As soon as Dad gets home we're going out to your favorite restaurant."

"I'd taken out some meat because Philip said he felt like grilling."

"Dad can grill tomorrow."

"Speaking of cooking, when am I going to meet my future daughter-in-law?"

Kennedy had told his mother about Lydia and her incredible cooking talent. He had also told her about Mustafa. Lydia had given him the telephone number of the lawyer who'd handled her niece's and nephews' adoption, and he'd placed a call to Caroline Bennington, who had agreed to accept the case, but warned him not to tell Mustafa about the ongoing process.

"After the surgery."

"When are you going to see her?"

"After the surgery," he repeated.

Diane, totally bewildered by Kennedy's response, asked, "Why?"

Kennedy met her questioning stare. "I don't like goodbyes." He knew if he went to Maryland to see Lydia he would never return to Alabama. "I'm going inside to change before Dad gets home."

He went inside the house that had been renovated to include a second floor with large bedrooms, a wraparound porch, a gourmet kitchen, an all-weather patio, and a library/office. Philip had refused his offer to buy them a house in an upscale community in Mobile because he liked the small-town ambience of Smoky Junction. In the end, the man who had become his father the year he turned four agreed to let him underwrite the costs for renovating and expanding the small white frame house he'd bought for his wife and stepson.

Kennedy climbed the steps to the second-floor bedroom he occupied whenever he stayed in Smoky Junction. The expansive sun-filled bedroom, with a sitting room, private bath, and antique furnishings beckoned one to come and stay awhile.

Reaching for the cell phone on his waist, he punched in Lydia's programmed number. It rang several times before he heard her voice mail message. "Hi, Lydia. This is Kennedy. I'm calling to let you know that I'll be here for a while longer. I miss you and . . . I love you."

He ended the call and tossed the phone on the bed. He shrugged out of his jacket, dropping it on an armchair. As he undressed he thought about the conversation he'd had with Marvin earlier that afternoon in his attorney's office. He'd agreed to give him a kidney, but on one condition. The older man would have to sign an affidavit that he would never contact Diane Anderson or her husband, Philip Anderson, again, or he would be subject to arrest for harassment.

Marvin had glared at him across the table for a full minute, then picked up a pen and signed the document. It was witnessed and notarized by the firm's paralegal before the parties involved got up and shook hands.

His mother spoke of letting go. He had let go of Nila. Lydia had let go of her past, and now Diane would be given the opportunity to let go of Marvin and give Philip what she'd withheld from him for more than thirty years—a marriage free of the encumbrances from her past.

Kennedy walked into the bathroom and turned on the shower, mentally counting the weeks until he would be reunited with the woman who had filled the space the other women he'd known couldn't.

Twenty-two

Kennedy closed his eyes, shutting out the blinding light overhead. He'd been prepped for surgery, and the drug they'd given him before he was rolled out of his room and into the operating room made him feel light-headed, weightless. He heard voices, male and female, and felt someone extend his left arm in an outward position.

He had spoken to Lydia the night before but did not tell her he was to undergo surgery the following morning for the removal of one of his kidneys. He'd heard the frustration in her voice when she asked if she was ever going to see him again. His words of reassurance that they would be reunited sounded weak until he asked her, "Why do you tug so hard at my heart—that space that other women couldn't fill?" Lydia was unable to reply because she'd begun crying. The last thing he remembered before he ended the call was her crying.

The anesthesiologist leaned over him. "Kennedy." His eyes crinkled above his mask when his patient opened his eyes. "You're going to feel a slight prick, and then I want you to start counting backward from a hundred."

Sighing heavily, he nodded. "One hundred, ninety-nine,

ninety-eight . . ." He reached eighty-nine, and then his world
went dark.

"What's up with your daughter?" Charles Lord asked his
wife.

Etta Mae shot her spouse of more than fifty years a look
that spoke volumes. "Why is it whenever one of your children has an attitude it's always *my* son or *my* daughter?
When is it ever *ours*, Charles?"

"It's your daughter because you understand them better
than I do. Remember, we had six boys before I had to deal
with the girls and their mood swings."

Andrea, cradling Sharon's infant daughter in the crook of
one arm, walked into the kitchen in time to overhear her father. "Daddy! Oh no, you didn't go there."

Charles sucked his teeth. "Yes, I did."

"We all know how disappointed Lydia is because the
owner of that new office building turned down her restaurant
proposal."

"That was months ago, Andrea. It's now the end of
November, and she should've gotten over it by now."

"Daddy, you know how sensitive she is," Andrea said in
defense of her baby sister. She smiled at the baby in her
arms. "Sharon is going to throw a fit if she sees me standing
here holding Jessica instead of putting her in her crib. She
complains that Orlando picks her up as soon as he gets
home, and now she doesn't want to be put down."

Etta Mae stood up and held out her arms. "I'll take her
upstairs." An upstairs bedroom had been turned into a nursery with the birth of her grandchild. The large room was out-
fitted with three cribs, two youth beds, and a set of bunk
beds.

A loud roar went up from the enclosed back porch where
most of the male family members had gathered to watch the
televised Thanksgiving Day football games. Their spouses

had congregated in the family room to watch their favorite movies. The sound of the front doorbell reverberated throughout the house.

"I wonder who that could be," Charles said. Whenever the family gathered together, the door was never locked.

Andrea motioned to her father. "Don't get up, Daddy. I'll see who it is."

She made her way out of the kitchen, down a hall, through an expansive entryway, and to the front door. She opened it, then went completely still. She recognized the tall man standing on her parents' porch. Her stunned gaze shifted to the young boy at his side, believing he had come to the wrong house.

"Yes?"

"I'm sorry to have come unannounced, but I'd like you to let Lydia know that Kennedy Fletcher and Mustafa Johnson are here to see her."

Andrea's mouth opened and closed several times before she was able to say, "Please come in, Mr. Fletcher." Kennedy and Mustafa walked into the entryway as Andrea disappeared into another part of the house.

Andrea walked into the family room. Everyone held their sides while laughing at the antics of the Wayans brothers' comedy hit *White Chicks*.

"Lydia, there's someone here for you."

She glanced away from the wall-mounted television screen. The last time someone had come to her parents' house to see her it had been Justin. Although she hadn't heard from him since his e-mail, she still expected him to pop up unexpectedly.

"Whoever it is, I don't want to see them."

"I think you'd better come and tell him that yourself."

A frown creased Lydia's forehead. She was missing the actors' witty dialogue. "Who is he?" she snapped angrily.

"You'll know him when you see him. He has someone named Mustafa with him."

Lydia jumped as if she'd been jolted by a bolt of electricity. "Kennedy?"

Andrea smiled. "Yes. He said he was Kennedy Fletcher."

Heads turned and all gazes were fixed on Lydia instead of the television screen.

"How do you know him?" Sharon asked.

Lydia rose slowly from a love seat, her knees shaking. "We met at camp."

Someone hit the Pause button on the remote, and everyone followed Lydia as she walked out of the family room.

Lydia saw him and Mustafa, the tears blurring her eyes making it difficult to see their faces clearly. She hadn't heard from Kennedy in almost a month, and she'd imagined every conceivable scenario: accident, another woman, or possible death. When he didn't call her for their regular Sunday night chat, she called him. After hearing his voice mail message three times, she'd given up and stopped calling.

Kennedy had lost weight, a lot of it. But he still was as handsome and virile as she'd remembered him. A smile trembled over her lips as she extended her arms.

Kennedy took two long strides and gathered Lydia to his chest. Smiling, he lowered his head and nuzzled her neck. "I told you I'd come, baby," he whispered against her moist, parted lips.

She placed tiny kisses all over his face. "You had me worried to death because I thought something had happened to you."

The sound of someone clearing their voice shattered the spell, and Lydia turned to find her father and brothers staring at her and Kennedy.

Mustafa peered shyly at the crowd of people staring at Mr. K and Miss Lydia.

Lydia moved between Kennedy and Mustafa, grasping their hands. "Daddy, I want you to meet two people who are very special to me. Kennedy Fletcher and Mustafa Johnson. Kennedy, Mustafa, my father, Charles Lord."

Kennedy offered his right hand to Charles. "I'm honored, Mr. Lord. Happy Thanksgiving."

Charles took the proffered hand, his eyes narrowing slightly. "Same to you, son. Have you eaten?"

Kennedy glanced over at Mustafa. "No, sir. We haven't."

"Well, come on in and sit down. We'll talk later."

The tense moment over, the crowd parted like the Red Sea and watched Kennedy and Mustafa as they followed Lydia and Charles into the kitchen.

"Yo, Juggernaut, what's up, man?"

Turning to his left, Kennedy stared at Orlando Gibson. "Hey, O.G. What are you doing here?" The two men shook hands, then hugged each other.

"I'm family. I'm married to Sharon Lord. What brings you here?"

Kennedy smiled at his fraternity brother. He'd first met Orlando at an Atlanta Greek Fest during his junior year in college. "Lydia and I are engaged."

Dwayne and Quintin exchanged knowing glances. "Lydia, why don't you fix your *fiancé* and Mustafa a plate, while we get acquainted with Kennedy?" Dwayne drawled softly.

Lydia glared at Dwayne, knowing what her brother was up to. They planned to execute Intimidation 101. "Okay. Mustafa, please come with me."

Kennedy followed Lydia's brothers to the rear of the house and into an enclosed back porch. She'd told him what he would encounter, and he was hard-pressed not to keep a straight face.

Dozens of eyes were trained on him as the men circled him. His gaze swept over those ranging in age from mid-fifties to late teens.

Slowly, methodically he removed his jacket and let it fall to the carpeted floor. Not taking his eyes off Dwayne, he motioned to him. "You first."

Dwayne's jaw dropped. "Say what?"

Kennedy assumed a fighting stance. "I learned a long time ago to take out the big one first. And after I drop you, then I'll take you, then you," he drawled, pointing at Lucien and Quintin.

"Who the hell are you to call me the big one!" Dwayne shouted.

Everyone laughed, some collapsing to the sofa, love seats, and chairs. They laughed until tears rolled down their cheeks.

Dwayne's youngest son threw an arm over his father's shoulders. "I've told you you need to lose that belly, Dad."

It was Kennedy's turn to laugh. Dwayne, still smarting, glared at him. "I can't believe you'd come up in my folks' place and roll up in my face like that."

Kennedy sobered quickly. "I told Lydia that if you don't start none, there won't be none. I came here to meet the family of the woman I plan to spend the rest of my life with, not get into a confrontation with her menfolk. Lydia doesn't need anyone's permission or approval to marry, but it would make things a lot easier if we all got along."

Quintin stepped forward, extending his hand. It was apparent the man Lydia planned to marry could not be intimidated. "Welcome to the family, brother."

One by one all of the men lined up and shook Kennedy's hand. Dwayne was last, smiling and pounding his back. Kennedy stiffened and clamped a hand over his right side.

"What's the matter?" Dwayne asked.

"I'm still recovering from a surgical procedure," he said between clenched teeth. Not only was he still in pain, but he also experienced recurring bouts of fatigue.

"Now, ain't you nothin'? How can you talk about kicking *my* ass when you're in no shape to take a punch, *my brother*?"

Quintin curved an arm around his brother's neck. "Let it go, Dwayne. What you need to do is come with me when I go to the gym."

"Hey, Ken, come sit down and watch this conversion play," Lucien Lord called out as he positioned himself in front the television.

Someone made space for him on a sofa. He sat down, slapping his knee and groaning with the others when the quarterback's snap was intercepted.

Kennedy was so caught up in the game and the camaraderie of the men in the room that he waved Lydia away, telling her he would eat later. She mumbled something about "football junkie," before she stalked back to the kitchen.

Her mother, sisters, and sisters-in-law, who wanted to know the 411 on her and Kennedy Fletcher, surrounded her.

Lydia lay beside Kennedy, her head resting on his shoulder. The light from a bedside lamp fired the flawless cushion-cut diamond set in a pavé band on her left hand. She wiggled her fingers, smiling.

"You can exchange it if you don't like it."

"No, Kennedy. It's exquisite. You have wonderful taste in jewelry."

He chuckled softly. "I have a confession to make. My mother picked it out for me."

"I'll make certain to thank her when I meet her."

Smiling, she recalled the events that followed Kennedy's surprise visit to her parents' house earlier that evening. He never made it to the kitchen to eat his Thanksgiving dinner. He'd become so engrossed in the football game that he wound up eating in front of the television.

Mustafa made friends easily with the younger children. Micah had appointed himself as Mustafa's mentor, and when Kennedy told him he was taking him back to Friendly Heights, he balked. Kennedy and Quintin conferred with each other, and after a lengthy discussion Mustafa went home with Quintin, Victoria, and their children for a sleepover.

Kennedy and Charles had gone for a walk together. After they returned to the Lord house, Kennedy had asked to see Lydia alone. He'd proposed marriage again, slipped the ring on her finger, and sealed his promise to love her always with a breathtaking kiss.

"I love you, my ring, and this house," she whispered near his ear.

The Regency-style house was built on a quiet tree-lined street in a suburb near the D.C.–Maryland line known as Friendship Heights. Kennedy had taken her on a tour of the six-bedroom, five-bath residence, surprising her because most of the rooms were empty.

"The house is yours to decorate any way you want." Shifting on his side, Kennedy faced Lydia. "When do you want to get married?"

She held his steady gaze. "You have a lot of explaining to do, Mr. Fletcher, before I set a wedding date."

He ran a finger down her nose. "What do you want to know?"

She touched the thin scar along the right side of his back. "How did you get this?"

"It's a long story."

Pressing her breasts against his chest, Lydia smiled. "We have all night, darling. Talk to me, Kennedy."

"My biological father needed a kidney."

She listened as Kennedy bared his soul, telling her everything about his childhood, the unrequited love affair between Marvin Kennedy and Diane Fletcher. His voice softened noticeably when he spoke of Philip Anderson, the man who'd become his father and mentor.

"Why did you give Marvin a kidney?"

Turning over on his back, Kennedy stared up at the ceiling. "I was the only compatible donor." He closed his eyes. "I could've said 'the hell with you,' because of how he'd treated my mother. But then I had to ask myself what if? What if I'd needed an organ and no one came forth to help me? My dad always told me, 'Think of the other guy, son, before you say or do something. If you don't like it, don't do it.' "

"How is Marvin?"

"He's recovering—albeit slowly."

"How are you doing?"

Kennedy threw an arm over his head. "I'm also recovering. I'm tired most of the time, but I'm told that's normal for someone who has lost an organ. I'm glad I won't begin coaching until the next school year."

"We don't have to get married this year, Kennedy. I'm more than willing to wait until the spring."

He shook his head. "I'm not."

Lydia stared at his stoic expression. "How about New Year's Eve?"

"Where?"

"Cabo San Lucas."

A smile spread across his face like the brilliance of the rising sun. "We can reserve several villas, fly everyone in a couple of days before, then marry on a yacht. How does that sound to you?"

Rising on an elbow, she stared down at him, complete surprise freezing her features. "When did you come up with this idea?"

"I researched Cabo San Lucas online, then contacted a travel agent who gave me the names of villas in the area." He met her gaze. "If you don't like the idea, then we could brainstorm together."

"There's no need to brainstorm, darling. I love your idea."

His eyebrows lifted. "You do?"

Leaning closer, she kissed him. "I do, I do, I do," she whispered over and over, knowing she would repeat the words again in another four weeks.

Twenty-three

Lydia Charlene Lord stood beside Kennedy Marvin Fletcher, repeating her vows under a half-moon and a star-filled sky. A warm breeze off the Pacific Ocean stirred the fabric of a pearl-colored, bias-cut silk crepe Narciso Rodriquez slip-dress-styled wedding gown. The unembellished beauty of the gown reflected her unique personality—simplicity.

She glanced up at Kennedy through her lashes and a se-cret smile softened her glossy lips. Their gazes met, fused, communicating a love that promised yesterday, today, and all of their tomorrows.

The ship's captain told Kennedy he could kiss his bride, shattering the hypnotic spell. Lowering his head, he circled her waist, pulled her up close to his chest, and kissed her, sealing his promise to love and honor her all the days of their lives.

Clutching a bouquet of gardenia, white roses, tulips, and peonies, Lydia trembled as the realization that she was now a married woman swept over her. The man holding her to his heart was the one in whose arms she wanted to go to sleep and wake up every day, whose babies she wanted to bear, whom she wanted to stand beside her during her successes and failures, whom she would grow old with, whom she would love forever.

"Darling," she crooned softly, "we'll continue this later."

"I can't wait," Kennedy whispered close to her ear.

Hand in hand, they turned to greet everyone who'd flown thousands of miles to witness their nuptials. All of Charles and Etta Mae's children, grandchildren, and great-grandchildren were in attendance along with Diane and Philip Anderson, Roger and Grace Evans, Neil and Rachel Lane and their daughters, Ethan and Joanna Bennington and their three children, and Mustafa. Kennedy had become Mustafa's legal guardian as his foster father.

Now that he'd become a father, Kennedy had softened his attitude toward Marvin. He invited him to the wedding, but Marvin declined, citing health limitations.

Charles Lord extended his arms to his youngest child. She walked into his embrace, her arms encircling his waist. "You look beautiful, baby girl."

Tilting her head, she smiled at him. "Thank you, Daddy."

He kissed her cheek. "Be happy, baby girl."

She nodded. "You know I will."

Kennedy pressed the flesh, kissed scented cheeks, slapped broad backs, and laughed loudly when teased about his wedding night. He'd kept his promise not to make love to Lydia until they were married. Sharing a bed or a shower on occasion tested the limits of his self-control, but he was resolute in his pledge.

The yacht floated over the calm ocean waters as a live band launched into an upbeat dance number that had everyone swaying and reaching for partners. Champagne and non-alcoholic beverages flowed from fountains as white-jacketed waiters passed out hors d'oeuvres to wedding guests who would welcome a new year on the ocean, under the stars in a foreign country.

Lydia found herself in her husband's arms as the clock ticked away the old year. She removed her veil and the three-inch strappy sandals, dancing barefoot on the smooth surface of the boat deck.

He spun her around. "Did I tell you how much I love you today, Mrs. Fletcher?"

Resting her head on his shoulder, she inhaled the hauntingly sensual fragrance of his cologne clinging to the fabric of his dinner jacket. "No."

Easing back, Kennedy stared at her. "I didn't?"

"Not as Mrs. Fletcher."

He pulled her close again, chuckling softly. "I'll be certain to show you later, Mrs. Fletcher."

"I can't wait. And I promise not to take advantage of you," she teased.

"Use me, darling. You won't get a complaint from me."

Kennedy stopped when he felt someone tugging on his jacket sleeve. It was Mustafa. "Are you asking to cut in?"

Mustafa had discarded his tie and suit jacket. Kennedy had selected him to be his best man. "No. I want to know if it's all right if I go back home with Chaz and Micah."

"You don't want to hang out here with us?"

"No. Please, Daddy, can I go back with them?"

Lydia and Kennedy went completely still, their stunned gazes fixed on the boy whom they hoped to legally adopt in the near future. It was the first time Mustafa had called Kennedy Daddy. Lydia looked at her husband as he struggled to conceal his shock.

Kennedy reached out and cradled the back of Mustafa's head. "Yes, son. You can go back with them. I'll call the airline and have them change your ticket." He smiled at the joy shimmering in his son's eyes. "Are you too big to give your dad a hug and kiss?"

Mustafa shrugged a shoulder. "I guess not."

Kennedy went to one knee and put his arms around Mustafa. Lydia pulled up the hem of her gown and braced a hand on her husband's shoulder, her arms covering his around the boy.

Mustafa hugged the man and woman who he prayed would become his mother and father for real and forever. He smiled at Kennedy, then Lydia. "You're the best dad and mommy in the world."

Quintin, professional photographer and commercial artist, raised his camera and captured the tender, poignant family scene for posterity.

"What are you smiling at?"

Turning, Quintin showed Victoria the image he'd captured on his digital camera. "What do you think?"

Victoria stared at yards of silk crepe from Lydia's gown flowing over the polished deck, the expression of serenity on Kennedy's face as he pressed a kiss to Mustafa's forehead, and the wide grin on Mustafa's face as he reveled in the love of his parents.

Blinking back tears, she smiled up at her husband. "It's beautiful, Quintin. You should think about painting it, then give it to them as an anniversary gift."

Quintin lowered his head and kissed his wife. "When did you get so smart?"

"I've always been smart, Quintin Lord. I was smart enough to stand still long enough for you to catch me."

"I thought you were chasing me."

Her eyes widened. "I never chased you, Quintin Thomas Lord."

"Yeah, you did, Vicky. Let's go ask Lydia."

"Don't you dare bother her now. We'll settle this later."

"How much later?" Quintin asked.

Going on tiptoe, Victoria kissed his mouth. "A lot later," she crooned.

Quintin managed to get off three more shots of his sister, his brother-in-law, and his nephew before they rose to their feet. He smiled. His sister had gone to camp to supervise a kitchen and had fallen in love.

Pride swelled his chest. Lydia told him she'd given herself two years to decorate her home and have a baby all before Lady Day's grand opening. With any other person he would've thought her crazy to put that much pressure on herself, but not Lydia. She had more ambition, determination, and competitiveness than any of the Lords.

There was no doubt Kennedy Fletcher had his work cut out for him, but something told Quintin his new brother-in-law was up to the task. He was the only one who'd bested them at their game.

Quintin glanced over at Lydia again. She and Kennedy stood off from the others, holding hands. When she turned and raised her face to accept her husband's kiss, he averted his gaze.

He went in search of his wife and children. The new year was fast approaching, and he wanted to hold on to his loved ones like the image he'd captured with his camera.

"Five, four, three, two . . . Happy New Year!" the ship's crew and wedding guests shouted loudly.

Lydia curved her arms under Kennedy's shoulders and buried her face against his warm throat. "I love you, Kennedy."

He tightened his hold on her slim waist. "I love you, too."

It was much later, after the yacht had docked and they retreated to their villa, that Lydia and Kennedy were able to demonstrate the depth of their love over and over again.

The flickering flames from dozens of votives reflecting off whitewashed walls competed with the glow of the moon that silvered every light-colored surface.

Lydia's gaze was fixed on the man sitting on the side of the bed on a rooftop terrace waiting for her. A smile parted her lips as she closed the distance between them. Kennedy had kept his promise that they would not make love again until their wedding night. Their wedding night had come along with new beginnings. It was a new year and they were husband and wife. A warm breeze lifted the delicate fabric of her nightgown before it settled back around the curves of her slender body.

Kennedy stood up, extending his hand. It had only been months, but unknowingly he'd been waiting years for this moment. Lydia Lord-Fletcher was his love, his wife, and his life. Everything he did, every decision he made he thought of her first.

He smiled when she placed her slender hand in his; he pulled her to his chest and buried his face in her hair. She had worn it up for the wedding, but now the heavy strands grazed the nape of her neck.

"Do you know how long I've waited for this?" he whispered close to her ear.

"Four months," Lydia whispered against his bare shoulder.

"No, baby. All of my life."

Curving her arm under her husband's shoulders, Lydia leaned into him. "I can't wait any more, darling."

Lydia didn't want to wait and neither did he, but they would have to wait because Kennedy wanted their coming together to last as long as possible. The weather was perfect, the setting perfect, and the woman in his embrace also perfect. Bending slightly, he swept her up in his arms and placed her gently on the bed, his body following her down.

Lydia closed her eyes and let her senses take over. She heard the soft lapping of the ocean as it washed over the beach, the fragrant scent of the frangipani and orchids growing in abandon, and firm muscle and sinew under her fingertips.

Kennedy's hands were everywhere: her hair, her throat, her breasts, and between her legs. Her breathing deepened as his weight and smell enveloped her in a sensual spell from which she did not want to escape.

Gathering the hem of her nightgown, Kennedy eased the silken fabric up her legs, thighs, waist, breasts, over her shoulders and then her head. She gasped when his mouth covered one breast, then the other, his teeth tightening on the nipples. He moved down the length of her body and staked his claim at the apex of her thighs. His hands and mouth had her writhing on the bed, as her breath came in long, surrendering moans.

Tears filled Lydia's eyes and flowed down her cheeks as gusts of desire shook her from her head to her toes. "Please . . . please . . . please." Her pleas floated upward and were carried out into the Mexican night on a tropical breeze.

Kennedy heard the soft pleading and moved up the length of Lydia's body. He knew she was close to climaxing and he wanted to join her when ecstasy hurtled them beyond reality.

Parting her legs with his knee, he eased his sex into her hot, wet body, groaning audibly as her flesh closed around his, squeezing and holding him until he exploded in a downpour of fiery sensations.

Once he was able to move, Kennedy reversed their position. Passions spent, they waited until their breathing resumed a normal rate, and still joined fell asleep as contentment and peace flowed between them.

This night was only the beginning—the beginning of all of their tomorrows.

Epilogue

Two years later . . .

> *The sports world A-list turned out for the grand opening of former Ravens running back Kennedy Fletcher's wife's restaurant Lady Day.*
>
> *Food critics were impressed with the décor, the ambience, and the eclectic menu prepared by executive chef Lydia Fletcher and assistant chef Neil Lane. Lady Day, named in honor of Baltimore's own Billie Holiday, is located half a mile from the Inner Harbor and claims an intimacy missing in most dining establishments. Reservations are suggested if you want to experience the most glorious dining experience.*

Lydia fell back on a mound of pillows and kicked up her legs. "We did it, darling."

Kennedy placed the newspaper on the bedside table and reached for his wife. "You did it."

He closed his eyes and nuzzled her neck. His life was better than he ever could've imagined. Lydia had opened her Lady Day. Mustafa Johnson was now legally Mustafa J.

Fletcher and in another three months they would increase their family by one when Lydia delivered a baby girl.

Kennedy's life had changed dramatically since meeting Lydia. He taught high school biology and coached the football team. He alternated checking Mustafa's homework and attending school-sponsored extracurricular activities with Lydia.

Whenever Mustafa stayed over at his cousins' during a school holiday or break, Kennedy and Lydia retreated to the house in the woods to rekindle a flame that never seemed to burn out.

Kennedy placed a hand over his wife's belly. He smiled when he felt the movement. He couldn't wait to meet his daughter. He'd promised Lydia he wouldn't spoil her, but he knew that was one promise he had no intention of keeping.

HOME SWEET HOME

If you and your neighbor have a difference of opinion,
settle it between yourselves and do not reveal any secrets.
—Proverbs 25:9

One

The large airy kitchen was the most functional room in Victoria Jones's newly purchased condominium apartment. A contractor had installed an additional microwave oven, two built-in, eye-level industrial ovens, a rotisserie, an eight-burner gas range with a grill and exhaust system, and a commercial walk-in refrigerator and freezer. These appliances were tools of her trade, and now she was ready to operate VJ Catering at its new location.

Baltimore, Maryland, was not very far from Washington, D.C., yet it was far enough away for her to begin a new life.

Baltimore was far enough away from Victoria's parents, who lamented relentlessly that it was time she consider remarrying.

It was far enough away from her friends, who had settled into a comfortable routine of coming home to a husband and children.

It was also far enough away from her ex-husband, his new wife, and their children. Children could have been born to her and Richard if she had been able to conceive again.

But none of that mattered any longer. She had begun anew—with a new home and a new enterprising business.

She walked up two steps from the brick-walled kitchen to

the expanse of the living and dining areas and up the curving staircase, with its decorative wrought-iron railing. At the top was a loft containing three bedrooms with Palladian windows and towering sloped ceilings.

Everywhere she turned in the apartment there was a sense of space and light.

How different, Victoria thought, this home was from the one she had abandoned when her marriage ended. She and Richard had lived in a stately English Tudor structure with dark walls, floors, and darkly colored leaded windows.

Elegance and tradition. That was what she and Richard Morgan exemplified as young Washingtonians. They were heirs to a dynasty, a dynasty of elite African-Americans who were as much a part of the Capital District's history as was the Washington Monument.

Pulling back her shoulders, Victoria sucked in her breath and exhaled slowly. It had been a while since she had thought about Richard, and thinking about him always brought pain. Somehow it was impossible to remember the good times they had once shared. She decided to exorcise Richard from her mind with the thing he detested most. Her dancing.

Climbing the staircase with a fluidity and grace that had come from a lifetime of classical dance training, she walked into the smaller bedroom she had designed as a dance studio.

Her reflection stared back at her from a wall of mirrored glass. Thick, chemically straightened hair was brushed back off her forehead to the nape of her neck. At thirty-one, she was five foot three, but a long and graceful neck and an incredibly slender body made her appear taller and much younger.

Dressed in a white leotard, matching footless tights, and faded pink ballet slippers, she moved over to the barre and began a series of stretching techniques. She no longer danced professionally, but years of training could not be erased even after the shattered bones in her right ankle. The orthopedic surgeon's prediction of a speedy recovery was realized but his conclusion that the ankle would never be strong enough to withstand the hours of practice demanded from a professional dancer also bore truth.

At twenty-one, a poorly executed *entrechat quartre* had cost Victoria Morgan a dance career, a tiny life nestled in her womb, and two years later, her marriage.

This morning she executed *pliés, jetés,* and several arabesques with relative ease. Forty minutes later the routine concluded with a perfect *tour en l'air*—one complete turn of her body and a graceful *révérence.* A satisfied smile touched her expressive full lips as silent applause roared its approval. She had given a flawless performance.

Her workout ended, as it did every morning, with a luxuriating shower and her velvety-soft skin glowing with a scented cream cologne of pungent flowers and woodsy oils. She slipped into a pair of ivory satin-and-lace bikini underpants and a matching demi-bra. Her hands faltered as her mind registered a low thumping sound reverberating off the bedroom walls.

It was music. There was no mistaking the deep moan of an organ, but it was the accompanying male voice singing a soulful ballad that transfixed Victoria. Whoever was playing the music had turned up the volume.

Throwing a tropical floral print kimono over her half-nude body, she raced out of the bedroom and down the staircase.

The sound of the music grew louder and louder until Victoria felt the pulsating bass in her chest. The only time she had known music to be as loud was when she attended concerts or dance clubs.

Flinging open the front door, she was met with the full force of the powerful sound. The door to the neighboring apartment stood open. There was no doubt her neighbor enjoyed his or her music—at full tilt.

She had closed on the purchase of the apartment more than three months before, but it had taken that long to renovate it before moving in, and she still had not met her neighbor on the two blocks of five row houses, each containing two duplex units.

Most of the units were purchased by young professionals under forty, the remaining to retired couples who no longer had to mow lawns, rake leaves, or shovel snow the occasional time it fell. However, it appeared as if her closest neighbor's development had been arrested at adolescence or the person had undergone some degree of hearing loss.

Victoria walked into her neighbor's entryway and froze. The sight that greeted her was a shock. The sound of the raucous music paled as she noted bundles of old newspapers, palettes of dried paints, and stacks of stretched canvases against every inch of wall space in both the living and dining rooms, discarded articles of intimate apparel—male and female—crushed pizza and take-out food cartons, fishing gear, and a large schnauzer, whose hot breath washed over her bare thighs.

The dog's luminous eyes were partially concealed under a fringe of shaggy black hair as it peered up at her. Victoria prayed the dog wasn't vicious. In any case, she did not want to make any sudden motion that would startle it.

Swallowing painfully, she managed a hoarse, "Nice dog." Her words were drowned out by the rhythmic pounding of the music.

The animal reacted to her friendly greeting by rising on its hind legs and resting both front paws on her shoulders. The weight of the powerful dog knocked her backward and she lost her balance, falling down onto a pile of soiled laundry. She struggled vainly to free herself from the tangle of clothes and the dog sitting comfortably on her middle.

"Let her up, Hannibal!"

It took several seconds before she registered the sound of the male voice. The command was soft, yet carried a ring of unyielding authority.

The man had not *shouted* at the dog because the music had stopped. She had been too startled by the scene she had come upon to realize the absence of the driving, pumping rhythm.

"Hannibal!"

As the dog obediently moved off her body, Victoria stared up at the tall figure looming above her. The man extended a hand and she grasped it. In one smooth, strong motion she was standing. Clear brown eyes in a bearded brown face the color of burnished oak narrowed in concentration. The direction of the man's gaze was fixed on a spot below her neck.

Glancing down, Victoria discovered her wrap hung open, permitting her rescuer a full view of her body in her skimpy undergarments.

With as much aplomb as she could manage, she retied the sash to the kimono. Tilting her chin, she frowned up at the man.

"Do you mind not playing your music so loud," she said haughtily.

"I like it loud," he retorted, a small smile softening his mouth.

She felt her temper flare. "Look, Mr. . . ."

"Lord," he supplied. "Quintin Lord." Grinning, he gestured toward the dog standing at his side. "Of course you've met Hannibal," he continued smoothly. "Hannibal's usually not so demonstrative with his affection. But being a male he just couldn't resist getting close to a beautiful woman."

Gritting her teeth, she warned, "Please keep the music down."

If possible, Quintin's smile widened, displaying a mouth filled with large white teeth. "I'm somewhat partial to Victoria's Secret myself," he remarked, lifting an eyebrow.

At first she thought he was asking her name, but then realized he was referring to her lingerie. Turning on her heel, she stalked out of his apartment and back into her own. She closed the door with a resounding slam but not before she heard a loud chuckle from Quintin Lord.

Victoria stood with her back against the door, trying to regain control of her temper. *He's rude . . . and he's a pig,* she thought. A pig who lives in a pigsty. And his dog was also rude. If she hadn't fallen on the pile of dirty clothes she could have broken her neck.

She made her way to the living room and flopped down on an oyster-white armchair with a matching ottoman. A moan escaped her. Quintin Lord had turned on his music again. The only consolation was that it wasn't as loud as it had been before.

Two

Quintin pushed the litter strewn about the living room into large green plastic bags. The two weeks away had dulled his memory. His last assignment must have left him more stressed out and dazed than usual. He made it a practice not to clean up until he completed a project, and, as evidenced by the number of take-out food containers he had gone through while doing the graphics for an ad agency pitching a new line of beauty products, the normal clutter now bordered on slovenliness. After he had completed the ads he promptly packed enough supplies to spend the next two weeks on his boat visiting the Florida Keys and several Caribbean islands.

Picking up a lacy bra, Quintin dangled it from a forefinger. Of all of the models he photographed, Alicia was the one who always seemed to leave an article of clothing behind. Smiling, he wondered if she ever ran out of underwear. The bra went into the plastic bag with the other discarded trash.

Thinking of underwear reminded Quintin of his new neighbor. The delicate white lacy triangles against her sienna-brown body had been a definite turn-on. He had painted and photographed more nude and near-nude women than he could count since becoming an artist. A woman's bare breasts, thigh, or derriere held as much excitement for Quintin Lord as a speck of lint on his camera lens.

But the beautiful woman with the perfect body who had moved in next door was different, very different.

Her face was small—oval—and her features were even. Everything about her was young and fresh—except for her eyes. They were large and haunted; seemingly haunted with a sadness that belied her young years.

Quintin picked up a windbreaker and tossed it onto a pile of soiled clothing. The motion forced the large schnauzer to move to another comfortable location. Visibly disturbed, the dog growled deep in his throat.

"Don't get too relaxed, Hannibal," he warned his pet. "I have to go to the supermarket and *you* have a date to be groomed." Hannibal growled again, burying his muzzle in the clothes.

Quintin shot Hannibal a look of indifference. "It doesn't matter to me, sport. I can always order take-out." Hannibal only ate canned dog food.

Hannibal rose to his feet, large black eyes trained on his master. To Quintin it seemed as if he and Hannibal were telepathically connected. The dog always sensed Quintin's mercurial moods, while he controlled Hannibal with a mere glance or hand signal; the two had been inseparable since he bought the puppy from his dog-breeder sister two years ago.

"I thought you'd see it my way," Quintin remarked, smiling.

He put out several bags of garbage for the day's pickup, then gathered the soiled clothing that had accumulated from the two-week sailing excursion, while Hannibal waited patiently.

The animal's short tail twitched in excitement as he led him out of the apartment to the four-wheeler parked in one of the garages at the rear of the row houses.

The late-spring sun was unusually warm and foretold of a characteristically hot summer. Quintin enjoyed the change of seasons, but found a special peace sailing miles from land, having only water, sky, and the feel of a deck, rising and falling, under his feet.

His next assignment was to create a series of ads for an African-American clothing designer whose popularity had come from her use of Moroccan beads, Ghanaian cloth wraparound skirts, and Kente cloth trimmings. He predicted the assignment would take three weeks, at the end of which time he would again feel the sensual roll of *Jamila*'s smooth deck under his feet for several weeks before again accepting a new commission.

Quintin made several stops, dropping off laundry before he deposited Hannibal at the dog grooming salon. There was an hour's wait before Hannibal would be ready, so he decided to have his own hair and a month's growth of whiskers cut at the unisex salon located in the minimall. What he enjoyed most about living in the Baltimore suburb was having every big-city convenience on a small-town scale.

Thirty minutes later, his close-cropped hair soft and shining from a shampoo and conditioner, and his brown jaw smooth from an expert shave, Quintin walked into a spacious air-cooled supermarket.

Seeing to his personal needs had always given him a sense of independence, and at thirty-seven he had no immediate plan to alter his lifestyle or change his bachelor status. All he needed was his work, his boat, and his dog to feel complete; as the fifth child in a family of six boys and three girls, he had been forced to carve out his own space and establish his importance and independence early within the Lord household.

He strolled up and down wide aisles, selecting cans and packages, tossing them aimlessly into his shopping cart. He turned into the dairy aisle and saw her.

His gaze moved slowly and sensuously over the curve of

her hips in the slim black denim skirt she had paired with a white T-shirt. Her shapely legs were bare and her tiny feet were encased in black leather flats.

Quintin felt the heat rush through his own body, recalling the woman's near-nude body earlier that morning.

Victoria glanced up and found a man staring at her. There was something vaguely familiar about him, but she could not place his face.

The man was tall, nearly six foot, and arrogantly handsome. His golden-brown face was deeply tanned, his hair cut close and brushed back off a high, wide forehead. A thick mustache obscured his upper lip while failing to hide the sensual fullness of his lower one. He smiled, and recognition dawned. He was her neighbor Quintin Lord!

Victoria chided herself for not recognizing him. There weren't too many men bold or secure enough to wear small gold hoops in *both* ears.

She shivered, not wanting to acknowledge the chill pervading her limbs was from Quintin Lord's penetrating gaze, but was the result instead of the cold air emanating from the freezer cases.

"Good afternoon, Mr. Lord," Victoria said with a deadly calm she did not feel as she perused the crisp khaki shirt he wore with matching slacks and tan deck shoes.

Quintin inclined his head, smiling. "Good afternoon, neighbor."

Victoria extended a small hand. "Victoria Jones."

He had unwittingly guessed her first name. He considered that a good omen.

He flashed a disarming smile, grasping her hand. "I'm sorry we got off to a bad start this morning. Please accept my apology."

She extracted her fingers from his warm grip, returning the smile. "Apology graciously accepted."

He peered into her overflowing shopping cart. "You must have quite an appetite."

Victoria laughed, the sound light and carefree. When her eyes crinkled, her gentle and delicate beauty hit Quintin full force.

"I'm having a housewarming celebration Saturday afternoon," she explained.

At least she hadn't said *we're* having a housewarming, he thought, ruling out a roommate or live-in lover.

Quintin continued to stare at Victoria, his eyes photographing her face and committing everything about it to memory. He had photographed and painted women much more beautiful than Victoria Jones yet there was something about her that haunted him, drew him to her against his will.

He glanced at his watch, then at the contents of his own shopping cart. He still had a few more items to select before picking up Hannibal.

"I'll let you finish up your shopping," he said to Victoria. "See you around."

Victoria nodded. "See you around," she repeated.

She watched Quintin as he moved down the aisle, admiring how well he wore his clothes. His apartment may have been a disaster but Quintin Lord's attire was clean and neat.

Victoria turned her attention back to the long list of items she had to purchase for the housewarming event only two days away. She was looking forward to having her friends over to her new apartment with an almost childlike excitement. It was to be the first time in a long time that the printed invitation read Victoria Jones and not Richard and Victoria Morgan.

She selected her dairy items before heading over to the produce section. Summer fruits were in season and she picked out the most appealing strawberries, blueberries, cantaloupe, several other types of melons, and a variety of fresh vegetables.

She completed her shopping and merely raised an eyebrow when the cashier totaled her purchases. As she handed the cashier three large bills, the bagger quickly and expertly packed her groceries. She thanked the clerk, then pushed her cart through the sliding doors and out into the early-afternoon sunshine.

A tall male figure moved beside her, grasping the handle to the cart. Victoria's short gasp of surprise was momentary. She glanced up at the smiling face of Quintin Lord.

"I thought you'd need help trying to fit everything in your car," he explained quietly.

She stared at the thick brush of hair covering his upper lip before her gaze moved to his strong neck.

"It'll all fit," she said, raising her gaze to meet his. "I have a minivan."

She had bought the vehicle when she'd started her catering business. There was no way she would be able to transport trays of food and serving pieces, stacks of linen, serving tables, and an occasional hired server in an ordinary car.

Quintin steered the cart out to the parking lot. "Then I'll help you load it," he said in a firm tone. "Where are you parked?"

Victoria quickened her pace to keep up with his long strides. "That's not necessary."

Quintin ignored her protest. "Where's your van?"

She knew it was useless to argue with him as she pointed to her right. "It's the navy-blue one in the first row."

She followed Quintin, opening the sliding side door and watching as he emptied the cart, stacking the many brown paper bags in the cargo area and on the fold-down rear seat.

Victoria noted the smooth ripple of firm muscle under the dark-brown flesh of his arms uncovered by the turned-back cuffs to his khaki shirt. She was fascinated by the fluid, graceful line of Quintin's body as he reached for, picked up, and put down each bag. Despite his height, she mused, Quintin Lord easily could have been a dancer.

Quintin pushed the empty cart into a line with others, then turned back to Victoria. He had felt her watching him, and he wondered what was going on behind her haunted gaze.

"I've performed my good deed for today. I do hope that

I'm *truly* forgiven," he said, his eyes crinkling attractively as he displayed his winning smile.

She arched a curving eyebrow. "For what?"

"For my inappropriate remark about your undergarments."

Victoria remembered his comment about her skimpy lingerie and a wave of heat flared in her cheeks. It was not his fault that she had been so scantily clad. And if she had not been so unnerved by the ear-shattering volume of his music she never would have walked into his apartment half dressed.

"Yes, Quintin. You're *truly* forgiven," she returned with a soft laugh.

Quintin leaned closer, the heat from his breath and body increasing the warmth in Victoria's. "See you around, neighbor."

Quintin's *see you around*, the small gold hoops in each ear, the thick brush of his silky mustache, and the graceful leanness of his lithe body nagged at Victoria on her drive home.

Something about Quintin Lord signaled a primitive warning for her to stay away from this very attractive male.

I hope he's married or he at least has a steady girlfriend, she thought, remembering the feminine underwear tossed recklessly on his living-room floor. That would serve as an excuse and a healthy reminder to keep Quintin Lord at a comfortable distance, for she could not permit herself to get close to a man again.

She had given Richard her love, her body, and her life, and it still had not been enough for him.

Victoria stared at the traffic light in the intersection, then glanced over to her left. Sitting in a four-wheeler waiting for the light to change was Quintin Lord. She studied his profile and turned away, pulling out into traffic as soon as the light changed from red to green.

She was too far away to see Quintin's expression in her rearview mirror. If she had, she would have been unnerved. But more than that she would have been shocked if she had known his thoughts.

Three

"Do you like her, Hannibal?" Quintin asked his lounging pet.

The dog raised his head, focused soulful eyes on his master, then lowered his shaggy head back to his front paws.

"What is it about her—this Vicky Jones—that's different?" Quintin questioned in his monologue with Hannibal. She's perfect, he thought. Victoria Jones was not classically beautiful, but she was perfect. He wanted to photograph her; he wanted a likeness of his diminutive neighbor for himself for an eternity.

As a skillfully trained commercial artist, Quintin knew what to look for whenever he photographed a subject: the right camera angle, the proper lighting—and the most effective ways to bring out the best in a subject without artificial props or retouching. This inherent skill made him tops in his field and highly sought after. He was discriminating in whom he accepted as a client, earning fees and commissions that far exceeded those of his colleagues while permitting him to act out his fantasies.

Sailing had been a boyhood craving. After he had worked enough years to save sufficient money, he had a boat built to his specifications. Now, at thirty-seven he discovered he had another craving—Victoria Jones. Without rhyme or reason he wanted the woman.

"Perhaps I'm going through a midlife crisis," Quintin continued to a silent Hannibal. Hannibal blinked slowly at Quintin with mysterious dark eyes.

"Hell, I'm too young for a midlife crisis!" Quintin sputtered. He flopped down to an armchair after pushing a stack of magazines onto the floor. Lacing his fingers together, he steepled his forefingers and brought them to his mustached upper lip. The two fingers stroked the thick coarse hair in an up-and-down motion.

He wanted Victoria Jones. He wanted to know her in every way possible. A part of his body stirred and he knew he wanted to know her in the most intimate way possible.

Quintin buried his face in his hands. He *was* going through a midlife crisis. It had been too long since he had lusted after a woman—any woman.

His sex drive was as healthy as any normal man's, but recently he hadn't felt driven to sleep with any particular woman.

He had proven to himself that he did not need sexual intercourse to exist.

No, he didn't need any woman to exist—that's what he'd always told himself—but some foreign, hidden emotion taunted him now, telling him that was not the case. Why hadn't he felt this way before meeting Victoria Jones?

Victoria felt a strange presence and she turned slowly. Standing outside of her kitchen was Quintin Lord's giant schnauzer.

The dog stood motionless, blinking at her through a fringe of shaggy hair. His tightly curling black coat had been stripped until the pale pink of his flesh was visible.

Crossing her arms under her breasts, Victoria smiled at Hannibal. "Just because I left my door open, that didn't mean you could walk in without an invitation."

The dog lowered its head and turned to walk away. "No!" she cried out. "You don't have to go." Much to her surprise, Hannibal turned and flopped down to the cool wood floor. Resting his muzzle on his front paws, he closed his eyes and began snoring.

"Well, I'll be," she whispered softly, wondering if Quintin knew the whereabouts of his pet. She realized he knew the dog could not have gone very far. The front door of the condominium was self-locking and she was certain only she and Quintin occupied the two duplex apartments.

Victoria busied herself putting away her groceries. The smell of wood still lingered in the spacious kitchen from newly hung oak cabinets. She rinsed fruits and vegetables before storing them away in the bins in the commercial refrigerator, mentally outlining her menu for the housewarming celebration. The dishes she planned to serve would demonstrate her expertise in the culinary arts. The Saturday gathering would be all the advertising she would need to start up her business.

The position of the sun's rays slanting through the kitchen's skylight shifted and Victoria glanced up at the clock over the sink. It was too late for lunch, so she decided on an early dinner.

Hannibal forgotten, Victoria washed, sliced, and set aside several boned chicken breasts. Quickly and expertly she counted out a generous portion of snow peas, then sliced a large carrot, yellow and red bell peppers, a celery stalk, and fresh shiitake mushrooms on a cutting board countertop. She added minced garlic and fresh ginger to a bowl of Oriental sesame oil and soy sauce, then ground fresh cilantro and shallots in a food processor, adding them to the marinade along with lemon juice, freshly ground pepper, and salt. She poured the mixture over the chicken, which would be ready for grilling within the hour.

Stepping over Hannibal, Victoria went upstairs to change her clothes. Slipping out of her skirt, she pulled on a pair of white loose-fitting Indian cotton slacks with a drawstring waist.

Minutes later she returned to the living room and put several CDs on a carousel. The apartment was flooded with the sensual voice of Luther Vandross.

Victoria's romantic mood was mirrored by the musical selections she had chosen: Vandross, Anita Baker, Brenda Russell, and David Sanborn. If she had felt stressful, her choices would have been different: Yanni, Andreas Vollenweider, or David Arkenstone. New Age music melted away her anxiety, transporting her to a sphere of fantasy.

It had been three years since she had been swept away by fantasy. At twenty-eight, she met a young man in France. They both had enrolled in a ten-week graduate culinary program at the La Varenne École de Cuisine, completing their courses successfully; however, their liaison did not survive the predictable summer romance syndrome.

Victoria had no desire to marry Masud and set up an eating establishment in his native Burundi. It also had not mattered to her that Masud was a true prince, the eldest son of a tribal chief, heir to both his father's throne and his millions. Prince Masud was quick to explain that his family owned the largest coffee plantation in the small, densely populated, land-locked African country.

She saw Masud off at Orly Airport, telling him she would always think of him as a special friend. Masud bowed over her hand and called her his queen.

She left Paris a week later and returned to the United States as a highly trained and skilled banquet and pastry chef. She spent another two years working for a prestigious Washington, D.C., hotel before deciding it was time she went into business for herself.

Returning to the kitchen, she looked around for Hannibal, searching the pantry, dining area, and the entryway. Shrugging her shoulders, she closed the door. The dog had probably gone back home.

Victoria completed the preparations for her dinner, making a Greek salad to accompany her main dish of grilled chicken with stir-fry vegetables. She busied herself for the next hour while the chicken absorbed the mixture, then, switching on the grill, she placed several strips on the red-hot grating, turning them quickly to prevent overcooking.

Victoria heard the soft chiming of her doorbell and went still. She made her way to the door and peered through the peephole. Recognizing Quintin Lord, she opened the door. Her pulse leaped as she surveyed his lithe form in a pair of paint-spattered shorts and an equally paint-spattered tank top.

"Yes?" Her voice was lower and more husky than normal, and for the first time Quintin noticed her distinctive southern drawl.

His gaze swept quickly over her face. "I'm looking for Hannibal. Have you seen him?"

Victoria opened the door wider. "He was here, but I can't find him now. I thought he had gone home."

Quintin shifted a black eyebrow, his gaze locked with Victoria's. "Do you mind if I try calling him?"

She stepped back, and Quintin walked into the entryway. Placing both forefingers in his mouth, he whistled shrilly. Seconds later Hannibal bounded down the stairs, tail twitching nervously. He jumped up and down against Quintin's thigh, excited to be reunited with his master.

Quintin scratched Hannibal behind his ears. "Hey, homey. What are you doing hiding out here?"

Hannibal responded by barking loudly and winding his way in and out between Quintin's legs.

Victoria laughed as she watched the dog's antics. It was apparent Hannibal was glad to see Quintin. Her smile faded slowly. As much as she did not want to admit it, she was also glad to see him. In his revealing outfit his sun-darkened body was exquisite.

She suddenly gasped loudly. "Oh, no!" Her food was

burning. Turning, she left Quintin staring at her retreating back as she raced into the kitchen.

She managed to salvage several strips of grilled chicken before they were charred beyond recognition.

"It smells wonderful," Quintin remarked, leaning against the entrance to the kitchen. He had followed her. His sherry-colored gaze swept over the furnishings in the large space. "And it looks as if you're ready to do some serious cooking in here," he added softly.

"I'm a caterer," she admitted, placing several more strips of chicken on the grill.

Quintin walked into the kitchen, carefully noting the ovens, commercial refrigerator and freezer, and the strange-looking utensils and culinary gadgets suspended from overhead hooks.

Resting a hip against a counter, he stared at Victoria's delicate profile as she concentrated on the grill. "What's your specialty?"

She smiled at him. "Everything. I'm a master chef."

"What did you have to do to become a master chef?"

"Demonstrate skills of an exceptional level in cooking, baking, presentation, cold foods, nutrition, and facility design." She sounded like an culinary school advertisement.

Quintin's impassive expression did not change. He never would have guessed her profession. He figured her for someone who worked with small children.

He took a seat on a tall stool near the cooking island, watching Victoria examine the strips of chicken.

"Was it difficult?" he asked without warning.

She turned slowly, taking her time in answering his query with one of her own. "Was what difficult?"

"Venturing into a field that has been dominated by men."

"I never let that deter me," she answered as honestly as she could. There were times when she met some opposition, but refused to let it thwart her goal to become a master chef.

Quintin leaned back, resting both arms on the back of the

stool. The motion caused the cotton fabric of his tank top to stretch across the expanse of his broad chest.

The sensual, unconscious motion was not lost on Victoria as she averted her gaze from his body. Quintin Lord was slim and loose-limbed, yet solid and muscled. It was evident he worked out regularly.

"Did you always want to become a chef?" he continued with his questioning.

Victoria shook her head, not looking at him. "No." She swallowed the rising lump in her throat. It was never easy to talk about her aborted dance career. It brought back too many other unpleasant memories.

"I was trained to be a dancer," she admitted.

Quintin gave her body a long, penetrating look. He glanced down at her tiny feet in a pair of white ballet slippers. Victoria felt her cheeks heat up as his gaze retraced its path, then lingered on her face.

"What kind of painting do you do?" she asked, giving him an equally bold stare.

She had to admit to herself that he was the most attractive man she had seen in a long time. There was something lazily seductive about his lounging stance. Her gaze moved to his mustached mouth and she wondered what it would be like to feel the hair on his upper lip against her own mouth. Would it tickle? Would it scratch? Or would it feel both rough and soothing at the same time?

"I'm a freelance commercial artist."

"Are you good?" she questioned quietly.

His eyes darkened with an emotion that seemed to drink in everything about her. "Yes, Vicky Jones," he replied just as softly. "I'm good. In fact, I'm very, very good."

She smiled, unaware of the captivating picture she presented. "I'm glad to know that," she replied, knowing he wasn't talking solely about his artistic ability.

"What medium do you work in?" she questioned.

"Primarily oil, acrylic, watercolors, and on rare occasions charcoal. Why do you ask?"

"I'm looking for several watercolors for my living room. I've gone to a few shops and galleries, but I haven't found anything I'd like to look at day after day."

Quintin moved off the stool and stared down at her up-turned face. The haunted look in her eyes was absent and in its place was openness and curiosity.

"I may have a few watercolors tucked away at my place. I'll try to hunt them up, then offer you a private showing."

Victoria sensed his teasing mood. "Are you serving hors d'oeuvres and champagne?"

He leaned closer, grinning broadly. "I'll supply the artwork and champagne. The only hors d'oeuvres I'd be able to offer would be chicken fingers with a plethora of plastic-packaged sauces. I'm willing to wager I have the most extensive collection of take-out menus of anyone within a three-mile radius."

Victoria laughed. "I'll supply the hors d'oeuvres."

Quintin grasped her right hand, pressing his lips to her soft palm. "Bless you, child."

She almost gasped aloud at the pleasurable jolt racing up and down her arm. The feel of the thick brush of hair on her sensitive flesh was intoxicating. She stared at his lowered head, unable to believe this man, her neighbor, could turn her on so easily.

"What time, Quintin?"

He raised his head, still holding on to her hand. His brow furrowed. "What?"

"What time do you want to show me your paintings?"

Quintin released her hand. Touching Victoria Jones and inhaling her feminine fragrance had unnerved him. "Seven," he said quickly.

"A.M. or P.M.?"

Regaining control of his emotions, he crossed his arms over his chest. "I jog at seven A.M. You're more than welcome to join me."

Victoria shook her head. "I don't jog. I broke my ankle ten years ago, and there are times when I can't put too much pressure on it."

"Are you all right walking?"

She nodded.

"Then we can walk tomorrow."

"Perhaps some other time," she suggested, tactfully turning down his invitation. Agreeing to see him to purchase artwork was one thing. Going for early-morning walks was something else entirely different.

"Then it'll be seven P.M.," Quintin countered. "My place or yours?" he asked with a wide grin.

Victoria remembered the clutter in Quintin's apartment. "My place—if that's okay with you."

"Your place it is. See you around."

Turning on his heel, Quintin turned to leave, whistling softly. Hannibal's head came up alertly and he pranced after his master.

Victoria followed after a few minutes and locked the door. She retreated to the kitchen, humming along with Luther Vandross's "Superstar," ignoring the little voice warning her to stay away from Quintin Lord.

It's not going to be that easy, she thought. After all, the man was her neighbor. There was no way she could avoid him even if she wanted to.

But she had to admit to herself that she didn't want to. Not yet.

Four

Victoria glanced around her living room, pleased at what she saw. Soft light from a floor lamp bathed everything in a warm pink glow. A sofa, love seat, and matching armchair in an oyster-white Haitian cotton cradled watered silk throw pillows in mauve and gray and complemented the pale-pink area rug on the highly polished wood floor.

The mouth-watering aromas from her day-long marathon cooking session had been extinguished by the highly efficient exhaust system, and newly opening pink-and-white tulips in a large vase filled the room with their fragrance.

She let out a soft sigh of relief. She had prepared all of the dishes she would need for her Saturday housewarming celebration: hors d'oeuvres, main and accompanying side dishes, and delectable desserts. The only dishes she hadn't prepared and refrigerated were the fresh green salads.

Lighting fat white vanilla-scented candles on the cherry-wood side tables, she stood back and admired her handiwork. The dining-room table had been set with a snowy linen cloth with elaborate cutout designs, translucent china, gleaming silver, and delicate crystal stemware.

Positioning a fork, Victoria examined it for even a dot of tarnish. Satisfied that everything was in order, she picked up a remote device and flicked on her stereo unit. The ballet score from Aaron Copland's *Billy the Kid* flowed from the speakers. She had danced the Americana ballet at fourteen, and along with *Swan Lake* and the *Nutcracker* it had immediately become one of her favorites.

When the doorbell chimed, Victoria glanced at the clock on the mantel over the living-room fireplace. It was exactly seven. *He's on time,* she thought, making her way to the door.

When she opened the door, Quintin's easy smile was slow in coming. He found it hard to believe the subtle change in Victoria's appearance could transform her ethereal femininity into one that virtually shouted its presence with the softly curling hair framing her face, the light cover of makeup highlighting her features, the shimmering white silk blouse and slacks covering her body, and the exotic scents clinging to her warm brown flesh.

His smile broadened and Victoria stepped aside. "Please come in," she urged, taking the bottle of champagne he offered her. "I'll put this in some ice."

He followed her into the dining room, admiring the soft shadows of the pink light reflecting off the pale walls.

Victoria settled the bottle of champagne in a large crystal bowl filled with ice, watching Quintin as he moved into the living room. He examined the photographs of her family on the mantel while she silently admired the graceful slimness of his male body in a black shirt and slacks.

He turned without warning and caught her intense stare. Victoria felt heat steal into her cheeks, but she did not drop her gaze. She pushed her hands into the hidden pockets of her slacks to hide the slight trembling of them.

He returned her bold stare, seemingly reaching into her very thoughts. He saw curiosity and some other emotion he could not yet define.

"Lovely," he said in a quiet tone. "You and your home," he explained when she shifted her eyebrows.

"Would you like a tour while the champagne chills?"

Quintin moved closer to her, pulling her left hand from the pocket of her slacks. He cradled her much smaller hand in his, squeezing her fingers gently. "Lead on."

Victoria registered the heat and strength of his strong grip and threaded her fingers through his. She smiled up at him. "We'll begin with the second level."

Hand-in-hand Victoria led Quintin in and out of the three rooms. He chuckled softly when he saw the room she had set up as her dance studio.

"Do you ever give private performances?" he teased.

She flicked off the light, shaking her head. "No."

"Not even by special request?" he insisted, standing very close to her.

"No!"

Victoria could have bitten off her tongue. She had not meant to snap at him, but she would never dance for an audience again. She would dance for one person—herself.

Quintin watched a myriad of emotions cross her face. "Was it that painful, Vicky?"

"The injury or my giving up a dance career?" She answered his question with one of her own. She did not add giving up a child she would never hold or a husband she had loved unselfishly.

"Everything. Everything that went along with giving up your dance career."

She managed a brave smile. "It was painful, but I recovered."

Quintin moved closer, trapping her body between his and the door. "I take that to mean that you're carrying no excess baggage from your past."

Victoria felt somewhat annoyed by his line of questioning. He was asking a lot from her. After all, he was only her neighbor—and a stranger at that.

Tilting her chin, she stared up into his sherry-colored eyes. "What you see is what you get," she answered in a flippant tone.

He flashed a devilish grin, his teeth showing whitely

under the thick mustache. "And just what is it you're offering, Miss Jones?"

"What any other neighbor would offer, Mr. Lord. A cup of sugar, picking up your newspaper or mail when you're on vacation, and perhaps bringing you a cup of hot tea if you're down with the flu."

He stepped back, surprise clearly written on his face. "Oh, those things," he replied.

"What else did you have in mind?"

Quintin shrugged broad shoulders under his black sand-washed silk shirt. "Nothing. Nothing," he mumbled.

He had barely registered the furnishings in the other rooms. He was too busy trying to sort out his reaction to Victoria Jones. What was it about his neighbor that made him feel and react like a gauche adolescent?

He was certain he was more worldly than she, but there was a strange wisdom about Victoria that made him doubt she would ever lose her cool no matter what the circumstances.

She had ventured into a career in what most considered a man's domain and she had survived. Not only was she beautiful, but she was also bright and confident.

"That concludes the tour," Victoria stated, leading Quintin down the hall to the staircase.

Quintin spent the next hour sipping champagne and sampling the exquisite hors d'oeuvres Victoria had prepared. He bit into a grape leaf stuffed with goat cheese, pine nuts, and currants. He followed that with smoked salmon and caviar on toast points.

"This is definitely X-rated food," he sighed.

"It is a bit sensual," Victoria agreed.

He thought of it as downright erotic. His lids lowered as he studied Victoria in the way he usually studied a model. The food she had prepared as well as the white silk outfit she wore were all erotic. Even her hair—curled softly around her face—was erotic.

He stared at her over the rim of his fluted glass, a slight smile lifting the corners of his mouth. "I must admit that I'm enjoying your music."

Victoria laughed openly. "I didn't think you'd appreciate my taste in music."

"It isn't something I would buy, but it'll do."

"What do you like?"

"The blues and R&B."

"Not that stuff you were blasting yesterday?" she asked, wrinkling her nose.

"Exactly. B. B. King, Otis Redding, Bobby Blue Bland, Wilson Pickett, Aretha Franklin, James Brown . . ."

"I get the picture," Victoria said, grimacing.

"What's wrong with them?"

"Nothing, Quintin."

He saw her lips twitch in amusement as she turned her head. "Could it be, Miss Victoria Jones, that you're lying to me?"

Victoria managed a straight face. "Never, Mr. Lord."

Quintin stared at her, pleased to note the sadness had left her gaze. He wondered who or what had hurt her so deeply that it was mirrored in her eyes. Reaching over, he refilled her glass with the pale, sparkling wine. He had refilled his own glass three times to her one, and he was beginning to feel the effects of the champagne.

"Would you like to view the paintings?" he asked. He had to get up, do anything except sit and stare at Victoria Jones. She was delicate. Hypnotic. Her body was tiny and perfectly formed, her face young and innocent. Her voice was soft, feminine and controlled; perhaps too controlled.

Victoria's large eyes widened perceptibly. "Yes, Quintin."

He rose to his feet, seemingly in slow motion. It seemed like hours, but it took only minutes for him to retrieve the drawings from the case he had left by his front door.

Hannibal blinked slowly at him, licked his whiskers, then promptly went back to sleep. Quintin had explained to Hannibal that he was going next door—alone.

Victoria cleared a portion of the dining-room table, and when Quintin returned, she watched him lay out the water-color drawings.

She caught her lower lip between her teeth as her heart pounded wildly. Quintin Lord was right. He was very, very good! The images seemed to jump at her while pulling her in at the same time. The soft muted shades of a lavender and indigo sky cradled the stark branches of white birch trees in the blazing splendor of a setting sun, firing the land with reds, raw sienna, ocher browns, and green.

Quintin felt, rather than saw, her reaction to the painting. "If you like this one the next one should really please you," he stated confidently.

He was right. That one was also a landscape, with purple hills and stark white birch trees swayed by the force of a rushing orange and yellow waterfall. Droplets of water dotted the trees like sprinkling snow. The background was mauve, pinks, and soft lavenders. Instead of an orange sun there was an orange moon. The painting was large; perfect for her living room.

"I want it, Quintin." She was hard pressed to keep the excitement from her voice.

He rested his hand on her shoulder in a possessive gesture. "It's yours."

Turning slightly, Victoria stared up at him. "How much do I owe you?"

"Nothing," he whispered.

"Nothing?" she repeated.

"Nothing, Victoria."

"No," she protested, shaking her head. "I can't—"

"It's a housewarming gift," Quintin cut in.

"But you can sell it—"

"I'll never sell it," he interrupted again.

Her feelings for this man intensified with every moment

she spent in his presence, but there was no way she wanted to be obligated to him—not for anything.

"Have you shown this to anybody?"

"No."

"Why not?"

Quintin shrugged a shoulder. "I never got around to it."

"That's why you haven't sold it," Victoria stated with a smugness she didn't actually feel.

His hand moved from her shoulder to her neck, then to her chin, lifting her face to his. "If you insist on buying it, then I'm more than willing to negotiate the terms, Miss Victoria Jones," he said, lowering his head.

Victoria felt the hardness of his chest against her breasts, the strength of his fingers around her waist, and the mastery of his mouth as it worked its magic on her lips.

She became a part of Quintin, feeling what she felt when she saw his paintings—being pulled in and floating in and out of hot and cool colors of orange and lavender.

The hair on his upper lip was startling, totally masculine and masterful. She groaned, inhaling, and her lips parted. His tongue moved tentatively into her mouth, then withdrew.

Raising his head slightly, he stared down into her startled gaze. "That was only the down payment. I'll take the rest in twelve equal installments," he teased with a smile.

Victoria's shoulders shook uncontrollably. She couldn't stop laughing as she rested her forehead against Quintin's chest. Slender arms encircling his waist, she collapsed against his body.

"You're impossible, Quintin."

He rested his chin on the top of her head. "No, Vicky, I'm good; very good."

Placing both hands against his chest, she gave him a gentle push. "I think I need some leverage in this deal."

Quintin's lids lowered slightly over his gold-brown eyes. "Are you proposing a counteroffer?"

"How would you like to put away some of your take-out menus for a while?"

His smile was wide and dazzling. "Are you saying you'll cook for me?"

She nodded. "I have to cook for myself, so I'll just prepare a little extra for you."

"You've got yourself a deal." He released her and reached for the painting. "I'll frame this and hang it for you."

"Thank you, Quintin."

He stared at Victoria, nodding. *Don't thank me,* he thought. He should be the one thanking her—thanking her because for the first time in a long time he wanted a woman, and wanted her for more than a sexual encounter.

The night had begun and ended well—for both of them.

Five

Victoria opened her apartment door early Saturday morning to the announcement of a flower delivery at the same time a tall, beautiful, pencil-thin woman quietly closed the door to Quintin's apartment. The woman flashed a mysterious smile, slipped on a pair of over-size sunglasses, and strutted sensuously down the hallway and out of the building.

Victoria exhaled, smiling. It appeared as if Quintin Lord was involved with a woman, and knowing this would remind her not get too involved with her neighbor.

The delivery of flowers from a local florist was quickly followed by a second delivery from a nursery that left a towering sequoia cactus, with a note from her parents. She directed the nurserymen to position the tree near the sliding-glass doors leading to a spacious patio, which spanned the length of the kitchen, living, and dining rooms. This signaled the delivery of several more large house plants and exquisite serving pieces she could use when entertaining.

She prepared green salads, set up the serving tables on the patio, thankful that the weather was warm, with sunny skies and a hint of a cooling breeze. Selecting background music, a variety of differing wines, arranging flowers, and wiping away a light layer of dust from the cherry-wood furniture took up most of the morning. Glancing at the kitchen clock, she knew she only had an hour before her guests were due to arrive. Since most of her friends lived in the D.C. area, she had decided on a luncheon instead of a dinner.

Forty-five minutes later, Victoria, dressed in a silk T-shirt in a flattering apricot color and a sweeping black silk chiffon skirt of many layers, opened the door to her father and mother.

At sixty-eight and sixty-six respectively, William and Marion Jones's exuberance and stylish elegance belied their ages. William, a former ambassador to Seychelles and Togo, and Marion, a former French teacher, had taken their newly retired status seriously. Both of them had become avid golfers.

"Welcome, Mom and Dad," Victoria said, greeting her parents warmly. "Thank you for the cactus."

Marion Jones's dark brown eyes darted quickly around the entryway as she made her way into the living room. "I like it, sweetheart," she said, examining the cathedral ceiling and the light pouring in through floor-to-ceiling windows.

William Jones folded his daughter into a rib-crushing embrace, lifting her easily off her feet. "You've done it, honey."

Victoria kissed her father's smooth jaw. "And you didn't think I could."

William smiled, nodding his head. "I knew you could. It's just that I feel better knowing you're not living alone in some isolated part of the city."

"I do live alone," Victoria retorted, frowning up at William after he'd released her. Aware of her father's outdated belief that women shouldn't live alone or that they needed a man to protect them, she quickly changed the topic. "Come and see how I've decorated the upstairs," she suggested.

Petite silver-haired Marion smiled. "William and I will look around. You stay here and greet your guests."

Victoria knew her mother was annoyed. She only called her husband William when that was the case. Normally she would have called him Bill or sweetheart. Everyone was a "sweetheart" to Marion Jones.

William and Marion ascended the curving staircase and the doorbell chimed again. Victoria answered the ring, releasing the building's outer door, then waited for her best friend to make her way down the hall.

Red-haired Joanna Landesmann reminded Victoria of a sparkling penny. Her short hair was a shiny copper, her friendly eyes a bright clear brown, and a light sprinkling of freckles stood out across her pert nose and sculpted cheeks.

"Welcome!" Victoria called out, greeting Joanna with a warm smile and kiss on her cheek. "Thank you for the beautiful flowers and the punch bowl."

Joanna returned the kiss. "Glad you liked them. You just don't know how many times I drove past this place and wanted to stop by. But I managed to quell my inquisitiveness and waited for today."

"My, my, my. Have you changed, Miss Landesmann?"

Joanna affected a moue. "One must grow up one day."

At thirty, Joanna was mature except when it came to affairs of the heart. The professional party planner always seemed to pick the wrong man to fall in love with. Her boyfriends took advantage of her generous nature, breaking her heart before Joanna realized it was she who did all of the giving in their relationship.

Victoria led Joanna into the kitchen. "Who are you in love with now?"

"No one, and I don't expect there will be anyone for a long time. I've sworn off men."

"For how long?" Victoria couldn't help smiling.

"It's been over two months." Joanna's expression was more serious than sad.

This disclosure surprised Victoria. She and Joanna had worked for the same hotel in Washington, D.C., and become fast friends from the first time Joanna, as banquet manager, conferred with Victoria, who as the sous chef monitored every station in the kitchen. The two women discovered they shared similar tastes in music, old movies, antique and craft shops. Like Victoria, Joanna eventually left the hotel to go into business for herself. Joanna still lived in D.C., but she and Victoria managed to get together every other month for lunch or dinner.

"What happened to that lobbyist, Jo?"

"I sent him packing. He was such a liar, and you know how I hate liars."

Victoria smiled. "Good for you."

Joanna returned her smile. "It felt good to give him his walking papers," she stated, glancing around the kitchen. "I don't believe this place. It's incredible."

Victoria nodded her thanks, experiencing twin feelings of pride and apprehension: pride because she was the only one controlling her career, but some apprehension because she desperately wanted her catering enterprise to be a success.

The front doorbell chimed again, and Victoria went to answer it. Over the next half hour it chimed many more times. By two o'clock everyone had arrived and settled down to sample the different dishes Victoria Jones had prepared for the guests who had come to wish her well in her new home and new business endeavor.

Nathaniel Jones, co-anchor on a D.C. cable news station, dropped an arm around his sister's shoulder. Leaning over, he kissed Victoria's cheek. "Do you think you can whip up something special for Christine's parents' fortieth wedding anniversary?"

Victoria glanced over at her sister-in-law who was engaged in an animated conversation with the elder Joneses.

"You have to let me know how many people I'm serving and whether you want a sit-down dinner or a buffet."

"I think a buffet dinner is preferable."

"How many, Nat?"

"Christine has compiled a list of sixty-two."

Victoria curved an arm around her brother's waist. "I'll fix something nice."

"Low-fat sauces, no-cholesterol desserts, and low-sodium cheese spreads for the middle-age matrons please," he teased.

"I'm going to tell Christine what you've said."

"No, Vicky, don't. She claims at least once a day that I don't like her family."

Victoria smiled up at her tall, well-groomed, handsome brother. "But you don't, Nat Jones."

"That's because they are puffed-up snobs."

"Look who's talking," she retorted, snorting delicately and walking away. Nathaniel Jones was so conservative that he had earned the name Clark Kent. It followed him throughout his years as a Washington, D.C., journalist and now as a popular television news anchor.

Victoria mingled among her guests, graciously accepting their compliments on her cooking. Many of them had taken the elegant business cards she had left on the side tables in the living room.

Her sister Kimberly was the first to leave. She had to return to Silver Spring to breast-feed her three-month-old son. Victoria handed her a decorative bag filled with several containers of food.

"This is for Russell. He called earlier and asked for samples."

Kimberly laughed. The last thing her high school football coach husband needed was food. It was a constant battle for Russell Abernathy to keep his weight under two fifty.

"Maybe I'll tell him you forgot to give them to me," Kimberly said.

"I won't lie for you, Kimm."

"I thought sisters were supposed to stick together."

"Not when my brother-in-law can power lift me with one hand," Victoria countered with a wide grin.

Kimberly shrugged her slender shoulders. "I guess it's the least I can do for him for babysitting."

"Kiss the baby for me, Kimm."

Kimberly noted the longing expression in her older sister's eyes. "I will. But why don't you come down and see him and kiss him yourself?"

Victoria averted her gaze. "I will. As soon as I settle in I'll be down."

It was a lie and both women knew it. Victoria had only seen her nephew once since his birth. She found it difficult to hold the tiny baby and not think of her own barren womb. She had come to the sad conclusion that she would never be able to claim as her own any baby she held.

Victoria hugged and kissed her sister. "Thank you for coming."

Kimberly held her close. "Thank you for inviting me."

The small crowd dispersed in groups of twos and threes over the next three hours, leaving Joanna and Victoria savoring cups of freshly brewed cappuccino.

Joanna anchored her feet on a rung of the tall stool in the kitchen. She licked a dot of frothy milk off her upper lip. "How would you like a partner?"

Victoria put down her cup, staring at her friend. "What are you talking about?"

Joanna blushed to the roots of her dark red hair. "Well, not exactly partners. But . . . something like a collaboration."

Resting her arms on the butcher-block countertop, Victoria's eyes narrowed. "What are you hatching, Jo?"

"I've done rather well putting together weddings, bridal showers, school reunions, and sweet sixteen parties. And I'm certain you're going to be a big success once word gets out that you cater these same events. And . . ."

"And?" Victoria asked when Joanna hesitated.

"I want to help you for helping me when I broke up with Addison Fletcher. What I'm trying to say is whenever I contract to do an event I'll recommend you as the caterer."

"That's not necessary, Jo. My business will come around in its own time."

"But why struggle to build it up when you can come out of the chute at full speed. I've managed to contract for at least two to three events a month and most of my contacts have been through referrals. I've even stopped spending money on advertising. I have a client who gives a luncheon for her bored and idle rich friends at least once a week. The woman spends nearly two hundred dollars a pop on flowers alone, while the firm that caters her food is horrific. They serve the same bland, boring food week after week."

Victoria picked up her cup, taking a sip of the fragrant coffee. "Apparently the bored and idle rich ladies are satisfied with the food being served."

"They can't be. They only come because Mrs. Sunny Calhoun is the social grande dame of Baltimore's National Preservation Society. Please, Victoria, let me talk to her about your services. She only has to try you once. If she doesn't like what you prepare she can always go back to the other caterers."

"Let me think . . ." The doorbell chimed melodiously, preempting what Victoria was going to say. "Excuse me, Jo."

She went to the door and opened it. Quintin Lord filled the doorway, an irresistibly devastating grin curving his mouth.

"Hi," Victoria whispered, her heart pounding loudly in her ears.

His gaze swept quickly over her face and body, missing nothing. "Hi," he returned, the single word soft and caressing. "I framed your picture. If you don't mind I'd like to hang it for you."

She stared up at him as if she had never seen him before. "If it's a bad time I'll come back later," Quintin said quickly.

Victoria inhaled sharply. Seeing Quintin Lord again was overwhelming to her senses. Whenever she was in his presence she couldn't ignore the tingle of excitement inside her. And at that moment it hadn't mattered that she saw a woman leaving his apartment earlier that day. This man—her neighbor—evoked passions she thought had faded when her marriage ended.

The realization washed over her. She wanted Quintin Lord!

"I . . . I have company," she stuttered.

Quintin pulled his gaze away from Victoria, focusing instead on the profusion of flowers, houseplants, and the seguro cactus near the patio doors. He had deliberately kept himself busy all day rather than think about her, but he had failed miserably.

When he least expected it, the image of Victoria Jones had crept unbiddingly into his mind, disrupting his concentration and causing his thoughts to wander. He had been so distracted that even his art students asked if he was feeling well. He'd said he was, but he wasn't.

He had spent the last twenty-four hours recalling the softness of her skin, the fragrance of her perfume, and the taste and feel of her mouth when he had kissed her.

Vicky Jones had gotten to him. The woman didn't appear to be the slightest bit interested in him, yet she had gotten to him.

I'm losing it, he thought, running a hand over his face, and at that moment he knew he had to do something without letting Victoria know what he had planned.

He lowered his hand, staring intently at her upturned face. "I'll come back later." He was so enthralled with her tiny body covered in silk and airy chiffon that he almost missed the tall red-haired woman making her way toward them.

Victoria noted the direction of Quintin's gaze and glanced over her shoulder. She turned back to him. "I'd like for you to meet a good friend of mine, Joanna Landesmann. Jo, this is Quintin Lord, my neighbor."

His attention temporarily diverted, Quintin extended his hand. "My pleasure."

Joanna grasped his hand, her clear brown eyes sweeping appreciatively over his face. "The pleasure is *mine,* Quintin."

Victoria registered a familiar tone in Joanna's voice. She was flirting with Quintin whether she was aware of it or not.

Quintin released Joanna's hand, his gold-brown gaze softening as he smiled down at Victoria. "I'll see you later." He nodded to Joanna. "Nice meeting you."

Victoria closed the door behind him, then turned to smile at a grinning Joanna.

"He's gorgeous," Joanna whispered.

"That he is," Victoria agreed solemnly.

"What are you going to do about it?"

"What in the world are you talking about?"

"Is he married?"

"I don't think so."

"Is he engaged?" Joanna continued.

"I don't know."

"Find out, Miss Jones!"

"Why should I?"

"Because you need a man."

Laughing, Victoria shook her head. "Now you're beginning to sound like my father. I don't need a man."

"How long has it been, my friend? Two, maybe three years?"

"And it'll be even longer, Jo. Right now I don't have time for a relationship."

Joanna folded her arms over her chest, giving Victoria a questioning look. "What's wrong, Vicky? You dated that representative from Ohio, but you broke it off just when the man was ready to propose to you. Then there was that undersecretary from the Defense Department who was here one day and gone the next."

Victoria wanted to scream at Joanna to mind her own business. There was no way she could explain to her friend that she didn't want to become involved with a man because the moment they mentioned marriage and children she rejected them. They'd want children and she couldn't have children, and there weren't too many men who were willing to adopt someone else's child.

Joanna glanced down at her watch. "I think I'd better be getting back before I run into D.C. traffic. Thanks again for the invite."

Victoria flashed a warm smile, then hugged Joanna. "Thank you for coming. And I promise I'll think about your offer to go in with you."

Joanna's face brightened with a smile. "Please do. I think we'd make a dynamic duo."

"Like Batman and Robin," Victoria quipped.

"Tarzan and Jane," Joanna countered.

"Abbott and Costello."

"Peaches and Herb," Joanna shot back.

"Desi and Lucy," Victoria said, giggling.

"Ike and Tina," Joanna sputtered.

"Not!" they both chorused, laughing.

Joanna picked up her large handbag. "I'm out of here."

Victoria walked her to the door and waited until she walked down the hall and out into the warm Baltimore evening.

The door to Quintin's apartment stood open, and Hannibal ambled out and sniffed at Victoria's legs. Leaning over, she scratched him behind his ears.

"Hey, Hannibal. How are you?"

Hannibal responded with a loud bark and moved closer to her.

"Don't jump, Hannibal," came a stern command behind her.

She turned around and smiled up at Quintin. "He didn't jump on me this time."

Quintin's gaze was fixed on her mouth. "I gave him a lecture about jumping on you."

"It's obvious that he's quite obedient."

Quintin shifted a black eyebrow. "He's been trained to obey."

Her heart started up its uneven rhythm again. There was a tangible bond between her and this man that was so apparent and startling, it robbed her of speech and reason.

His gaze moved with agonizing slowness from her mouth to her throat, then down to her chest. Victoria felt her breasts tingle against the silky fabric of her T-shirt.

The man was making love to her without touching her. How was that possible?

She stared back with longing and there was no way she could hide her desire for him from him.

"Have you eaten?" she asked, her voice a throaty whisper. Quintin shook his head, not daring to speak, move, or break the spell he'd woven without his being aware of it.

Victoria swallowed painfully. "I'll fix you a plate."

Quintin had to move. She walked past him and into her apartment, leaving him staring after her, his fists clenched tightly.

Turning, he walked stiffly into his apartment, his rebellious body betraying him. He'd lied. He wanted Victoria Jones for herself and for sex. He *was* lusting after the woman.

Six

Victoria stood at the doorway to Quintin's apartment, holding a tray filled with several covered dishes. Hannibal rose from his lounging position at the door, his soft whining alerting Quintin someone had invaded the canine's territory.

"Come in, Vicky."

She stepped into the entryway, noting most of the previous clutter was missing; however, half-completed canvases were still lined up against the living-room walls while a camera perched on a tripod was positioned in the middle of the room.

Quintin appeared and took the tray from her hands and placed it on a table. "Are you going to join me?"

"No," she said quickly. "I've eaten."

"How was your housewarming?"

"A smashing success."

Quintin shifted his eyebrows. "A smashing success," he repeated, smiling. "You sound like a Brit."

Victoria gave him a saucy grin. "Would you prefer that I'd said it was all that?"

Throwing back his head, he laughed. "I never would've thought you'd know any street slang."

"Why?" She managed to look insulted.

"Because of your taste in music, Miss Jones."

"What's wrong with my taste in music?"

"It's all wrong. It has no feeling, no passion and no soul."

"And yours does?"

"Yup," he said smugly. "You can feel my music. It pulls you in and sweeps you along with the rhythm, not releasing you until the last note fades away."

"That's your opinion, Mr. Lord."

He sobered. "And it's my opinion that you're a fabulous cook and a very beautiful woman."

Victoria was caught off guard by his compliment, but somewhere she managed to find herself and her voice. "Thank you, Quintin."

He nodded, smiling. "At least we can agree on that," he said softly, staring back at her in a waiting silence. "I'd like to contract your services for a dinner party."

"When, where, and for how many?"

Quintin slipped his hands into the back pockets of his jeans. "Wednesday evening. Here, and dinner for two."

Victoria's breath caught in her lungs. He had just complimented her, then within the same breath asked that she cook for him and another woman. She recovered quickly.

"What do you want me to prepare?"

"I'll leave that up to you?"

"You must have a preference—fish, poultry, or red meat."

"A shellfish appetizer and a poultry entrée. Any vegetable and dessert you choose will do."

"Do you want me to provide wine or liqueurs?"

"Yes to both. In fact, Victoria, I want you to select everything from the food, to the music and anything else I'd need to make a favorable and lasting impression on a woman."

She forced back a grimace. The Cheshire cat grin on the face of the woman leaving his apartment earlier that morning spoke volumes. Her expression indicated not only had Quintin impressed her, but he had also satisfied her.

She flashed a false smile, admitting to herself that she couldn't afford to be distracted by romantic notions.

"You intend to entertain a woman in this . . . this . . . this . . . *hovel*?"

Quintin shrugged wide shoulders. "I paint, Miss Jones, not keep house."

"Then you should hire a housekeeper," Victoria shot back, not caring whether he heard the censure in her voice.

"Hire one for me," he countered, struggling not to laugh.

"I'll do just that." Victoria spun around on her heel and walked out of his apartment and back into her own, the sound of his laughter following her and echoing in her head.

When she slammed her door, she thought how the sound resembled the crack of a rifle.

Fool!

She had been a fool to give Quintin Lord even a passing thought even though he had kissed her. Besides, they had nothing in common; they were complete opposites.

Maybe Jo was right. She had been without male company for too long and she was desperate.

But she wasn't desperate; she was alone by choice not because she couldn't attract a man.

Her eyes widened and she bit down on her lower lip to keep from laughing hysterically when she thought about attracting a man.

She would make certain Quintin Lord wouldn't pay any attention to his long-legged date or his meal.

Wednesday night would be a night to remember—for everyone.

Victoria inspected Quintin's kitchen and living and dining rooms, declaring it all clean and tidy and paid the cleaning woman she had called for her services.

"It looks rather nice, doesn't it?" Quintin remarked as he stared down at the shining surface of his dining-room table. "I don't think I've seen the top of this table for months."

That's because you live like a slob, Victoria thought. She managed to give him a saccharine grin.

"I'm going to take Hannibal over to my sister for the night," Quintin stated evenly, examining her enchanting profile.

"Why? Doesn't he like your girlfriend?" she questioned. Hannibal stared up at her, whining softly.

"They like each other a little too well and I don't want to compete with my pet for a woman's attention."

Turning, she glanced up at Quintin. Hannibal might like Quintin's girlfriend, but Victoria doubted she would make a similar impression with the woman. "What time do you want me to serve dinner?"

"Eight. If you need to set up anything before then, just walk in. I'll leave the door open."

"I'll probably begin setting up about seven forty-five." She wiggled her fingers at him and gave him a wink. "I'll see you later."

Victoria wasn't as concerned about the dishes she had selected for Quintin's dinner party as she was about her own appearance. She had prepared everything she was to serve Quintin and his dining partner, but she didn't have much time to fix her face and hair.

She showered and washed her hair in record time. But she used the better part of an hour to blow dry her hair and curl it with a curling iron. The tiny curls bounced around her head and forehead as she picked them out with her fingertips.

Victoria moisturized her body with a creamy, scented lotion and added a dot of perfume behind her ears, at the base of her throat, on her inner wrists, and behind her knees.

A mischievous smile softened her lush mouth when she eased her slender body into a white tank dress. The body-hugging garment revealed every curve of her petite frame. She had changed underpants several times before she found a pair that would not show under the snug dress. The dark brown lace bikini panties were as equally risqué as the dress that ended six inches above her knees.

Making up her face, utilizing the professional techniques she'd learned years before when she had performed on stage, Victoria highlighted her best features.

Satisfied with the results, she slipped her bare feet into a pair of black patent-leather sling-back sandals. The three-inch heels made her dress appear even shorter. All the better, she thought.

Running her fingers through her hair again and fluffing the curls, she smiled at her reflection in the bathroom mirror. She washed her hands, dried them, then descended the stairs to serve Quintin Lord and his date.

At exactly seven forty-five Victoria pushed a serving cart into the neighboring apartment. Quintin was nowhere to be seen. She spread a lace tablecloth over the dining-room table, and set the table with china, silver, crystal, and cloth napkins. Next, she arranged a bouquet of delicate yellow roses in a crystal vase that doubled as a centerpiece. Lemon-scented candles, dimmed overhead chandelier, a bottle of white wine chilling in a silver bucket, and a compact disc playing soft music set the mood when Quintin finally made his way down the staircase.

He saw the vision in white bending over the table, rearranging glasses and silverware, and he nearly lost his footing. Victoria was clothed, yet every curve of her body was outlined by the form-fitting tank dress. She couldn't have turned him on more if she had been naked.

He stared numbly, appraising her perfect legs in the high heels. The muted light caught the smooth darkness of her exposed flesh, making it a shimmering brown satin.

His gaze moved slowly over her flat belly, her rounded hips, and the soft fullness of her small breasts.

Victoria glanced up. When she saw him, her smile flashed sensuous and mysterious. "How does it look?"

"Beautiful. Beautiful," he repeated, coming closer.

Somewhere in the living room a clock chimed softly. It was eight o'clock.

Victoria stared up at Quintin, stunned by his appearance. Again, he was dressed in black, but this time his attire was linen instead of silk.

His jaw was clean-shaven, his hair soft and shiny, and the smell emanating from him was clean, manly, and intoxicating.

"Your date is late," she stated quietly.

Quintin's hands came up slowly and his fingers curved around her bare upper arms. "No, she isn't." He stared deeply into her eyes. "You're my date, Vicky."

Victoria would've fallen if Quintin hadn't tightened his hold on her arms. He pulled her closer until her breasts were flattened against the hardness of his chest.

Lowering her head, she began to laugh. So much for making his date jealous. Her plan had backfired.

"You tricked me, Quintin."

Pressing his mouth to her forehead, he kissed her curls. "I'm sorry about that. I'll try and make it up to you," he crooned.

Tilting her chin, she stared longingly into the depths of his sherry-colored eyes. "How?"

"I'll begin with this." His head came down and his mouth covered hers gently yet masterfully.

Her slender arms wound around his waist, her feminine heat and fragrance sweeping over him.

The feel of his thick, silken mustache sent shock waves throughout her nervous system as his tongue searched out hers, capturing it in a dance of desire.

Quintin cradled Victoria's face between his hands, afraid to touch her body, for if he touched her he would never have the opportunity to romance her. She would end up sharing his bed. It wasn't that he didn't want to sleep with her, but it was too soon. She was different from the other women he had gone out with, and that was something he could not forget.

Victoria felt the heat, a ripple of excitement, and the rising passion. Her whole being seemed to be poised, waiting for something she hadn't experienced in a long time.

She was waiting for fulfillment—a fulfillment that was just out of reach.

A fulfillment she wanted to experience, but not yet. It was too soon.

"Quint, please," she murmured against his searching, questing lips.

Quintin's fingers threaded sensuously through her hair, his fingertips massaging her scalp and causing her nerves to come alive in a warm, tingling sensation.

Unconsciously, she pressed closer while praying he would release her. If he didn't let her go she would embarrass herself. She didn't want to beg him to make love to her.

He released her mouth but not her head, and Victoria buried her face against his hard chest, trying to bring her emotions under control.

"I think I've just paid for the watercolor—in full," she breathed out in a heavy sigh.

"I don't think so, Vicky."

"Why?" she crooned, inhaling his after-shave.

"You tried to seduce me."

Pulling back, Victoria stared up at him. "I did not try to seduce you."

"Then what do you call this . . . this postage stamp-size garment pasted on your body?"

She managed to look insulted. "It's a dress, Quintin."

"Yeah, right. And I'm Michelangelo di Lodovico Buonarroti Simoni."

"And I love your ceiling," she countered softly.

"Don't try to change the topic, Miss Jones. Were you or were you not trying to seduce me?"

"No," she answered truthfully. She wasn't trying to seduce Quintin. She just wanted to make his date jealous. "Come, it's time to eat."

What Quintin wanted to eat was not on tonight's menu, but this wouldn't be the last time Victoria Jones would find herself in his arms. After all they were neighbors and there was no way they could avoid each other.

Seven

Victoria felt Quintin watching her every motion. She was thoroughly embarrassed. She had worn the skimpy dress to divert some of the attention away from his so-called date but unknowingly she had garnered his attention—all of it.

Bending down, she unloaded a lower shelf of the serving cart and placed a bowl of three-pepper salad on the table, along with an accompanying lobster, papaya, and avocado salad on crisp red-leaf lettuce leaves.

Straightening, she folded her hands on her hips, the toe of one shoe tapping angrily on the floor. "Have you seen enough?"

Biting down on his lower lip to stifle his laughter, Quintin nodded slowly. "For now." He extended a hand. "Come sit down. I won't have you waiting on me."

"But you're paying me to wait on you," she retorted.

"There's going to be a slight modification. Tonight I'm paying for your cooking and your company."

Taking his hand, Victoria allowed him to seat her. He took a chair to her right at the head of the table, flashing a grin.

"I knew what you were up to the moment I saw you in that dress," Quintin confessed.

"You . . . you couldn't," Victoria sputtered, heat flaming her cheeks.

Lowering his chin, he gave her a long, knowing look. "You didn't dress like that the other night when you invited me to your place, so I figured you wanted to make a statement."

Bracing her elbows on the table, she rested her chin on her fists. "What did I want to say?"

His gaze swept leisurely over her face. "That you're *all* woman, Vicky Jones."

Oh, how wrong you are, she thought. *I may look like a woman but there is something missing.*

Schooling her features not to reveal her inner turmoil, she managed a false grin. "Guilty as charged."

Quintin reached for the bottle of wine and removed the cork effortlessly. He poured the fragrant pale liquid in her glass, then filled his own. Lowering his head slightly, he gave her a sidelong glance. Victoria found the gesture not only charming but endearing.

"Do you dress like *this* for other men?" His voice was quiet, and heavy with sarcasm.

Victoria unfolded her napkin and placed it on her lap. "On occasion," she replied truthfully.

"On how many occasions?"

Her lashes swept up and she gave him an innocent look. "A couple," she answered with a shrug of a bare shoulder.

Quintin's mouth tightened under his mustache. Victoria Jones was a flirt *and* a tease.

"May I make a request, Victoria?"

She raised her delicate eyebrows, giving him an expression of innocence that disarmed him immediately. "Of course, Quintin."

"I . . ." He hesitated, not wanting her to think he was domineering or a chauvinist. He chose his words carefully. "Will you not wear that dress or anything quite that fitted if you . . . you agree to go out with me."

Victoria glanced down at her dress. "You think this is too tight?" she asked with an incredulous look on her face, unable to resist teasing him.

"You bet your . . ."

Her head came up slowly. "My what?" she drawled with an exaggerated flutter of her lashes.

Quintin's thunderous expression vanished when he realized she was teasing him. Leaning closer, he trailed his left hand over her silken cheek. "You can bet your tutu it's too tight."

Both of them laughed at the alliteration and their laughter set the mood for the evening.

Quintin was effusive in his praise as he tasted each dish she had prepared. He had never developed a taste for avocado, but its pairing with the flaky succulent lobster meat and the sweet papaya juice in a tarragon vinegar and delicate olive oil sauce changed his mind.

He took a forkful of hoppin' John, biting into a succulent shrimp. "Oh, Vicky," he moaned, closing his eyes. "This is better than my mother's."

"I decided to add a Cajun touch with the shrimp and spices," she informed him.

Quintin took another forkful. "Yup. I think you've outdone Mrs. Etta Mae Lord."

Victoria laughed at Quintin's boyish banter. He looked like a child in a bakery. "I take it your mother is a good cook?"

"One of the best," he admitted. "She had enough practice cooking for a husband and nine children."

She blinked slowly, her mouth gaping. "You're one of nine?"

"Six boys and three girls," he said proudly.

"You could've been a baseball team."

"The Lords were quite a handful. However, no one, and I mean *no one*, crossed Etta Mae Lord. She made certain we were clean, cooked wonderful meals, and kept everyone in line with just a look. It was my father who was the teddy bear. His favorite saying was, 'Etta Mae, let up on them. After all, they're only children.' He had no way of knowing that if his wife had let up on the children he probably would've had to ask permission to enter his own house."

Victoria's eyes were crinkled with laughter. "Where are you in the birth order?"

"Fifth. My folks had six boys before they got their first girl. Then they decided to try again and it was another girl and then another."

"Why did they stop at nine?"

"They ran out of bedrooms. Our house had six bedrooms, including a nursery, and my mother felt two kids to each bedroom was enough. She believed the eldest boy and girl should have their own rooms, so that left the others to double up."

"It sounds as if you had a lot of fun."

Quintin smiled, nodding. He cheerfully related the scrapes and episodes they managed to hide from their eagle-eyed, perceptive mother, who at times threatened she was going to find a job outside of the house and leave her offspring to fend for themselves.

"Her threat was taken quite seriously," he continued. "My mother had a nursing degree, and she could've always worked per diem at a local hospital, but she gave up her career to become a homemaker. So whenever she talked about getting a *real job,* we always solicited our dad's support, and he firmly made his point when he told Etta Mae he worked a sixteen-hour day just to make certain his wife could stay at home and take care of his children."

"What does your father do?"

"He owns an auto repair shop." Quintin registered Victoria's serene expression and slight smile. She was delicate and alluring, and it was the first time she appeared totally relaxed and at ease with him.

"Tell me about the Joneses." He took a sip of wine, silently admiring the flickering glow of the soft candlelight on her satiny skin.

"There's not much to tell," Victoria began. "I'm one of three, and the middle child. I have an older brother who is a journalist and a younger sister who's a teacher.

"My parents are both retired and they're thinking about a second career as amateur golfers."

"What were their first careers?"

"My mother was a French teacher and my father worked for the State Department. He was an ambassador to Seychelles and Togo."

This disclosure intrigued Quintin. "Did you live in Africa?"

"No," she replied, shaking her head. "My father was too uneasy about the political structure of these newly independent countries to have his family live with him on a permanent basis. We visited on our school holidays and during the summer."

"It must have been fascinating." Quintin's expressive gold-brown eyes were shining. "I've always wanted to be part of a sailing expedition to Africa."

"Sail?" Victoria gave him a skeptical look. "Why not fly?"

"Because I'd rather sail." Leaning back slightly, he crossed his arms over his chest. "I have to admit that I like sailing more than anything else in the world. It's become somewhat of an addiction."

"How long have you had this addiction?"

Resting his arms on the table, he leaned closer to Victoria. "All of my life, Dr. Jones," he whispered quietly.

"Have you done anything to assuage this somewhat unusual craving, Mr. Lord?" she returned in a soft, soothing tone, playing along with him.

"Yup," he replied, nodding slowly.

She leaned closer. "How?"

"I bought a boat."

It was Victoria's turn to arch her eyebrows. "A sailboat?"

"A cruiser."

"Where do you keep it?"

"I have a slip down at a marina near the harbor. Have you ever been to the Keys?" She shook her head in the negative. "How would you like to sail down one weekend?" he asked.

Victoria stared at the expectant expression on Quintin's face. She wanted so much to refuse his offer but couldn't. His easygoing, relaxed manner was stirring and magnetic. With Quintin she never had to be on guard. She could be who she was without measuring every word or every gesture. She could be Victoria Jones and no one else.

"I'd like that very much."

Quintin let out his breath slowly, nodding, and his bright smile mirrored his intense pleasure. Everything he'd planned was falling into place. His newest craving was about to be assuaged. He would have Victoria Jones where he wanted her—on his boat, out on the ocean, miles from land.

"Do you have anything planned for next weekend?" he queried.

She mentally visualized her calendar, remembering she had to plan for her brother's in-laws' wedding anniversary fête.

"No. I'm free," she confirmed.

"Good. We'll leave early Friday morning and come back Sunday night."

Victoria ignored the warning that drew her to Quintin Lord, telling herself that he was her neighbor and they were complete opposites. There was no way she could become involved with him. Like the other men who'd been in her life since she'd ended her marriage, she would keep him at a distance.

It was with much reluctance Quintin dropped his gaze from Victoria's face, asking, "What's for dessert?"

Victoria rinsed the dusting of flour off her hands and picked up the telephone after the fourth ring.

"Miss Jones?" came an unfamiliar female voice on the other line.

"Speaking," she answered, cradling the receiver between her chin and shoulder.

"Miss Jones," the woman continued, "your name and number were given to Dr. Pearson by Mr. Quintin Lord, who's here recovering from emergency oral surgery."

Victoria's stomach made a flip-flop motion. "Is . . . is he all right?"

"He's fine, Miss Jones. It's just that he won't be able to drive home because of the anesthesia. Dr. Pearson would like to know if you'd be responsible for seeing that Mr. Lord gets home."

She glanced up at the kitchen clock. It was nearly four o'clock. "Of course." She wrote down the address of the oral surgeon, then hung up. Seconds later she dialed the number to a local taxi service, giving them her address and telling them to pick her up in ten minutes.

After changing into a pair of jeans and a yellow T-shirt, Victoria brushed her hair and covered it with a matching yellow painter's cap.

She hadn't seen or heard from Quintin in two days. He'd escorted her back to her apartment the night of their dinner party, giving her a chaste kiss on the cheek and a generous check to cover the cost of preparing dinner and the cleaning woman's services.

The following morning there was no thumping music coming from the neighboring apartment or the sound of Hannibal's barking. The next day was a repeat of the day before. Victoria rang Quintin's doorbell, but received no response. Shrugging a shoulder, she returned to her own apartment, temporarily dismissing her elusive neighbor.

The taxi sped through downtown Baltimore, weaving dangerously in and out of rush-hour traffic. She paid the driver and walked into a modern office building.

Making her way through the mass of humanity flowing out of the air-conditioned building and into the city's humidity, Victoria found an elevator that took her to the eighth floor and the professional offices of Dr. Arnold Pearson.

Dr. Pearson handed her a printed sheet of paper. "Please follow the instructions on this page, Miss Jones. It is imperative that Mr. Lord not rinse his mouth for twenty-four hours. He shouldn't smoke, drink hot liquids, or attempt to drink through a straw. I don't want him to interfere with the normal clotting process; however, if there's excessive bleeding be certain to call my emergency number. Please remind him that he's to come back in a week for a follow-up visit. I'm also going to give you a prescription for a pain reliever. He's to take one tablet every four hours as needed."

Victoria stared numbly as the dentist handed her a prescription. She had to fill the prescription, drive Quintin home, then see that he followed all of the oral surgeon's instructions.

Slipping the prescription in her pocket, she smiled up at the dentist. "May I see Mr. Lord?" She followed him to a small room. Quintin lay on a bed, eyes closed and the left side of his face swollen from the packing cushioning his gum and jaw. Moving to his side, she touched his hand. His drug-glazed eyes opened immediately as he managed a grimace.

Victoria's delicate fingers went to his forehead, and she noted the growth of whiskers on his unshaven cheeks. Smiling, she leaned over his prone figure, her warm, haunting fragrance washing over him and helping Quintin to temporarily forget his discomfort.

She had come. He didn't know why, but somehow in the drug-induced nightmare he'd just experienced he thought she wouldn't come.

"I'm taking you home," she said quietly.

Quintin nodded and allowed Victoria to help him from the bed. Leaning heavily against her, he dropped an arm over her shoulders and placed one foot in front of the other. An emotion he'd never felt before struck a vibrant chord in him. He had deliberately stayed away from Victoria for the past two days, sailing aimlessly along Chesapeake Bay until an unexplained pain in the back of his mouth forced him back to land. Leaving Hannibal with his sister, he drove to the dentist. After a brief examination he had undergone emergency oral surgery for an impacted wisdom tooth.

He'd run from Victoria, but it had been useless. He needed her and he wanted her; but more than that he realized he was falling in love with her.

Eight

Quintin spent the next sixteen hours groping through a fog of darkness, warmth, and a softly crooning female voice. The only thing he was certain of was that he wasn't in his own bed. The scent and softness that was Victoria Jones surrounded him each time he surfaced from his drugged sleep.

Opening his eyes, he turned his head slowly. A hint of a smile crinkled his eyes but not his frightfully swollen jaw. It took herculean effort but he pushed himself into a sitting position. The motion caught Victoria's attention and she raised her head from the book she had been reading.

"Good morning." Her voice was soft and inviting.

Quintin mumbled a good morning, falling back weakly to the mound of pillows behind his head.

Victoria rose from a pale-green-and-white striped love seat and made her way across the bedroom to the bed. Bright sunlight pouring through the floor-to-ceiling windows shadowed her figure in brilliance as she moved closer to where Quintin had spent the night sleeping comfortably with the aid of the white pill she had given him.

Sitting down on the bed, she placed a cool hand on his forehead. Her dark eyes moved quickly over his face. The gauze packing had been removed from his mouth, yet the left side of his face remained grotesquely swollen, and some discoloration was evident along his jawline.

"Are you hungry?" Her warm breath washed over his face.

Quintin nodded. It had been more than twenty-four hours since he had eaten. The toothache had begun the morning after his dinner date with Victoria but he had ignored it. The throbbing pain continued off and on, prohibiting him from eating any solid foods. The discomfort grew progressively worse until he was blinded by the pain, and what he couldn't understand was that his last dental examination four months ago hadn't picked up anything.

"I'll make something soft for you to eat." Her gaze was filled with gentle concern. "Do you want something for the pain?" Victoria questioned.

"No more," he moaned, shaking his head. He didn't like the feeling of helplessness and not being in control. The tooth was gone, and it wouldn't be long before the pain would also disappear.

Victoria walked out of the bedroom, making her way down the winding staircase. After leaving the dentist, she had managed to get Quintin into his four-wheeler and struggled to support his sagging body enough to secure him with the seat belt. He'd slept while she stopped at a pharmacy to fill the prescription, waking only when she parked the auto at the rear of their house. He remained conscious long enough for her to open the door to her apartment where she pulled and pushed him up the staircase. She had decided to let him sleep in her guest bedroom so that she could monitor his recovery, but they never made it. Quintin collapsed at the top of the stairs, nearly crushing her when she fell under his solid body. It took another ten minutes to anchor her hands under his shoulders to pull him across the floor and into the bedroom that was closest to the staircase—her bedroom.

Quintin lay on the carpeted floor for an hour before waking again. He'd mumbled incoherently as she coaxed him onto the bed and removed his clothing. He swallowed one of the pills and promptly fell into a deep, painless slumber.

She had spent the night on the convertible love seat, sleeping fitfully and listening for a sound from the bed. Quintin had slept without waking throughout the night while she awoke feeling fatigued and aching. Her well-conditioned body had suffered the effects of her trying to move a man who weighed at least one hundred and seventy-five pounds.

Victoria returned to the bedroom with a bowl of luke-warm creamy oatmeal filled with applesauce and milk. She set the tray down on the bedside table, then handed Quintin a warm cloth and towel to clean and dry his face. When she sensed he seemed embarrassed by the gesture, hesitating to take the cloth, she turned her back to straighten the bed covering.

"Feeling better?" she asked, folding back the white eyelet comforter.

"Yes-s," he slurred, managing to wash his face, though unable to open his mouth comfortably.

She turned back to him, taking the cloth and towel. Smiling, she placed the tray across his lap. "You have another six hours before you'll be able to rinse your mouth with warm saltwater."

Quintin picked up a spoon. "I need to shave and take a shower," he mumbled.

Victoria smiled at him. "After you eat I'll help you."

His eyes widened and he shook his head. "No." He wouldn't mind Victoria helping him shower or even sharing a shower with her, but only if he was in control of his every thought and action.

She saw the frown settle into his features as he stared back at her. Her gaze inched down from his face to his bare chest. The sheet had fallen to his waist, and for the first time Victoria Jones felt the impact of the sensuality of the half-naked man in her bed. His shoulders were broad, his chest hard and furred with coarse black hair which tapered down to a narrow line over a flat belly, and his arms were long and ropy with lean, hard muscles.

She had realized all along, of course, Quintin Lord was a man but it was only now that she saw him as all *male*. She herself was female; a female who had denied her femininity for years. When had it all happened and why had she allowed herself to wallow and drown in self-doubt?

"If you fall and hurt yourself in my shower I'll finish you off before you can sue me," she threatened sarcastically.

Quintin lowered the spoon and closed his eyes. He tried smiling, but could produce only a grimace. Opening his eyes, he stared at the angry expression on her face. "I won't fall," he said, raising the spoon and scooping up the oatmeal. He watched Victoria watching him. By the time he'd emptied the bowl her frown had disappeared.

Leaning over him, she took the tray. "Hurry up and get better, Quintin. I'm not very good at playing Florence Nightingale. I'm a chef not a nurse," she snapped, fighting her growing attraction for him.

He stared at her mouth, recalling its soft sweetness and the nectar he had tasted over and over. He loved her mouth; he loved her perfect little body, and he was in love with Victoria Jones.

His mind clear for the first time in hours, he quickly calculated what he needed to do to make Victoria his.

"I'm sorry," he apologized, and fell back on the pillows. Sighing, he turned his face away from her, closing his eyes.

Victoria felt properly chastised. She hadn't meant to snap at him. Oral surgery was not something any person welcomed. But she couldn't help her responses or her unexplained hostility. Quintin Lord was in her house, in her bed, and she didn't want him in either place. Or did she?

Feelings she felt long dead were back. After her divorce she refused to date, concentrating instead on her new career. Only Masud had been able to penetrate the shield she'd erected, but once the summer ended and she left Paris, the shield was back in place.

She had dated occasionally while she worked in Washington, D.C., but she never permitted the relationships to develop to a point where there would be talk of marriage or babies.

Victoria didn't mind a relationship—one that would remain platonic. She wanted Quintin Lord as her neighbor, not as her lover.

She sat down on the side of the bed. "I'm the one who should apologize, Quintin." She didn't see him smile. Patting his bare shoulder, she said, "I'll get all the things you'll need to shave."

Quintin waited for Victoria to leave, then, on shaking legs and wobbly knees, made his way into her bathroom. Bracing his back against a wall, he managed to shower and wash his hair without falling. Wrapping a towel around his waist, he returned to the bedroom, noting that Victoria had made the bed. She had turned back the sheets and laid out a change of clothes for him. His shaving equipment was on the bedside table.

He needed her and she had come. She had comforted him and given him sustenance, and she had done it because he was her neighbor.

He recalled Victoria's statement when he asked what she was offering. *What any other neighbor would offer, Mr. Lord. A cup of sugar, picking up your newspaper or mail when you're on vacation, and perhaps bringing you a cup of hot tea if you're down with the flu.*

Dressing slowly, Quintin's thoughts were filled with Victoria Jones. She had admonished him about his music and the untidiness of his apartment while she teased, flirted, and seduced him. She was a beautiful and enchanting enigma he wanted to make his own.

Victoria had recovered from the startling realization that she was inexorably drawn to her neighbor by the time she reentered the bedroom. Quintin lay on the bed, wearing a

T-shirt and jeans, his bare feet crossed at the ankles, reading one of the Walter Mosley's Easy Rawlings mysteries she had left on the table next to the love seat.

He glanced up from the book, the fingers of his right hand going to his cheek. "Do you mind if I finish this chapter before you shave me?" Quintin asked through clenched teeth.

She swallowed hard and met his bold stare. He was pushing it.

"But you said you'd help me, Vicky." His voice was low, his expression contrite.

She didn't know whether to scream at Quintin or turn on her heel and walk out of the room. Having a wisdom tooth removed should not have rendered him an invalid.

Folding her hands on her narrow hips, Victoria sauntered over to the bed. "What else do you want me to do for you?"

Quintin closed the book and placed it on the bed. Exhaling heavily, he closed his eyes. If it wouldn't hurt so much he would've roared with laughter. She was on to him.

"It's not what I want you to do for me. It's what I want you to make for me."

She stood over him, staring down at his handsome face. "What?"

He reopened his eyes. There was just a hint of a smile inching the corners of her mouth upward. "Brownies. Double fudge chocolate, please."

"With or without the walnuts?"

"No nuts, please. Remember, I can't chew."

Victoria pushed her right fist under his nose. "You may not have a choice, neighbor, because I'm ready to feed you a knuckle sandwich."

Quintin reached for her hand and placed it along his swollen jaw. The silken skin on the back of her hand grazed the stubble of hair on his cheek.

Closing his eyes, he inhaled the haunting, cloying fragrance of the perfume on her wrist. His fingers tightened gently on her hand as he pulled her closer, losing himself in her delicate, feminine warmth.

He was floating again, this time without the aid of the painkiller. The images he had glimpsed in his dreams sprang to life.

Effortlessly, he pulled Victoria up over his body until her breasts were molded to the solid hardness of his chest. She lay rigid, her cheek pressed to his throat. Counting off the seconds, Quintin waited for her to relax before she sank into the cushioning of his protective embrace.

"Quin-tin?" His name came out low and hesitant.

His left arm moved from her waist to her shoulders, making her his captive. When his left hand cupped the back of her head, the gesture elicited a soft sigh of pleasure from her parted lips.

"I just want to hold you, Vicky."

And I don't want you to let me go, Victoria replied silently.

She wanted Quintin to hold her. The warmth of his arms was so masculine, so comforting. And it had been a man's protection that she missed most of all.

She had learned her assertiveness and independence from her mother, but Marion Jones had constantly reminded her daughters that there were times when a woman needed protection only a man could offer.

Marion's advice was manifested during the ten weeks Victoria lived in France completing her graduate studies. Having Masud as her companion thwarted the advances of other men and permitted her to feel completely safe.

"Vicky," he moaned against her hair. He was in pain. His jaw ached and his heart bled. His craving for Victoria Jones had surpassed his craving for sailing. He desired her body but he wanted the whole woman more. Her warmth, fragrance, and her soft curves enveloped him, and despite his claim that he didn't have to sleep with her, his own body hardened with desire.

Smoothly and unhurriedly, he eased her down to lie beside him, his breath coming quickly. "I need a pill," Quintin gasped. He had to rid himself of the pain in his jaw and the shadow of foreboding tightening the muscles in his chest; something told him that for the first time in his life he would not get what he wanted. Some unnamed emotion whispered that Victoria Jones was beyond his grasp.

Nine

Quintin stared up at Victoria through half-lowered eyelids, his chest rising and falling evenly. The pain medication was working slowly. Slowly enough for him to savor the pleasure of her shaving him.

He had been too shocked to protest when she had straddled his thighs and lathered his face with shaving cream. Her warning of "don't move and don't say a word" was heeded as he rested his back against the pillows and yielded to her gentle touch.

The three-day growth of whiskers itched unbearably, and he did not want to risk further discomfort by scratching his bruised and tender jaw. The only time he neglected to shave was during an extended sailing trip. A beard and a hat shielded his face from the damaging rays of the sun and the bite of saltwater.

He was sailing again, but this time without a boat, drifting into nothingness. The last thing he remembered before Morpheus claimed him was the pressure of Victoria's hips pressing intimately against his groin as she bit down on her lower lip in concentration; he remembered that and his own body's uncontrollable response.

Victoria's hands stilled, her body stiffening. Quintin was

asleep but there was no way she could mistake the swelling pushing up against her buttocks. He was asleep while another part of his anatomy was awake and throbbing.

She had shaved him quickly, her hands steady, using the skills she had acquired to bone meats and prepare intricate and elaborate pastries and desserts.

Wiping a tiny spot of cream from his chin, she slipped fluidly off his prone form. She had tried leaning over Quintin to shave him, but hadn't been able to find a comfortable position or angle. Exasperated, she straddled him, hoping he would be asleep before she finished.

Standing beside the bed, she surveyed her handiwork, then splashed a cooling astringent onto his chin and cheeks. The discoloration along his left jaw was darker and more pronounced, while the swelling did not appear as severe as it did earlier that morning.

Victoria examined the man sleeping in her bed, wondering what it was about him that drew her to him like a fragile moth to a hot flame.

Her attraction to Quintin Lord was swift and unexpected, so unlike the slow, simmering attraction she had had for her ex-husband.

She had grown up loving Richard Morgan. He and her brother were good friends, but it wasn't until she turned fifteen that Richard acknowledged her as a member of the opposite sex. Before that time she had been Nat's little sister. She accepted Richard's grandmother's engagement ring on her eighteenth birthday and they were married a week after she had turned twenty.

It had been a fairy-tale romance culminating in a fairy-tale wedding between the descendants of two of Washington's oldest black families.

It ended because Richard wanted children to carry on the Morgan name—his own flesh-and-blood children, and it was only then that she realized Richard had married her not because he loved her, but because she was the daughter of Ambassador William Jones. Richard had always been impressed with the number of foreign dignitaries who visited the Joneses' opulent D.C. residence for formal dinner parties.

Victoria wondered if Quintin wanted children. She also wondered if people who grew up in large families wanted large families of their own.

She surveyed his relaxed features, finding his face more boyish in sleep. The tiny lines around his intense, penetrating gold-brown eyes were missing. The grooves around his mouth that were so attractive whenever he smiled were barely perceptible; however, the silkiness of his neatly barbered mustache that failed to conceal the sensuousness of his lower lip was as hypnotizing in sleep as it was in wakefulness.

Leaning over, she pressed a gentle kiss to his mouth. "Feel better, sweetheart," she breathed into his mouth. Quintin stirred briefly, then settled back into sleep.

Victoria sat on the high stool in the kitchen, telephone receiver cradled between her chin and shoulder while she made notations on a pad balanced on her knees. A slight frown dotted her smooth forehead.

"Why are you being stubborn, Nat?"

She had been arguing with her brother about the menu for his in-laws' anniversary celebration.

"It's not me, Vicky. It's Christine who says she doesn't want anyone to go away hungry."

"Okay," Victoria conceded. "The meat dishes will include butterflied lamb, smoked and fresh hams, roast turkey, and roast beef."

She heard a loud sigh come through the line. She had mailed her brother and sister-in-law a sample menu of what she would prepare for the anniversary celebration, but Christine Jones had rejected it, ignoring Victoria's suggestion that a summer fête called for a menu of lighter fare—broiled meats and fish, vegetable salads, and fruity desserts.

"Thanks, Vicky. You've just saved my marriage."

"You spoil your wife, Nathaniel Jones," Victoria teased.

"That's because I love her," Nat said in an even tone.

There was a pregnant silence before Victoria spoke again. "I'm glad you do, Nat." She smiled. The most secure feeling in the world was loving and being loved.

Could she love Quintin Lord and have him love her back?

What was the matter with her? She didn't want to fall in love. Or did she?

"Love you a bunch," she said softly, then rang off.

"Vicky?" The raspy male voice broke into her thoughts, and the subject of those torturous thoughts stood at the entrance to the kitchen, leaning against the arched doorway.

Victoria surveyed his bare feet, faded jeans riding low on his slim hips, and the stark white T-shirt stretched across his broad chest.

She left the stool and moved fluidly to his side. Her arm went around his waist and she led him over to a large wrought-iron table with matching chairs with plump black-and-white striped back and seat cushions.

"How are you feeling?" Her warm breath washed over his ear after he was seated.

"Hungry," he growled with a smile.

Victoria stared at his hair, and for the first time she realized how black it was. A soft, glossy, tightly curled midnight black. "How old are you, Quintin?"

Raising his head, he looked up at her. "Thirty-seven," he said without hesitating. "Why?"

She shrugged a shoulder. "Just curious."

His gaze captured hers. "What else are you curious about?"

"Nothing else." Her voice was calm, gentle.

"I'm single," he continued as if she hadn't spoken. "I have no encumbrances from my past. No ex-wives or children."

"Do you want children?" She didn't know what made her ask the question.

He measured her with a cool, appraising look. "I never gave having children much thought in the past. But now I don't think I'd mind a little Lord or two underfoot."

She had her answer. He wanted children. Turning away, she returned to the cooking island, ladling a simmering portion of creamed broccoli soup into a bowl.

Quintin devoured two bowls of the flavorful soup, feeling stronger than he had in days. His gaze followed Victoria as she stood at a counter measuring ingredients into a large aluminum mixing bowl. Four smaller aluminum bowls were also lined up on the counter.

He moved from the table and stood beside her, watching as she strained a mixture she had heated into a small bowl.

Noting dishes filled with ground pistachio nuts and coconut, he asked, "What are you making?"

"Gelato."

Quintin moved closer, his chest brushing her shoulder. "What is gelato?"

Victoria smiled up at him. "Italian ice cream."

"An Italian ice?"

"No, a cream. It's made with a custard base. When you add ingredients like espresso beans, hazelnut-and-chocolate candies, fresh coconut, or mascarpone cheese the result is an intense flavor. Gelaterias are as popular in Italy as fast-food restaurants are in the States."

Arching his eyebrows, Quintin gave her an expectant look. "Can I sample it?"

He reminded her of a little child who couldn't wait for his mother to finish with the cake batter so he could lick the mixing bowl.

"What flavor do you want?"

His eyes widened. "I have a choice?"

She laughed. "Yes, you have a choice."

"Vanilla."

"Vanilla," she repeated. "Can't you come up with a flavor that's not so conservative?"

"But I am conservative, Victoria," he protested.

She patted his chest. "Not quite, Quintin Lord. Not with both of your ears pierced."

His hand went to the small gold hoop in his right ear. "You don't like the earrings?"

Victoria wanted to say she liked the earrings in his ears; she liked his hair, his eyes, mouth, and she liked everything that made Quintin Lord the man he was.

He looked at her as if he were photographing her with his eyes, and the smoldering flame she saw in his gaze startled her. Unconsciously, she moved closer to him, both palms flattened on his solid chest.

A soft, mysterious smile tilted her mouth upward. "I like your earrings very much," she replied softly.

Quintin folded her in a protective embrace, his fingers splayed over her back. His heart was pumping low and steady. Her arms slipped up and circled his strong neck, bringing her even closer.

He swayed slightly and Victoria pulled back. "Sit down before you fall down," she ordered in a quiet voice.

Quintin obeyed. He wasn't going to fall down. What he wanted to do was fall into bed with Victoria and stay there for the rest of his life. He wanted to hold her, kiss her, and brand her with the love he had never offered another woman.

Victoria removed a plastic container from the commercial walk-in freezer and scooped out a serving of mascarpone gelato. She poured a cup of hot espresso over the scoop, then placed the dish in front of Quintin.

"Mascarpone gelato served *affogato*."

Picking up a spoon, Quintin swallowed a portion of the frozen Italian cream cheese drowned in espresso coffee. His hand halted and he stared across the table at Victoria as she sat down with her own dish of gelato.

Registering his startled expression, she smiled. "Exquisite, isn't it?"

Nodding his head in stunned silence, Quintin returned

her smile. Within minutes he finished the mascarpone gelato and extended the empty dish. "More."

"Keep eating and you're going to get fat," Victoria warned, picking up his dish.

"I'll jog longer," he replied, licking the spoon.

She served him another flavor, blood orange, the taste reminiscent of a Creamsicle. Quintin took his time eating this one, savoring the taste of creamy sweet red oranges.

Victoria was pleased with Quintin's reaction to the gelato. She intended to introduce the dazzling popular Italian dessert to her new clients.

"What others flavors have you created?" he asked after he finished his second serving.

"Ricotta, banana, lemon, apricot, espresso, chocolate varieties, ginger, and a very wicked zabaglione. I usually make the fruit varieties when they are in season."

"What is zabaglione?"

"It's made with marsala wine, egg yolks and sugar," she explained. "It can be served as a sauce, dessert, or a beverage."

Quintin smiled. "It sounds wickedly rich and fattening."

"What it can be is wickedly potent."

Like you, Quintin mused. Delicate, beautiful, and potent.

Rising to his feet, he stared down at Victoria. "I think I've intruded on your hospitality long enough. I'd better be getting back to my place."

Victoria rose with him. It seemed strange to her that, just a few hours ago she couldn't wait for him to go home. She realized the more time she spent with Quintin the more she liked him. But she didn't want to get too used to his company; she didn't want to need him.

"I'll check on you later," she promised.

Quintin gave her a long, penetrating look, then flashed a shy smile. "You won't have to check in on me. I'll be back for my double fudge chocolate brownies," he said, wiggling his eyebrows. "Without the nuts, please," he added as Victoria folded her hands on both hips.

She stuck her tongue out at him and he blew her a kiss, prompting a smile from her. When he left her apartment she was still smiling. Wrapping her arms around her body, she closed her eyes and swayed sensuously to a tune in her head, not realizing it was the Anita Baker hit "Just Because."

Ten

Quintin climbed the staircase to his bedroom and sat on the bed. The telephone answering machine on the end table registered four calls. Pushing a button, he listened to the recorded messages: one from his mother, two from his sister Sharon, and one from Ethan Bennington.

He returned the calls, reassuring Etta Mae Lord he would not miss the family's Memorial Day celebration. He smiled after hanging up because for as long as he could remember since he turned twenty-five he was reminded to bring a young lady with him. His mother had become relentless about his marrying and adding to her growing number of grandchildren.

The call to Sharon allayed her fears that he had not succumbed to complications brought on by the oral surgery. She laughed nervously after he teased her, then reported Hannibal was well and didn't seem to miss him very much. He told her he would pick the schnauzer up in a few days and rang off.

The return call to Ethan proved puzzling. "I've got some good news, but I think I'd rather tell you in person," Ethan stated. "Are you going to be home tonight?"

Quintin touched his swollen jaw. "I'll be here, buddy."

"I'll see you in twenty minutes."

Quintin hung up, wondering about Ethan Bennington's good news. Ethan was the director of a Baltimore cultural center that established the criteria for recreation and community centers throughout the Baltimore metropolitan area.

The two men had met four years ago at a city-wide cultural exposition. Ethan had displayed several antique pieces from his private collection of furnishings dating back to seventeenth and eighteenth-century colonial America, while Quintin showcased his coveted daguerreotypes and prints of black army regiments from the Civil War through World War II. What had begun as an interest in each other's passion for art turned quickly into a friendship of mutual admiration and respect.

Staring down at his bare feet, Quintin remembered he had left his shoes in Victoria's bedroom. His eyes lit up as he remembered bits and pieces of the last twenty-four hours: Victoria caring for him—her gentleness and her annoyance whenever he tested her patience.

He loved the way her eyes narrowed as she faced him down and the soft, sweet scent of her body. He loved everything about her. He was deeply and inexorably in love with his neighbor.

Ethan Powell Bennington's generous mouth opened and closed several times before he whispered, "What happened?"

"Wisdom tooth," Quintin replied, opening the door wider and stepping aside to let Ethan into the entryway.

Staring back at Quintin, Ethan let out an audible whistle. "It looks as if you ran into a roundhouse right."

I'd be willing to run into a roundhouse right if only to have Victoria Jones nurse me back to health, he thought.

Ethan walked into the living room, stopping short. "What happened to the clutter?"

"Cleaning woman," Quintin explained.

Ethan gave him a skeptical look. "I can remember the

time I offered you a gift of a cleaning service and you turned it down. What brought this on?"

"I wanted to impress a young lady," Quintin replied candidly.

"Do I know her?"

"No."

"Then she must be special."

Quintin managed what could be called a smile. "She's very special," he confirmed.

Ethan clamped a well-groomed hand on Quintin's shoulder. "There's hope for you yet. When will I meet her?"

"Soon enough. Can I get you something to drink?"

Ethan stared at Quintin, smiling widely. "I'll have a brandy." He walked over to the sliding-glass doors leading to the patio and stepped out into the warm twilight. Within minutes Quintin handed him a snifter of premium French brandy. "Where's yours?" he asked, noting only one glass.

Quintin folded his body down to a rattan chair. "I'll pass. I'm taking a painkiller."

Ethan took a matching chair, then took a sip of the brandy, his eyes narrowing as he stared over the rim at Quintin. Placing the glass on a low table, he crossed an ankle over a knee.

"I'd like to ask a favor of you, Quintin."

"All you have to do is ask, buddy."

Ethan turned away, and the waning light softened the distinct outline of his patrician features. Ethan Powell Bennington exemplified breeding and wealth, and as a result of those qualities he had become a most eligible bachelor among Baltimore's social elite.

"I've asked my sister to handle Ryan's adoption, and when it's finalized I want you to be his godfather," he stated quietly.

If Quintin hadn't known how serious Ethan was about the young boy who'd spent most of his ten years in foster and group homes he would have laughed at his friend. But he didn't.

"I'd be honored, Ethan," he replied without hesitating.

Turning, Ethan extended his hand, grinning broadly. "Thanks, buddy."

Quintin took the proffered hand, pumping It. "When do you expect everything to be finalized?"

"Caroline's hoping it will not take more than six months. I'd like to be able to take 'my son' home for good before Christmas."

"I'm certain Ryan is as anxious to have you for a father as you are to have him as your son," Quintin replied.

Ethan let out his breath slowly, closing his eyes. The anxiety he had felt for months had begun to subside. His wish was about to come true—even if he had to wait another six months.

Having disclosed his good news, Ethan and Quintin talked for an hour, discussing the upcoming plans for the cultural center's fifth anniversary.

Quintin promised he would supervise the set decoration project the art students planned for the drama club skit. He had become a volunteer when he offered to teach an art history course twice each month during the school year; once he convinced the young children that a nude statue or model was art and not pornography he was able to open their young minds to a world where art told the history before many cultures had a written language.

Night had fallen as Ethan prepared to leave. "Ryan keeps asking when you're going to take him out on your boat."

Quintin winced. He should've known better than to promise the child and not deliver. He knew it had to be soon because he was scheduled to begin a shoot in two weeks.

"If you're free next Saturday and if the weather holds we can go out a few miles."

He had planned to sail down to the Keys with Victoria, but knew that was now impossible because he had to return to the oral surgeon late Friday afternoon.

"You're on, Quintin."

Ethan thanked him again, then left for his two-bedroom cottage in a Baltimore suburb across town.

Quintin returned to sit on the patio, watching the clear nighttime sky and registering the differing sounds of chirping crickets and the noisy buzzing of cicadas. The golden glow of light spilled out onto the concrete floor of the neighboring patio. Only a wrought-iron railing separated the two residences.

"Vicky," he whispered. As if she had heard him the sliding-glass doors opened and she stepped out into the warm night.

He didn't move, blending into the shadows and watching her as she moved fluidly to the railing and peered out in the direction of the tiny lights surrounding the Olympic-size swimming pool belonging to the residents of the duplex units.

She had changed from her jeans and T-shirt to a light-colored gauzy dress that left her shoulders bare. The bodice crisscrossed her breasts and skimmed her tiny waist before flowing out around her calves.

Quintin was stunned, unable to move or breathe. His lungs burned and nearly exploded before he exhaled and melted back against the hard rattan of his chair. Every line of her body was revealed in the diffused light—the curve of her waist, the roundness of her hips, and the slim length of her thighs and legs.

Her hair was pulled back and secured in a twist, allowing him an unobscured view of her lovely face. He didn't know how long he watched her, but even after Victoria had turned and reentered her apartment he continued to see her.

Double fudge chocolate brownies forgotten, Quintin returned to his living room and picked up a sketch pad. Within minutes the image of the vision imprinted on his brain came to life. He worked for hours, sketching and erasing before the likeness of Victoria Jones came alive on the large sheet of paper.

Streaks of dawn had pierced the nighttime sky when

Quintin finally made his way up the staircase to his bed. He slept deeply, only waking to the chiming of the doorbell.

Victoria listened for a sound of movement, then rang again. Quintin hadn't returned for his brownies the night before and she thought maybe he had forgotten about them. She had shrugged it off until the thought that perhaps he had fallen and injured himself startled her out of sleep. Tossing restlessly until the sky lightened with the dawn of a new day, she showered, dressed, and went to seek out her neighbor.

His door opened without her knocking, and she stared up at a blurry-eyed Quintin Lord. "Good morning," she said cheerfully.

Quintin ran a hand over his hair. "Good morning," he mumbled back.

Trying to appear nonplussed at seeing his half-clothed body, she shrugged her shoulders. "Just checking to see that you're okay." She pulled her gaze away from the jeans he had slipped on. He had zipped them but hadn't bothered to snap the waistband. His belly was flat with corded muscles visible under the feathering of coarse hair disappearing under the denim fabric.

"I'm fine," he said, covering his mouth and a yawn.

She handed him a small shopping bag containing his deck shoes, shaving equipment, and the bottle of pain medication.

"Breakfast will be ready in half an hour. If you're not ready I'll leave it outside your door."

"I'll be ready," he grunted, taking the bag. He waited until she returned to her apartment before he closed the door.

Seeing her again, up close, confirmed that he had captured a remarkable likeness when he had sketched her. He only had to modify the slight tilt of her chin whenever she glanced up at him and soften the curve of her lower lip before he transferred the sketch to a canvas and completed it with vibrant oils.

He had already thought of a name for his masterpiece:
"Night Magic."

Quintin sat opposite Victoria at the table on her patio. He
had surprised her by stepping over the railing separating the
two patios, seating her after she had set the table.

A cooling breeze lifted her unbound hair around her face.
This morning she had worn a bang swept across her forehead, the back and sides curving loosely under her chin and
along her nape.

Her gaze swept slowly over his face. "Your jaw is looking
a lot better this morning."

Quintin nodded. "Much of the swelling is gone, but the
bruise looks hideous."

Victoria uncovered a dish of steaming-hot grits. "Even
with the bruise you can still turn a few heads, Adonis," she
teased, spooning a portion of the grits onto a plate. She uncovered another dish with fluffy yellow scrambled eggs.

Leaning back on his chair, Quintin smiled. "It sort of
gives me a rugged look, don't you think?"

"It looks as if someone rocked your chops."

"Some doctor named Pearson did," he replied, his eyes
crinkling in amusement.

"Remind me to kiss it later and make it all better."

"I'm going to hold you to that promise, missy." He gave
her a sensual smile, filling his own plate with grits, eggs, and
creamy butter.

Quintin downed the grits, eggs, a serving of applesauce,
and two cups of coffee, then leaned over the table, asking,
"Where are my double fudge chocolate brownies?"

Victoria bit down on her lower lip, smiling. "Where do
you put all of your food? You should weigh at least two hundred pounds."

"I'm not far from it. I weigh in at one eighty-six."

His weight was deceiving. She thought he'd weighed between one hundred seventy and seventy-five. No wonder she could hardly move him.

"I see why you jog," she replied.

"Do you want to walk tomorrow morning?"

"Before or after breakfast?"

"Before, of course," he said.

Raising her chin, Victoria nodded. "Okay. Seven," she confirmed.

Quintin caught her gaze and held it, noting the shape of her eyes, the curve of her cheekbones, and the fullness of her soft sensual mouth. Victoria Jones had the sexiest mouth of any woman he had ever kissed.

"I'm afraid there's going to be a change of plans for next weekend."

Victoria gave him a puzzled look. "What's next weekend?"

"Our excursion to the Keys. We're going to have to put it off until another time."

"That's all right, Quintin."

"There will be another time, Vicky." She smiled demurely, lowering her gaze. "But the weekend doesn't have to be a complete waste," he continued. "I'm planning to take *Jamila* out on Saturday. I've invited a good friend and his son, if that's all right with you." But before she could reply he added, "Why don't you invite a friend or two, then we can have a pre-Memorial Day celebration."

"How large is *Jamila?*"

"Large enough. It sleeps four and the deck can easily accommodate twelve."

Victoria filled her cup with coffee. "Where did you come up with the name *Jamila?*" She wondered if he had named it after a girlfriend.

"It took months before I found just the right name. I finally found it in a book of baby names. It's from Somalia and it means 'beautiful'." He didn't say that if he had to come up with a name for it now it would be Victoria.

"You remind me of a modern-day Paul Gauguin. I can imagine you sailing to a tropical island where you'd spend the rest of your life painting and drinking coconut milk."

"I've seriously thought about it."

Leaning forward, Victoria studied his solemn expression. "Do you ever think you'll leave Baltimore?"

"Maybe one day." He shook his head slowly. "But not now."

Her heart pounded an erratic rhythm. She was venturing into dangerous territory with her line of questioning. What did she want from Quintin? What did she want for herself?

"Why not now, Quintin?"

Because of you, Vicky, his head screamed. Because there would be no way that he could leave her. Not now. He loved her. Didn't she know—couldn't she tell that he loved her? Didn't she realize he was going just a little crazy because he had never been in love before.

"I've met someone . . ." he began.

Victoria felt as if he had knifed her. There was no reason for the pain, but she felt it as surely as if he'd picked up the knife on the table and driven it into her heart.

"A woman?" she asked hoarsely.

"Yes, Vicky."

A bitter jealousy stirred inside her. Suddenly she hated the tall, graceful woman she had seen leaving his apartment.

"She's a lucky woman," she said in a quiet whisper.

Quintin's grin was slow in coming. "I'd like to think she is. However, I think I'm the one with all of the luck."

Victoria finished her coffee, then rose to her feet. "I'd better get your brownies before you haunt me."

She made her way back into the house, Quintin's low chuckle of laughter following her. It wasn't until she reached the kitchen that she felt the prickle of tears behind her eyelids. She had been deceiving herself. She was falling in love with her neighbor.

But it was all for nothing because he was in love with another woman. Why did she always pick the wrong man to fall in love with?

First Richard and now Quintin. She might be older now, but she certainly wasn't any wiser.

Eleven

Quintin followed Victoria into the kitchen, watching as she placed moist brownie squares in a colorful plastic container and covered it. He also noted several large trays filled with fried crab cakes. Two other trays were filled with potato salad. An industrial roll of colorful plastic wrap rested beside the trays.

Quintin's eyes glittered with amusement. "How about I sample the crab cakes and potato salad to see if they're good," he drawled, reaching for the trays.

Moving closer to him, Victoria slapped at his right hand. "Don't you dare touch that! I left some out for you."

He affected a pout. "Where are you taking those?"

"These are going to church for . . ." She broke off, hands on both hips. "Wait just a minute, Mr. Lord. Before I moved in here you existed on greasy, additive-filled, artery-clogging swill and now I can't prepare a crouton without you wanting to sample a crumb."

Quintin reached for Victoria, molding her feminine curves to his length. "You've spoiled me," he crooned, smiling down at her upturned face.

Victoria's gaze caressed his features, lingering on the sweeping arch of his thick black eyebrows, the tiny lines around his large laughing eyes and the sensual curve of his masculine mouth.

"I'm considering unspoiling you," she teased.

"Too late." His head lowered and he nuzzled her neck.

"I'll move away," she continued, her voice low and halting as his mouth moved slowly over her hair.

"I'll follow you, Vicky. I'll sail the world searching for you."

Her arms going around his slim waist, Victoria melted against his body, luxuriating in the unyielding strength that was Quintin Lord's.

She wanted the man! She wanted him more than she had ever wanted Richard. She wanted to know what it was about Quintin Lord that drew her to him.

Closing her eyes, she gave in to the powerful passions coursing throughout her as Quintin sculpted her body with his fingers. He was the artist, the sculptor molding and shaping her to his will.

Quintin was certain Victoria could feel his trembling, his tentativeness. He wanted and needed her so badly he was lightheaded. Victoria Jones filled his every waking and sleeping moment. She had possessed him and controlled him.

"Quintin." His name was a strangled cry. He moaned in response, his hands busy cupping her hips and pressing her to his heated groin.

"Quintin," she repeated.

His breathing was heavy and ragged. "Don't move—not yet," he pleaded. He wanted her to know that she aroused him—that she had the power to turn him into a weak-kneed trembling mass of uncontrollable passion.

Victoria felt his maleness surging against her thighs. She felt the tension turning his muscles into bands of steel. She was experienced enough to know that the moment of sexual sparring had evolved beyond their control. All that was needed was a blink, an intake of breath, or a spark before they dissolved into a precious and profound oneness.

"I need you, Vicky," he murmured against her ear.

She stiffened. She didn't want him to need her; she wanted him to *want* her. Richard needed her, and not once had he ever said that he wanted her. If she was going to become involved with Quintin it had to be because they both wanted each other.

"Let me go, Quintin."

"Vicky."

She pushed against his solid chest. "I said, let me go!" This time her tone was layered with a chilly warning.

He released her, stepping back and staring down at the set of her mouth. Victoria Jones was upset. But what had he done? He had only told her the truth.

Turning away, Victoria picked up the box of plastic wrap. "I'll see you later."

Quintin watched as she pulled out enough rose-colored plastic to cover a tray of potato salad, then he turned and silently made his way out of her kitchen. Returning to his own living room, he flopped down on a dark-brown leather chair and cradled his face in his palms.

Had he moved too quickly? Had he assumed she would fall into bed with him because she had allowed him to kiss her? Lowering his hands, Quintin stared at the screen he used as a backdrop for a photography shoot.

He had to remind himself that Victoria Jones was different. Different from any other woman he had ever met. He couldn't rush her into bed.

A wry smile curved his mouth. He would wait her out. She wasn't going anywhere and neither was he.

Victoria directed the four young men to her van and watched as they unloaded the trays of crab cakes and potato salad. Her housewarming celebration had borne fruit. One of her friends had called frantically the night before with an announcement that her grandmother's arthritis was acting up and the elderly woman couldn't prepare the crab cakes and potato salad she had promised for her church's revival festivities.

Victoria had checked her inventory on the computer that rested on a counter in the kitchen, sighing in relief. She had had enough lump crabmeat and potatoes on hand to fulfill the request. It had taken her a long time to set up the disk listing the items, quantity, and the purchase date, but it had proven invaluable. Within minutes she knew whether she could prepare any dish on very short notice.

"Thanks, Victoria, for helping out my grandmother," Nadine Erskine said, smiling broadly. "Grandmama never would've been able to hold her head up again if Sister Sara started gossip saying that she used her arthritis as an excuse not to make her special dishes. There's been an ongoing feud between my grandmother and Sister Sara Barnes for years. Sister Sara claims no one can make crab cakes or potato salad the way she does."

Victoria laughed. "But is Sister Sara good?"

Nadine nodded. "She's good, but not as good as my grandmother. The only one I know who can make better potato salad is you," she stated, handing Victoria a check.

"Then tell your grandmother not to tell anyone that I prepared the salad if she wants to keep her reputation." Victoria took the check, slipping it into her blouse pocket.

"I would, but I can't count on Grandmama. She'll probably sing your praises to the top of the tent, and after that you won't be able to keep up with the orders that'll come your way. These ladies can be so competitive."

"Well, I can't say I won't appreciate the business," Victoria remarked. She reached into the van and withdrew a decorative black-and-white striped shopping bag with VJ Catering and her telephone number inscribed in black script along each white stripe. "This is a little something for you, Nadine."

Nadine took the bag, peering down at its contents. "What is it?"

"Vanilla and chocolate wafer points and an Italian ice cream. Keep the ice cream frozen until you're ready to eat it.

Then you should soften it slightly in the refrigerator before serving it."

Holding the bag in one hand, Nadine threw her arms around Victoria. "Thanks, girlfriend. For helping my grandmother and for the goodies."

"Anytime." She hugged Nadine back.

She returned to her vehicle and backed out of the parking lot. The lot was filling up quickly with people who had come to the large Baptist church for their week-long revival marathon. The program had listed popular evangelists as well as unlimited food for all who came to praise the Lord while testifying to His good works.

Victoria drove through downtown Baltimore, finding it hard to believe that it had been just two days since she picked up Quintin from the oral surgeon. He had spent only a day in her apartment but it could have been a week. Her emotions went into double overtime whenever she was with him. What was there about the man that wouldn't allow her to keep her balance?

There was one thing she was certain of concerning Quintin. She was never bored with him.

Victoria slid back the sliding screen door and stepped out onto the patio. She made her way to a chaise longue and picked up the Sunday newspaper. She'd planned to spend the afternoon reading the paper and relaxing.

An hour later it was the ringing of the cordless telephone on a wrought-iron table that pulled Victoria out of sleep. She had dozed off.

Sitting upright, she reached for the receiver, hesitating when she saw Quintin reclining on a matching chaise less than three feet away from her.

"What are you doing here?" Her voice was heavy with sleep.

Quintin pointed to the ringing telephone. "Answer the phone, Vicky."

Victoria snatched up the receiver. "Hello."

"Who set you off, Vicky?" asked a familiar female voice.

"I'm sorry, Jo." Victoria lowered her voice to keep a grinning Quintin from overhearing her conversation. "Something just startled me." She saw Quintin frown when she referred to him as *something*. "What's up?"

"What are you doing next Saturday?"

Victoria remembered she had promised Quintin she would go out on his boat with him. "I'm invited to go sailing," she informed Joanna. "What did you have in mind?"

There came a loud sigh through the wire. "Nothing as exciting as a sailing expedition."

"How would you like to come along?"

"Are you sure?" Joanna questioned.

"Of course I'm sure, Jo. I was told I could invite a friend." Quintin's frown deepened further with the mention of "friend." "We'll be leaving early Saturday morning, so why don't you stay over Friday night."

"You're on. I'll call you before Friday and let you know what time to expect me."

"Good. I'll talk to you later."

Victoria returned the phone to its cradle, smiling. "I've invited a friend for Saturday."

"So I heard," Quintin mumbled angrily.

Why the hell did he have to open his big mouth and tell Victoria that she could invite a friend? Now he was going to have to call on all of his self-control not to snap this Joe's neck if the man . . .

He groaned inwardly. Tossing Joe overboard on Saturday would be too late. The man was going to stay with Victoria Friday night.

Quintin couldn't clench his teeth without experiencing discomfort so he reclined on the chaise, closing his eyes.

Getting next to Victoria Jones was as difficult as trying to pick fleas off a dog's back. He had to come up with a way to win her love.

Victoria assumed a similar position on her chaise, also closing her eyes. "Is there something you wanted, Quintin?" she asked in a lazy tone.

Yes, there is, Quintin thought. He wanted her to be his wife and the mother of his children. A fist of shock squeezed his heart before letting go. How had it happened? How had he so quickly, deeply, fallen in love with Victoria? "I want my brownies," he said instead.

She sat up quickly, staring at him. "Why didn't you take them this morning?"

Quintin didn't move or open his eyes. "You threw me out before I could."

She folded her hands on her hips. "I didn't throw you out."

"You said 'I'll see you later.' I took that to mean I was dismissed."

Swinging her legs off the chaise, Victoria stood up and glared at him. "You and those damned brownies!"

"For shame, Vicky. Swear words on Sunday," he teased.

Victoria went into the house, cursing the man in English and in French.

Twelve

After walking with Quintin Monday morning Victoria did not see him again until early Saturday, and it wasn't until he pounded on her door and she opened it to see him standing there did she realize how much she had missed him.

"What are you trying to do, wake the dead, Quintin Lord?"

"We're supposed to cast off at sunrise, matey," he said with a wide grin.

She couldn't help smiling back at him. The bruising and swelling along his jaw had disappeared, no longer marring the face she had grown to love. Yes, she could admit that to herself. He loved another woman, yet she was in love with Quintin Lord. It had taken time away from him to realize that she wanted and loved him.

She loved his masculinity, his teasing nature, and his creative brilliance. And she also had come to realize that he was so easy to love. There was nothing complicated about the man.

He was dressed in white: shorts, T-shirt, and deck shoes, and his sherry-colored gaze swept quickly over her attire of tan walking shorts, orange T-shirt, and matching orange Bass canvas shoes. The tan painter's cap on her head would protect her face from the hot sun.

Victoria opened the door wider. "The food chest is in the kitchen."

"I didn't ask you to cook," he said, smiling down at her lovely face. "I'd planned for us to dock somewhere and pick up lunch."

She patted his muscular shoulder. "My treat."

Leaning over, he raised her chin and placed a light kiss on her mouth. Thanks, Vicky."

Joanna Landesmann walked into the entryway the moment Quintin kissed Victoria. She stopped short, watching his fingers curve gently around her friend's upper arms. Then, without warning, Victoria was in his arms, her body molded intimately to his. Retreating quietly, Joanna went back to the kitchen, her face mirroring the satisfied grin of a cat who had just devoured a dish of sweet cream.

Quintin deepened the kiss, his tongue searching the warm softness of her mouth. Her lips parted, delighting him as her tongue met his in an intimate heated joining.

Again he had stayed away from Victoria Jones, but to no avail. His desire for her had not waned nor had his love diminished. What he felt for her was real—real and passionate, and it wasn't until he'd been away from her for two days that he realized he was jealous. Insanely jealous of this Joe she had invited to stay with her. This Joe she had invited to sail on *Jamila*.

Well, if Joe wanted Victoria Jones he had to come through Quintin Lord, because he had no intention of losing her. Besides—what the hell kind of name was Joe? Joseph or Joel maybe, but not plain old run-of-the-mill Joe.

Victoria curved her arms under Quintin's and clung to his shoulders, abandoning herself to the whirl of sensations gripping her mind and body.

He devoured her mouth and she returned his hunger with a similar passion. "Quintin," she murmured, trying to catch her breath.

Pulling back, he registered the startled look in her large dark eyes. "You were past due on your payments for the watercolor, Vicky. I decided to collect the late charges." He swept the hat from her head and buried his face in her hair.

Victoria rested her forehead against his chest, holding back laughter. "You didn't say anything about late charges or interest."

His hands were busy caressing her back. "You didn't read the fine print, Miss Jones."

"What other hidden charges did I miss?"

Holding her at arm's length, he studied her face thoughtfully. "There's one more, but I can't reveal it at this time."

"I'm going to report you to the state's attorney general for fraudulent business practices, Mr. Lord," she teased.

He smiled. "Lawsuits are known to take years to settle."

"I have time, Quintin."

His smile faded as a serious light filled his gaze. "So do I, honey. I have nothing but time."

Victoria knew his statement held a double meaning.

"What time are we sailing?"

They sprang apart at the sound of Joanna's voice. Quintin stared numbly at the woman with short red hair.

"Do you remember my friend, Jo Landesmann?" Victoria asked.

Quintin managed several croaking sounds until he recovered. Joe was not a Joe but a *Jo*. "Of course," he said, extending his hand. He was certain both women heard his sigh of relief.

Jo took the proffered hand, drinking in his sensual smile. He was more than gorgeous. He was magnificent.

"I'm ready to ship out, Quintin," Jo replied, finding her own voice.

Unlike Victoria and Quintin, Joanna wore a pair of white cotton slacks and a long-sleeved cotton gauze navy-blue shirt. She had learned not to expose her fair skin to the sun.

Jo pointed to a large canvas bag near the door. "That's also going aboard."

Quintin looked from the bag and back to Jo, then to Victoria. "What on earth are you two taking along? I invite a couple of guys and they bring what they have on their backs. Meanwhile, you ladies bring everything including your vanity mirrors. Out on the sea we usually rough it."

Victoria smoothed back her hair, then replaced her cap. "Just take it, please," she drawled in a bored tone.

Quintin held out his hand. "Give me your keys, Vicky. You and Jo wait outside while I bring everything out and lock up here."

As if they'd rehearsed it, Victoria and Joanna saluted Quintin. "Aye, aye, sir."

The two women waited until they were outside and seated in Quintin's four-wheeler before collapsing in hysterical laughter.

"Did you . . . did you . . . see . . . see his face when I pointed to the bag?" Jo sputtered.

"Yes-ss," Victoria hiccuped. "Here he comes," she whispered as Quintin came down the front stairs with the bag atop the chest. Hannibal bounded down behind him and waited patiently at the curb while Quintin opened the tailgate. He secured the chest and bag, then lifted Hannibal into the cargo area and secured the tailgate door.

Walking around to the passenger side of the vehicle, he opened the door. Motioning with his hand, Quintin ordered, "Vicky, you ride up front with me."

Before she could reply, he pulled her from her seat and settled her in the one beside the driver. He slammed the door, glaring at her through the open window. His angry expression registered: *Don't start none—won't be none.*

Victoria glanced over her shoulder at Jo, but the redhead was busy crooning to Hannibal. Had she forced Quintin to lose his temper? This was another side of him she had never seen.

Fifteen minutes later Quintin pulled up in front of a small cottage in a wealthy Baltimore suburb. A profusion of wildflowers surrounded the property enclosed by a white picket fence. At exactly six o'clock a man and a young boy emerged from the house.

"Take a look, ladies," Quintin said. "Two males and no bags," he taunted.

Victoria did not reply, but gave Quintin a smug smile. She intended to make him beg before she shared anything she and Jo brought along for the trip.

A light breeze ruffled the man's brown wavy hair, and as he neared the four-wheeler both Victoria and Jo were staring openly at him.

Quintin waited until the two were seated on the backseat beside Jo before he made the introductions. "Victoria Jones, Joanna Landesmann. Ethan Bennington and his son Ryan." There was a chorus of hellos and smiles.

Victoria longed to turn around and glance at Ethan Bennington and his son but quelled her curiosity. To use Jo's expression, the man was "gorgeous."

Ethan had what she thought of as classic good looks. His face was finely chiseled—each feature exquisitely defined and balanced. However, Ryan Bennington looked nothing like his father. Where Ethan was fair, Ryan was dark. The young boy's coloring was a rich mocha-brown, his black hair thick and tightly curling, while his features were indicative of his biracial heritage.

Ethan's hazel eyes swept over the cargo area. "I thought you weren't going to bring anything, Quintin."

Quintin glanced up at the rearview mirror. "I didn't. The booty belongs to the ladies." Ethan's gaze went from Jo to Victoria before he turned away, hiding a smile.

The gesture was not lost on Joanna and Victoria, and they silently acknowledged that Ethan Bennington would also join Quintin as a beggar before the sun set.

Jo kept up a steady stream of conversation with Ryan, who after some urging revealed he was ten and had just completed a sixth-grade curriculum even though he was in the fifth grade.

All conversation came to an abrupt halt when Quintin parked and directed everyone to the slip where his *Jamila* was moored.

"Why didn't you tell me it was a yacht?" Jo whispered in Victoria's ear.

"He told me it was a cruiser," she whispered back.

"It's a *yacht*," Jo insisted, staring at more than thirty-five feet of gleaming white hull.

Ryan was equally impressed as he stood on the pier, eyes wide and mouth gaping.

"It's all gassed up and ready to go, Mr. Lord," reported a wiry man. The network of fine lines on his tanned, leathery face was a testament of too much sun and salt water.

Quintin patted the man's back. "Thanks, Patrick."

"When can I expect you back, Mr. Lord?"

"Probably before sunset."

Patrick saluted. "Good sailing, folks."

Quintin helped Victoria, Jo, and Ryan up the ramp while Ethan carried the chest and the large canvas bag on board. Hannibal, as familiar with the deck of *Jamila* as he was with his home, made his way across the teakwood deck and settled down in a cool area under the pilothouse.

"Where do you want these?" Ethan asked, still holding the chest and bag.

"Both go in the galley," Victoria said, watching Quintin as he sat down on the deck and removed his shoes.

Standing and walking over to a closed compartment, he lifted the top of a chest and withdrew five life jackets. Extending a bright yellow one to Ryan, he said, "Put this on."

Ryan stared at the jacket, pouting. "I can swim."

"So can I," Quintin retorted, "but I have a healthy respect for the ocean."

"Put it on, Ryan." Ethan's voice was soft, yet held a ring of authority that warned Ryan not to challenge him.

The boy took the jacket and slipped it on. His dark mood lifted slightly once he saw that all of the adults did not seem to mind that they had to wear the life jackets.

The rising sun was high in the late-spring sky when Quintin lifted the anchor and maneuvered the ship out of the harbor and into Chesapeake Bay.

Victoria stood at the railing with Jo, watching the fleet of boats in the harbor grow smaller, then disappear altogether. The feel of the rising and falling deck under her feet was hypnotic, and giving in to the urge she sat down and removed her shoes. The teak deck was soft as old suede, and warm from the sun.

I always wanted to be a part of a sailing expedition to Africa. She remembered Quintin's statement as she ran a hand over the smooth polished railing.

Shifting slightly, she stared up at Quintin as he stood in the pilothouse, bare feet slightly parted and sunglasses shielding his eyes from the rays of the bright sun glinting off the choppy water as he steered his beloved *Jamila* out into the Intercoastal Waterway.

Everything about him was confident and relaxed. He lived his life exactly the way he wanted to live it. He painted, sailed, and came and went at will.

She thought of his girlfriend, and wondered why Quintin hadn't invited her to sail with them. A wry smile curved her lips. She hoped the woman was worthy of Quintin's love.

Victoria was unaware that Jo had moved away to talk to Ryan and that Quintin had taken her place at the rail until she heard, "Awesome, isn't it?"

Victoria jumped at the sound of the familiar voice. "Who's piloting—"

"Ethan took over," Quintin interrupted, staring down at her delicate profile. "Have you got your sea legs yet?"

She took a step back from the railing and rose on her toes, arms outstretched, and affected a second position ballet pose.

"Good enough, Captain Lord."

Quintin was transfixed by the graceful move, his gaze glued to her legs and the incredible arch of her bare feet. "Very good," he replied. Moving closer, he pulled her to his side, his right arm holding her captive. "When are you going to dance for me, Vicky?"

She felt her blood run cold. She would never dance again—not for Quintin and not for anyone.

"Never," she replied, pushing against his firm grip.

He wouldn't let her escape. "Why not?"

She didn't answer, her gaze fixed on the water.

Quintin saw a flicker of pain. It was the same pain he had noticed the first time she spoke of giving up dancing. "What made you give up your dance career? Maybe I should rephrase the question. Who made you give up your career?"

Victoria could have been carved out of marble as she stood at the railing, unmoving. "It wasn't who or what, Quintin. It was a lot of things. Things that are too complicated to explain."

Lowering his head, Quintin pressed his mouth to her ear. "Try me, Vicky. I'm a good listener."

Victoria surprised Quintin when she clung to him, burying her face against his T-shirt. "I can't, Quintin. I can't tell you now."

His arms tightened around her waist. "I'll wait, Vicky. I'll wait until you feel comfortable enough to tell me. And whatever it is, it can't be so bad . . ."

She put her fingers over his mouth, stopping his words. "No more," she ordered quietly.

Quintin captured her fingers and kissed each one before running his tongue over her soft palm, eliciting the trembling response he sought from her.

Pulling her hand free, she gasped, "Quintin, don't. You act as if there's only the two of us on this boat."

Removing his sunglasses, he stared at her. "If that were the case, then I would be faced with a dilemma. Do I drop anchor and make love to you on deck or try to go below where I'd take you in one of the cabins. Yes, Vicky, I want you."

She wasn't given the opportunity to reply because he walked away, leaving her staring at his broad back.

Swaying slightly, she leaned against the railing and tried valiantly to bring her emotions under control.

He knew. Without a doubt he knew that she wanted him to make love to her.

It didn't matter that he was in love with another woman. It didn't matter that she would never marry Quintin or give him children. All that mattered was that they wanted each other. Sharing her body with Quintin was inevitable. The only question that remained was where or when.

Jo escorted Ryan across the deck. The boy's tightly closed eyes and swaying gait indicated the ship's rolling motion was upsetting him.

Ryan's knees buckled, and Ethan rushed to him, lifting him effortlessly into his arms. Sandy's eyebrows furrowed in concern. "Are you all right, son?"

Ryan nodded. "My stomach keeps moving, Ethan."

"Take him below and I'll fix him something that'll settle his stomach," Jo volunteered.

"Stomachaches are for girls," Ryan mumbled, turning his face toward Ethan's broad chest.

Ethan chuckled, his hazel eyes sweeping from Jo to Victoria. "Stomachaches aren't just for girls. Men get them, too."

Victoria watched Ethan, Ryan, and Jo disappear below the deck of the ship, shaking her head. Males, she thought. The moment they left the womb they became sexist.

She remained on deck, inhaling the saltwater and enjoying the feel of the sun until it became too hot.

Climbing down into the hatch, she was surrounded by smooth and gleaming wood walls and doors. The door to one cabin stood open and she saw Ethan sitting on a bunk while Jo sat on another beside Ryan, coaxing the child to drink the liquid in the cup she held to his mouth.

Moving closer to the bow, she discovered a large galley, modern and fully equipped for a life at sea. Victoria had sailed before on sloops, catamarans, and tenders. She was more than aware of the cost for these vessels. It appeared as if Quintin Lord had spared no expense for what he called his *"addiction." Jamila* was an exquisite sailing ship.

She unpacked the large chest, storing perishables in an

ample refrigerator. She emptied Jo's large bag and extracted cooking utensils and china.

Thirty minutes later, the hold of the ship was filled with the aroma of frying bacon and simmering coffee. Freshly baked croissants were wrapped in a clean towel and left warming in a small oven.

It took several seconds, but Victoria registered silence and stillness. The engines had stopped.

She heard the sound of someone clearing his throat, and she turned to find Quintin and Ethan crowding the doorway to the galley.

"Breakfast smells good," Quintin quipped with a wide grin. Ethan nodded in agreement.

Jo pushed the two men aside and washed her hands in a stainless-steel sink. Taking a half-dozen eggs from a carton, she cracked them in a large aluminum bowl.

"What time do we eat?" Quintin questioned.

Victoria glanced over at Jo, who nodded perceptively. "You don't," they chorused in unison.

"We . . . we don't," Ethan replied, his voice nearly breaking in disappointment.

Victoria folded her hands on her hips. "You 'men' didn't want the 'ladies' to bring anything. I remember Captain Lord saying that men only bring what's on their backs when they go sailing, not vanity mirrors."

Ethan's attractive dimpled chin dropped as his gaze swung to his friend's face. "No, man, you didn't say that, did you?"

"Answer your first mate, Captain Lord," Victoria taunted.

Ethan crossed his arms over his chest, glaring at Quintin as Jo beat the egg mixture with a wire whisk.

Victoria's hands were busy sectioning oranges into halves, a sly smile lifting the corners of her mouth. *Beg, Quintin,* she ordered silently.

Ethan stepped into the galley, his tall frame making the space appear smaller. "Apologize, Quintin," he threatened, his gaze fixed on the strips of bacon on a large platter. The aroma of brown sugar and cinnamon rose from the crisp, golden-browned meat.

"Quin-tin," Victoria drawled.

"No!" His reply was adamant.

Ethan panicked. "Hell, I'll apologize." Bowing slightly from the waist, he bobbed to Victoria and Jo. "I'm sorry, ladies, if I offended you."

Reaching over, Jo picked up a stack of plates and handed them to Ethan. "Please take these up on deck."

Ethan, ignoring Quintin's scowl, took the plates and pushed past him. Jo picked up a tablecloth, a stack of cloth napkins, and a handful of cutlery and followed Ethan.

Quintin stalked into the galley and trapped Victoria against a wall. "You're a wicked woman, Victoria Jones."

She stared at the middle of his chest, biting back laughter. "Beg, Quintin," she crooned.

Bracing a hand on either side of her head, he leaned forward. Lowering his head, his mouth grazed her cheek. "You don't know how much I want you, Vicky. Please let me make love to you."

She pounded his shoulders with her fists. "Not that kind of begging, Quintin."

He caught her small fists, grinning. "That's the only kind of begging I know." He noted the set of her stubborn little chin. "Okay, Victoria Jones. I apologize for my off-color, sexist remark. Now can I eat?"

Rising on tiptoe, she kissed his mouth, running her tongue over his lower lip. "Aye, aye, sir."

Quintin watched as Victoria cooked the eggs to a soft yellow fluffiness and turned them over into a dish that would keep them warm. He helped carry a jug of freshly squeezed orange juice in cracked ice and the basket of croissants up on deck.

Ethan had helped Jo set the table with a white-and-blue checkered tablecloth and cobalt-blue napkins. The blue-and-white color scheme was repeated in the bone-white china plates with shimmering cobalt-blue trim. The wind had settled down to less than three knots, and when the four adults sat down at the table, Quintin had to admit to himself that the presence of the two women added a touch of class that *Jamila* had not experienced in the past.

Ethan lay on a deck chair, his bare feet crossed at the ankles. Closing his eyes, he smiled. "Did you beg good, buddy?"

Quintin didn't stir from his lounging position. "Think I didn't? Etta Mae Lord didn't raise no fool."

"Is Victoria the one?"

Quintin, his gaze fixed on Victoria as she sat on the deck playing cards with Jo and Ryan, smiled. "Yes."

Crossing his arms over his chest and settling into a more comfortable position, Ethan grinned. "Good choice, buddy."

Thirteen

Jamila prowled the waters of the Chesapeake for hours until Quintin dropped anchor at Cape Charles. Everyone was ready for a light lunch.

Victoria lifted a curling french fry from Quintin's plate. "I can't believe I'm still hungry," she confessed.

"Sailing always gives me a tremendous appetite," Ethan said, reaching for the hamburger on Ryan's plate.

"Hey!" Ryan cried out. "I wanted that."

Ethan took a large bite out of the burger. "I'll buy you another," he replied after swallowing. "Better yet, what do you say we pick up a half dozen lobsters and go back to my place and have cocktails and lobster under the stars?"

"Sounds good to me," Quintin replied, his gaze fixed on Victoria's face.

Ethan smiled at Jo. "Will you join us?" She stared at him through the lenses of her sunglasses.

"I'd love to," she agreed.

"I'll have the lobster, but I'll pass on the cocktails," Ryan quipped.

Everyone laughed at Ryan's serious expression. Ethan dropped an arm around his son's shoulders and hugged him. Ryan returned the affectionate gesture while at the same time retrieving what was left of his burger from Ethan's plate.

He stared at the half-eaten grilled beef patty. "I think you're better than Popeye's Wimpy, Ethan."

"I'll Wimpy you," Ethan growled, holding Ryan's head in a loose headlock and rubbing the knuckles of his right hand over the boy's hair.

Victoria smiled at the good-natured teasing between Ethan and Ryan, but she thought it odd that the boy insisted on calling his father by his given name. She glanced over at Quintin and he returned her stare, winking.

"We can sail into Norfolk and pick up the lobsters, then head home," Quintin stated.

Ethan winced. "I don't think Hannibal will appreciate a half dozen live lobsters on board. Remember when he attacked the bushel of the crabs?"

Quintin groaned. "Don't remind me," he said, relating how he and Ethan had gone out on *Jamila* for her maiden voyage and picked up a bushel of crabs at a wharf along the Virginia coast for a fish-fry later that evening.

"The basket was covered, but Hannibal was transfixed by all of the thrashing and scratching, so he decided to investigate. He tipped the bushel over, and crabs were everywhere. Most of them had made their way successfully back to the ocean before I could drop anchor and help Ethan retrieve them."

Victoria, Ryan, and Jo laughed until they were breathless as Ethan described in great detail the sound of their claws clicking like castanets on *Jamila*'s highly polished deck.

"Quintin went absolutely ballistic because they were ruining his deck. But what I couldn't understand was that he was picking up the little buggers and pitching them back in the basket while screaming, 'Throw the scavengers overboard, Ethan.' Meanwhile, Hannibal was running around barking like he was possessed, his toenails leaving long jagged scratches every time he came to an abrupt stop whenever a crab turned in his direction."

Quintin nodded. "*Jamila*'s maiden voyage was quite a catastrophe. We managed to salvage about two dozen crabs, and I had to have the deck refinished before I could take her out again."

Jo, wiping her damp eyes, said, "I guess lobster is out."

"Not if it's lobster tails," Victoria replied.

Ethan's smile was dazzling. "Good call, Victoria. How many can you eat, buddy?" he asked Quintin.

"Three if they're small."

"Ryan?"

Ryan puffed up his narrow chest, his brow furrowed in concentration. "Four if they're small."

Ethan gave him a skeptical look. "Victoria?"

"Two."

Ethan turned to Jo, his expression impassive. "How about you, Jo?"

Jo's expression was equally closed. "Two."

Victoria glanced from her friend to Ethan, wondering why the redhead was so subdued with Quintin's friend. Had Ethan said something to her that turned her off?

"Twenty tails should be enough, wouldn't you say, Quintin?"

"Ask Victoria. She's the master chef."

Ethan leaned back on his chair, realization widening his gaze. "No wonder breakfast was so incredible. Victoria Jones, you can cook for me anytime."

Quintin's jaw clenched. "No, she can't," he countered softly.

"Why not?" Ethan had missed Quintin's challenge.

"Because she cooks for *me.*"

Ethan's body stiffened. At thirty-eight, he was more than experienced enough to recognize territorial possession, and he had just stepped over the boundary.

Victoria felt her face heat up as Quintin, Ethan, and Jo stared at her. Ryan was still too young to understand the sexual undercurrent surrounding the adults at the table.

Ethan's gaze returned to Quintin and he nodded, acknowledging the other man's claim. He turned to Victoria, flashing his charming smile. "Do you cater events?"

"I do." She managed to give Ethan a polite smile. "If you have something in mind I'll give you my number and we'll talk at another time."

The heat had left her face, but she still felt rage coursing through her chest. Quintin did not own her. He had no right to assume she would cook only for him. After all, cooking was her profession and livelihood. The look she shot Quintin said, "We'll talk later."

Quintin rose to his feet, aware that he had angered Victoria. He knew her well enough to note the narrowing of her eyes and the set of her mouth.

He hadn't meant for his statement to come out the way it had, but he hadn't been able to help himself. He had allowed jealousy to cloud his judgment even though he knew Ethan would never attempt to come on to Victoria.

He would apologize to her, or if necessary he would beg. He was becoming quite proficient in the begging department.

Coming around to her side of the table, he helped her to her feet. Leaning over, he sang softly in her ear, "Ain't too proud to beg."

"Quintin, behave," she gasped, taking a sharp breath and glancing around to see if the others had overheard him.

"I am," he whispered back, grasping her hand and leading her down the pier toward *Jamila*.

Forgetting about her earlier anger, she smiled up at him. "You just won't do right."

Without warning, he bent down and swung her up in his arms singing loudly, "Do Right Woman, Do Right Man."

Burying her face between his strong neck and solid shoulder, Victoria laughed until the tears flowed down her cheeks.

Quintin's theatrics set the mood for the return trip. The

four adults launched a repertoire of golden oldies to show tunes while Ryan lounged on deck beside Hannibal, shaking his head in amazement.

He pressed his face to Hannibal's ear, whispering, "It's enough to make me seasick again. Grown-ups are whacko."

The informal gathering began in earnest with Jo arranging a bouquet of white roses and irises from Ethan's garden for the large table set up in the rear of the cottage. She also cut several bunches of scented herbs, adding a delicate fragrance to the humid night air.

Quintin placed tall beeswax candles in a half dozen antique Spanish lanterns and hung them from nearby trees. He also filled amber-colored votive glasses with white votive lights. Lighting them, he placed the flickering lights strategically at one end of the table.

Victoria and Ethan had claimed the cooking duties, broiling the lobster tails, preparing a dipping sauce and a salad of torn red leaf lettuce, dandelion leaves, and roasted red peppers in a balsamic vinegar dressing. She also quickly and expertly turned two overly ripe avocados into a spicy guacamole. Jo helped, slicing sourdough bread and brushing each slice with garlic butter, then warming it in the oven.

Later there was only the sound of a classical guitar composition coming through the speakers set up outdoors as the diners concentrated on devouring everything put out on the table.

The setting sun and the flickering of fireflies and the candles created a mood that was quiet and almost ethereal. Ethan had served an excellent vintage white wine, and after two glasses Victoria reclined on the grass beside Ryan and stared up at the lanterns.

"You cook better than Ethan," Ryan stated, matter-of-factly. "And he's a good cook."

"I'm only good because I've been trained to cook."

Turning his head slightly, Ryan stared at her profile.

"Maybe you and Ethan can get married, then both of you can cook together."

Victoria turned her head slowly and stared at the tortured expression on the young boy's face. "Your father isn't married?"

Ryan bit down on his lower lip. "Ethan is not my father. Well, not yet anyway. He wants to adopt me, then he'll be my father and I'll be his son. It's going to take a long time. I told him it would go faster if he had a wife, but he says he doesn't need a wife to adopt me."

Victoria swallowed painfully. Now she knew why the child referred to Ethan as "Ethan."

"He's right, Ryan. Nowadays a person doesn't have to be married to adopt a child."

"But it would go faster if he was married. I like being with Ethan. I hate going back to that . . ."

Victoria sat up and stared down at Ryan. His eyes were tightly closed, as if he willed tears not to fall. "Back to what, Ryan?"

"Back to that place." He bit down on his lower lip. "People steal my things!"

Without thinking, Victoria pulled the child from the grass and held him gently. "Don't give up, Ryan. Ethan wants you as much as you want him."

The boy's large, dark eyes were trusting. "Are you sure?"

She nodded slowly. "Very sure. I don't know Ethan very well, but I can see that he loves you."

"I love him, too."

Victoria was surprised that a child his age could express his feelings so openly to a stranger. Hugging him, she kissed his forehead. "How about dessert?"

Ryan groaned and pulled out of her loose embrace. "I can't. I ate two lobster tails."

Victoria had only been able to eat one. Ethan had purchased twenty lobster tails, each weighing close to one pound. The meat from the uneaten tails could easily be used for a salad or a bisque.

Quintin sat with his back propped against a large oak tree, watching Victoria and Ryan. An indescribable feeling had tightened his chest when he saw her fold the boy in her arms. The gesture was so tender, so touching, that it stunned him, and at that moment he thought of her suckling his child at her breasts.

And if he thought what he felt for her was just infatuation it was easily dismissed. He *did* love her. He loved her with an emotion that went so deep, he would not have been able to put it into words.

He tore his gaze away from her and smiled. Ethan and Jo sat at the table talking quietly. Victoria's friend was quiet and shy. Almost as shy as Quintin before you got to know him well.

Hannibal ambled over to Quintin and lay down beside him, muzzle on his master's thigh. Quintin scratched his pet behind the ears, closing his eyes. The day had been successful. He had taken *Jamila* out to sea with Victoria; at one time he would have been content to sail with Hannibal, but now sailing would not be the same unless Victoria was aboard.

A satisfied smile curled his lips under the mustache as his thoughts were filled with a tiny woman with clear red-brown skin, liquid eyes, and a full mouth.

At that moment Quintin made himself a promise. He would marry Victoria Jones before the New Year.

Fourteen

As the votive lights burned out, the flickering candles in the lanterns provided the only source of illumination in the encroaching darkness, competing with the stars in a navy-blue sky.

Ryan had fallen asleep, his head resting against Victoria's shoulder. She shifted to a more comfortable position and cradled the boy to her breasts, smiling.

The day had been wonderful. She had fallen in love with *Jamila*. The ship was exquisitely designed to provide the utmost comfort.

Her smile broadened. Quintin had proven to be an excellent captain and host, and she knew that she loved him with all of her heart. Her smiled faded slowly as she tried comparing her feelings for Quintin with how she had felt about Richard.

Richard Morgan had always been unreachable, unattainable. Maybe that was why she'd had a crush on him. Richard was older than her by eight years and that alone was attraction enough. He was an "older" man.

He was older *and* controlling. The selection and the decorating of their home was the only area where she had

had absolute authority. Richard Morgan did not trouble himself with something he considered "a woman's domain."

He abhorred her dance career, tolerating it only because he knew if he wanted Victoria Jones, he had to accept her profession. He felt dancers—even ballet dancers—were a degenerate lot without a shred of morality.

Victoria wanted to dance from the first time she saw Tchaikovsky's *Nutcracker.* She began dancing lessons at eight, and became a professional at twelve when she earned the coveted role as Clara in an all-black adaptation of the popular Christmas ballet.

If only Richard had waited he would have had his wish. She was forced to give up her dance career, but what Victoria hadn't known until that time was that he wanted an heir more than he resented her dancing.

Sighing, Victoria dropped a kiss on the top of Ryan's head. She held a child who was crying out for a mother and father, and she wanted a child. Even if she couldn't bear a child she was more than willing to adopt one. A child who would be more special than one who was of her own flesh because she would be given the option of choosing. If she had had a child with Richard she would have accepted and loved it unconditionally. But with adoption she could select the sex, age, racial designation, or ethnicity of her son or daughter.

Ethan and Ryan were blessed. They wanted each other enough to wait; wait forever if necessary.

"Is he heavy?"

She started, staring up at Quintin who hunkered down beside her. "No." Her voice was low and breathless.

Quintin smiled, noting the startled look in her eyes. The candles in the three overhead lanterns sputtered, casting a soft glow across her features.

"Are you ready to go home?"

"Yes," Victoria replied, returning his smile. She hadn't realized she was tired until she sat down. She had been up before dawn rolling dough for the croissants.

Quintin eased Ryan from Victoria's embrace, lifting the boy. He walked over to Ethan, depositing him in his foster father's outstretched arms.

"We're going to push off now," he informed Ethan.

Ethan nodded, smiling. "Thanks for everything, buddy."

"My thanks to you, too, for the lobster. We must do it again."

Ethan arched an eyebrow. "Only if it's the same crew."

"Same crew," Quintin confirmed, smiling at Jo.

She lowered her head, blushing furiously in the waning light. "Thank you, Ethan."

"The pleasure has been all mine," he returned, his gaze fixed on her lowered head. His attention was diverted as Victoria moved over to stand beside Quintin. "I hope I'll get to see you again, Victoria."

She gave him an open smile. "But of course." Her gaze swept over Ryan. "You have a wonderful son, Ethan."

Ethan tightened his grip, pulling Ryan closer to his chest. "Thank you. He's the most precious thing in my life."

"It's been great, Ethan," Jo said, her mysterious smile hinting of something left unsaid.

Ethan nodded. "Same here."

Quintin led Victoria, Jo, and Hannibal back to his four-wheeler. There was complete silence on the return trip. Everyone was exhausted from a day filled with sun, saltwater, and rich food.

Jo refused Victoria's offer to spend the night, claiming she had to be back in Washington to coordinate a wedding breakfast.

She hugged Victoria while Quintin put her overnight bag in the trunk of her car. "I'll call you tomorrow night," she whispered conspiratorially. Turning to Quintin, she rose on tiptoe and kissed his cheek. "Thanks for everything, Quintin."

Quintin gathered her to his chest and kissed her forehead. "Does this mean you're willing to sail with the tyrannical Captain Lord again?"

"Aye, aye, sir."

He released Jo, chuckling under his breath. Victoria's friend was all right.

They waited until Jo drove off, then walked up the stairs to their respective apartments. Victoria opened her door and Quintin carried the chest into the kitchen, placing it on a counter.

"Are you up to walking tomorrow morning, Vicky?"

She offered a tired smile. "Of course."

Quintin pulled her to his chest, kissing her cheek. "Sleep well."

She stared at his back as he walked out of the kitchen. Minutes later, she turned out the lights and made her way up the curving staircase to her own bedroom. She checked the messages on her answering machine, bathed, fell into her bed and was asleep within minutes.

Victoria lay awake, listening to the sound of rain pelting the windows. She had slept fitfully. She had been bone tired but dreams about Richard and Quintin attacked her relentlessly throughout the night.

Pressing her face into a pillow, she groaned. Sleep was elusive, so she decided to get up.

Not bothering to go through her stretching routine at the barre, she headed for the bathroom and stood under the cool spray of the shower until her flesh was beaded with an icy exhilaration. There was something to be said for a cold shower.

She toweled herself dry and creamed her body. The doorbell chimed melodiously as she pulled a slip dress over her head. Glancing at the clock on the bedside table, she winced. It was seven o'clock. Quintin was insane if he thought she was going to walk in the rain. Skipping lightly down the stairs in her bare feet, she opened the door.

"Good morning, beautiful."

Victoria returned Quintin's sensual smile, her gaze sweeping over his tall frame in a single glance. This morning he wore a pair of jeans, bleached a near white from numerous washings, and a white tank top that displayed his well-toned upper body to perfection. His feet were bare.

"Get back into bed, Vicky," he ordered, holding up two large white shopping bags.

"What are you doing?"

"Don't make me beg, Vicky."

She crossed her arms under her breasts, grinning. "Beg, Quintin," she crooned. "I love it when you beg."

He headed toward her and she backpedaled to the staircase, deciding to play along with him. "Aren't you going to tell me why you want me in bed?"

"I'll show you," Quintin replied, turning suddenly and walking into her kitchen.

Victoria retreated up the staircase to her bedroom. She straightened the sheet on the bed, turned back the blanket and fluffed up the pillows. She slipped into bed seconds before Quintin strode into the room carrying a tray, setting it down across her lap.

"There's nothing more romantic than sharing breakfast in bed on a rainy day." Leaning over, he dropped a kiss on the top of her head. "You can start without me."

Victoria uncovered a Styrofoam container. It was filled with a stack of buckwheat pancakes. The tray also held packets of butter, coffee creamer, maple syrup, plastic utensils wrapped in a paper napkin, and a Styrofoam cup of steaming black coffee.

Quintin returned, carrying his own tray. He balanced it while getting into bed beside Victoria. "Why don't you select something nice to listen to while we eat," he suggested, motioning with his head at the radio on the table on her side of the bed.

Victoria lowered her chin and peered up at him from under her lashes. "My, my, my. Aren't we bossy this morning."

He settled back against the pillows. "I brave the elements for my neighbor to bring her breakfast and what does she do? Nag, nag, nag."

"What your neighbor is going to do is kiss you passionately after she finishes her breakfast," she promised.

Quintin's lips curved up in a smile. "You break your promises, Victoria. There was another time when you promised to kiss my cheek and make it all better."

She gave him a sidelong glance. "I'll keep it this morning."

His hands stilled and he stared at her profile. "This is *one* morning that I'll make certain you keep it."

Victoria tried concentrating on her breakfast as the heat from Quintin's body seeped into hers.

She couldn't believe she was sitting in bed with Quintin casually eating a stack of fluffy pancakes from a take-out restaurant as if it something they did every morning.

"Nice music," he mumbled after taking a swallow of coffee. Victoria had selected a station that played soft, easy-listening music. The melodious strains of a musical rendition of "Midnight Train To Georgia" floated from the speakers.

"Wonderful pancakes," she complimented. The buckwheat cakes were light and flavorful.

"The cook down at Ray's Diner is exceptional," Quintin explained. "When I walked in this morning everyone asked if I'd been away."

"Did you tell them that you now have your own private chef?"

Leaning over, Quintin kissed her ear. "No. That's our secret."

Victoria glanced up, registering the merriment in his gaze. "What other secrets are you hiding?"

"I have a cleaning woman."

She nearly spilled the coffee in her container when she brought it up to her mouth. "You *what?*"

He flashed a pained expression. "You wounded me deeply when you called my place a hovel. I happen to know what hovel means, Victoria."

She felt her face burn with embarrassment. "I didn't mean . . ."

"Yes you did mean it," he countered. "And you were right. And you're not the first woman who has commented on how I keep my house."

Victoria wondered if that woman was the one he was in love with. Was she also turned off by the piles of clothes and clutter strewn throughout the spacious apartment.

"My mother has refused to come to visit because she's ashamed by how I live. Her house is always spotless and she can't understand how I can live with clothes on the floor and trash piled up for days."

"The woman is your mother?" Victoria couldn't help smiling.

Quintin nodded. "The one and only Etta Mae."

She laughed. "I think I like Etta Mae."

"How would you like to meet her?"

"When?"

"Tomorrow. We usually all get together for a Memorial Day cookout. Etta Mae has been after me for years to bring a 'nice girl' with me."

Victoria felt her pulse quicken. Why hadn't Quintin asked his leggy girlfriend to go with him to his family's holiday gathering?

"I'll pass this time," she said.

"Are you busy tomorrow?"

"No," she answered honestly.

"Then why not come with me?"

Because a man usually doesn't bring a woman to meet his family, especially his mother, unless he's serious about her, she thought.

"I don't want to intrude," she said instead. "It's going to be a family gathering."

Quintin stared down at her hands, noting the slight trembling. He placed his larger hand over hers, squeezing gently. "If your parents asked you to bring someone to a family celebration and you asked me, I'd go and not once would I feel like an intruder, Vicky. I'd be your guest."

How could she tell him that she was willing to sleep with

him, but nothing more than that. That their relationship would be similar to the one she had had with Masud in Paris.

Girding herself with resolve, she nodded. "Okay, Quintin. I'm ready to meet Etta Mae."

"She'll adore you," he stated, squeezing her fingers before releasing them.

Both of them finished their breakfast in silence, the sound of music competing with the rhythmic beating of the falling rain.

Quintin took both trays, swinging his legs out of the bed. "Don't go away," he ordered softly.

Victoria couldn't go anywhere if she tried. She was too full. Hanging out with Quintin Lord was going to make her fat.

Sliding down under the blanket, she closed her eyes and smiled. He had become so much a part of her life in the short time since she had moved into the apartment that she found it difficult to remember when he hadn't been there. In only three weeks he had become so inexorably involved in her life that she didn't know where it began or ended.

There were times when he disappeared for days, but she still felt an invisible, tenuous thread weaving them together. She hadn't wanted to fall in love with Quintin Lord, but she had. However, she was realistic enough to know that she could not plan a future with him. She would take what he offered and give him what she could in return, and when it was over it would be over.

Quintin reentered the bedroom and turned off the bedside lamp. The gray sky and falling rain darkened the room, not permitting light through the Palladian windows.

He slipped into the bed beside Victoria, pulling her gently into his arms. Her heat and fragrance washed over him as he inhaled deeply.

Victoria nuzzled her nose to his warm throat. "Thank you for a wonderful breakfast," she breathed out softly.

"You're quite welcome." His voice was low and soothing.

"You were right," she said after a long, comfortable silence.

"About what?"

"Having breakfast in bed on a rainy day is very romantic."

"Hmmm," he groaned, settling her against his body and pulling her left leg over his jean-covered thighs.

Victoria wiggled until she found a comfortable position against the hard male body. His arms tightened around her back and minutes later she fell into a deep, dreamless sleep.

Quintin rested his chin on the top of Victoria's head, luxuriating in the press of her tiny body against his. Nestled in his arms, asleep, she was so soft and trusting. He held her, her head resting on his shoulder until he, too, fell asleep.

The sound of their breathing, the music coming from the radio, and the incessant tapping of rain against the windows swallowed them whole in a cocoon of love and peace.

Fifteen

A rumble of thunder shook Victoria, and she came awake with a violent start.

"It's all right, darling. It's only the storm."

She blinked in the darkness, trying to reorient herself. Relaxing, she snuggled closer to Quintin. "How long have I been asleep?"

His fingers trailed over her back. *"We've* been asleep for over an hour," he said softly near her ear.

"You're not good for me, Quintin."

He chuckled. "Why not?"

"Eating in bed, then falling asleep. I'm going to get fat," she complained.

"You'll never be fat," he retorted, pulling back and trying to see her features in the darkened room. "Maybe you'll gain some weight in the hips, but never fat." His hands cradled the fullness of her buttocks. "I wouldn't mind if you added a few inches to your caboose."

Her face heated up. "Quintin!"

He laughed openly. "Some men like legs, others big breasts. I prefer cabooses." His right hand searched under the hem of the skimpy cotton slip dress, grazing the backs of her thighs. It continued its slow, deliberate journey, ending with his fingers splayed over the triangle of satin hiding her femininity.

Quintin's gentle touch sent currents of desire racing through Victoria. His hand continued its exploration, sweeping over her belly and breasts. Her entire body was on fire, flushed with pinpoints of simmering heat.

"Quintin," she moaned. Whatever else she wanted to say was left unsaid as his hand came up, his thumb going to her chin. Exerting the slightest pressure, he opened her mouth.

His tongue traced the outline of her mouth with an agonizing slowness before it slipped through her parted lips. His tongue worked its magic, moving in and out of her mouth and precipitating a familiar throbbing between her thighs.

She had become a lump of soft clay with Quintin Lord the sculptor. He could mold her into whatever shape and form he desired.

Victoria couldn't get close enough to him as she pressed her full, aching breasts to his chest. It was as if her clothes burned her sensitive flesh. She was on fire—everywhere.

Her hands searched under the cotton fabric of his tank top, fingertips feathering over the solid muscles in his broad chest and leaving tracks in the thick mat of chest hair. The hair on his body excited her. Richard's skin had been almost as smooth as her own.

"Vicky. Oh, Vicky," Quintin chanted hoarsely, his hands roaming intimately over her breasts. Withdrawing his hand, his mouth replaced his fingers.

Gasping aloud, she arched. Her nipples exploded in a pebble hardness against the ridge of his teeth. Writhing beneath him, Victoria couldn't stop the moans from escaping her parted lips.

Quintin, his mouth fastened to one breast then the other, murmured a silent prayer he could prolong the foreplay. His body was on the verge of exploding.

He had fantasized about Victoria Jones from the first moment he saw her, and knowing that fantasy was to be fulfilled was an awesome thought to him.

The storm raging outside matched the rising passion of the two lovers as their private world was rocked with one discovery after another.

Quintin undressed Victoria, quickly removing the slip dress and her bikini panties, while she struggled to pull his tank top over his wide shoulders. Brushing her hands away, he rose to his knees and divested himself of his shirt, jeans, and briefs. Pushing the mound of clothes to the floor, he reached for her.

The thunder rumbled and shook the heavens while the sky and the bedroom were lit up by the flash of lightning, but it did not match the searing passion of Victoria and Quintin.

Quintin moved over her, his hands beneath her hips. She felt his hard pulsing length against her belly, and her breasts tingled against his hair-roughened chest.

She caressed the length of his back, aware of the unleashed power in his strong male body.

He trailed a series of slow, shivery kisses down her neck, whispering her name. She breathed lightly between parted lips, crooning, "Quintin. Oh, oh!"

He answered her, taking her right hand and pressing it to his groin. Her fingers circled him, squeezing gently.

The breath rushed from Quintin. His body was rigid with poised ecstasy. His hand covered hers and he guided his throbbing sex into her wetness.

She moaned softly and he cradled her face between his palms, kissing her mouth. "I'm sorry, baby. I had no idea you were that small and tight."

Victoria, eyes closed, felt every inch of Quintin as her flesh sheathed his. The enormity of their act washed over her. What was she doing? He didn't love her. He was in love with another woman.

Quintin sensed the change in Victoria. He could not continue. He didn't want to make love to her. He wanted her to make love *with* him; make love to each other.

Supporting his greater weight on his elbows, he pressed his lips to her ear. "What's the matter, darling?"

Victoria's arms went around his strong neck. She wanted to cry; cry because she loved him so much. She buried her face in his throat, breathing heavily.

"Do you not want me to make love to you?" he asked when she didn't respond.

She shook her head.

Quintin doubted whether he would have been able to withdraw from her body; even though he hadn't moved he was close to erupting within her.

His eyes opened and he groaned audibly as realization swept over him in a cold wave. It was the first time—the very first time—that he hadn't protected the woman during a sexual encounter.

"Vicky . . . Vicky," he repeated, his heart pounding loudly in his ears. He was certain she could hear it. "I'm sorry. I should've protected you."

"I won't get pregnant," she stated, allaying his fear.

Quintin took that to mean she was utilizing a form of contraception. Exhaling, he smiled. "And I can assure you that I'm not carrying any sexually transmitted disease."

"Thank you, Quintin." Her tone was expressionless.

His passion dissipated like someone letting the air out of a balloon. He couldn't make love to her—not now. Withdrawing, he reversed their positions. She lay on his chest, flesh against flesh.

"Do you want to talk about it, Vicky?"

"No." Her voice was soft and void of emotion. What she wanted to say was that she loved him; she loved him enough to want to spend the rest of her life with him, that she wanted to become his wife, that she would be willing to become the mother of all of the children they wanted to adopt. But that was not going to happen because he was in love with another woman; another woman would become his wife and the mother of his biological children.

Reaching down, Quintin pulled the sheet up over their bodies. He held her tightly in the darkened bedroom until they fell asleep for the second time that morning.

* * *

Victoria awoke, her body covered with moisture. The heat from Quintin's body was overpowering.

She couldn't believe she had fallen asleep on top of him; her legs nestled within his.

"Where are you going?" he asked as she tried slipping out of his arms.

Her nose grazed his mustache as he lowered his head to stare down at her. "I need a shower." He released her and she slid off the bed.

Walking into the bathroom, she opened the door to the shower stall and turned on the water, adjusting the temperature and the flow of water.

Stepping into the stall, she closed the door and raised her face. The warm water sluiced down her hair, flattening it to her scalp. She rinsed away the scent of Quintin's body, then reached for a bar of fragrant hard-milled soap.

She soaped her body, shampooed her hair, but before she could add her customary instant conditioner the shower door opened and Quintin joined her.

The soft overhead light permitted Victoria to see what the darkened bedroom had not revealed. The breath was sucked out of her lungs as her gaze swept over Quintin's naked body. He was Michelangelo's David come to life.

He gave her a shy smile. "I thought you'd need someone to do your back."

Her large eyes crinkled in laughter as she turned around. Quintin moved closer, pressing his chest to her back, his arms circling her waist.

"I'm going to do your back," he crooned softly against her ear, "and your neck and your breasts." He punctuated his promise, his fingers splaying over her soap-covered breasts.

His fingers began their own magic, sweeping slowly over the small firm globes of flesh until her nipples hardened. He turned her around and panting, her chest heaving, she pressed her cheek to his shoulder.

Quintin's lids lowered over his gold-brown eyes as he felt

his passion for Victoria spiral again. He had lain in bed, cursing himself for not making love to her. She hadn't said he couldn't make love to her, and the image of her naked and writhing beneath him propelled him from her bed.

He wanted Victoria Jones. But more than that, he loved Victoria Jones!

Brushing back the strands of wet hair clinging to her forehead, he smiled down at her. "I love you," he whispered reverently.

Victoria would have fallen if he hadn't been holding her. Her lower lip trembled as she melted against his strong body. "Quintin!" she breathed out, not believing what she had heard.

Her arms went around his neck and she arched her feet until she was standing on her toes. Her mouth closed on his as her love flowed from her to communicate silently that she also loved him.

Quintin was overwhelmed by her response. His hands encircled her waist and he picked her up. Holding her with one arm, he used one hand and guided his member into her tight, warm pulsing body as water flowed over them. Her hot flesh closed around him and he groaned audibly.

Victoria tightened her legs around his waist, leaning back in his strong grip. Knowing Quintin loved her increased her desire and she responded to him, giving him everything, holding nothing back.

Her body felt hot, then cold and then more heat. She breathed in deep soul-shattering drafts of air as Quintin quickened his thrusts, their bodies finding a tempo that reached a shattering crescendo.

Quintin's back, pressed against a tiled wall, made a downward journey. He took Victoria with him. He couldn't believe the passion shaking his legs and not permitting him to stand. He sat on the floor of the shower stall, his body joined with hers. The cooling water temperature did not cool his desire. Long, strong fingers encircled her tiny waist, and he guided her up and down over his blood-engorged sex.

He kissed her deeply, his tongue keeping the same rhythm as his thrusting body. He heard her gasps of pleasure, and his own gasps and moans joined Victoria's.

He had known the moment he saw her that she was different—she was the one.

Victoria moaned aloud with erotic pleasure, Quintin's hardness electrifying her. She rose and fell to meet him in an uncontrolled passion, and then it happened. Waves of ecstasy swept over her as she ground her buttocks against his thighs. Heat rippled through her. There was no way she could disguise her body's reaction to his lovemaking.

Quintin's passion rose to meet and overlap hers when he exploded inside her body. The heat clouded his brain, singed his body, and he surrendered all that he had as liquid passion poured from him and bathed her with love.

They sat on the tiled floor, breathing heavily while the falling water cooled. Victoria laid her forehead against Quintin's chest, trying to catch her breath.

She couldn't believe her response to him. She had never responded to a man with such abandon. Smiling, she savored the feeling of complete satisfaction.

Quintin's breathing slowed. He experienced twin emotions of shock and contentment. He had never taken a woman the way he had just made love to Victoria, but never had he experienced the feeling of sweet satisfaction that made him almost as helpless as a newborn.

He didn't know where he found the strength, but he gathered Victoria from the floor of the shower stall and rinsed her hair and body. The water was icy cold when they finally stepped out of the stall.

They laughed like small children, drying each other's bodies with thick fluffy towels. Victoria admired the beauty of his male form as she drew the terry-cloth fabric down his spine.

She kissed his shoulders. "You have a very nice butt, Mr. Lord," she crooned, her fingers gripping his firm hips.

Quintin nearly choked. He spun around, taking the towel from her loose grip. "You're wicked, Vicky."

Arching her eyebrows, she smiled up at him. "I don't think so, Quintin. I don't believe I have a wicked bone in my body."

Moving closer to her, he pulled her head to his chest. "And what a fabulous little body you have."

She rubbed her nose against his chest hair. "You've just confirmed something you told me the night you promised to show me your watercolors."

"What's that?"

"You *are* good, Quintin. Very, very good."

They made their way back to the bedroom and the bed. Both of them were content to lie beside the other, holding hands, lost in their own private thoughts.

They made love for the second time, this joining a slow and tender one. They slept again, sated, and when they awoke their passions had been slaked—until the next time.

It was early evening and the rain had slacked to a soft-falling mist. Victoria sat beside Quintin on the patio enjoying the warm damp night. The candles flickering in the living room cast a golden glow through the screen of the sliding patio doors.

Quintin tightened his grip on Victoria's shoulders and kissed her hair. She had allowed it to air dry. Spending the whole day with him hadn't given her the opportunity to blow it out or curl it. She had complained, but he told her she looked beautiful with any hair style, coiffed or au naturel.

Victoria felt Quintin's mouth on her ear. He was as passionate and tender out of bed as he was in bed. A foreign emotion welled up within her and she felt tears prick the backs of her eyelids.

Shifting and pressing her lips to his, she whispered, "I love you so much, Quintin."

He stared down at the shadowy outline of her face. Lowering his head, he kissed her closed lids, catching the salty tears on the tip of his tongue.

"I was so afraid you wouldn't or couldn't love me," he confessed.

"It's so easy to love you," she retorted. "What I was afraid of was that you were in love with the woman I saw leaving your apartment a few weeks ago."

He pulled back, frowning. "What woman?"

"A woman who can claim a pair of stilts for legs."

Quintin remembered whom Victoria was referring to. "I don't get involved with models," he replied in a serious tone.

"You told me you'd met someone and—"

"That someone was *you*," he interrupted. Quintin studied her bowed head, realization dawning quickly. "Is that why you wouldn't let me finish what we had begun earlier this morning?" She nodded, and Quintin laughed. "If we're going to have a normal relationship, Vicky Jones, then we're going to have to be honest with each other. No secrets. Okay?"

She smiled up at him. "No secrets," she repeated.

Sixteen

Quintin's "I grew up in farm country" was confirmed as Victoria sat beside Quintin, staring out through the windshield at the passing countryside. They had left Baltimore's city limits twenty minutes before, and the landscape changed along with the sizes of the homes and surrounding properties. She noted the grazing cows, barns, horses, bales of hay, tractors, pickup trucks, and other farm vehicles behind fenced-in areas and along the shoulder of the road.

Quintin turned off a local two-lane road, shifted in four-wheel drive, and maneuvered up a rutted unpaved hill. Hannibal rose from his lounging position in the cargo area and barked excitedly.

"Hannibal!" Quintin admonished, glancing quickly over his shoulder and glaring at his pet. Hannibal sat down on his haunches, panting.

"He seems pretty excited," Victoria remarked, watching as a large white three-story house came into view. Several hundred feet of lush green lawn surrounded the house like a thick carpet.

"Watch him take off like a bullet as soon as I open the door," Quintin warned. "If Hannibal could talk he would call this 'Hannibal's Big Adventure.'"

"Somewhat like a kid going to Disney World?"

"Exactly," Quintin replied, laughing. "It'll take him a week to recover from all of the attention he'll get from my nieces and nephews."

"He sounds like a real party animal." Quintin groaned at her pun, shaking his head. "I thought it was funny," Victoria retorted, managing to look insulted.

He slowed the Jeep, then parked. Leaning over, he pulled her from her seat and she lay half on and half off his chest and legs. Lowering his head, he pressed a tender kiss on her pouting mouth.

"I love you," he whispered, watching wonder light up her gaze. Every time he confessed his love to her it seemed as if it surprised her; it was as if she did not believe him.

Clutching his wrists, Victoria held on to Quintin, not wanting to let him go. The past twenty-four hours had been a time of discovery; it was as if she had discovered passion for the very first time in her life. A passion that was strong and spontaneous.

"I love you, too, darling."

Shifting slightly, she returned his kiss, her tongue sweeping over his mustached mouth.

Quintin jerked back as if he had been burned. "Do that again and I'll turn around and go back home," he threatened, grinning.

"And have your mother angry with me for keeping her son away from a family outing? I don't think so, Quintin Lord."

"I'd tell her I couldn't help it."

"Forget it."

He released her, shifted into gear and drove around the side of the large farmhouse where automobiles of every make and model were parked in rows of twos.

Quintin came around and helped Victoria from the four-wheeler, and she was met with a variety of tantalizing odors lingering in the warm late-spring air.

Hannibal sprang from the back of the Jeep as soon as

Quintin opened the cargo door, racing around to the back of the farmhouse.

A large white tent was erected under a copse of massive oak trees. Situated under the tent were two long wooden tables with benches crowded with adult couples, young adults, and a number of small children.

Victoria heard the words, "Quintin brought a girl" the moment gazes were turned in their direction.

"Hey, Quint," hooted Dwayne Lord. "Aren't you going to introduce us to your lady, or are you trying to keep her all to yourself?"

"Wait your turn," Quintin warned his brother, steering Victoria toward his parents.

Etta Mae Lord greeted them warmly. She was a tall, gray-haired, large-boned woman without an ounce of excess fat. Her gold-brown eyes were bright and intelligent.

"Welcome." She held out her hands to Victoria.

"Thank you, Mrs. Lord." Victoria went into her embrace.

"Etta Mae," the older woman insisted.

"Etta Mae," Victoria repeated, hugging her in return.

The Lord matriarch assessed her son's date, nodding and smiling. It had taken Quintin too many years to count to bring a woman to a family celebration, but he had chosen wisely. The petite woman with the large dark eyes reminded Etta Mae of a fragile doll.

Victoria turned to Quintin's father who was only an inch taller than his dynamic wife. She was completely charmed by the gentle nature of Charles Lord. There was something about him that reminded her of Quintin.

After the introduction to Quintin's parents, Victoria met his brothers, sisters, nieces, nephews, and the fiancés, fiancées, boy and girlfriends of the single family members. Within minutes she was referred to as "Quintin's girlfriend."

Sharon Lord captured Victoria's arm, declaring she was to be her hostess. "Quintin told me all about you," she confessed with a bright smile. "He said you took care of him when he had to have his wisdom tooth pulled."

She returned Sharon's smile. The resemblance between Sharon and her brother was startling. "He was a very good patient," Victoria confessed in all honesty.

"So it's not gratitude that made him bring you today?"

Victoria recalled their wonderful lovemaking, shaking her head. "I hope not."

"I hope not, either," Sharon said with a slight frown. But the expression disappeared as quickly as it formed. "I'm Hannibal's mother," she continued. "I'm a dog breeder, and Hannibal comes from a long line of pedigreed champion giant schnauzers."

"Do you show dogs or breed them?"

"Right now I'm just breeding them. But if I can convince Quintin to let me sire Hannibal to an exquisite pure black bitch schnauzer next month I'd be willing to train and show the best of their litter."

Victoria smiled as Quintin approached and handed her a glass of lemonade. "I'm willing to bet that my little sister is bending your ears about her dogs."

She took the glass. "Sharon was telling me that she wants to breed Hannibal."

Quintin curved an arm around Victoria's waist, winking at Sharon. "I have to ask Hannibal whether he's ready to become a papa."

"Once Onyx comes into heat he'll be ready," Sharon countered. "After all, he's a male, and aren't all males always ready to breed, dear brother? Are you blushing, Quintin Thomas Lord?" she teased, peering up at him.

Quintin's mouth tightened under his mustache as he glared at his sister. "Are you hungry, Vicky?" Not waiting for her reply, he steered her in the direction of the tent.

Victoria leaned against his side, her breast pressing against his arm. "She's right, darling. You're always ready."

Lowering his head, he whispered against her ear, "I have to be to keep up with you, sweetheart." Now it was Victoria's turn to feel the heat in her face. "I'll always be ready for you," he continued softly. "I'm ready now."

She looked up at him, her gaze registering the simmering passion lurking beneath his impassive expression. Her lips parted and she inhaled, feeling her breasts swell against the cotton fabric of her oversize T-shirt.

They could have been the only two people under the large tent as they were caught up in a dizzying spell of longing. Surreptitious glances were cast in their direction, conversations tapering off until there was complete silence. A young child whimpered and was quickly hushed by its mother.

Victoria was the first one to notice the strained silence, her gaze sweeping over the assembled guests. Unconsciously she moved closer to Quintin, and his arm tightened around her waist.

"I want Victoria on my team," he said smoothly, breaking the silence.

"No mixed teams this year," Lydia Lord reminded Quintin. At nineteen she was the youngest child of Charles and Etta Mae. "We decided last year that if you brought a girl it would be the girls against the guys."

Quintin shook his head. "I sure hate to see women cry."

"No more than I hate to hear men gnash their teeth." Lydia retorted, hands on hips.

Quintin released Victoria and made his way slowly toward Lydia. "Now why did you have to go there, Lydia? Why did you have to talk about teeth?"

Lydia sprinted out of his reach. "If the shoe fits, then wear it, Quintin Thomas Lord."

"The pig is ready," Charles Lord called out from outside of the tent, and everyone picked up a plate and made their way over to the pit where a whole pig had been roasting since before sunup.

The whole group was sprawled on the grass under trees, napping and relaxing after devouring mounds of potato salad, roast pork, barbecued chicken, cole slaw, and marinated vegetable salads. It would be another two hours before the annual baseball outing began. After the game everyone would sit down for dessert. Victoria had contributed to the dessert menu with three homemade sweet potato pies.

She sat on the ground under a tree, watching an infant crawl away from its mother in her direction. The barefoot little girl wore only a diaper and a sleeveless undershirt.

Victoria froze as the baby came closer, her heart pounding uncontrollably. Quintin was sprawled beside her, asleep.

The infant stopped and reached out with a tiny, chubby hand. The round dark eyes closed, filling with tears. A weak cry followed.

She felt the baby's frustration, but was paralyzed. She wanted to reach out and pick up the little girl, but her hands refused to follow the dictates of her brain.

Quintin came awake immediately. He glanced from his niece to Victoria. Sitting up, he picked up the infant and cradled her to his chest.

"Hey, hey, princess. It's all right," he crooned. The baby stopped crying, sniffling against his chest. He nestled her in the crook of his arm and placed a kiss on the tiny girl's forehead. "Uncle Quintin will take care of you."

Victoria watched in awe. The baby seemed to recognize her uncle's face and smiled, revealing four tiny white teeth.

"What's her name?" Her voice was low and breathless, and she was wary.

"Gabrielle."

"A beautiful name for a beautiful little girl."

Quintin handed Gabrielle to Victoria. "Hold her."

Victoria felt faint and her mouth seemed suddenly to be filled with cotton. *No, Quintin,* her head screamed. *I can't.*

"It's okay, Vicky. She won't cry." He thrust little Gabrielle at her and Victoria had no choice but to take her.

Gabrielle sensed Victoria's tension and began to fret again. "Don't cry. Please don't cry," she pleaded, trying to soothe the baby.

Gabrielle's whimpers turned to laughter, surprising Victoria. She smiled back at the tiny round brown face. "You are so adorable." The baby dropped her head to Victoria's chest and snuggled against her breasts.

The stiffness left her limbs, and she began to relax. Lowering her chin, she kissed the top of the baby's softly curling damp hair. Gabrielle had that clean smell exclusive only to a baby. She thrust a fist into her mouth and within seconds had fallen asleep.

Quintin moved closer to Victoria, dropping an arm over her shoulder. "What is it about you that children fall asleep in your arms? First Ryan and now Gabrielle. You remind me of the paintings of the Madonna with child."

She closed her eyes, not responding. He had no idea how difficult it was for her to hold a child, knowing every child she held would never be from her own body.

Richard's caustic words attacked her and she tightened her grip on Gabrielle's soft rounded body. *I want out of this marriage. Victoria. I need a woman who can give me children. My children, not someone else's throwaways.*

She shivered slightly as Quintin pressed his mouth to her ear, the silken hair on his upper lip sweeping over the sensitive flesh of her lobe.

"I want you so much," he whispered passionately. What he didn't say was that he wanted her as his wife and the mother of his children.

Victoria smiled, not opening her eyes. He wanted her and she wanted him. She loved him and he loved her. At that moment life with Quintin was wonderful and perfect.

Victoria stood in a huddle with Quintin's three sisters, four sisters-in-law, and the girlfriend of his only single brother discussing strategy. All of the women wore black baseball caps with a large white L printed on the front.

"Victoria, you're new at this, so I need to warn you that the guys cheat," Sharon explained. "There's nothing too low or dirty they won't do in order to win. And that means they'll slide into you when you're covering a base, or whoever's going to be their catcher will block the plate even if he's not holding the ball." Her sherry-colored eyes glowed with excitement.

"We'll play three full innings, but if no one scores, then we'll play another three. Now, let's go out there and kick some booty!"

Victoria jogged out to second base. The expansive field in the back of the farmhouse had been turned into a baseball diamond many years ago. The grassy knoll beyond a low wooden fence some two hundred feet from home plate was designated as home-run territory. Lines of white chalk down the right and left fields outlined fair territory from foul.

Adjusting her cap and pounding her glove, Victoria leaned forward and concentrated on the first batter. She smiled. Quintin was the lead-off batter.

The annual Memorial Day baseball game had developed with some hard and fast rules: an underhand pitch was utilized with the larger softball along with the lighter weight aluminum bat, and Charles Lord stood behind the plate as the perennial umpire while Etta Mae kept score.

Teenage and preteen offspring sat on benches, cheering for their parents, aunts, and uncles.

Lydia went into her windup, and a wicked curve sailed close to Quintin's chin. He glared at her and crouched lower in his batting stance; he took the next pitch, but his bat made contact with the third one and it sailed over Victoria's head and out into center field. Sharon came up with the ball and threw it to Victoria a second after Quintin's foot made contact with the bag.

He smiled at Victoria. "Hi, beautiful." She ignored him, pounding her glove and watching as Quintin's oldest brother stepped into the batter's box.

Lydia, experienced with the masculine gender's strategy of taunting basemen, glanced over her shoulder. She lowered her head, watching as Quintin took a sizable lead toward third base. Without warning, she turned and fired the ball into second base. Victoria caught the perfect throw and tagged Quintin before he could lunge back to the bag.

"You're out!" Victoria screamed, leaning over a prone Quintin. He raised his head and glared at her. "Get off the field, handsome. You're holding up the game," she taunted.

"You'll pay for that," he threatened softly, rising to his feet and adjusting his cap.

"I can't wait."

He moved closer to her. "I'll make you beg."

"I can't wait," she repeated before he turned and loped off the playing field.

The game continued with no one scoring through the first three innings. The next three became intense as the women scored first with two back-to-back doubles in the bottom of the fifth inning. The men came back with two runs in the top of the sixth.

Sharon, Victoria, and Lydia were the scheduled batters for the bottom of the sixth inning. Sharon led off, exploding the first pitch over the fence at center field. All of the women gathered at home plate and waited while she circled the bases in a slow, victorious trot.

Play was resumed after the brief celebration. Victoria felt the tension as she gripped the bat and stepped into the batter's box. Moisture had formed between her breasts and ran in rivulets down her belly under the T-shirt. Her team had tied the score.

Dwayne went into his windup and pitched a missile past her chest. She stepped out of the box and inhaled deeply. Lydia's boyfriend pounded his glove loudly behind her. "Let's see another one just like that one, Dwayne!" the catcher shouted.

Dwayne complied, and the next pitch landed in the exact same spot. "Strike two," Charles intoned.

Victoria concentrated and crouched. The next pitch connected with the bat and sailed out into left field. She ran toward first base, her gaze on the ball. The left fielder lost the ball in the grass and she wound up on third base with a stand-up triple by the time it was relayed to the catcher.

"Nice hitting and nice base running," Quintin crooned behind her. "I was waiting for you to make it to third base all afternoon."

"Why?" she asked, not turning around.

"So I can do *this!*" Moving closer, he nuzzled the back of her neck.

"Quintin!" She remembered Sharon saying that the men would employ any trick to win.

"What would you do if I kissed you right now?"

"You can't interfere with the runner," she retorted. Lydia had stepped into the batter's box.

"I'm not interfering with the runner, Vicky. I just want to kiss my girlfriend."

Victoria took several steps up the third base line toward home plate. "I didn't know I was your girlfriend."

"You're more than my girlfriend," Quintin countered.

Victoria was not given an opportunity to ask what she was to Quintin because she was off and running as soon as Lydia's bat made contact with the ball. The shortstop fielded the ball and threw it to home plate.

Less than six feet from the plate, Victoria realized she was going to be out. The catcher was crouched to protect the plate and tag her. She increased her speed, springing and jumping over his head. She scrambled back and touched home plate just under his tag.

Charles Lord crossed his arms over the runner and catcher, shouting, "Safe!"

Seventeen

The victory celebration was loud and boisterous. Victoria was dubbed the female Ozzie Smith for her acrobatics on the playing field, and the members of her team lauded over, taunted, and jeered their male counterparts.

"Next year we're playing with mixed teams," Lucien Lord declared.

Lydia frowned at her oldest brother. "No way, Lucien. You guys just can't stand to lose. If you'd won you wouldn't be crying about having mixed teams."

"This is the first year we haven't had mixed teams," Lucien complained.

"And it won't be the first time the guys will lose, either," Sharon stated smugly.

"How were we to know that Quint's girlfriend was a gymnast," Dwayne grumbled, frowning.

"I'm not a gymnast," Victoria protested, unable to believe the men were so competitive.

"What are you?" every male member of the team chorused. Everyone except for Quintin. He leaned against a tree, arms folded over his chest, smiling.

"Tell them, Vicky," he urged.

She glared back at him. "I will not. Just because you lost

doesn't mean the women should have to justify we have superior playing skills."

"You tell them, girlfriend," Lucien's wife shouted.

"Why can't you men accept defeat?" It was Etta Mae's turn to bond with the winning female team. "You lost, gentlemen. Case closed."

"Dad . . . Dad, are you sure Victoria touched the bag before the tag?" Lucien would not concede defeat.

Charles Lord nodded slowly. "You lost, Son." His voice was soft and final.

Gloves and bats were gathered and placed in several large plastic milk crates. The annual Memorial Day baseball competition was over until the next year.

Everyone filed into the farmhouse and waited in turn to use the two and a half bathrooms there to wash up before sitting down to enjoy dessert.

"Who made the potato pie?" the female voice shouted to be heard above the din in the large kitchen. "Etta Mae, did you make the pie?"

"Not me," Etta Mae replied.

Sharon took a bite of her slice of sweet potato pie. "This is not Mama's pie. Who made the pie?"

Quintin, sitting beside Victoria at a large oak table, stared at Victoria's impassive profile. She was not going to admit she had baked the pie.

Gabrielle's mother cradled the baby on her hip while cutting a small piece of pie from her husband's plate. "Are you sure this isn't your pie, Etta Mae?"

"Even if I could make the filling as creamy and spicy as this, I've never been able to roll out my crusts this thin," Etta Mae confessed.

Lydia nodded. "Mama's right. This is not her crust."

"Who made the potato pie?" Lucien's fifteen-year-old son walked into the kitchen, his mouth full.

"Weasel out of this one," Quintin whispered close to Victoria's ear.

She glared at him, eyes narrowing. "You better not say anything." Her voice was low and threatening.

"Mama, Vicky's threatening me," he wailed, concealing a grin.

"Grow up, Quintin," Etta Mae admonished.

Quintin's grin grew wider. "She's threatening to beat me up if I tell that she made the sweet potato pies."

There was a stunned silence, everyone's gaze fixed on her flushed face.

"What *don't* you do well?" Sharon questioned, glancing from Victoria to her brother.

"She's perfect," Quintin announced proudly.

"You've got that right," Dwayne confirmed under his breath. He earned a solid punch to his shoulder from his girlfriend for his comment.

Victoria was besieged with questions about how she made her crust and what ingredients she added to the mashed sweet potatoes to achieve its distinctive taste. It wasn't until half an hour later that she escaped to the outdoors.

The air had cooled down considerably with the setting sun as she made her way across the front lawn. Many of the young adults and small children sat on the grass in groups of twos and threes, talking or arguing softly and cheerfully. A few of them called out to her as she passed, and she acknowledged them with a smile and a wave.

The Lords were a dynamic and somewhat overpowering family. She wasn't used to the noise and energy they seemed to expend effortlessly.

Charles and Etta Mae were not only tolerant, but they were proud of their children and grandchildren. There was no mistaking their pride with the fun-loving, good-natured family unit.

"Victoria, may I talk to you?"

She turned, smiling at an excited Lydia. "Of course."

The nineteen-year-old was tall and willowy as a young sapling. The only feature she shared with Quintin was her eyes. They were the same gold-brown shade and were framed by long thick lashes.

"I'd like to ask a favor," Lydia began shyly.

Victoria smiled, trying to put the young woman at ease. "Ask."

"I'd like to work with you. What I mean is, will you teach me to cook . . . prepare certain dishes? I'm majoring in culinary arts with a minor in restaurant and hotel management. I just completed my first year," she rushed on, "and I'd love to get some hands-on experience."

"Are you working now?"

Lydia shook her head. "I've applied to several restaurants, but no one has hired me. I've told them I'll do anything. Wait or bus tables. Even wash dishes. But everyone that I've spoken to said they don't want to train me, then have me leave when classes begin again in the fall. I want experience, Victoria. Nothing else."

Victoria was charmed by Lydia's enthusiasm. She was older than Lydia when she decided on a career in the culinary arts, and her own enthusiasm had been similar.

Her business enterprise was in its infancy stage. She knew it would be only a matter of time before she'd need an assistant. An assistant she would have to train, and one she could depend on.

"Do you attend a local college?"

"Yes."

"Will you be available on weekends during the school year?"

"Yes."

A slight frown appeared between her eyes as she considered Lydia's proposal. "I can't pay you much—"

"I don't want any pay," Lydia interrupted.

Victoria smiled, shaking her head. "Okay. Can you start tomorrow morning?"

"Yes, yes, yes!" Lydia clenched her hands, then bit down on her lower lip.

"Be at my place tomorrow at ten o'clock."

Lydia lowered her hands and took a deep breath. "Where do you live?"

"Next door to your brother. I'm his neighbor."

When Lydia squealed, several people turned and glanced over at her. "I don't believe it. Lucky for you, Victoria. As Sharon would put it, 'You've got the pick of the Lord litter.' Both Sharon and I agree that Quintin is our favorite brother. He always spoiled us and we're *very* protective of him."

Victoria smiled. "You think Quintin needs protecting?"

"Not really," she confessed. "It's just that I've always thought Quintin is very special. He wasn't anything like my other brothers who forced every guy who got up enough nerve to date my sisters to run a fierce gauntlet."

Victoria thought of her own brother's reaction when he found out that Richard had asked her out. Richard had to reassure Nat that he had no intention of sleeping with his sister unless they were married.

"What did they do?" she asked Lydia.

"They usually met them at the door and described in detail a slow form of dismemberment, starting with the fingers, if they even remotely entertained the notion of seducing their sisters. It took a while before the word got out that they were bluffing."

She couldn't help herself as she burst out laughing. Lydia curved an arm around her shoulders and hugged her.

"Thank you again. I'll see you tomorrow morning."

Lydia returned to the house and Quintin watched Victoria as she stared at his sister's retreating figure. He hadn't been able to talk Lydia out of approaching Victoria about becoming her apprentice. He didn't want her to feel obligated to hire his sister because of their relationship. Thinking of sleeping together, he couldn't wait to be alone with her again.

He made his way over to Victoria, his step light, his stride loose and fluid. Curving an arm around her waist, he led her away from the house.

"Did you hire her?"

Victoria wound her left arm around Quintin's waist.

"Yes."

"You didn't have to." His voice was low and soothing.

"I know I didn't."

"Don't let her get away with—"

"Don't worry, Quintin," she cut in. "I'm not going to coddle her. She'll work and work hard. Lydia will only be successful if she's serious about wanting to become a chef."

Pulling her closer, Quintin leaned over and kissed her forehead. "Good."

"And I'll not tolerate any interference from you if I have to reprimand her."

Stopping, he turned to face her. "I will not interfere. You have my word on that."

Victoria's wide-eyed gaze was fixed on his face, taking in everything that was Quintin Lord and everything about him that permitted her to love him so freely.

She smiled up at him, leaning toward his tall, strong body. "I'm glad I came today. I've had a lot of fun."

Quintin's hands cradled her upturned face. "I'm sure you and the ladies had a lot of fun kicking the stuffing out of the Lords with that little ballet maneuver. You're lucky I didn't tell the Lords that you were a dancer."

Her fingers went to his strong wrists. "You act as if I did something illegal, Quintin. Major-league ballplayers go through ballet maneuvers as a part of their physical training."

"We're not major-league ballplayers."

"I can see that. But maybe if the Lords were professional players they would learn how to lose without moaning and pouting. Why is it so hard to admit the ladies beat you?"

His eyes narrowed in intensity. "Because we're very competitive," he stated, his voice taking on a serious tone.

Lowering his hands, he grasped her hand and led her out to the grassy baseball field.

"What you've seen today is what every male Lord had to experience when growing up," he began. "My mother gave birth to nine children over a span of twenty-two years. Some of us were only eleven months apart, others two years, and the next child always had to fight for attention and independence. My sisters had it a lot easier. They've grown up protected and indulged by everyone. Therefore, they are a lot less competitive."

Victoria concentrated on placing one foot in front of the other. "Are you saying that you didn't have a happy childhood?"

Quintin stopped and shook his head. "No, Vicky. I had the best childhood anyone could ask for. I was wanted, loved, provided for, and encouraged to be whatever I wanted to be. I knew I wanted to be an artist since I was about ten and my father paid for my art lessons. There was never a question that he wouldn't agree to do it."

Squeezing her fingers gently, he continued walking. "I suppose we get our competitiveness from Etta Mae. This land belonged to her family. Her great-grandfather bought three acres of farmland, raising a breed of cattle that were resistant to most diseases while yielding lean tender meat.

"As his profits increased he bought up more adjacent lands until he and his brothers had a small empire of nearly a thousand beef and milk cows spread out over more than six hundred acres. By the time he'd educated his children and grandchildren the family's interest in breeding livestock dwindled until the land was sold off in large parcels. All that is left is ten acres."

There was a quiet, comfortable silence as they made their way over the land on which thousands of hooves had trampled. Ancient trees, with massive trunks and sweeping branches, broke up the monotony of grassland. Quintin sat down under one of the trees, pulling Victoria down with him.

Easing her back to the grass, he smiled down at her, running a forefinger over her nose and down to her lips.

"I've wanted to do this all day," he confessed seconds before he covered her mouth with his.

She felt the comforting crush of his weight as he covered her body, reveling in the taste of his mouth and his strength. Her ardor rose quickly and her fingers gathered the fabric of his T-shirt, pulling it up where she kneaded the hard muscles in his broad back. Her breath rushed out between her lips in short gasps.

She wanted him! The gush of wetness between her thighs startled her. His touch, his kiss, was enough to make her ready for him.

But she couldn't make love to him now. Not on the ground, and not where someone could discover them.

"Quintin, please," she moaned as his tongue plunged recklessly into her mouth.

Quintin's right hand searched under her T-shirt, capturing a firm, ripe breast, and, without warning, his mouth replaced his hand. She arched, keening, pushing the distended nipple farther into his mouth.

"Quintin, no!" The nipple slipped from between his teeth, his head coming up, and Victoria saw something in the depths of the gold-brown gaze she had never seen before. There was passion but there was also an expression of fevered abandonment. A heated frenzy lurking just below the surface, ready to ravish her mind as well as her body.

Closing her eyes, she pulled down her shirt. "Let's go back," she said hoarsely.

Rolling off her body, Quintin came to his feet and extended his hand. "Let's go *home*."

Eighteen

"My place or yours?" Victoria asked, opening the front door. Quintin followed her down the hall to their apartments.

"Mine," he replied.

"Let me get something to change into and I'll be right over."

Quintin pulled her against his body. "You don't need clothes."

"I'm not going to walk around naked," she protested.

"I like you naked," he countered, grinning.

"You're an animal." Her tone was a teasing one.

He pressed a light kiss to her mouth. "Wrong, Vicky. Hannibal's the animal, and even he's going to have his share of fun for the next few weeks."

Quintin had given in to Sharon's plea that he permit her to breed Hannibal with her prized Onyx. Hannibal would spend the next two weeks with Onyx before the bitch came into heat, hopefully with successful results.

Victoria opened the door and made her way into her apartment. She'd left the air-conditioning on and the high-ceilinged spaces were cool and refreshing.

It took less than fifteen minutes to check her answering machine and gather a change of clothes and her personal toiletries. A message from Jo confirmed that Sunny Calhoun wanted VJ Catering to provide the food for her upcoming Wednesday afternoon luncheon, and the call from Ethan Bennington asked that she call him Tuesday morning at nine-thirty. He left the number to the Greater Baltimore Cultural Center before the message ended.

The throbbing rendition of Percy Sledge's "When A Man Loves a Woman" flowed from hidden speakers as she walked through the open door to Quintin's apartment.

A slight smile softened Victoria's mouth. His apartment was immaculate, verifying his claim that he had hired a cleaning woman.

"You're just in time. I filled the tub for your bath." Quintin came down the staircase wearing only a pair of cut-off jeans. He slung a damp towel around his neck.

Victoria smiled up at him. It hadn't taken Quintin long to recognize her routine. She always showered in the morning, but preferred a leisurely bath before going to bed.

"Tonight you're in for a real treat. I'm going to give you a massage."

"I can't wait," she crooned, winking saucily and moving past him up the staircase.

Victoria lay facedown on the bed. Quintin knelt over her and gently kneaded her calves and the backs of her thighs. His strong fingers had dissolved the knotted muscles in her neck and shoulders, then worked their magic down her back to her legs.

The pungent fragrance of her body cream lingered in the air as she gave in to his expert touch, moaning sensually. She was so relaxed, Quintin had to repeat his query.

"No, you're not hurting me," she slurred.

Lowering his chest to her back, he covered her body, supporting most of his weight on his elbows. "You have an exquisite body, Vicky. I'd love to paint you in the nude."

She froze, her eyes opening. "No."

"The painting would only be for me," he whispered against her ear. "It would become a part of my private collection."

"You have a private collection?"

Quintin nodded. The picture of her on her patio was nearly completed. It was the first of many he intended to paint with Victoria as his model.

"How many paintings do you have in your private collection?"

"Just one."

"Is it a nude?"

"No. The subject is clothed."

Victoria swallowed loudly. She wasn't a prude, but she never considered sitting for a portrait—especially not a nude.

Quintin rolled off her body and pulled her to his side. His gaze was fixed on her mouth. "I don't want frontal nudity. I'd have you sit on a chair in profile, one leg draped over the other. The focus would be on your legs and feet. Your arms would be crossed over your breasts with your hands cupping your elbows. Your head would be tilted back, showing off the curve and length of your neck and the fragile bones of your jawline. I'd paint you from the left side because that's your best angle."

She was flattered her wanted to paint her, but she didn't feel comfortable knowing anyone would be able to view her nude body.

"I'm sorry, Quintin. I can't. I—"

"That's all right, darling," he interrupted. "Forget I asked."

The fingers of his right hand lifted several strands of hair from over her ear, his touch as light as the brush of a butter-fly's wing. A slight smile lifted the corners of his mouth under his mustache.

"What are you staring at?" she asked, capturing his gaze with her own.

"You."

The heat rose in her cheeks. "Why?" Her voice had dropped an octave.

"Because I like looking at you."

"Do you like what you see?"

His lids came down slowly as his grin widened. "Very much."

She returned his smile. "I'm glad."

His hand moved from her hair, down to a bare shoulder, and still lower to her waist, pulling her to his body until her bare breasts were flattened against his chest. His warm breath filtered over her mouth.

"Don't move. There's one thing I forgot to do to you."

Victoria lay on her back, staring up at the ceiling. Never had she felt so loved, so adored and pampered.

Quintin returned, sitting down on the side of the bed. A slight smile played at the corners of his sensual mouth. "I have to fluff you up."

She jerked, not knowing whether to laugh or turn away in shame. Quintin wielded a small comb, the teeth moving tentatively over the thick, dark tangled hair between her thighs.

He shifted his eyebrows as a full grin creased his face. "Now, it looks very nice. Take a look, Vicky. See how fluffy it is."

She half rose, cheeks filled with fire, surveying his handiwork. "Nice," she managed to croak.

"How do you taste, Vicky?"

Closing her eyes against his intense penetrating stare, she shook her head. "I don't know."

Quintin's hands moved up her thighs, cupping her hips. "You've never been tasted before?"

"No," she shuddered, visibly shaken by his erotic questioning.

She hadn't lied. Richard was the first man she'd slept with, and their lovemaking had been satisfying. Richard had been experienced, but he had also been very traditional.

"Do you want me to tell you how you taste?"

She sat up, her fingers catching in the hair on his chest. She was unable to hide their trembling from Quintin. She wanted him!

For the second time that day he had her aching and trembling for him.

"Do you?" he repeated.

Hiding her face in his throat, Victoria inhaled the cleanliness of his flesh, savoring the masculine smell of his freshly showered body.

Every nerve in her body tightened and screamed with desire. She ached with unleashed passion.

"Yes." The single word was a tortured moan.

Holding on to her, Quintin reached out and dimmed the lamp. If he was going to introduce Victoria to another level of sensuality, then he had to put her at ease.

He knew inherently that Victoria Jones was capable of grand passion, and he wanted to be the one to unleash that passion. He wanted to wipe away the memory of any man who had claimed her before. He wanted to be the last lover in her life.

He wanted her to want him as much as he wanted her, and he wanted her to want him in her life until they both ceased to exist.

"Relax, baby," he crooned, smoothing her hair off her face and easing her back down to the bed. "Let me do all of the work."

Closing her eyes, Victoria let her senses take over. She heard Quintin remove his cut-off jeans and drop them to the floor. She felt him move over her body, his greater weight comforting and protective.

"Stay with me, Vicky."

She nodded, not opening her eyes. She moaned once as his mustached mouth sought out her exposed throat. The brush of the hair on his upper lip over her throat was startling. The sensation of his mustache against her silken flesh intensified as he moved down her chest.

Her hands curled into tight fists. His tongue on her breasts, coating them with moisture, beaded the areola and brought her nipples into instant prominence. He alternated licking them with blowing his breath and rolling the swollen nipple between his teeth. She cried out once, but then bit down on her lower lip to stop any further sound.

"That was very good," he murmured, inching down her body.

Victoria's legs were trembling uncontrollably by the time he explored her flat belly. She went rigid when his hot breath seared the furred triangle between her thighs.

Sliding down the bed, Quintin gently forced her legs apart. He heard her first gasp of shock, but it was lost in the ensuing sobs of passion as his mouth worked its magic.

Writhing, Victoria couldn't stop her hips from moving as her body vibrated with liquid fire.

Her rising passion threatened to consume her before she reached fulfillment, and that fulfillment was poised, teasing, and hypnotic. She felt the hysteria of delight radiating from every pressure point in her body while her nerve endings screamed relentlessly.

Her head thrashed back and forth on the pillow and a cry was torn from the back of her throat.

"Quintin!"

He registered her desperation, her fear, and he acknowledged his own burning, pressing need to bury himself in her body.

Moving fluidly up her trembling form, he entered her in one smooth strong thrust of possession.

His own breath was coming quickly through parted lips. He felt her warm, wet, throbbing flesh close around him and he trembled uncontrollably.

Victoria was pulling and sucking him in. He didn't know where she began and he ended. Her legs encircled his waist, allowing him deeper access. She was driving him crazy. But if he was going to lose his mind he wanted her with him.

Victoria felt every muscle in Quintin's upper body straining; she heard his deep, labored breathing; she felt the dizzying pumping of his heart against her breasts, and she savored every strong thrust of his hips against hers.

She found his mouth and tasted herself on his lips. A moan of ecstasy escaped her when his large hands slipped under her hips, holding her tightly as he drove into her with a frenzied pumping motion.

She soared higher and higher until she exploded in a shower of shivering delight, whispering his name over and over. Before her sighs of completion faded, Quintin's unrestrained cry of passion filled the room.

He collapsed heavily on her body, gasping for air, reversing their positions. Victoria rested her cheek on his damp chest, trembling uncontrollably.

Quintin's breathing slowed and her trembling subsided, then stilled. Both of them were smiling broadly.

"Quintin?"

"Hmm-mm?"

"How did I taste?"

He opened one eye, peering down at her upturned face. Her smile was that of a completely satisfied woman. Lifting a shoulder, he shifted his eyebrows. "I suppose it was all right." He pulled a sheet up over their moist bodies.

Her face burned in embarrassment. She should've never asked. He didn't like it.

"You were delicious," he admitted after a lengthy silence.

Victoria wanted to punch him for teasing her. Shifting to face him, she pressed a kiss to his hard shoulder.

Without warning, she went rigid. "Quintin?"

"What is it?" He sat up suddenly.

"There's a furry animal in the bed." Her voice was a strained whisper.

Quintin pulled back the sheet, searching the large bed. "Where, Victoria? Where is it?" he repeated, fearful that maybe a rodent had gotten into the house.

Victoria moved quickly to his side, her right hand searching between his thighs. "Here it is," she said, cradling his sex in her splayed fingers.

He stared down at her hand as realization dawned. She was only teasing.

All levity waned quickly when he grew hard and heavy in her hand. Their gazes met and locked. Rising to her knees, Victoria curled into the curve of his body and kissed him deeply.

"I love you," she confessed seconds before he eased her back to the pillows.

"Not as much as I love you," he rasped, devouring her mouth and demonstrating the depth of his feelings for her.

He didn't ask the question that plagued his every waking moment. He couldn't wait until he felt the time was right to ask Victoria Jones to become his wife.

Victoria led Lydia Lord into the kitchen five minutes before ten o'clock. Lydia had arrived early. That was a good sign. The young woman would be punctual and dependable.

"I'll show you where everything is, but first I want to show you my calendar for the next week." A large calendar indicating three months at a glance was filled with notations.

"I have a new client," Victoria began. "Mrs. Calhoun holds a weekly Wednesday luncheon for about a dozen women, ranging in age from the mid-fifties to late sixties. I always consider age when preparing a menu. I'm certain these women are watching their weight as well as blood pressure and cholesterol readings.

"And that means I'll prepare low-fat, low-sodium, and high-fiber dishes. But that doesn't mean that the dishes won't be attractive or palatable."

Lydia studied the calendar. "What will you serve for her luncheon tomorrow?"

"I'm considering a spiced chicken salad over shredded

lettuce, sliced cucumber, and tomatoes. The chicken stays moist and full of flavor because it's prepared in a yogurt marinade. There's another salad known as a Wensleydale salad. It's made with shredded white cabbage, red pepper, Wensleydale cheese, thinly sliced scallions, and black olives. The dressing is a mixture of plain yogurt, coarse-grained mustard, and honey."

"That sounds fabulous."

"Any cheese I use will be a low-fat. Then there's always a summer green salad of romaine, oak leaf, dandelion, or sorrel leaves. Sometimes I add very young and tender spinach leaves."

Lydia's dark eyes glittered with excitement. "What about the entrèe?"

"Most likely shrimp creole with a rice pilaf. But for those who cannot eat shellfish, I'll offer a grilled chicken breast with the pilaf."

"Dessert?"

"Peaches cardinale, a summer fruit compote, or gelato."

"Sounds delicious."

"Now let's go shopping. I have to prepare for an anniversary celebration this coming weekend. I want to show you how I select different cuts of meat. Our first stop will be a wholesale butcher."

Victoria spent the better part of an hour showing Lydia her kitchen and explaining what pots and what utensils were used for the preparation and cooking of certain dishes. The young woman was a quick study, jotting down notes in a small binder.

Watching Lydia's hands as she made a notation, Victoria frowned. "You're going to have to cut your nails."

Lydia's head came up quickly, then her gaze shifted to her long, delicate fingers. Her nails were long and shimmered with a bright red color.

"No polish, either," she continued. "No one wants to see flecks of red on their freshly whipped cream or eat particles of uncooked meat or poultry with their fresh lettuce leaves from the residue left under your nails."

Lydia nodded. "Do you have a nail clipper, polish remover, and an emery board?"

Victoria patted the younger woman's shoulder in a comforting gesture. "Come with me."

She had heard the same lecture the first day she attended classes at the culinary school in Washington, D.C. The instructor had listed the do's and don't's on a chalkboard, and long fingernails headed the list of don't's.

One of her male classmates teased her relentlessly, dubbing her "Sally Hansen" until she beat him out for first prize during a pastry-making competition. That was the beginning of many awards she garnered before winning a full graduate scholarship to attend the La Varenne École de Cuisine in France.

"You're going to be very good," she told Lydia after she had clipped, stripped, and filed her beautiful nails.

Lydia managed a strained smile. "How do you know that?"

"Because you want to be successful, Lydia. And you have enough Lord competitiveness in you to make sacrifices in order to achieve that success."

"Thank you for believing in me, Victoria."

She wanted to ask Victoria whether she was aware that they were to become family in the very near future. Both she and Sharon agreed that Quintin was in love with Victoria, and the possessive look in his eyes indicated he would not let her go without a battle. The look was a familiar one. All of the Lord brothers had had a similar look just before they asked the woman they had fallen in love with to marry them.

"Let's get busy," Victoria said, picking up her own notebook filled with items she had to order for a very busy week of cooking and baking.

Nineteen

Victoria and Lydia spent the morning and early afternoon selecting cuts of beef, lamb, smoked and fresh hams, and poultry from a wholesale meat packer. The butcher wrote down her explicit instructions as to how she wanted the meats dressed and when they should be delivered. Lydia stood by, watching and listening intently.

When they returned to the minivan, Victoria headed straight for the fish market. "There will come a time when all I'll need to do is call in my order to the butcher and he'll know how I want the meat cut and dressed."

"What about the fish people?" Lydia asked.

"I'll pick up the fish because it's a lot easier to buy and prepare."

Lydia stared out through the windshield, her brow furrowed in concentration. "It seems as if there's so much to learn."

"It appears that way in the beginning. I never thought I would learn the differences between all of the salad greens," Victoria admitted. "There's arugula, Belgium Endive, and Wirloof. Then there's Bibb, Boston, and iceberg lettuce. Cabbage comes in red, green, ruffly savoy, and Chinese. And you must remember that Belgium endive or Wirloof taste different from the bitter-tasting curly, flattened heads of regular chicory or endive. Dandelion, escarole, romaine, watercress, and spinach are also seen in many of today's salads."

"What would you prepare if you were cooking for vegetarians?" Lydia questioned.

"I'd steam my vegetables or blanch them and use them in a salad."

Lydia continued questioning Victoria, eager to learn.

"What vegetables would you use?"

"Cucumbers, red and green bell peppers, red and white radish, all varieties of tomatoes, scallions, asparagus, green and wax beans, broccoli, cauliflower, carrots, celery, white turnips, kohlrabi, snow peas, zucchini, mushrooms, red and Spanish onion, fennel and bean sprouts," Victoria paused. "The list is endless. Fruit salads can also be used to satisfy vegetarians as well as those who eat meat."

She glanced at Lydia's profile. "Ready to quit?"

"No," Lydia replied quickly. "Someday I want to own a gourmet, four-star restaurant."

Victoria nodded, remembering the different stations she covered while learning the restaurant business. Before she worked her way up to sous chef she had worked at the grill, sauté, pasta, and pastry stations. She demonstrated remarkable skill as a garde manager when she supervised all cold food preparation, including sandwiches and salads. Preparing elaborate salads had become her specialty.

The two women spent less than fifteen minutes selecting large succulent shrimp for the creole and a half-dozen softshell crabs for their dinner later that evening.

On the return trip home Lydia was quiet, reviewing the notes in her small binder while Victoria's thoughts were of Quintin.

They had made love again earlier that morning just as the sun rose to herald the beginning of a new day. After their pulses slowed and their breathing returned to normal, they lay together, limbs entwined and hearts beating as one.

Quintin had whispered over and over that he loved her; loved her more than he had ever thought it possible he could love any woman. She registered the deep passion in his voice and cried silently. He comforted her, believing her tears were an expression of joy. He never knew of her fear; a fear that he would want something from her that she was unable to offer him.

Lydia sat between her brother and Victoria on the patio devouring soft-shell crab sandwiches with red-pepper mayonnaise, a salad of mixed greens with sun-dried tomatoes in a honey-mustard sauce, iced tea made with a refreshing bubbly seltzer, and several scoops of hazelnut gelato.

"Do you eat like this every day, Quintin?" Lydia asked.

"Just about," he admitted, dabbing his mouth with a cloth napkin.

Lydia shook her head. "It's like dying and going to heaven."

Flashing a smile, Quintin stared at Victoria. "I die and go to heaven every time Vicky and I . . ." He broke off quickly when he realized what he was about to say. Lowering his gaze, he grimaced as both women stared at him.

"When you and Vicky do what, my darling brother?" Lydia teased.

Not bothering to answer, Quintin stood up and began clearing the table. Victoria and Lydia stared at his retreating back, then burst out laughing, the sound following him into the apartment.

They sobered, then Lydia offered to help clean up. Victoria refused, saying, "You'd better call it a day. You have a lot to digest before you come back tomorrow. If you get here around eight I'll have you help me prepare the dishes for the Calhoun luncheon. You'll only work half a day tomorrow, because you're going to need all of your energy for Thursday and Friday. You'll probably be on your feet each day for about six to eight hours."

Lydia nodded. Lowering her chin, she smiled shyly. "Can I have another serving of gelato before I leave?"

"I'll give you some to take home."

Lydia was overjoyed when she was given the choice of choosing the flavors. She selected a quart of mascarpone and zabaglione.

"Good choice," Quintin said, smiling at his youngest sister.

"You've tasted these?" she asked him.

Crossing his arms over his chest, he nodded slowly. "I've had the extreme pleasure of tasting *every* flavor."

Lydia stared at his flat midsection. "Be careful. You know how hard it is to keep your weight down as you get older."

"Go home, fresh mouth!" His smile belied his sharp tone.

"I'm going, I'm going," Lydia whispered, walking on tiptoe across the kitchen, carrying a bag with the gelato.

Victoria and Quintin, arm-in-arm, followed Lydia to the outer door. They watched as she settled herself behind the wheel of her Honda Civic, and waved to her as she drove off. She returned their wave through an open window.

Quintin pulled Victoria against his side. "How was she?"

"She's good, Quintin." Turning in his embrace, Victoria smiled up at him. "Let's go for a walk."

Quintin nodded. He returned to his apartment to get his keys. Minutes later, he and Victoria walked outside together enjoying the warmth of the twilight and smiling at other couples who had decided to take advantage of the warm evening.

They walked for a mile in silence before retracing their steps. As they neared their block, Quintin broke the silence saying, "I'm not going to be able to see as much of you in the next few weeks as I'd like. I have to do a shoot of a clothing designer's latest creations. If I can get the project completed in three weeks I'll be lucky."

She squeezed his fingers. "That's not going to be a problem because my calendar is also filling up."

He stopped and cradled her face between his hands, exhaling audibly. "When I do a shoot I really get wrapped up in my work, and I just don't want you to think that I'm avoiding or ignoring you."

"Don't worry about me, Quintin. I'm a lot more secure than you think." At that moment she was, not knowing that her statement soon would be replayed in her head, over and over, haunting her relentlessly.

Quintin slipped from Victoria's bed two hours before dawn, brushing a light kiss across her soft lips. "I'll see you later tonight," he promised.

He kissed her again and reached for his jeans. Making his way down the staircase, he walked out of her apartment and into his own.

An unexplainable shiver of apprehension swept through him as he walked into the bathroom. He went through the unconscious motion of shaving, looking at his reflection staring back at him in the mirror.

He hadn't made love to Victoria either the night before or that morning. She hadn't asked him to nor had she intimated that she wanted to be intimate with him. She seemed content to lie beside him, one leg draped over his thigh. She had been unusually quiet, and instead of trying to draw her out, he permitted her to withdraw from him. And when he left her bed he somehow felt her withdrawal was complete.

Showering and dressing quickly, he loaded his cameras, canisters of film, and tripod into the Jeep. He drove down quiet streets, heading east toward the ocean. Streaks of pink and pale blue were just beginning to brighten the sky as he pulled into a parking area along a stretch of sandy beach.

Four tall, emaciated-looking models stood on the sand, clutching cups of steaming liquids and pouting. Their bodies were swaddled in flowing robes and caftans. Quintin nodded after he gave them a quick glance, then began setting up his equipment.

He recognized the preening divas. Each one thought she

was more beautiful and more photogenic than the other. He found them too thin, too vain, and much too superficial; however, behind the camera lens they were transformed into delicate, colorful butterflies and peacocks.

A slight smile softened his mouth. He much preferred Victoria Jones's looks. She was soft and totally feminine. Her face was enchanting, her body sensual, and her legs perfect. He found it hard to believe she had come into his life, filling a void he didn't known existed.

Checking the light with a meter, he adjusted the lens on the camera positioned atop the tripod. In another ten minutes there would be enough light to begin photographing.

He signaled the director, and a short, slightly built man dressed in white waved his hands at the sullen women.

"Ladies, ladies. We're ready." His voice carried easily over the soft lapping waves.

In unison, cover-ups were discarded. The wardrobe mistress took them and disappeared into a tent a short distance down the beach.

The models were dressed in colorful wraparound skirts in a Ghanaian cloth. The skirts revealed flat stomachs, hipbones, and inverted belly buttons. A half dozen strands of large Moroccan beads hung from long, thin necks, modestly covering four pairs of small brown breasts.

Quintin checked the light again. The rising sun cast a golden shield behind the women, turning their varying shades of brown skin into pearlized satin.

Peering through the camera lens, Quintin motioned with his right hand. "Ryanna, show me more of your right shoulder. That's it. Vashit, raise your chin just a tad. Good," he crooned.

The four women raised sticklike arms covered with circles of brass and wood, and posed—lips pouting, eyes hooded, bare feet arched. Their narrow bodies swayed to the sounds of drums coming from the speakers of the large portable tape player next to the dress designer.

Satisfaction lit up the face of Abayomi Koffigoh as she

watched the models come alive in front of the camera. Business was good enough for her to hire top models to show off her latest creations, and good enough for her to hire one of the best photographers to shoot them.

Her dark eyes narrowed behind the lenses of her sunglasses. When she had interviewed Quintin Lord for the assignment he was friendly yet very businesslike. He ignored her veiled attempt to attend a dinner party at her home and she had shrugged off his refusal. He probably didn't like women, she had mused.

Quintin used two rolls of film before the models retreated to the tent to change into their next outfit. He shot another six rolls before the sun bore mercilessly down on the women's exposed skin and the director decided to wrap up the shoot for the day. Weather permitting, they all agreed to meet the following morning for more beach scenes.

"If you want me here tomorrow somebody had better do something with my hair," screamed one of the models.

Without turning around Quintin knew the strident voice belonged to the quixotic Alicia Sherwood. The exquisitely photogenic woman always left her calling card whenever he shot her at his apartment: a delicate scrap of underwear.

"What's wrong with your hair?" Abayomi asked.

Alicia waved a delicate hand. "These braids are pulling my eyes up without the aid of cosmetic surgery. In other words, they're too damned tight."

Abayomi managed a saccharine grin, successfully concealing her rising annoyance with the temperamental model. "I'll make certain your hair is rebraided."

"Thanks," Alicia drawled, her large eyes fixed on Quintin's back. "See you tomorrow, Quintin," she crooned.

He turned around and graced her with a warm smile. "Alicia." Turning again, he picked up the leather bag with his equipment and slung it over his shoulder while grasping the tripod in his free hand. He headed back to the parking lot. The next four to six hours would be spent in the darkroom in his apartment, developing the film and making up contact sheets. Then later that evening he would see Victoria.

Just knowing he would see her made the day spent away from her worthwhile.

Twenty

Victoria sat across the table in her dining room, her chin resting on the heel of one hand, staring at Ethan Bennington's lowered head. The luncheon dishes she'd served Mrs. Calhoun and her guests that afternoon had been an unqualified success, and the dinner meeting with Ethan promised more success for VJ Catering. He wanted her to cater the cultural center's fifth anniversary celebration.

Ethan scrawled his signature across the bottom of a check. "This should cover the cost of the food and your services," he said, handing her the check. "If it's not enough please let me know."

She stared at the amount. The check drawn on his personal account far exceeded the amount she'd need to purchase, prepare, and serve food for the confirmed two hundred invited guests.

Placing the check, facedown, on the table, Victoria smiled. "It's enough, Ethan."

"I . . ." Whatever he was going to say was interrupted by the chiming of the doorbell. He rose to his feet as Victoria pushed back her chair.

"Please excuse me."

When she opened the door it was to find Quintin standing in the doorway, smiling down at her.

"Hey," he said softly.

"Hey yourself," she countered, taking his hand and pulling him into the entryway. "You're just in time to see your friend before he leaves."

Quintin tightened his grip on her fingers, pulling her back. "What friend?"

She urged him forward. "Come and see."

He followed her to the dining room, his mouth tightening noticeably when he saw Ethan rise to his feet, extending his hand. "What's up, buddy?"

That's what I want to know, he thought angrily. What the hell was Ethan doing in Victoria's apartment? Why was he eating at her table?

There was only a pulse beat of hesitation before Quintin extended his hand. "Not much. What's up with you?"

"I'm trying to pull everything together for the anniversary celebration," Ethan explained. His hazel eyes were fixed on Victoria.

"I suppose you want Victoria to handle the food."

Ethan nodded. "It's a done deal. She *will* cater the banquet dinner."

Quintin felt only partially relieved that Ethan and Victoria were discussing business. Why couldn't Victoria meet Ethan at his office? Why did he have to come to her home?

Victoria watched a myriad of expressions cross Quintin's face. His voice was strained, his manner stiff and formal. She wondered if his shoot had gone badly. Moving to his side, she slipped her hand in his. He squeezed her fingers.

Ethan, noticing the intimate gesture, reached up and buttoned the top button on his light-blue button-down shirt and tightened his navy-blue silk tie.

"I think it's about time I made it home. I still have a list of contributors to call before next week."

"How are the donations going?" Quintin asked him.

A slight frown creased his forehead. "Slow. But I'm sure

they'll come in as promised. I've made calls to a few of my old Wall Street buddies to throw a few extra dollars this way for a good cause. They keep telling me I was a fool to give up the excitement of playing the market to beg for money for a not-for-profit operation, but there's no way I'd ever go back to that style of life."

Quintin gave him a warm, open smile for the first time. "Instead of making thousands of dollars a day in commissions from buying and selling stocks for wealthy people, you're now soliciting funds from them to keep your center's doors open."

Ethan nodded. "It sounds crazy, but at least I can sleep soundly at night knowing I'll never have to be tempted by those insider trading scams that might cost me not only a career but also my freedom." He walked over to Victoria and smiled down at her. "Thanks again."

Her right hand touched his shoulder in an affectionate gesture. "You're welcome, Ethan. I'll see you to the door."

Quintin waited in the dining room while Victoria escorted Ethan out of her apartment. He let out his breath in a ragged shudder. He had considered punching out his best friend because he found him alone with Victoria. Burying his face in his hands, he shook his head. What was the matter with him? He was losing it . . . he'd *lost* it.

He was feeling what he had felt the first time he met Victoria Jones; as if he were undergoing a midlife crisis. Then he had wanted a woman who was a stranger; but now Victoria Jones was no longer a stranger to him; he was her lover.

Lowering his hands, he stared at the patio doors across the living room. At first he wanted to get to know her, then he wanted to sleep with her, and now he wanted to marry her. For the first time in thirty-seven years he wanted a woman for a wife—his wife.

He had satisfied his craving for sailing with *Jamila,* and he had found companionship with Hannibal. Women—they were there when he *needed* them. And that was how he had viewed women in the past—he needed them. But only now did he *want* a woman. He wanted Victoria because he loved her with his every fiber of emotion. It was only now that he had to examine his feelings. Feelings of confusion, possessiveness, jealousy, insecurity, and fear tortured him. He wanted Victoria every hour, every minute, and every second of the day.

Even his work was off. The results of the early-morning shoot revealed that after he'd developed the film in his darkroom. Alicia Sherwood, his favorite model, looked wooden and hideously stiff, and the subsequent call to the designer revealed his dissatisfaction with the modeling session.

The excitement he normally felt when photographing a subject was missing. It was that excitement with its accompanying rush of adrenaline that made him better than most commercial artists. He was a perfectionist, and his best was never good enough.

He managed a wry smile. He had a second chance to redeem himself. Abayomi Koffigoh had agreed to repeat the shoot.

He turned, his smile widening as Victoria walked gracefully into the dining room. She wore the same slip dress she had worn the morning he first made love to her. It revealed the silken skin of her shoulders, arms, neck, and back. It ended mid-calf, but failed to conceal the perfection of her legs.

Victoria returned Quintin's smile, moving into his outstretched arms. Tilting her head back, her gaze swept slowly over his face. "How was your day?" It was the same question she used to ask Richard when he returned home from his hectic Georgetown law practice.

Quintin brushed his lips over hers. "Horrific until now." He deepened the kiss, his tongue slipping between her parted lips.

She moaned sensually, and a shudder shook his body. His hands went to her head, fingers threading through her unbound hair. Victoria moaned again as his fingers massaged her scalp, sending chills up and down her body.

"Quintin," she murmured weakly against his searching mouth. "I have work to . . . to do," she managed to gasp.

"So do I," he shot back, swinging her up in his arms.

"I do," she insisted, moaning against his chest.

"I'll help you," he countered, taking the stairs to her bedroom two at a time.

Pressing her lips to his hot throat, Victoria closed her eyes. "You can't cook," she whispered.

Those were the last three words she uttered until he had stripped the dress from her body, undressed himself, and positioned his naked body over hers, trembling uncontrollably. The corded muscles in his arms, the wild, glazed look in his eyes frightened and excited her at the same time.

"Oh," she muttered as he entered her in a smooth, strong thrusting motion of his hips.

Once sheathed in her moist heat, Quintin felt a rush of reason clear away the fog clouding his mind. He was back in control. The image of the first time he had made love to her swept over him, and he relived their erotic coupling in her shower stall.

Savoring the oneness, his hands framed her face and he placed gentle kisses on her closed eyelids. "I love you, darling," he crooned reverently. Her eyes opened and she stared back at him. "Please don't leave me." His fear of losing her had surfaced.

A slight frown made vertical slashes between her eyes. "What are you talking about, Quintin?"

Lowering his head, he buried his face between her neck and shoulder, inhaling the familiar fragrance of her perfume. The scent was Victoria: soft, sweet, hypnotic, and feminine.

"I've never craved a woman the way I crave you," he began quietly. "It's frightening, Vicky. You're not like an inanimate object that can be replaced when it wears out or is used up. You're a human being. You feel and react to people and situations."

"What are you trying to say?" she asked after a moment of silence.

"What I'm trying to say is that I'm afraid of doing or saying something that will cause you to send me away."

Her frown deepened. "I still don't know what you're talking about."

"Ethan."

"What about Ethan?"

Raising his head, Quintin caught her startled look. "I wanted to hit him," he confessed.

Her gaze widened. "For what?"

"For being here with you."

Victoria swallowed several times, trying to form the words rendering her speechless. "You . . . you think I'm—"

"I'm jealous, Vicky," he interrupted. "I know I have no right to be, but I'm jealous of every man who talks to you. I even thought that your friend Jo was a Joe. A Joseph kind of Joe."

She wanted to laugh, but didn't. Quintin's expression was one of pain. Her fingers touched his mouth. "Get a grip, darling. I'm with *you* and not some other man."

He lowered his head again. "I know," he mumbled. "But even if you decide to see someone else, remember he'll never love you the way I love you."

Her arms tightened around his neck, holding him close. "I love you, Quintin. I love you the way I've never loved any man." It was the truth. Though she had been infatuated with Richard, she knew she had never loved him. Not the way she loved the man she held to her heart.

"And I love you," he groaned, feeling the blood pool in his groin again as his flesh swelled for a second time within her.

He wanted to take her quickly, passionately, but he tempered his hunger, savoring the taste of her body as his mouth explored her throat, shoulders, and the firmness of her small breasts.

Quintin was always amazed how quickly her nipples hardened against his tongue and tightened between his teeth.

Making love to Victoria was exciting and as essential to him as eating and breathing. Each time he shared her body he thought of it as an honor and a privilege.

Victoria, eyes closed, gave in to the feel of Quintin filling every available inch of her body. His weight, hardness, and fullness evoked spasms of unbelievable pleasure that raced throughout her with no place to escape.

Her breath came quickly, rendering her helpless as the shudders of excitement swept her from head to toe. She felt heat, then chills at the base of her spine, between her legs, in her breasts, and in her head.

I'm going to go crazy. The litany began in the back of her brain, spinning faster and faster until she felt as if she *would* go crazy if Quintin didn't bring her to the pinnacle of fulfillment.

His movements quickened and both of them were out of control. She screamed blatant sexual demands and he complied, doing what she had pleaded with him to do. Holding nothing back, Quintin ground his hips to hers, allowing her to feel his strength, his hardness and the strong, pulsating length of his maleness as he drove into her yielding flesh over and over.

Without warning, her name was torn from the back of his throat and his movements quickened until his cries were joined by hers in a duet of unrestrained ecstasy.

Quintin withdrew and slid down the length of her moist, heaving body and buried his face between her trembling thighs and gently drank from her flowing well of feminine delight. Her shock was boundless as he renewed her desire and she soared and exploded again and again as his tongue caught the nectar of her musky sweetness.

Spent, sated, and exhausted, she fell asleep with Quintin lying between her thighs, his arms around her legs, holding her possessively.

Quintin lay motionless, unable to believe what he had just shared with Victoria. The beautiful witch made him do things to her he had never done with any other woman. She had woven a spell over him that made him helpless to resist her. He had fallen in love with her and would love her forever, and he knew he couldn't wait to ask her to marry him. He had to have her as his wife before the end of the year!

Twenty-one

"Are you certain you're all right?" Lydia asked Victoria for the second time that morning. She watched her move more slowly than usual and yawn incessantly.

"I'm just a little tired," Victoria confessed. She didn't want to tell Lydia that she and her brother had spent most of the night making love.

She gave Lydia a tired smile. "Check the computer and see how many cans of cherry filling we have on hand."

Lydia went over to a corner of the kitchen that had been set up as an office. She had learned quickly that every can, box, or sack of food in Victoria Jones's kitchen was inventoried on labeled disks. At any given moment Victoria would know if she had enough of any ingredient on hand to prepare whatever was requested by a client.

"You have one sixty-four-ounce can left," Lydia called out.

"That's enough for four pies," Victoria said. "Add cherry pie filling to the list." Cherry pie was Christine's parents' favorite pie and Nat had insisted she make enough for the invited guests and one for the honored couple.

Taking the last can of pie filling from the pantry, she opened it and poured the contents into a large aluminum bowl. Lydia rejoined her at the cooking island, watching as she ground whole nutmegs and added them to the filling.

"Nutmeg enhances the flavor," she explained to a rapt Lydia.

"Are you going to make lattice-tops or two-crust pies?"

"A lattice-top is visually more attractive. I'm going to show you how I make my pie crust so it's thin and flaky while still holding the filling."

Lydia, daring not to divert her gaze, watched as Victoria measured sifted flour into a bowl, added a pinch of salt, vegetable shortening, and butter.

"The butter gives the crust added richness." She blended the shortening and butter with a pastry blender until the mixture was crumbly, then sprinkled cold water over the mixture a tablespoon at a time until the pastry mix held together leaving the sides of the bowl clean. Lydia counted every spoonful of water.

Flouring the marble countertop, Victoria then divided the large ball into four and rolled out each ball until it was smooth and thin. She laid the rolling pin across the center of each pastry circle, gently folding half of it over the pin before transferring them to the pie pans.

Lydia was given the task of cutting pastry strips and weaving them evenly across the tops of the filled pie pans. She accomplished it so easily and quickly, Victoria felt secure enough for her to mix and roll out crusts for the apple and pecan pies Nat and Christine had also requested.

The two women worked throughout the morning and afternoon, preparing and freezing pies, trays of potato salad, cutting and marinating vegetable dishes, putting up batches of dough for breads and rolls, cutting out, baking, and decorating butter cookies.

"Tomorrow we prepare the meats and bake the cake," Victoria informed an exhausted Lydia as they both lay on lounge chairs on the patio.

"If I survive," Lydia moaned, closing her eyes.

"Are you ready to quit?"

Lydia sat up quickly. "Oh, no. It's just that I can't remember standing on my feet so many hours at a stretch."

"Running your own catering business is not easy. You have to prepare everything," Victoria explained. "When you work in a kitchen with other chefs you'll have a specialty. The chef at the sauté station will only concern himself with sautéed items, as well as the sauces and side dishes that appear on the same plate. The chef who oversees the pasta station is responsible for all pastas and accompanying sauces, as well as potatoes. If you decide to become a pastry chef you'll also have assistants, and your responsibility will be all desserts and some breads."

"What did you like best, Victoria?"

A slight smile softened her mouth. "Being the executive chef. I liked devising the menus and recipes. In other words, I determined the food's personality."

"I only hope I'll be half as good as you."

"You'll be better," Victoria stated honestly. "You have a natural bent for cooking. I sort of backed into it."

Lydia shifted, leaning on one elbow. "You didn't plan to become a chef?"

"I was trained to be a dancer," Victoria revealed. "I decided to go into the culinary arts when I broke my ankle. I didn't like cooking as much as I enjoyed seeing the presentation. I believe food should not only taste good but look tempting."

Lydia nodded, remembering the lunch Victoria had fixed for them: curried chicken balls on lettuce leaves, prosciutto-wrapped asparagus, Brie on stone wheat crackers, and fresh blueberries in cream.

"Would you rather prepare for buffet dining or a sit-down dinner?"

"Buffet dining. The presentation can be much more attractive and the variety of dishes appeals to a lot more people. With a sit-down dinner there's only a choice of the usual prime rib, chicken, or fish. With Saturday's celebration there will be everything from fresh and smoked ham to roast turkey, potato salad, mixed greens, fried okra, shrimp with blackeyed peas, deviled eggs. The list goes on and on. There's usually less waste with a buffet. If I prepare just one tray of let's say fried okra and it goes quickly, then everyone will move on to something else."

"What kind of cake are you going to make?" Lydia question.

"A double chocolate wedding cake."

"Double chocolate?"

"White chocolate and milk chocolate pound cake," Victoria explained. "When the layers are cut, both white and milk chocolate pound cake are revealed."

"That sounds incredible." Both women turned to see Quintin stepping over the wrought-iron railing. "Can I have a few samples?"

"This is called stepping over and entering instead of breaking and entering," Victoria teased, smiling up at Quintin.

Leaning over, he brushed a kiss on her lips, then moved over to Lydia and kissed her cheek. "How's it going, squirt?"

"I can make a pie crust like Victoria's," she said proudly.

Cocking his head, Quintin smiled at his sister. "You have the best for a teacher."

"She's incredible," Lydia said, her voice rising in excitement. "I'll be able to open my own restaurant right after I graduate. Daddy said he'll give me the money to set everything up."

"I suggest you try saving some of your own earnings," her brother suggested. "You appreciate things a lot more when you make a personal investment."

Lydia rose to her feet, shaking her head. "You sound like Mama."

"That's because she said the same thing to me when I was your age."

"And you'll probably say the same thing to your children."

Quintin smiled, his gaze shifting to Victoria. He missed the flicker of pain that crossed her face when Lydia menioned children. He probably would say the same thing to the children he hoped to have with her.

"I hope I do," he said quietly.

"You hope you say the same thing or you hope you have children?" Lydia asked.

His gaze was fixed on Victoria. "Both."

It was all Victoria could do not to scream that she would never have his children. Her smile was forced as she stood up. "How did we go from food to babies?"

"I don't know, but I'm going home where I'm going to soak in a hot tub for an hour," Lydia said. "Whoever said cooking for a living is easy is a bald-faced liar."

"Thinking about quitting?" Victoria and Quintin chorused in unison.

Lydia flashed a sassy smile. "Never!" Turning, she went back into the living room. "See you tomorrow," she called out over her shoulder.

Quintin took the lounge chair she had just vacated, closing his eyes. "How was your day?"

"Tiring. And there's more tomorrow."

"Is there anything I can help you with?"

Victoria stared at his profile. "Yes, there is."

"Ask away, Vicky."

"Could you please sleep in your own bed tonight—alone?"

He sat up, blinking at her as if he had never seen her before. "Why?"

"Because I'm bone-tired, Quintin. I can't spend the night wrestling with you, then spend eight hours on my feet without feeling fatigued. I've waited a long time to set up my own business not to want to do well."

A muscle throbbed noticeably in his jaw. She had called their lovemaking wrestling. Was that all it was to her—wrestling? Offering him her body meant that little to her.

"Are you saying that I'm ruining your business?"

"I'm not saying that, but . . ."

"Then what the hell *are* you saying, Vicky? Spit it out!

You're an intelligent woman who never has a problem saying what you mean."

Her temper rose to meet his and she sprang to her feet. "Go away, Quintin, and leave me alone!"

He recoiled as if she had struck him. His body was rigid and his eyes widened in shock. She was sending him away. The fear he verbalized the night before had become a reality.

She didn't wait for him to step over the railing separating the two apartments as she turned and walked back to her place, closing the patio doors.

The soft click of the lock severed his trance, but it was another full minute before he reacted and made his way back to his own patio. He sat down on a chair, staring out into nothingness until the sun set, the sky darkened, and a red haze around the moon indicated a threat of rain for the next day. He ceased to think and feel, unable to believe what had happened.

Victoria stood under the spray of the shower, sobbing. It was the only place she could hide without Quintin hearing her from the neighboring apartment.

He wanted children. He wanted a baby and she couldn't give him a baby.

Sitting on the tiled floor of the stall, she cried until her sobs turned to whimpers, then to halting hiccuping sounds. She was drained.

The water turned cool, then cold, and her teeth began to chatter uncontrollably. Somewhere, somehow, she found the strength to rise from the floor and turn off the water.

She couldn't stop her teeth from clicking as she made her way out of the bathroom and into the bedroom, and without bothering to dry her body she lay across the bed and fell asleep.

The next morning she awoke, eyes swollen, her throat raw, and her limbs chilled from the air-conditioning. Glancing

t the clock, she knew she only had an hour before Lydia ar-
ived.

Reversing her daily ritual, Victoria soaked in a tub of hot
water, swallowed a couple of aspirins with a glass of orange
uice, then followed it with a cup of strong tea.

Lydia's expression registered shock when she noticed
Victoria's puffy eyes and drawn cheeks but kept her silence.
She didn't have to be as wise as Etta Mae Lord to know
something had occurred between Victoria and Quintin.

Victoria was her employer and she knew she couldn't
overstep the thin line that separated business from personal.
But not so with Quintin. He was her brother and she loved
him fiercely. She would discover what he had said or done to
Victoria to bring about the pain she unsuccessfully tried to
conceal each time she glanced at her.

She liked Victoria; liked her enough to have her as a sister-
in-law.

Twenty-two

Victoria experienced a ripple of excitement for the firs
time in two days as she maneuvered her minivan down th
driveway to the rear of the large Washington, D.C., tow:
house. She had not seen Quintin after their Thursda
evening spat and the damp and rainy weather on Friday ha
not lifted her dark mood. But early Saturday morning th
rain had stopped and the hot weather returned with
promise of clear skies and a brilliant summer sun.

Christine Jones met Victoria and Lydia as they began un
loading trays of food from the van. A nervous tic tortured th
woman's left eye.

"Calm down, Christine," Victoria said softly. "We hav
everything under control."

Christine hugged Victoria and kissed her cheek. "I hop
everything turns out okay. Believe it or not, my parents knov
nothing about this."

Victoria hugged her back. "Then it should be a wonderfu
surprise. This is my assistant Lydia Lord."

Lydia, smiling proudly, extended her hand. "Hello, Mrs
Jones."

Christine shifted her eyebrows, taking the proffered hand
"Please call me Christine. Nat's mother is Mrs. Jones."

"Where do you want us to set up, Christine?" Victoria questioned.

"Outside. Nat had the patio cleaned early this morning before the tables and chairs were delivered."

Victoria nodded. "I'm expecting two waiters from a local agency. When they arrive please send them to me."

"Will the four of you be enough to serve sixty-five people?" Christine asked.

"More than enough. Remember you have your own bartender, so I'll carve meats, Lydia will serve cold food, one waiter will serve hot food, and the extra person will float."

"You're the expert. I won't interfere."

"Can I sample the goods?" Nat Jones asked, coming out of the house and grinning broadly at his sister. He folded Victoria in a bear-hugging embrace, lifting her off her feet.

She kissed him on the mouth. "Why do you guys want samples all the time?" She thought of Quintin always wanting to sample what she had prepared. The thought swept the joy from her face.

"Because we're guys," he rationalized, easing her back to the ground.

She caught Lydia's hand, pulling her forward. "This is my assistant, Lydia Lord."

Lydia's mouth dropped slightly. "Aren't you Nathaniel Jones from the cable news channel?"

High color suffused Nat's sculpted golden-brown cheekbones as he stared at Lydia. He was never completely at ease with his celebrity status away from the television station. "Yes," he finally admitted.

"May I have your autograph, Mr. Jones?"

Nat winked at Lydia, whispering, "Later."

The offer surprised Victoria. Her brother always kept his professional life separate from his personal life. He was secure enough never to let them overlap.

The two waiters arrived, assisting Victoria and Lydia as they unloaded the van and set up the Sterno heaters under the trays of hot foods.

Victoria personally supervised the unloading of the cake. It was baked in four separate layers and decorated with white chocolate butter frosting. She had used a large decorating bag, utilizing five metal tips to make the curls and pipe the grapevine and flower designs. White chocolate curls and shavings would grace the third and top layers.

More than a dozen round tables, each seating six, with attached umbrellas, were positioned around the Joneses' large backyard. The area for serving food and beverages was also shaded by a tent.

By one o'clock the first guests began arriving, and Christine had calmed down enough to become the gracious hostess.

The two waiters greeted the guests with trays of cold shrimp with an accompanying cocktail sauce, deviled eggs, mushrooms stuffed with crabmeat or smoked ham and seasoned bread crumbs, crab puffs, chow-chow, a variety of cheeses and crackers, and a spicy guacamole.

William and Marion Jones arrived with their usual flair, Marion declaring the food looked too good to eat.

She made a big show of kissing and hugging Victoria. "Sweetheart, you've outdone yourself," she gushed.

"Thank you, Mom." Turning to Lydia, she introduced her to her mother as her assistant.

Marion curved an arm around Victoria's waist. "Now, you listen to what all my daughter teaches you, and one day you'll be quite good."

"That is my intention, Mrs. Jones."

Marion gave her a warm smile, nodding, then turned to Victoria. "Sweetheart, I wanted to let you know that your father and I are giving a little something at our house for the head of the Togolese Union for Democracy two weeks from today. Perhaps you remember him. Mr. Kodjo was the former secretary-general of the Organization of African Unity."

"I remember him well."

"Well, he's agreed to come and he's bringing his nephew Yaovi. You do remember the very handsome young man who studied economics and international law at Oxford. He was always very interested in you."

How well she remembered Yaovi—she and every other woman on the African continent. Yaovi was spectacularly handsome. He claimed the most sensual eyes and mouth of any man Victoria had ever seen.

"How can I forget him," she said with a mysterious smile.

"I'm not trying to play matchmaker, sweetheart, but I just wanted to let you know in case you decide to come without an escort."

"I suppose your 'little something' will be a formal dinner?"

"Of course, sweetheart."

"I'll be there, Mom."

"With an escort?"

Closing her eyes briefly, she thought of Quintin. How she wished she could bring him with her, but she knew that was not possible. The break had been quick and bloodless. There was no way she wanted to reopen the wound.

"Without an escort," she finally said. "Let Yaovi know that I'm looking forward to seeing him again."

Marion clasped her delicate hands together, smiling. "Wonderful. Now, Lydia, please serve me some of Victoria's wonderful potato salad."

Lydia spooned a helping of potato salad onto Marion Jones's plate, frowning. She had overheard the conversation between Victoria and her mother. She had also noted the expression on Victoria's face when her mother had spoken of the man named Yaovi. She had to let Mrs. Jones know that her daughter wasn't interested in this Yaovi because she was in love with her brother.

Lydia knew she had to act and act quickly.

Victoria tipped the two waiters, thanking them for their help. Both of them requested that she ask for them again whenever she catered another event in the D.C. area. She promised she would. The two young men were Howard University students and supplemented their meager incomes by waiting tables and serving parties.

Sitting in the van beside Lydia, Victoria smiled at her. "Well, do you still want to be a chef?"

Lydia nodded, smiling a tired smile. "More than ever before. Even though you prepared all the food, I felt a personal satisfaction seeing everyone eat. I can't believe there weren't any leftovers."

She had to agree. The invited guests had come with prodigious appetites, devouring every morsel of food in sight. If she hadn't removed the top layer of the cake for the honored couple their guests would have eaten that, too.

"It was a success," she said softly.

"The first of many successes," Lydia replied.

Both women were quiet on the return drive to Baltimore. Victoria refused Lydia's offer to help unload the van, saying she would unload it the next day. She slipped several large bills into the younger woman's hand as she sat in her tiny Honda CRX.

"It's a tip," she said before Lydia opened her mouth to protest. "Thanks for your help."

Lydia stared at the money. "I should be the one thanking you. I should pay you instead of you paying me."

"Maybe one day you will pay me."

A sly grin teased Lydia's mouth upward. "Maybe I will."

Victoria watched the red taillights from the car as it pulled away from the curb, then turned and retreated to her own apartment. She was past being exhausted, and she knew the exhaustion wasn't just from not getting enough sleep or from standing on her feet for hours.

The fatigue was emotional. She had soared to great heights with Quintin. It was only when she fell that she realized the enormity of their separation.

She had looked forward to seeing him, hearing his voice and having him hold her to his body. He lived only a few feet from her yet she felt as if they were separated by miles.

She loved him—loved him with an intensity she had never felt for another man; and she knew she would never love another man the way she loved him.

Since her divorce she'd been sure she never wanted to remarry. But she'd found herself thinking of marriage again. Thinking that this time it would be different. She could have a career that her husband respected; and he would be willing to share in her successes as well as her failures.

He would want her for herself and not for the children he hoped she would give him to carry on his name and his genes.

Not the child Richard wanted to nurture and mold into what he had failed to become.

The child Richard wanted that would be an object of vanity—a miniature clone of him.

Her steps were slow and heavy as she made her way up the stairs to the front door. The pounding rhythms hit her the moment she stepped into the hallway. Quintin was playing his music full tilt.

Victoria didn't know how it happened, but she alternated pounding on his door with her fist while ringing his doorbell.

The door swung open, and she stared up at a bearded Quintin. His gold-brown gaze swept quickly over her, missing nothing. "What?"

She registered the sharpness in his bored tone, but refused to back down. "Turn it down."

He shifted an eyebrow and yawned. "Good night, Miss Jones."

"I'll call the police," she threatened.

"Good."

Turning away, she opened the door to her apartment and slammed it as hard as she could. Pressing her back against the door, she bit down hard on her lower lip. She was torturing herself. Just seeing him again was torture, so she decided the best way to get over Quintin Lord was not to see him again.

But that didn't prove as easy as she thought it would be. Her nights were filled with images of him and their passionate lovemaking. The images were so real that she awoke in a sweat, her heart pounding and her body throbbing.

Victoria sat across from Joanna in a D.C. restaurant, drinking from a glass of iced tea. The mysterious smile on Jo's face revealed more than what the redhead was saying.

"So, Ethan has hired you to plan the center's fifth anniversary celebration?" Victoria repeated the news her friend just revealed.

"Isn't that a gas?"

"He or the idea?"

Jo blushed furiously. "Both," she admitted with a sigh. "Victoria . . . Victoria . . ."

"That is my name," she teased.

"Well . . . well, it goes a little farther than business."

Victoria decided not to make it easy for Jo. "Are you saying you and Ethan are involved?"

Her flush deepened. "Well—not really. We've had dinner a few times."

"Dinner at his place?" Jo nodded. "Well, the man happens to be a wonderful cook."

"It's not only his cooking, Victoria. It's Ethan."

"What's wrong with him?"

"Nothing. He's perfect. As perfect as a man can get, I suppose." Jo's gaze was fixed somewhere over Victoria's head. "I don't know how to say this."

Leaning over, Victoria grasped Jo's hands, holding them firmly. "Are you trying to say that he's not into women?"

"Oh, no! No never." She pulled her hands free.

"What is it?"

"He's somewhat shy. He has the most exquisite manners, and he does all of the right things, but he hasn't . . ."

Victoria threw back her head and laughed. "He hasn't tried to get you into bed," she finished perceptively.

Jo nodded again. "I hope it's not me."

"It's not you, Jo. It's the man. You're so used to the slobs who take you out to dinner, then expect you to be their dessert that you don't recognize a real man when you finally meet one. Did you notice the furnishings in his house? They're heirloom pieces. And we both know he didn't pick up that Rodin sculpture sitting in his living room at a thrift shop. Even without seeing Ethan's portfolio you know he's anything but ordinary."

"I don't want to get hurt, Vicky."

"You won't if you don't give him your heart." *Unlike me with Quintin,* she thought.

"You're right. I've thought myself in love so many times that this is all new to me."

"He may be preoccupied because he's waiting for Ryan's adoption to go through. Just let Ethan establish where he wants the relationship to go."

Jo shrugged her shoulders. "You do know that Quintin is going to be Ryan's godfather once the adoption is final."

"No, I didn't," she answered truthfully.

Jo gave Victoria a long, penetrating look. "Aren't you seeing Quintin?"

"Why do you think I'm seeing him?"

"Because I know what I observed the day we went sailing, Vicky. I saw the man with his tongue down your throat." She ignored Victoria's slight gasp. "And I know that he hasn't been the nicest person to be around lately."

Victoria slumped against the padded back on her chair, frowning at Joanna. "So this little dinner date is not about Ethan, but about Quintin and me. Did Ethan tell you to discuss Quintin with me?"

Jo nodded, biting down on her lower lip. "I wanted to talk to you about *Ethan,* and when I mentioned I was going to see you for dinner he suggested I ask you about Quintin."

She felt some of her tension ease. "Thank you for not lying, Jo."

Leaning forward on her seat, Jo asked, "What happened between the two of you?"

"I haven't seen him for a week."

"Why?"

"Because I can't ever give him what he'd like to have."

A frown creased Jo's forehead. "What is that?" she asked quietly.

She exhaled, her eyes darkening with pain. "A child."

The natural color faded from Jo's face, leaving a liberal sprinkling of freckles. "You're kidding, aren't you?"

"No." Victoria shook her head for emphasis. "I had an accident ten years ago, a very serious accident, and after I woke up in the recovery room I was told that I'd never have children. My husband left me because I couldn't give him a child." Her expression hardened. "I don't intend for another man to do that to me again."

"But the two of you could've adopted a child."

"Richard wanted his own children. His exact words were, he didn't want 'someone else's throwaways'."

"He sounds like a horse's ass," Jo snapped, her eyes shooting sparks of copper fire.

She couldn't help smiling. "Don't tell anyone, but he is."

Both women dissolved in a paroxysm of laughter, lifting the dark mood. Jo signaled their waiter and ordered two glasses of white wine.

Victoria took a sip of her wine, then leaned over the table. "What has Quintin done to make Ethan solicit you to be his envoy on this mission of peace?"

"It's more like a mission of mercy. I'm here to save the children. Quintin volunteered to help with the stage sets for the big production number and apparently he got into a confrontation with one of the older boys. He complained to Ethan that he wasn't going to take anyone 'getting up in his grill,' and the next time Quintin tried it the two of them would settle it outside—in the back."

"Grill?"

"His face, Vicky. Ethan had to translate the term to me, too."

"How did Ethan handle the situation?"

"He talked to the kid for a long time and finally got him to calm down. He was less successful with Quintin. He hasn't seen Quintin nor has he returned his phone calls since last Saturday."

"That was the last time I saw him, too. He was playing his music loud enough to wake the dead and when I threatened to call the police he called my bluff."

"Did you call them?"

"No. But he did turn it down ten minutes later."

There was a long pause before Jo spoke again. "What are you going to do, Vicky?"

"Go on with my life as if Quintin Lord never existed."

Frowning slightly, Jo stared at Victoria, giving her a look that said she didn't believe her. "Are you sure?"

Victoria blinked slowly, nodding. "Very sure." And at that moment she was.

Twenty-three

Victoria considered talking to Quintin about bullying young kids, but each time she approached his door she turned around and reentered her own apartment.

She remembered his confession that he wanted to punch Ethan when he discovered him in her apartment. She found it difficult to associate Quintin with violence. It seemed so out of character for him especially when she recalled his gentleness and tender lovemaking.

The dilemma was solved for her. As she sat out on her patio she heard the doors of his apartment slide open. Sitting in the darkness, she blended into the shadowy night.

"Quintin." Her soft voice carried easily in the stillness. She heard his sharp intake of breath and smiled. He didn't answer her, and she continued. "There's a nasty rumor going around about you threatening to take someone out in the parking lot behind the cultural center. Don't you think you're a little old to be brawling like a thug? And especially with a kid."

"Are you willing to take the kid's place, Miss Jones?"

"Of course not. I've never brawled like a common—"

"What came out of *his* mouth was common, Miss Jones," he said, interrupting her. "For your information I merely warned him about using foul language in front of the girls, and he said something about his First Amendment right to free speech. I merely gave him a choice: clean up his mouth or he was off the project."

She felt her face burn in embarrassment and she was grateful for the cover of darkness. "I'm sorry, Quintin. I suppose I only heard half of the story."

There was only the sound of chirping crickets and the occasional slapping sound of tires from a passing vehicle before Quintin spoke again. "Apology accepted."

A slight smile lifted his mouth. He couldn't see Victoria, but his nostrils had detected the scent of her perfume. She was so close yet so far away.

The past week had been hell. He wanted to go to her and hold her, to kiss away the bitter words they had traded. He wanted her and he needed her. But more than that, he loved her. He'd never stop loving her.

When Lydia had called him and read him the riot act, he retaliated by hanging up on her. He then retreated into a world of silence, not answering his phone or returning calls.

He was hurting, he was bleeding, and the woman who could stem the flow was sitting less than twenty feet away. She could heal him, could make him whole.

"Good night, Quintin."

Her quiet voice floated toward him, and he held on to the sides of his chair to keep from going to her. "Good night, Victoria."

He registered the soft click of her door, then he did what he had been doing for a week: he sat out in the darkness until the sky lightened.

Victoria received an unexpected call from her sister the morning of their parents' dinner.

"Why don't I pick you up and we'll drive down to D.C. together," Kimberly Abernathy suggested.

"Wouldn't it be better if I pick you up, Kimm? After all, you're closer to D.C. than I am."

"I'm already in Baltimore. I'm leaving the baby with Russell's mother."

"How is she going to feed him?"

Kimberly laughed. "I'll pump enough milk to last him until I get back. I've got my figure back and I'm ready to do some serious partying."

"What time should I expect you?"

"How about three?"

Victoria glanced at the clock on the bedside table. "Make it four. I have an appointment to have my hair done at eleven."

"Four it is. I'll see you then."

She hung up, staring at the dress she had planned to wear to the dinner party. It was an exquisite evening ensemble with vertical bands of dark sapphire, blue velvet, and black silk chiffon with long sleeves, a fitted bodice, a velvet neckband. The full, gored skirt was made for dancing. The vertical bands, ending at the waistline, covered her breasts and her breastbone. The body suit she had purchased to match her own skin tone provided a modicum of modesty. Three inches of silk heels in a sapphire blue completed the outfit.

Like Kimm, she was also ready to do some serious partying. But unlike Kimm she was free to flirt with whomever she pleased. Perhaps if she flirted enough she would be able to forget about her neighbor.

Victoria stared at her reflection in the mirror on the dressing table. The soft light in the bedroom where she had grown up was flattering to her expertly made-up face. Her hair had been cut close to her scalp and curled into a cap of loose ringlets. The haircut made her eyes appear larger, and the overall effect made her look younger than her thirty-one years.

The cocktail hour was to begin promptly at seven, leaving her less than ten minutes to dress. She slipped into her dress and pulled up the zipper, artfully concealed in one of the velvet bands in the back. She stepped into her heels, then fastened a pair of sapphire-and-diamond earrings which had belonged to her great-grandmother in her pierced lobes.

A babble of voices, male and female, American and foreign, drifted up from the living room as she made her way down the carpeted curving staircase in the Joneses' magnificent Georgian-style home.

She caught a glimpse of colorful African prints along with the traditional tuxedo. She had grown up watching her father attend and preside over formal dinners for many African dignitaries in the thirty years he had worked for the State Department.

She spotted Yaovi immediately. He towered over most of the men in the room. She also recognized the cut of his suit. Yaovi had always favored his Armani suits over the traditional African garb.

Unusually large dark eyes followed her progress across the room as yards of black-and-sapphire chiffon floated out around her legs. A full, sensual mouth smiled, revealing perfect white teeth.

Yaovi excused himself and met Victoria halfway across the room. He grasped her hands, kissing her fingers. "What a vision," he crooned, lowering his head in a slight bow. "Victoria, you are more beautiful than I remembered."

The burgundy lip color on her mouth shimmered as she pursed her lips. "Yaovi—always the charmer."

He released one of her hands and pressed his left one to his heart. "You wound me, Victoria. You know I'd wait a lifetime for you. The last time we met you were taken."

She tilted her chin, drowning in his obsidian gaze. "And how many wives do you have now?"

He managed to look insulted. "I have not taken a wife."

"What are you waiting for?" She knew Yaovi to be at least thirty-five.

"You." The word rolled smoothly off his silken tongue.

"I'm afraid you'll have to wait forever because the lady happens not to be available."

Victoria froze, and if Yaovi hadn't been holding her hand she was certain she would've fallen. Turning slowly, she stared up at Quintin Lord.

"What are you doing here?" she whispered.

Quintin reached out and extracted her hand from Yaovi's. "Thanks, buddy, for watching over Victoria. I'll take over now."

Yaovi stood speechless. He managed to nod as he watched the man lead Victoria Jones away. His shock was temporary, for within seconds a woman strolled over, draping her bare arm over the fabric of his expertly tailored suit jacket. Smiling, he lowered his head to listen to her quiet voice. His deep laugh floated over the woman's ear and she winked knowingly up at him. He reached for a glass of champagne from a passing waiter, handed it to her, then claimed a glass for himself.

Victoria pulled against Quintin's strong grip, but she knew she couldn't free herself without making a scene. Especially not in front of her parents or their guests.

Her stunned gaze swept over Quintin, taking in the single-button black tuxedo jacket, silk banded-collar, white shirt, black dress trousers, black patent-leather dress slippers, and the single diamond stud in his left ear. He had traded his gold hoops for the brilliant tiny diamond.

"To answer your question as to why I'm here . . ." He took a glass of champagne from a waiter, gave it to her, and, without releasing her hand, took one for himself.

"Yes," he continued, "why I'm here. I received a rather cryptic message on my telephone answering machine saying that if I didn't want to lose the woman I loved to a magnificent, British-accented, English-speaking African gentleman who travels to Milan once a year to replenish his wardrobe, then I'd better show up here at seven tonight. And it appears that I arrived just in time, Vicky."

"You can't be talking about Yaovi?"

"Was the man drooling over your hand Yoda?"

"Yaovi, Quintin," she corrected.

"Whatever," he drawled. "Now, drink your champagne

and act nice, darling. Then we'll disappear for a few minutes and talk."

She tried pulling away from him. He had no right to barge into her parents' home and embarrass her. "Let me go, Quintin."

He tightened his grip, his lips curling under his silky mustache. "Please, Vicky, don't make me act common in front of your parents and their esteemed guests."

"You *are* common to come barging in here," she retorted.

Quintin took a sip of champagne, his gaze fixed on her beautiful, delicate face. "Must I remind you that I was invited. How else would I have found you. Drink your champagne, love. It happens to be an excellent vintage."

She took a sip from the fluted glass, feeling the heat flood her face and neck as she watched everyone in the room staring at her and Quintin.

"Come with me," she ordered, leading him in the direction of her father's library. He preceded her inside the large room and she closed the door behind them.

Turning to face him, Victoria found she couldn't keep her hunger for him from showing. Even though she knew it was wrong to be alone with him, at that moment she was helpless to resist the tall man standing less than three away. He had affected his own style of formal dress, and the overall effect was devastatingly appealing. The collarless shirt, the absence of a tie, and the earring said Quintin Jones was his own person; a person who would throw convention to the wind if there was a cause he truly believed in.

He glanced around the library, quickly assessing the photographs lining the wall. His gaze lingered on the portraits of distinguished men dressed in the height of fashion from the mid- to late-1800s.

Turning back to Victoria, Quintin held out a hand, taking her glass and putting it down on a polished mahogany side table with his. "Please sit down, Vicky."

She grasped his hand and permitted him to seat her in a brocade armchair. He took a matching one, facing her.

Crossing a leg over his knee, he stared at her. "Don't you have something to tell me?"

Victoria crossed her legs, too, allowing him a glimpse of silk sapphire-blue pumps from under the flowing yards of black-and-blue chiffon. "I don't know what you're talking about.

"Don't you?"

"Don't answer my question with a question, Quintin."

He continued to stare at her, unblinking. After a deafening silence, he lowered his gaze and laced his fingers together.

"Something is bothering you; something that goes a lot deeper than you trying to make a go of your catering business. I've also had time to think about your evasiveness whenever I asked you about your dance career. You're hiding something from me, and you're hiding from yourself."

Her eyes narrowed slightly. "You're wrong."

"Am I, Vicky? The only time you're not hiding is when we're in bed. Only when we make love do I get to know the real Victoria Jones. Then you hold nothing back. But outside of bed you're cautious, guarded, and sometimes distant. Leaning forward, he held both of her hands, not permitting her to escape. "Who did this to you?"

She looked at her hands cradled in his and smiled a sad smile. "No one did it to me, Quintin." Her voice was barely a whisper. "I did it to myself. I permitted someone to define who I was."

"Who was he?"

"My ex-husband."

"What happened, darling?"

Her head came up, and she met his intense gaze. "I told myself I wasn't a woman." She related details of her accident and Richard's subsequent reaction to her not being able to bear his children.

Quintin tightened his hold on her hands and pulled her fluidly from her chair and onto his lap. He cradled her gently to his chest and buried his face in her hair.

"He was a fool, Victoria," he finally said after her whisered words faded. "You're more woman than any woman ve ever known. The only thing I'll say is that I love you and at I want you as my wife."

"Quintin," she sobbed against his chest, "you still want e even if I can't give you a child?"

His hands searched under her chin, raising her face. He rveyed the unshed tears in her eyes. "Is that why you sent e away? Because you can't have children?"

She nodded, closing her eyes. She couldn't bear to see the ok of revulsion on his face. Richard hadn't been able to nceal his when she told him that she would never bear a hild.

Quintin's expression was taut before a look of amusement ftened his mouth. His arms became bands of steel around er waist. "You little fool. Do you think I want you because I ant children?" She nodded shyly. "Well, you're wrong, liss Victoria Jones. Don't you think if I wanted children I ould've had some before now?"

"But . . . but . . ."

He covered her mouth with his fingers, then replaced em with his mouth. He deepened the kiss as she twisted on is lap, her arms going around his neck.

"Quintin." His name came out in a sighing groan while is lips explored her eyelids, the curving slope of a cheekone before finding her mouth again.

"You beautiful, silly witch. My loving you and wanting to arry you had nothing to do with children," he said softly gainst her ear. "If you decide you want a child we can alays adopt. There's no shortage of black children looking r a home filled with love. And that's what we would have, icky, a home filled with love."

Pulling back, she smiled up at him. "And don't forget decious food."

He returned her smile. "And a beautiful mother."

"And a wonderfully talented, handsome father."

"And a few neurotic pets," he added.

There was no way Victoria could conceal her joy as s
melted against his chest, her head resting on his shoulder.

"When do you want to get married, Quintin?"

"How about next week?"

"That soon?"

He pressed a kiss to her hair. "You'd rather wait?"

Biting down on her lower lip, she thought about t
agony of waiting. She shook her head, smiling. "No."

"Your place or mine?"

"For what?"

"Where do you want to live?"

Extracting herself from his embrace, Victoria stood
and began pacing, the flowing skirt of her dress floating (
around her feet in a cloud of shimmering blue-black.

"I have to have my kitchen," she mused aloud.

Crossing his arms over his chest, Quintin studied t
graceful outline of her body. "And I have to have my dai
room."

"But I also need my room to work out at the barre."

Rising to his feet, Quintin went to her and folded h
against his body. "I guess you win. What we can do is kno
down the wall separating the two apartments and join t
lofts. Or we can keep the apartments for professional pu
poses and buy a little place somewhere in the country."

Tilting her face to his, she kissed his chin. "I kind of li
being a neighbor."

Lowering his head, Quintin intoned, "Thou shalt n
covet thy neighbor's house; thou shalt not covet thy neig
bor's wife, nor his manservant, nor his maidservant, nor l
ox, nor his ass, nor anything that is thy neighbor's."

She laughed. "I guess that means we'll have to buy a lit
place somewhere in the country."

"I thought you'd see it my way." He took a quick glance
his watch. "We still have time before dinner is served to
your folks know that we plan to get married."

"There is something I need to know before we go back

"What is it?"

"Who called you and left the message on your machine?"

"Your mother," Quintin replied smugly.

A shock flew through her. "My mother? But how? She ever met you."

"Lydia told her about us, and apparently the meddling little brat was determined to have you as a sister-in-law."

Victoria's mouth quirked with humor. "I knew there was omething I liked about her right away."

"That's exactly how I felt about you the moment I saw ou," Quintin confessed. "Especially since you were so willng to show me what I would get if I managed to get you to ll in love with me."

A frown wrinkled her brow. "What are you talking bout?"

Quintin dropped a kiss on the end of her nose. "You were orawled on my living room floor wearing the tiniest pair of anties . . ."

Victoria stopped his words as her mouth covered his, olding her length to his. They were breathing heavily when ey parted.

Arm-in-arm, they made their way to the living room, love hining from their eyes and joy filling their hearts, to an- ounce their good news to the world.

Epilogue

Victoria opened the door, shivering slightly as the co
winter air swept into the room. The flames from a roari
fire leapt as the burning logs crackled loudly when spar
flew up in a shimmering red-gold display.

"Merry Christmas. Come on in."

Ethan, Joanna, and Ryan filed into the room, ar
ladened with gaily wrapped packages.

"Merry Christmas to you, too," Ethan said, a wide sm
on his handsome face.

"Welcome, welcome," Quintin greeted his guests. I
handed Ryan a small, squirming puppy with a large red be
around its neck. "Merry Christmas, Ryan."

The young boy cradled the black ball of fur to his che
his eyes filled with delight. "Thank you, Quintin."

"You're quite welcome," he told his godson. "Hanniba
very proud of this little guy, so make certain you take go
care of him."

"I promise I will." The child's joy was boundless.

Quintin then took coats, hats, gloves, and scarves fro
the three while Victoria placed the packages under t
sweeping branches of a live, decorated evergreen.

"Everything looks so nice," Jo remarked, taking in the furnishings in the Lord living room.

Ethan, walking to the fireplace, glanced up at the painting over the mantel. "When did you do this one?" he asked Quintin.

Quintin placed a hand on his friend's shoulder. "I did the sketch the night you came to ask me to be Ryan's godfather."

"It's magnificent." His hazel eyes studied the painting. "If you ever think of selling . . ."

"It's not for sale, buddy. It's a part of my private collection." There was another painting he had done of Victoria, but that one was not for public viewing. Victoria had agreed to sit for him after they had been married for a year. He considered the nude portrait his finest work, but he had kept his promise not to show it. It hung on a wall in their bedroom.

"I think it's time I commission you to do a family portrait," Ethan stated solemnly.

Quintin's teeth shone whitely under his mustache. "Do I hear what I think I'm hearing? You and Jo?"

Ethan nodded. "She's agreed to marry me. Ryan was overjoyed when I told him that she would be his mother."

"I'll do the portrait, and I'll give it to you as a wedding gift."

Ethan extended his hand. "Thanks, buddy."

Quintin shook the proffered hand. "You're welcome, buddy."

His gaze drifted over to Victoria as she sat on a love seat with Joanna, admiring her engagement ring. It had been a year and a half since his neighbor walked into his apartment wearing practically nothing under a robe while issuing a demand that he not play his music so loud.

Victoria glanced up and met his gaze, and a mysterious smile touched her sensual mouth. Pursing her lips, she winked at him.

He returned her knowing wink. Ethan had Ryan and Joanna, and they had each other.

But that would all change in the upcoming year. They'd decided to adopt a child. There was more than enough love in their hearts for any child who would be fortunate enough to claim them as parents.

About the Author

The author of more than forty titles, native New Yorker Rochelle Alers has earned legions of readers since her blockbuster favorite *Hideaway* made its 1995 debut. A multiple award-winner, Rochelle is the recipient of the first prestigious Vivian Stephens Career Achievement Award for Excellence in Romance Novel Writing, and the first Zora Neale Hurston Literary Award conferred by the Zeta Phi Beta Sorority, Inc. One of her women's fiction titles is now required reading in several universities. You can contact her at *roclers@aol.com*.